TWO STRAIGHT-SHOOTIN'
WILL COOK WESTERNS
FOR ONE LOW PRICE!
"Will Cook's Westerns are first-rate!"
—Wichita Falls *Times*

FORT STARKE

"Diablito's here now," said father, "but for a reason."
This puzzled Regan. "Gentry?"

Now it was my turn to wonder as father shrugged and
replied, "Gentry has killed more Apaches than the Mexican
Army. It's my theory that wherever Gentry is, Apaches will
be found. And now they know that Gentry's in this district.
I believe that that's why they're trying to isolate Starke.
Gentry has come here before, and he may come here again."

Regan looked scared. "What's going to happen, sir?"

"There's no telling," said father grimly.

FIRST COMMAND

"I will speak for my people," Limping Deer said. "What
right have you to steal our cattle? You stole our land, made
war on us. Now we will not see our food taken!" He waved
his arms wildly. "All white men are liars, thieves! You will
give us the cattle!"

"There will be more cattle," Travis said. "It will only
be a few days, a week. You can wait. You won't starve."

"Limping Deer does not wait. He will have cattle today!"

"You will wait!" Travis said sternly. "I do not bargain
with you, Limping Deer. It is the white man's law under
which you must live, and it is my law you will obey now."

Other *Leisure Books Double Westerns* by Will Cook:
LAST COMMAND/APACHE AMBUSH
BULLET RANGE/IRON MAN, IRON HORSE

Will Cook
FORT STARKE/
FIRST COMMAND

LEISURE BOOKS **NEW YORK CITY**

Dedicated To
Henry Wilson Allen, who knows why

A LEISURE BOOK®

March 1994

Published by special arrangement with Golden West Literary Agency.

Published by

Dorchester Publishing Co., Inc.
276 Fifth Avenue
New York, NY 10001

FORT STARKE Copyright © MCMLIX by Will Cook

FIRST COMMAND Copyright © MCMLIX by Will Cook

Printed in the United States of America.

FORT STARKE

1

ALL THAT day a brassy sun hung furnace-hot, seemingly motionless, and even as it made its last flaming dip toward the horizon, the heat remained, reflected from the gray adobe walls of the fort and bouncing from the tawny dust of the parade. I was sixteen that year, which was a fine age for a boy, if he lived in Chicago or Cincinnati, or anywhere except Fort Starke. Then it was a poor year, a year when the Apaches hid behind every clump of sacaton grass and wrote a legend in blood across a vast and parched land.

My name? Melvin Lunsford, if it matters. There was a question in my mind whether I would ever live to be seventeen, and what does a boy of sixteen leave behind to be remembered by?

One look around made me wonder, for we were alone, with no one to chronicle a soldier's last act of heroism, or the futility of his dying. The adobe wall was warm against my back as I rested there, on the palisade ramp with the other soldiers. Around me, in a wide perimeter, sun-bleached planks and empty cartridge cases, and men.

I wasn't a soldier, not at sixteen, but I was Army, born to it, bred to it, and I understood a soldier's duty and his fear. Fear was a common commodity at Fort Starke, with Diablito surrounding us, biding his time so he could come over the wall again, and kill a few more men, thin us out a little more.

From where I sat I could see my father, who commanded Fort Starke. He rested his long-barreled cavalry pistol on one knee, a neat row of cartridges handy before him. Bob Van Orden was beside him. He was a civilian, one of the lost and strayed who took refuge behind our walls so he could die with us rather than alone.

The soldiers? They sprawled awkwardly, trying to sleep, trying not to think and trying not to remember what it was like on the outside, away from the push and press of the military form.

5

Below, on the parade, four men lay blanket-covered; we always buried our dead after dark. I sat with my legs out straight, hands idle on my thighs, trying to figure what day it was. As though the day mattered. Someone farther down spoke and heads turned, then we listened. That is the first thing you do when there are Apaches about—listen.

You could hear scratching—like a rat trying to eat a hole in a packing case. The post was old and the adobe was crumbling on the outside of the wall, exposing the vertical logs, and what wasn't exposed was dug away with the points of spears or sharpened sticks. That was the Apache way of climbing, to insert their fingers in between the logs and inch up, like a bear going after honey.

One by one, the soldiers cocked their Springfields, the locks clicking dryly in the silence. Let them dig: that was the common thought. Let them dig and climb—and then lean over the wall and fire straight down, when their hands are occupied.

Kill the Apaches while they climb!

I watched my father; he would give the order. And he did. With a cry the wall became alive with us rearing up, shooting, falling back as nearly a dozen babe-naked Apaches swarmed over. Sergeant McGuire, who stood three paces to my left, came against a painted buck, his arm blocking a flailing knife. McGuire's lips pulled back from his teeth and spittle made a froth around his mouth as his fingers clamped hard on the Apache's throat.

The shooting was ragged and brief. A soldier fell off the wall, locked to an Apache, and they struck the parade below with a sound like a sack of meal being flung into the back of a sutler's van.

McGuire threw the dead Apache back over the wall as though he were too filthy to remain on our side of the post.

Someone fired a random shot that snapped off the wall near my head, leaving a pucker in the adobe, and the smell of dust. A young soldier standing next to me cried out in a lonely voice, clapped his hands over his stomach, then sank to his knees. Slowly he bent forward until his forehead touched the bare planks, rolled onto his back and stared vacant-eyed at the evening sky.

Bob Van Orden had both his pistols working—then suddenly the shooting stopped and a silence seemed to pour over the post. From the post infirmary, Doctor Bickerstaff ran with his cracked leather bag. He saw me, made a motion with his hand, and I went down the first ramp ladder that was handy.

Father and Sergeant McGuire were gathering the wounded, lowering them to the parade. A detail came down the ladder, led by Sergeant Haukbauer. The men were gathered on makeshift litters and carried to the infirmary.

Doctor Bickerstaff took me by the arm. He was German and dedicated, and quite impersonal about death. "Mein boy, are you all right?"

"Yes, sir," I said. I wasn't all right and I wondered if I ever would be again, with my world all torn up and scattered around me. It was one thing for a mature man to face the prospect of dying, and quite another for someone who is sixteen, whose values are not firmly established, and whose life is only just beginning.

Bickerstaff shook me. "I vill need help. You haf been a *gut* student of medicine, Mel. You vill help, ya?"

What could I say to him? That this had never been my idea of medicine? I suppose I had some foolish notion of standing by a bedside, mouthing platitudes and making miraculous cures. Certainly I never considered bullet-ripped bodies and a man's screams in my ears as I tried to make half an arm out of a shredded mess.

Doctor Bickerstaff and I went on to the infirmary. Haukbauer and his detail carried the litters. I didn't particularly want to go there, for I did not want to see my mother, or Paul, my brother. He was my remaining brother, for Reed was dead and hastily buried as though it would be better for all of us if we forgot him. But I couldn't forget him, and I knew mother couldn't. Maybe she blamed me, I don't know. She had a right to. If I'd kept him off the wall when the Apaches came over . . .

But I hadn't kept him off, and now he was dead.

Bickerstaff's office contained a strong odor of antiseptics. He stood aside as Haukbauer and the detail placed the wounded on the floor. My father came in as Bickerstaff made his brief examinations.

Bickerstaff said to me, "See vat you can do."

Father watched as I cut away Trooper Nielsen's shirt. The wound had been inflicted with a knife, a deep slash across his chest, nearly severing the pectoral muscle. He was conscious and I wished that he wasn't for I had to suture. I went to a cabinet where Bickerstaff kept his set of beautiful curved needles and sutures.

"Where is your mother, Mel?" father asked, and I looked at him

"I haven't seen her," I said and began to repair the damage to Trooper Nielsen's chest. You have to suture deep, to gather

7

together the bottom of the wound, then take a stitch on the surface. One deep, one shallow; I made thirty-four before Trooper Nielsen fainted.

Father still remained in the doorway, looking much older than I remembered. Fatigue branded his face, etching deep lines around his eyes and lips. "Mel, I have another patient for you."

I scanned him quickly, thinking he'd been wounded, but that wasn't what he meant.

"He's Apache."

He watched me, and I knew what for. Hate can burn with frightening intensity after killing has been done, and I was no exception.

I said, "Can he be brought here?"

"I'll have McGuire do it," he said and went out.

Trooper Calabash had a fractured arm, and I set it without the blessing of anesthetic—Doctor Bickerstaff was using our fast-dwindling supply for chest and abdominal surgery. After splinting the fracture, I tried to tell Bickerstaff about the Apache, but he was too occupied trying to get the head of the arrow out of Corporal Clayton's stomach.

Sergeant McGuire and a trooper carried the Apache into the room; Bickerstaff stopped for a heartbeat to stare, then went on with his work. The Apache was conscious and he looked at me with hate-filled eyes. Had he not been so weak I believe he would have fought me as I bent to examine his wound. He had been shot in the chest, and from the bubble of pink on his lips I knew that a lung had been punctured, but there was no exit wound. The bullet had to come out.

I went to the cabinet for Bickerstaff's nickel-silver probes and a salver of disinfectant. McGuire was holding the Apache's arms and I bent down. He looked up as someone stepped into the doorway.

My mother stared wide-eyed at the Indian, then said, "I heard there was one of those savages in here."

Before anyone could stop her, she picked up a tall wooden stool, lifted it high, then swept it down, trying to hit the Apache on the head. McGuire blocked the blow with bunched shoulders and the chair splintered with a vibrating crack. With a cry of rage, mother flung herself at the Apache, but McGuire caught her and led her sobbing from the room.

Had I been less numb from the tension of the siege, I would have been unable to help anyone; but as it was, I probed with the steadiest of hands while the Apache lay there, alive in his eyes, sweat popping from every pore. I got the bullet out and bandaged the wound.

8

Sergeant McGuire came back, rubbing his head and working his shoulders. His glance touched the Apache.

"Will he live?" he asked.

"If we can keep him in bed," I said. "How's ma?"

His lips pulled down briefly. "She's had a time of it." His grin was brief and a little strained. "Ain't we all, bucko." Then he wheeled and went out.

There was nothing more I could do—for all my two years of study with Doctor Bickerstaff, my skill was considerably limited. Leaving the dispensary, I stood in the early darkness of evening, looking up at the wall where death became a momentary thing.

The silence was vast and deep and frighteningly peaceful. There was the question of tomorrow—tomorrow if it would ever be again for me. Yet at sixteen a boy does not like to think of dying—living is vastly more important and exciting.

And I suppose that's what I should tell you about, the living, not the dying, for the last occupies such a brief portion of our existence.

Yes, it is the living I must relate now.

2

WHEN I look back along the avenue of years it saddens me to find that so little remains that was my father's. Of course there are his stem-winder, his pistol and saber, but these are without particular value. I imagine a gun collector would give fifty dollars for the long-barreled Colt .45, and perhaps a fancier of edged weapons would pay thirty dollars for the fine Castellani saber. Once a watchmaker offered to buy my father's stem-winder so he could hang it in his window to indicate the progress made in this exacting craft.

That my father failed to leave a substantial inheritance is common knowledge among those who knew him, and for some this marked him a failure. But what he bequeathed to us—my mother and my brother—cannot be evaluated in dollars; the memory of the man is beyond value. Strangely, I can no longer call to mind his exact image; he was not a man who cared to have his photograph taken. He used to say man's vanity is his downfall. But I still remember his early gray hair and his mustache, and the eternal aroma of good cigars. A curse, my mother called them, especially when she had to sweep up the ashes my father always dropped, but she never demanded he go to the front porch to smoke, as many wives required their husbands to do.

Once father's cigars nearly made him famous; I guess the story was popular in the army for thirty years. Sergeant Terry McGuire, who had been in father's troop long before I was born, first told it to me. Father's patrol had been ambushed by Arapahoe near the north fork of the Arikaree River—outnumbered, pinned down, and soon to be overrun. But in the close fighting the chief made the grave mistake of smashing a pocketful of father's Havanas with his warclub. Infuriated, father went after him and drove his saber clean through the Indian, and the others were easily routed without a leader.

Sergeant McGuire used to tell the story often, and he considered it hilarious, but mother would pull her lips tight and say she didn't think it was funny at all, warning McGuire not to repeat it again in front of the children.

But he always did.

There are times when I can bring back the sound of my father's voice, and he is very close to me then. But most of all I remember that he was tall and straight-standing and that the troopers loved him. He used to say that the test of a man's ability to command was best judged by the length of time troops stayed with him. A good commander could keep men; troopers soon transferred out of a poor outfit.

1890 is a year I'll never forget, for that was the summer we drove Diablito, the Apache, back into the waiting arms of the Mexican army. Or perhaps I'll never forget it because I was sixteen and my world was falling to pieces and there was nothing I could do to save it.

Diablito was the last of the bad Apaches—Geronimo had been sent to a Florida prison, and the Apache threat was over —at least everyone thought so until Diablito ran north across the Arizona border.

And that was my father's department.

In the record he was listed as Lunsford, James Gillette, Lieutenant Colonel, 3rd United States Cavalry. That doesn't tell much about the man, what he was or what he stood for, and I guess you could say that's the reason I'm writing this after all those years have passed into the shadows.

There isn't much left of Fort Starke. A few adobe walls still stand crumbled with the years. On a recent visit I could still see the deep ruts worn into the hard adobe, ruts cut by

10

the iron-shod wheels of the water wagon making the trip from spring to palisade compound. But in 1890 Fort Starke was a part of Arizona Territory, part of the United States government, a two-acre adobe-walled plot planted on the southern edge of a parched and dreary desert. During the day this desert shimmered into a heat-hazed infinity under a molten sun. But in the evening a cotton-smothering desert darkness engulfed everything and the wind came up with its push and cry and everyone forgot the blistering hours.

We lived in the big house—the commanding officer's house—with my mother and two younger brothers, Reed and Paul. And our dog Fleas. An abomination, father called him, but I recall that he was the one who always fed him at the table. He repeatedly forbade us to keep Fleas in the house, but he was the one who brought his old greatcoat from the attic and allowed Fleas to sleep on it behind the kitchen stove.

Nelson A. Miles was the commanding general, father's boss. I suppose he's remembered best because he chased all the Apaches out of Arizona, the bad ones at least. The rest of them were placed on the reservations to the north where they were taught to farm and hated every minute of it. But there was still Diablito on the loose, and this must have worried General Miles some, for he ordered father to capture him.

I remember that morning. The sound of the wind pestering a loose shutter woke me and for a time I lay there, staring at the kalsomined ceiling, now a dismal gray in the predawn darkness. In the other room across the hall I heard my father stomping into his boots. So I edged back the covers, and put bare feet to the cold floor not wanting to wake Reed, who was eight and a light sleeper. I heard father go down the stairs and into the kitchen, so I dressed and slipped out of the room.

The lamp on the kitchen table had been lighted spilling a yellow glow through the doorway and into the hall. Father was by the stove, pulling on his suspenders with one hand and feeding wood into the stove with the other. Fleas left his bed, stretched and came toward father who bent to stroke his hoary muzzle. My father turned toward me, his eyelids pinched half-shut against the stab of light. He closed the stove lid and listened a moment to the mounting roar. "You're up early, Mel."

"The wind woke me," I said.

Father consulted his stem-winder. "It's only a little after five." Then he shrugged and slipped the watch back into his

11

pocket. I didn't say anything, just waited until he put a match to his morning cigar. Mother always said that he wasn't fit to live with until he had his cigar, and I guess she was right. But then, we had all learned not to pester her until she'd had her morning cup of coffee.

Father opened the back door and stood there looking at the dark parade and the quartermaster sheds beyond. Fort Starke wasn't such a bad place—I hardly recalled any other, having lived here nearly eleven years. Reed and Paul had been born here.

I moved across the room to stand by my father. The wind scuffed sand along, grating the weathered adobe, banging an unhooked door somewhere near the officers' picket quarters. In the middle of the parade the flagpole halyards *thrummed* steadily.

The barracks were a darkened lump of low buildings crouched against the west palisade wall. Dark now, but in an hour reveille would sound and the post would come awake. My father often stood this way when the post was quiet, watching and listening. He reminded me somewhat of Doctor Bickerstaff, the regimental surgeon, feeling the pulse of a patient, and I guess Fort Starke was father's patient, for he knew every complaint that weakened it, and every force that made it strong.

Finally his glance moved on to the bachelor officers' mess, now sporting lamp-bright windows. He tipped his head down to look at me and spoke in that soft way I liked. "Ready for your coffee, Mel?"

"Yes, sir."

You have to understand that mother was definite in her opinion that sixteen-year-old boys should not drink coffee, but there were mornings like this when father walked quietly around mother's rules. I guess my father's gift was his way of making a person feel a little older and a little more important than he actually was. I'd watched him do this to the regimental bugler, who was only seventeen. A quiet word from my father and the bugler would fancy himself the most man in the troop.

We cut across the parade corner, my father walking easy and loose and me straining to imitate that walk. Inside the mess two cooks labored over a blistering stove while the round-bellied mess sergeant sat at a long table, finishing a plate of fried eggs.

When father stepped into the dining hall, the sergeant jumped to his feet. "Mornin', sir!" He sent his yell into the kitchen. "Rafferty, bring the colonel his coffee!"

12

"Two cups," father said quietly, and Sergeant Gleason went into the kitchen. Rafferty brought the coffee, then went back to the bake-oven heat where Sergeant Gleason found a dozen tasks for him.

The coffee was strong enough to float a bullet, and scalding hot, but it was the way father liked it; I tried not to make a face as I drank mine. There was little talk; father was never a man to throw words around unless he had something important to say.

He puffed his cigar to a sour stub. Then he said, "I may buy you a horse of your own this year, Mel. Would you like that?"

I could only stare. When a dream becomes reality it is always a little stunning. He smiled through a cloud of cigar smoke. "I think you're ready for the responsibility."

"I'll take good care of him, sir," I said.

He squinted his eyes. "How are you getting along with Mr. Biers?" He paused, and when he did I had the feeling that he was seeing things far away, things I could never see. "Are you getting your lessons done on time?"

"Yes, sir."

"Mr. Biers tells me that you've been studying Latin and German with Doctor Bickerstaff. You spend most of your time at the infirmary. Do you like the doctor, Mel?"

"Yes, sir. He lends me books."

Father's glance swung to me; his eyes were squeezed half-shut. Shards of brightness came from their depths. "What kind of books? Latin?"

"Some Latin, sir. But biology mostly, in German. He—lets me use his charts too, when I need them."

"Charts?"

"Of bones and muscles, sir." I paused, understanding that I was leading myself into an area better left unmentioned, but a young boy's great desire pushes all else aside, even what judgment he has. "Father, could I have a microscope instead of a horse?"

There was a spittoon at the end of the table and father got up to drop his cigar. Then he stripped the wrapper from a fresh one. His glance came over the flame, a deep, penetrating glance.

"You never told me about this, Mel. I thought you wanted a horse."

"I do, but I'd rather have the microscope, sir." I was ill at ease and he saw it. He sat down again.

"Doctor Bickerstaff spoke to me the day before yesterday," father said softly. "He says you're a brilliant student." He

13

paused to build a wreath of cigar smoke around his face. "You're growing up, Mel. And I guess you're growing away from me, and I don't want that. It occurs to me that you've made up your mind what you want to be, and it isn't a soldier, is it?"

I couldn't look at him. "No, sir."

"Why didn't you tell me, son?" When I didn't answer, he added: "Because you thought I'd be disappointed, Mel?"

"Yes, sir. I know what you always wanted."

He waved his hand, and I fell silent. For a moment he sat rotating the cigar between his lips, and I could see that he *was* disappointed.

Finally he said, "I'm a few months from forty, son—that must seem ancient to you. It seems a long time to me when I look back and remember you, newborn, my first son." He smiled. "I had a young man's dreams and a young man's pride. I wanted you to be a soldier so I could sit in the audience and see you graduate from the same platform as I. That was foolish, son, for no man can require another to live over his life."

"But you always talked about—"

"Just talk, son. I've never lied to you, Mel. I did want you to be a soldier, but there are other things besides soldiering. Don't blame Doctor Bickerstaff for telling me—he was proud of you, and that made me angry, for he had the pride I should have felt. It wasn't your choice that hurt, Mel. It was the fact that you no longer cared to trust me." He reached across the table and rumpled my hair. "Don't hide Bickerstaff's books any longer, son. And tell your mother—she'll be proud of you."

Then he got up and took both cups to the kitchen, putting them in the sink. Father smiled mildly at Rafferty's look, motioned me to come along, and we went out the side door.

There was a light in regimental headquarters, and before the squat building stood an ambulance and ten-man detail. Father looked at this a moment and said, "The general's getting ready to leave. I have goodbyes to say. Better get home—your mother will be up."

"Yes, sir," I said and walked away. At the back door I paused just long enough to see him cross headquarters porch and go inside.

Mother was in the kitchen, a gray woolly robe tight about her. It is unfortunate that we can never recall our mothers as they looked young, but instead remember them as being a little careworn and tired. I do recall that she was slender and shapely, a small woman—thirty-some and not trying to

14

hide it. Her hair was brown with reddish lights in it and her eyes were that shade of gray that is almost blue.

I let the screen door bang, and she turned to look at me. "Where's your father?"

"At headquarters, seeing General Miles off."

"You've been to the officers' mess," she said and came close. "Let me smell your breath." She sniffed. "Coffee! Melvin Lunsford, I ought to take a shingle to you—" Then she turned away. "Oh, what's the use? Your father would give you a dime for not crying. I suppose if he drank whiskey you'd want to lick the cork."

"I only had a small cup," I said, feeling that this was something I had to defend. "I'm nearly grown!"

"You're only sixteen, and you'll march right up those stairs and see that your brothers get to breakfast. I've never seen such slowpokes."

Experience had taught me not to argue. Sergeant Terry McGuire always said that my mother would have made a good top sergeant, and I guess he was right. No one ever disobeyed her. One man tried, a sutler's assistant at Fort McDowell. Mother took his sass, then went home for father's riding crop. The rest is history in the army. The way I understand it the sutler's assistant was ashamed to show his face on the post after having been run off by a woman.

By the time I got Reed and Paul downstairs father had returned; I could hear his soft, deep voice in the kitchen. Mother was at the stove, arranging fried eggs on a platter. Father had finished washing at the sink and now stood dripping water on the floor, while mother stopped and searched out a fresh towel.

The dawn was growing brighter, invading the gloom, pushing back the glow of the kerosene lamps. Near the flagpole the regimental bugler blew reveille, the tones sparkling bright in the stillness. Then the post began to come alive.

Fleas came from behind the stove and put his front paws on Reed's shoulders, knocking him down. He began to wrestle with the dog.

"Sit at the table, boys," mother said, "and leave the dog alone."

Through the window came the first streaks of sunlight. I watched it spread across the flatness, the first warning of another scorching day. Reed and Paul were all action and noise, crowding each other to get to the table. Father gave them what McGuire called his 'parade ground glance' and they quieted immediately.

He said, "Why don't you give that dog a bath, Mel?"

"He don't like water, sir."

Father's mustache hid his smile, but I saw it lurking in his eyes. "That feeling is not confined to dogs," he said. He took our plates, filled them, then saw that each of us had a full glass of milk, which was pretty much a luxury in Arizona before the turn of the century.

"Mr. Wynant's milk cow got into a dandelion patch," mother said. "The milk's bitter as gall."

"I'll speak to the sutler," father said. "He knows a rancher up above who's been selling milk." Father's eyes came up to mine. "Did you tell her, Mel?"

"No, sir."

"Tell me what?" mother asked.

Reed, who always talked too much, said, "Melvin's got a secret, Melvin's got a secret!"

"Oh, shut up," I said. "You don't know anything about it."

"Let's not bicker," mother said.

"I'm not bickering," I said. "It don't concern him, that's all."

"Doesn't," mother corrected, then repeated it. "Doesn't. Pay attention to what Mr. Biers teaches you, Mel. Now tell me." She folded her hands and waited as she always did when she expected the exact truth from someone.

"I've been studying with Doctor Bickerstaff," I said. "I want to be a doctor when I'm older."

Mother's eyes darted to father as though she feared an explosion, but father kept on eating.

"Jim, you knew?"

"Bickerstaff spoke to me about it," father said quietly. "This is not a boy's idle curiosity, Cora. Mel has done well with his Latin and biology. Bickerstaff feels that the boy will make a fine doctor."

"But—that's not what you wanted, Jim. That's not what you planned. Why, from the day he took his first step you said—"

Father put down his knife and fork. "I've said a lot of things, Cora. But it's what Mel wants that matters. He went to Bickerstaff because there was a need in him that only Bickerstaff could fill. I want him to be a doctor, Cora, if that's what he wants."

Later in life I came to understand some of the reasons women cry, but that day I was baffled when mother put her apron to her face. Father smiled and went on eating, while Reed, Paul and I sat there, wondering what had happened to bring this on. Several times father slipped his arm around mother's shoulders and reassured her.

Finally she stopped crying and smiled at me in a way I had never known before, as though I were the answer to some secret longing. She looked at me, although she spoke to father.

"We'll have to send him East, Jim. In a few years, when Bickerstaff thinks he's ready. Colby is a good school—it was near my home. Fine doctors come from Colby, Jim."

"We'll see," father said. "We'll see in a few years."

Fleas, whose eyes never left father at mealtime, edged up to a station near the knee. A moment later father's hand dropped to his lap, and Fleas swallowed heavily, then licked his chops.

"Jim," mother said, "if you don't stop feeding that dog at the table you'll never train him!" We began to giggle but her glance silenced that. "Boys, hurry or you'll be late for school. Since Mr. Biers takes time from his quartermaster duties to instruct you, the least you can do in appreciation is to be prompt."

Then father said what I'd hoped he'd say. "Cora, I'm taking to the field for a day or so, and I'd be pleased if Mel came along."

Mother always had a ready objection each time father wanted to take me on patrol, but Terry McGuire's timely arrival cut her short. He came in without knocking, which was his habit, and to head mother off even further, father said, "there's two eggs left, Terry."

McGuire scraped back a chair and sat down. His glance was quick, darting, like the needle of a compass. He saw my mother's tight-lipped expression and my expectant face, so he mussed my hair and grinned. "Ah, no thanks, sor, but I'll be havin' some of that fine smellin' coffee."

Mother got up and brought a cup and saucer, pouring for him. "Don't bother to flatter me this morning—it'd be wasted."

McGuire's eyes sparkled like polished leather buttons. "Now, ma'am, you know I'm not the kind of man to turn a honey-phrase."

"You didn't kiss the Blarney Stone," mother said. "You swallowed it."

"She got up and stood near the sink with brush and comb. We hurried down the rest of the rancid milk and Paul and Reed lined up to have their hair properly combed and shirt tails tucked. Mother herded them to the front door. Her voice came down the hall. "Now study your numbers, Reed —I'll not have Lieutenant Biers saying you're lazy. And Paul, don't fight with Captain Shirley's boy—it all comes back to your father." The door banged and they raced off the porch, mother's voice following them. "Paul, there's wood to fetch for Mrs. Latham if you expect to be paid!" She came back into the kitchen, taking her place at the table. "What I need is one more."

"That can be arranged," father said, smiling.

Mother shot a short, embarrassed glance at me, then got up quickly and began to gather the dishes.

Sergeant McGuire had his coffee "saucered and blowed." I remember him as a blocky man, heavy as the bole of an oak. Thirty-four years of army trouble had drawn deep lines in his face, and the hooks and diamonds on his sleeves were frayed from the years he had carried his top soldier's rank.

McGuire said, "The gen'ral got up early this mornin', didn't he? Did he make any mention of the paymaster's stage, sor? It's been three months now since I've had a drop of—" he glanced quickly to me—"me medicine."

"You'll live longer without that poison," mother said.

"Try your credit at the sutler's," father suggested.

"I'm ten dollars in debt now, sor," McGuire admitted. "It was after that attack I had last month, if you care to recall, sor."

"Was that when you nearly got put in the guardhouse?" I asked.

McGuire gave a forced chuckle. "Ah, we'll not be talkin' about that, lad." He could switch subjects quite well, and did. "Did the darlin' gen'ral get away on schedule, sor?"

"On the minute," father said. "However he left us with a job."

"How's that, sor?"

Father's glance moved to mother, then back to McGuire. "He wants us to capture Diablito."

"The divil!" McGuire exclaimed. "But he's a Mexican Apache, sor."

"He has been staying in Mexico," father amended. "But the Mexican Army's been after him for months. General Aguinaldo of the general staff wants Miles to apprehend him; Diablito is forming the annoying habit of ducking into Arizona every time the Mexicans press him too close. And I agree with Miles—Diablito has to be captured, if and when he comes across again. There are plenty of Apaches in Mexico, all peaceful, but a leader like Diablito could recruit them. Miles doesn't want that possibility left behind."

This brought McGuire up short. "Left behind? Are we movin' out?"

"Within thirty days," father said quietly. "That's unofficial and will be until Miles sends us a telegraphic order

18

from Camp Bowie." Mother had turned and was standing there, listening. "We're leaving for good, Terry, and Miles wants nothing remaining that could cause a mess later."

"But there'll be some Army left in Arizona, won't there, sor?"

"Small, scattered detachments," father said. "Reservation police duty, little more."

"Thirty days," McGuire said, as though he found it unbelievable. "Seems I've been here all me life, sor."

"A long time," father admitted. He was looking at mother. She put the dishtowel aside. "Jim, you're not fooling? I wouldn't want you to fool about this."

Father frowned. "Cora, I didn't know you hated it here. The heat's bad, and you've had to do without—"

Mother sat down, her hands folded in her lap. "It's not hate, Jim—I'm Army and can take the bad with the good. It's just that so much has changed. The boys are growing fast and I can't keep up with them any longer. Once I could teach them, but they've outgrown my knowledge. Mr. Biers will be able to carry them another year—after that I don't know what. I just want to be near a town, Jim. Not a town like Douglas with a saloon on every corner—I mean a town where there's a church and a proper school. Am I wrong to think like that?"

"No," father said. "I'm sorry it hasn't been better, Cora."

She got up and went back to the dishes. "It'll be something to think about, going somewhere else. Before, I never dared to think. It's a kind of luxury now."

McGuire finished his coffee and took the cup to the sink. Nearly every morning he did this, took his cup to the sink after mother had finished drying, and every morning she tried to frown her disapproval. McGuire was a part of our lives.

"I want Wade Hastings in command of the second section," father said. "We'll depart in an hour. And see that Mel gets a gentle horse."

"Aye, sor," McGuire said, starting for the door. But he paused there and looked at me. "Bring your twenty-two, lad. We'll flush some game." His glance touched father. "Is it all right, sor?"

"He can take his rifle," father said, and peeled the wrapper from a cigar. As I said, he knew exactly how to make someone happy.

After McGuire left, father got up and walked over to mother. He put his hands on her shoulders, turning her to face him.

19

His voice was very gentle. "Just thirty days, Cora. Whether we catch Diablito or not, it's still just thirty days."

"That won't be long to wait," she said. I remained at the table, all ears. Then she turned to me. "Don't just sit there, Mel! Get your things. And wear those tin pants; I don't want you tearing up your good corduroys. Scoot! When your father says an hour, he means it! The cavalry isn't going to wait for you!"

3

MANY BOOKS have been written about the cavalry, and most of them are tales of dress parades and courageous charges. This makes, of course, exciting reading, but such spectacles were the smallest fragment of a soldier's life as I observed it. Other writers must have recognized this one-sided picture, for there are other stories, of army tedium and dull routine, broken only by fragments of gaiety. This, too, was a part of the army, but only a part.

The way writers tell it, a patrol riding from the post was an occasion for flags to fly and the regimental band to play. At Fort Starke, the departure of a patrol was always a quiet affair, even during the time of General George Crook and the big Apache trouble. And the only ones who watched were the wives of the men riding out and, of course, the commanding officer, who always acted like a man regretting the necessity of throwing so puny a force against so strong an enemy.

That was the way it went when Sergeant McGuire assembled C Troop of the 3rd on the southwest corner of the parade. Lieutenant Wade Hastings was inspecting. I was glad father had chosen Hastings for his second in command. Wade Hastings was a special kind of man to me. He always treated me as an equal and what sixteen-year-old can ignore that? He was a very tall man, an easy officer with the enlisted men, and if they habitually took advantage of his good nature, it was forgivable because he always managed to get the job done. I could not recall his ever losing his temper.

I was all for joining Hastings, but mother stopped me on the porch for her last-minute fussing. "You're sure your canteen's filled? You can't expect the troopers to share theirs with you." Her hands fluttered about, checking buttons, making sure I had everything. Mothers have a way of doing things. It can make a grown man feel like an irresponsible idiot.

"Now, don't pester your father," she warned for the tenth time. "Sergeant McGuire will look after you—Lord knows your father has enough to worry about without your bothering him."

Lieutenant Hastings had the troop in line, dismounted. "I have to go," I said, and gave her one of those hurried kisses that slide off the cheek. Then I clutched my rifle and canteen and ran across the parade.

As I raced past Hastings, he said, "A little more soldierly, there!" I popped into place beside Sergeant McGuire and when I looked at Hastings he was laughing.

The sun was young in the sky but an early heat pressed down, beating through the weave of my shirt. Sweat gathered under my hatband. Father came from regimental headquarters, his saber clutched against his leg to keep it from thumping around. He gave the troop one sweeping glance, saw the things that needed to be seen, then turned to Wade Hastings.

"Mount informally, Lieutenant."

Any other officer would have mounted them by the book, especially with the commanding general hardly clear of the post, but father ran his troop his way, and I never knew him to be influenced to the contrary by rank.

But before we could mount, Lieutenant Ludke came trotting up. "Sir," he said, saluting father.

Wade Hastings gave the hand signal for the troop to remain in place.

"Yes, Mr. Ludke?"

"I must apologize for approaching you in this manner, sir—"

"We can dispense with the formality," father interrupted. "What do you want?"

Ludke was new; his duty at Fort Starke had begun only two weeks before. He did not know father, or how to talk to him.

"As you know, sir," Ludke began, "I'm engaged."

"I didn't know," father said, "but I congratulate you."

"That isn't what I wanted to talk about, sir," Ludke said. Father smiled. "Mr. Ludke, you brought up the subject."

This threw Ludke into a flounder. He looked helplessly at Wade Hastings, then tried a new tack. "Sir, I was wondering if you would send a telegram when you reach Fort Redoubt.

I'm expecting my fiancée, a Miss Lilith Shipley, to arrive in Tucson, and I would like to leave word for her."

"Mr. Ludke," father said, "we have a telegrapher in the ordnance building. I suggest you send your message yourself."

"The telegraph is down, sir."

A frown wrinkled father's forehead. "It was working last night—I sent a message to Camp Lowell telling them of General Miles' departure." He looked at Wade Hastings. "Did you know about this?"

"Yes, sir. But I thought you knew—I told Major Regan to tell you." He paused. "Shall I attend to the repair now, sir?"

"Confound it, no!" Father said, glancing at his watch. "I mean to depart as scheduled. Mr. Ludke, see that the telegraph gets fixed. If Major Regan questions you on the matter, say that I gave you a direct order."

"Yes, sir. I'll take care of it."

To Hastings, father said, "Mount up."

Father swung up, and we settled in the saddles. He led us at a walk to the main gate. Along officers' row and in front of the enlisted men's sections, women stood in silence, watching us. This was a familiar sight to me, and whenever I recall a patrol leaving, I always think of them standing there, their faces stone-patient. This was a woman's role in the army, to carry the burden of uncertainty with endless patience. Rarely did the women leave the post and they mark time from the moment their husbands left until they returned. Or until there was no more hope of their returning.

The gates of Fort Starke swung wide for us, then closed. Before us stretched the desert, endless sand, thirty-eight miles to the nearest water and Fort Redoubt where 41 men and two officers guarded a hundred miles of border. And nearly forty miles in the other direction, Fort Savage stood sentinel duty, the only settlement between Fort Starke and Fort Yuma.

But neither place was father's destination.

We moved in an easterly direction, and the land around us was that shade of tan that is almost cream in the bland sunlight. A land of cactus and stunted brush, and now and then a dust devil stirred up by a freak turbulence in the otherwise motionless air. As the sun climbed, a smashing heat mounted and, faced with the glare, the horizon shimmered until it was undefinable. By midmorning we seemed surrounded by trackless waste—I could no longer see Fort Starke behind us, nor could I have placed it accurately by pointing. All the troopers rode with their hats pulled low over their eyes and each had daubed dirt on his cheekbones to cut the bouncing glare. For better than ten miles we followed a line of telegraph poles leading to Fort Redoubt. Then we swung away, putting these on our left flank.

The column was a line of dull sounds, jangle of equipment, protest of dried leather that no amount of saddle soap seemed to help in the hot months. Dust drifted up and hung in the still air to blend with the nitrogen of horses and the sweat of men.

Father put out a point, three troopers who rode nearly a half mile ahead of the column. Sergeant McGuire kept turning his head, looking back and out to the flanks. He always did this when on patrol and I suppose it was a habit left over from the days when any journey through this country was the beginning of an adventure that had no certain happy ending.

I watched for small game with my repeater ready, but nothing stirred. At noon we again picked up the line of telegraph poles leading to Fort Redoubt and father halted the troop. The men were given "at rest," and fell to their rations. Father called Wade Hastings forward from his section. "Have one of the signalmen shinny up that pole and rig a jump connection."

"Are you going to call Redoubt, sir?"

"I'm going to try to raise Starke," father said. "It would be interesting to know where we stand, Wade. Can the operator at Starke receive?"

Trooper Peterson went up the pole, cut into the wires at the insulator and dropped his line down. Corporal Melanowski attached his key and began rattling away to a mute length of wire. Father stood by, watching. Wade Hastings rolled a cigarette.

Finally Melanowski said, "Not a damned thing, sir."

"Keep trying," father said. He turned to McGuire. "Get my map case." When McGuire brought it, father found a map and spread it on the ground. "We'll alter our line of March to due south, Wade."

"That'll put us on the border by late afternoon," Hastings said. He squinted his eyes and scanned the distance. "This route will take us into the pass, sir. You're not going to cross into Mexico, are you?"

"We'll stay on this side," father said. He raised a sleeve and wiped the sweat out of his eyes. He turned to watch Melanowski who still labored over the key. When Melanowski finally shook his head, father turned back to Hastings. "The Mexicans have a signal picket stationed in the pass.

23

We'll set up the heliograph before it gets dark and ask them to relay a message."

"To Starke?"

"To Fort Savage," father said. "I want them to try and send a message over wires from the west. If they get through we'll assume there's a wire down between Redoubt and Starke."

"And if they don't get through?"

"Then I'll worry," father said. "Communication can become vital, Wade—don't ever forget it."

"Do you want me to send the signal detail on ahead? They could relay a heliograph message to the nearest Mexican telegraph. I think there's one at Frontieras. You'd have your answer by nightfall."

Father shook his head. "The sun's too hot for fast traveling. Besides, there's plenty of time. If we can make contact with the Mexicans we'll have an answer by midnight. I can telegraph for another squad. If they arrive by midnight, I'll know we have a down wire." He paused to gaze at the inscrutable distance. "Then again, there's Diablito. We have to find out where he is."

"You think the Mexicans know, sir?"

"They've been chasing him," father said.

McGuire put my thought into words. "Suppose they've chased him into Arizona, sor?"

Father's voice was even and unconcerned. "Then we have a bad Apache to catch, Terry."

The noon rest ended, and the troop mounted. We began the push south. The sun was vertical, a column of heat that left every man slouch-shouldered and lightheaded. Recalling those times, and the heat, I still marvel at those men, the fifty-cent-a-day regulars. I marvel at their magnificent strength and quiet devotion to duty. They were, as father often said, dirty, drunk, and disrespectful, but when he recounted the times they stood together in the face of death, his voice would grow soft and his eyes shiny. And it was then that I knew for certain how he loved a soldier.

Through a dreary, dead-heat afternoon we marched, seeing nothing. Finally father halted the troop and dismounted them. "Camp here," he told Terry McGuire. "Pickets, a ground rope. Squad fires." He pointed to me. "Stay in camp, Mel."

"Yes, sir."

Night bivouac for a cavalry troop was a busy time and there were no idle hands. Wade Hastings gave me the job of breaking dry brush for his fire, seeing as how I was to share

24

it with him. An hour passed before the troopers began to settle down, but the signal detail worked on with the heliograph. When my chores were finished, I walked over to watch. Father, Wade Hastings, and Terry McGuire were there.

The land around us was no longer desert, and the farther south it extended, the more broken it became, soon running to towering peaks. The corporal in charge of the heliograph worked it a few times to make sure he had the sun-catching mirror properly focused.

"All ready, sir. What shall I send?"

"A standard identification signal," father said. "The Mexicans will answer if their picket's manned."

"Yes, sir. Shall I send it steady?"

"For the first hour," father said. "If you get no reply, try five-minute intervals until the sun is gone." He glanced at the sky, his eyes squinted. "You have a good two hours left, Melanowski."

There was a rapid blinking of the shutters, clacking out a silent message of light across the miles of land.

"Can I stay here?" I asked.

"If you keep out of the way," father said and moved back to camp, McGuire and Hastings following closely.

I pushed a few small rocks aside and sat down. Waiting never seemed very exciting to me, and the Army did a lot of that; it was the story of a soldier's life. The sun was dropping, but there was little letup in the heat, and there wouldn't be any until around ten at night.

A half hour dragged by. Melanowski turned the shutter over to a private and squatted beside me. He uncorked his canteen and took a long pull before wiping his mouth with his sleeve. He was a young man, a second hitch man still wondering why he had signed over. I didn't know much about him, but that was not unusual, for there is something anonymous about the line trooper—the uniform makes them seem alike, and after awhile you stop trying to differentiate between one and another. They were either good soldiers or bad soldiers.

"You're startin' early in life," he said to me. "Better try farmin' when you get older. Better than this."

"Don't you like the Army?" I asked.

He grinned and sweat was pinched from the wrinkles near his lips. "Love it, kid. That's why a man signs over."

The private who operated the heliograph yelled suddenly. We scrambled to our feet. Father and Wade Hastings came on the run. I stared, and then I saw it, a pin point of light, blinking, speaking across the miles.

"They've acknowledged, sir," the private said. "What shall I send?"

"This," father said, handing him a paper. While the operator blinked out the message, father explained to Wade Hastings. "I've asked the Mexicans to relay the message to the telegraph at Frontieras. I figure an hour there, then another to get through from Frontieras to Fort Savage. If the line's up, Ludke will be here by midnight with a small detail."

The private stopped sending. "They've acknowledged, sir. Message on the way."

"Now ask for a meeting. Time and place."

The private worked the shutter, and when the message came back, Melanowski wrote furiously, his eyes darting between light flashes and paper. Finally the blinking stopped and Melanowski handed the message to father, who read and pulled at his mustache.

"Sergeant," father said, "get up a four-man detail, four that can stay out of the wine bottle. Sergeant Haukbauer can remain in charge until we get back." His glance touched me. "You can come along if you like. Do you good to see how the other half lives."

"What's going on?" Hastings wanted to know.

"An invitation," father said, smiling. "General Jesus Azavedo has invited us to supper, which was more than I bargained for." He pulled out his stem-winder and glanced at it. "I believe we can make it by eight o'clock if McGuire doesn't dally."

And Terry McGuire was never a man to do that. He made his four-man selection, all serious-faced teetotalers, then had the horses brought in from the picket line. Sergeant Matthew Haukbauer, a tall, prim-faced man, stood at attention while father told him what he expected in the way of discipline. I didn't know Haukbauer too well, for he was a man inclined to solitude. But father liked him. Not very original, father used to say, but as reliable as a railroad watch. But that was father's way, to expect the best of a man, and generally that's what he got.

From his saddlebag, father took a bottle of the sutler's best wine. He said, "I expected to do business with a captain and this would oil the rollers. However, it will make a nice gift for the general. Not his brand perhaps, but it's very good."

Sergeant McGuire looked at the wine. "What a thing for a man to see, sor, and me havin' such a terrible thirst."

"Then I'd better take charge of it," father said. He mo-

26

tioned us into the saddle and led out, pushing south, alternating between the trot and the walk. Father was very careful of the wine, but during ten minutes of dismounted traveling he handed it to McGuire.

"If that seal is broken when we arrive, you're a private."

"Aye," McGuire said sadly, and I knew this was a trial for him; his payday habits were well known in the army. Every time the paymaster's stage arrived at Starke, McGuire would show up at the house smelling like a hot mince pie. Mother would hustle off Reed and Paul and get cross with him, while father steered him to the barracks to sleep it off. Mother always wanted to know why father didn't do something—reduce McGuire to private—but father would say that every man has a weakness; we have to overlook these small things.

The land was now one layer of ripped rock piled on more rock and as we passed between huge outcroppings, heat radiated from them like the sides of a hot stove. Twice I saw lizards sunning themselves and once raised my gun for a shot, but father's glance warned me not to.

"You're in someone else's back yard," he said and I put the rifle away.

An hour of this rough going brought us into high ground and when I looked back I could no longer make out our night bivouac position. The sun was below the rim of the land and the sky blushed to blood in the west. A faint breeze began to stir, lifting small particles of dust.

Hastings said, "Reception committee, sir," and pointed.

Then I saw them, a small detail of Mexican regulars, green coats faced with bright red, and plenty of brass buttons, all highly polished. An officer led them and he came on at a trot, reining in amid a shower of dust. He was a gay, smiling man with a long waxed mustache and eyes as bright as polished ebony. He wore a fancy coat with long epaulettes; there was a profusion of silver on his saddle.

"Buenos tardes, señores." He removed his hat with a flourish. *"Capitán* Estobar, at your disposal."

Father introduced himself, and Lieutenant Hastings. Then Captain Estobar said, "This way, *señores. Andale*—the general is impatient for his food."

We followed him into the Mexican camp. Their army was not like ours and a good second lieutenant fresh from the Plain above the Hudson would have made a few changes. I had heard Terry McGuire say often enough that if the Mexicans fought the way they made love, no army could beat them. He must have known what he was talking about for there were more women in the camp than men. A huge fire marked the center of the bivouac and around this couples danced and drank. I wanted to stop and watch but father decided there were things going on he didn't want me to see, so we went on to the general's tent.

What I remember most about General Jesus Azavedo was that he lived pretty high on the hog. He was a man accustomed to luxury and made certain he had plenty of it on hand. Knowing my father and the opinions he held toward people who demanded servants to wait on them, I expected him to show some displeasure, but he was too much of a diplomat for that. But I knew that Jesus Azavedo was not my father's kind of officer; he preferred men like General George Crook, who always shined his own boots.

Father presented the wine. "California, General. From Sonoma Valley."

"Ah!" Azavedo beamed. "Spanish, of course. A fine vintage." He seated himself at a long table already sagging under the weight of food. His servants began to bring in platters, and the general kept them hopping, slicing meat, filling glasses.

For fifteen minutes we ate without talk. When the general's monstrous appetite seemed dulled, he turned glittering dark eyes on me. "Who is this young cock, my colonel? So young to be a soldier."

"This is my oldest son, Melvin," father said.

"*Buenos tardes,*" I said, and Azavedo's smile threatened to split his fat cheeks. He seemed delighted when I spoke to him in Spanish and for several minutes the questions and answers flew back and forth. How old was I? Was I going to be a soldier like my father?

But he hadn't invited us to his camp to listen to my Tucson Spanish. We were there to eat, it seemed, and the general did very well at it. Ham, chicken, three slices of beef, and nearly a quart of wine had little effect on his bottomless stomach. But it gave him the strength to talk.

"You are concerned about the Apache, no?"

"Only if there is room for concern," father said. "And General Miles feels there is."

"Sssshhh!" Azavedo said. "Everyone is concerned. General Aguinaldo of the general staff is concerned, but that is easy for him, sitting in his office in Mexico City. Me—" he thumped his chest— "I have to suffer the inconvenience of field duty."

"How long have you been camped here, sir," father asked.

"Let me see—nearly a week now. Yes, a week."

"And Diablito?"

"That Diablito—a ghost! I have chased him until my troops are exhausted. But catch him? No, *señor*. He is named well—the devil is his father."

"Has he been raiding?" Wade Hastings asked.

"Raid?" General Azavedo spread his fat hands, now quite greasy for he preferred to eat with his fingers. "Last month he struck near Frontieras. Eight dead and two women carried off. Then he vanished like smoke. But I have Diablito trapped in these mountains now, my colonel. Of course he is waiting for me to leave before he comes out."

"General Miles doesn't want him in Arizona," father said. "That's why I wanted to speak to you, General, to formulate some plan of capture."

"*Por Dios*, I want to kill him!" Azavedo wiped his fingers on the tablecloth. "But that is unimportant now. I can only pursue him; he crosses the border at will."

"Then suppose you pursue him and let me capture him," father suggested.

"*Si*, but I grow weary of the chase."

Father took a sip of wine, then peeled the wrapper from a cigar. He raised up from his chair to bend over the candle for his light, then sagged back and puffed for a moment. "General, I'll betray no confidence when I tell you that the United States Army is pulling out of Arizona soon. There won't be more than three full troops left behind. If Diablito comes across, we'd never be able to stop him."

"I could not agree more, *señor*."

Wade Hastings listened intently, for this was the first he had heard about moving. But he said nothing.

"Working together is the only way," father said. "Do you agree, General?"

"*Si*. Do you have a plan?"

"A rough sort of thing," father admitted. "Little more than a sketch of general operations. We do not dare to take an armed military force across each other's borders, but I think we can squeeze Diablito pretty tight between us."

"*Por Dios*, we could! We could hold him at the border, the mouse caught between two cats."

"I suggest that you concentrate your troops here at the pass," father said. "Instead of pursuing him in column, spread your forces here to block him; this pass is one much used by Apaches, and they're not much for departing from custom."

General Azavedo beamed. "That can be done, my colonel. But when he enters your country?"

"We'll be waiting for him," father said. Wade Hastings was frowning, full of questions he dared not ask. "I'll dispatch two troops for extended duty as soon as I return. Give me a day and a half to get them into the field."

"And if the devil doubles back, *señor?*"

Father smiled. "Then we'll drive him into your waiting arms, General. Keep your signal pickets manned, and we'll keep in contact with you. Look for our signals an hour after sun-up and at noon. Also an hour before sundown."

General Azavedo heaped praise on my father, calling him a military genius, but what really made him happy was father's willingness to do all the work and leave the credit.

"I go to give the orders," Azavedo said and excused himself.

As soon as he left the tent, Wade Hastings said, "For God's sake, sir, you're not going to trust that—"

"You're talking about a general," father reminded, half-smiling. "I haven't lost my mind, Wade; I think I played this close to my chest. The question is where Diablito will cross. I know now. He'll cross here because the general is guarding the pass, and it will be a matter of pride that he sneak past the general's sentries."

"By golly, sir, I think you've hit it!" Hastings smiled. "But remember that's a general you're using for bait."

"Yes," father said, smiling. "Don't ever try that with lieutenant colonels."

Azavedo returned, a man highly pleased with himself. "*Señores,* the order has been given." He saw down and began eating again.

Until now I hadn't paid much attention to the noise of the camp; there was so much of it that it became like all constant sounds, soon ignored. But the silence was so sudden and so complete as to be beyond ignoring. Even the general paused with wine glass half-raised, his head turned to the tent opening.

A lieutenant hurried in, bending over to speak softly in the general's ear.

"What?" Azavedo roared. His face became rage-choked. "Get him out of here! I'll not permit him in my camp!"

Wade Hastings looked at father, who shrugged ever so slightly.

Full of apology, the lieutenant departed and I could hear him speaking to someone, his softly pleading Spanish pushed aside by rough bass tones. Then the tent opening parted and the tallest man I had ever seen came in. He carried an enormous rifle, one of those new Winchester .50-100 Express calibers. When he saw father and Wade Hastings he stopped and set the rifle down, while his right hand lifted to the bone-handled Remington belted to his waist.

"The damned night's full of surprises," he said. "McGuire glared at me when I came through the camp." His glance touched me, then passed on to Wade Hastings, who sat as stiff as a coiled spring. "Am I going to have trouble with you, Wade?"

"I'll leave it up to the colonel," Wade said. "But any time is all right with me, Gentry."

"We'll have no trouble in this camp," father said sternly and Gentry's hand dropped away from his revolver. I stared at the man, feeling that I should know him, yet equally positive that I had never laid eyes on him before. He had a bundle under his left arm and he stepped up to the general's table. Gentry wore buckskin pants, something of an oddity in 1890. His moccasins were Apache and the elbows of his cotton shirt were worn through.

His face was most fascinating—I had never seen an expression so bold. At first I thought it was the scar running across his cheek that gave him that half-savage appearance, but then I decided it was his eyes. They were wide-spaced, a deep brown, and completely without expression. Gentry was not an unhandsome man and I supposed that a barbershop shave would have made him appear almost respectable.

Then Gentry did a thing so bold as to leave us stunned. Even my father, who was rarely surprised, watched with a sharp attention. With his right hand, Gentry reached out and swept the table clean of dishes; General Azavedo stiffened, ready to call his guards, but the light in Gentry's eyes forbade it, or I guess they dared him to call them but the general was not up to it.

Opening the bundle, Gentry dumped the contents on the general's table. For a minute I couldn't make it out, just a lot of hair. Then the sweet rottenness hit me and I knew what the bundle contained.

And I knew who Gentry was and what he was. I knew from the talk, and guessed the rest from the talk that had been hushed so I wouldn't overhear.

This was the renegade whom everyone hated. Gentry, the last of the Apache-scalp hunters.

In a voice that was cool and detached from all emotion, Gentry said, "I'll take three thousand pesos for this lot. A hundred pesos apiece."

4

THE WAY Gentry put his hands on his hips and waited, insolent and very calm, told me better than words could how dangerous a man this was. His eyes held General Azavedo as effectively as if he had pressed a saber point to the latter's throat. The general could not hide his fear—it flared in his round, chocolate-colored eyes, and quivered in the slack fall of flesh on his cheeks. He made me feel soiled and ashamed, because in the army I knew, courage was as commonplace as coffee in the morning.

General Azavedo moved his stubby hands in small aimless circles. He licked his lips once, then looked quickly to father as though he expected him to do or say something.

When father offered nothing, Azavedo said, "Such an amount I do not have, Señor Gentry."

"You have it," Gentry said. "Pay it to me so I can get out of this stinking boar's nest."

Father's voice was easy. "Don't give him one *centavo*, General."

Gentry swung his head toward father and I held my breath; a man does not tease a rattlesnake without the risk of getting bit. Yet Gentry's eyes did not change—they were without anger. He was a man whose actions were mathematically deliberate, the result of some warped, impersonal logic understood only by himself. I couldn't help wondering if his eyes had looked the same when he killed the Apaches for their scalps.

"Better keep out of this, Jim." His voice was a bass drone. He stood there, six and a half feet tall, towering over us all. "You're in the wrong pasture to give orders."

"Don't ever question one of my orders when I'm in mine then," father said. He scraped back his chair and stood up, moving around Wade Hastings and me to face Gentry. "Why don't you just get out of this camp and take the Apache hair with you?"

"After I get paid," Gentry said.

"What's the money to you?" father asked. He wasn't the

least bit afraid of Gentry and I could have popped a few buttons from pride. Hastings and the general sat motionless and I knew Gentry had them backed down. Hastings would have denied this to his dying day, and he would have fought Gentry at the drop of a hat, yet he was afraid. But father felt none of this, no urge to tangle with Gentry.

He puffed his cigar and spoke as calmly as if he were checking quartermaster supplies. "Who are you fooling, Gentry? You never kill for the money. You stink of death. There's death in your talk, in your habits. It's soaked into your pores so deep soap won't clean you."

Gentry listened with complete concentration, and when father finished, turned back to Azavedo. "Let's see the pesos." He was certainly a single-minded man. General Azavedo bent, gave beneath the pressure, then snapped his fingers to summon his lieutenant.

When the officer hurried in, Azavedo said, "Bring three thousand pesos. *Andale!*"

The lieutenant went out. Father rotated his cigar between his lips and said, "Don't pay him, General. Maybe he'll quit when there's no longer any money in it."

"I must obey the law," General Azavedo said with resignation. "If he didn't get the money from me, he would go to another official and say that I refused to pay."

"Let him," father said. "That's an outdated, savage law—it doesn't fit the times." He placed his hands flat on the general's table. "General, can you blame the Apaches for raiding when a man like Gentry can legally hunt them down? He keeps Diablito stirred up. Without Gentry, Diablito would settle down. He knows he can't win."

"You going to preach, Jim?" Gentry asked.

Father didn't even look at him. He straightened, disgusted with this business. "How many Apaches do you estimate he's killed, General?"

Before the general could hazard a guess, Gentry said, "Over a hundred." This was not a brag, just a cold statement of fact, like a report of last night's poker winnings.

Father whirled to face Gentry and he was angry. "How can I appeal to you? What can I say that will penetrate your shell of hate?"

"Nothing," Gentry said. "We don't understand each other any more, Jim. We're both fighting the Apaches, only the methods are different."

"The reasons are what's important," father said flatly. "Gentry, you're no longer a member of the human race."

33

"I kill Apaches," he said. "You've killed Apaches. Does your way have more honor than mine?"

"You flatter yourself," father said.

Gentry chuckled, his glance swinging to me. "I'll leave it up to the kid." The candlelight bounced from his eyes, leaving an animal glitter in the dark depths. "Do I scare you, kid?"

For an instant I couldn't decide which was worse, my fear of this man, or the dread that I'd show it. I swallowed hard and found that I had a voice. "Not as much as you think you do."

He smiled, and it was a pleasant break in his expression although his eyes did not change. "You got a tiger here, Jim. Been some time since I saw any of your brood up close." To me he added, "I once held you on my knee, boy, but you wouldn't remember it."

I looked at father. "Is that so, sir?"

"Yes. You were very young," father said. Then he turned again to Gentry. "What do you live for? Because you think you'll meet another Apache?"

"That's something," Gentry admitted. "Who has a better right than I have?"

Father blew out a long breath and turned back to his chair. He sat down. "Maybe you did at one time, but you've worn the reasons out." His glance came up, and there was a very plain warning in it. "Don't ever shoot an Apache on my side of the fence."

"I'll try to remember that," Gentry said. He half-turned when the lieutenant returned with the sack of pesos. "Count 'em," he said and waited until the general had them arranged in neat piles. Then he scooped them into the sack and fastened it to his belt.

"What do you do with the money?" Wade Hastings asked.

Gentry's flat glance settled on the lieutenant. "Is it your business?"

"No," Hastings admitted, "but I'm curious. You stay out of towns and don't spend anything."

"I save it," Gentry said. "I've been in the mountains going on six years now, hunting Apaches, and every peso I've earned has been salted."

"You don't have enough to buy a shirt," Hastings said. "Look at you. What do you spend it on, Mexican women?"

Gentry gave Hastings a dead man's stare, and he stayed completely motionless for a full minute, teetering on some hidden edge of violence. Then he blew out his breath and pointed to the scalps. "Took me eleven months to get those. That's the last, Jim. My word on it."

"The word of a stinking animal," Hastings said. He was a man afraid, yet to prove to himself that he wasn't, he tried to pick a fight.

"That's enough of that!" Father spoke quickly. He regarded Gentry from behind a veil of cigar smoke. "Can a man ask why you're saving this money?"

The tall man pursed his lips, then shook his head. He picked up his rifle and turned to the tent opening. "I hate talk," he said.

Father was instantly on his feet. "Gentry!" And the tall man came around like an animal at bay, the bone-handled revolver half drawn from his holster. "Once you killed a man for speaking of the past," father said. "I'm going to speak of it now. Are you going to kill me for it?"

"Don't say anything," Gentry said. "Once we were friends, Jim. I still remember that, so don't say anything to make me forget."

"The money won't change a thing," father said. "It won't buy *her* back or buy you into the human race."

"I didn't expect it would," Gentry said. "Good night, gents." His glance touched Azavedo, then Wade Hastings. "I expect it'll be some other time, Lieutenant. You got something in your mind that will have to come out."

"You just pick it," Hastings said.

"I'll let you do that," Gentry said.

"Please, *señor*," Azavedo said. "Leave my camp."

"Why, sure," Gentry said and the tent flap dropped. It was then that I became conscious of holding my breath, and let it out with a rush. Father puffed his cigar, completely relaxed. I noticed sweat on Wade Hastings' forehead, and he was fumbling with the flap of his pistol holster, trying to rebutton it.

"Some day I'll put a bullet through him," Hastings said.

"Why?" Father turned. "What would that solve? Do you think he'd care? He's been dead for six years, as dead as a man can get and still not know it. It's something no one talks about. Maybe if we had, Gentry would have been different."

"He's a trouble-maker," Hastings replied strongly, "you said so yourself. We'd all be better off with him dead."

I guess Wade was really riled by the contempt Gentry had shown for him. It was the first time I ever recalled seeing him mad, but father ignored it.

After glancing at his stem-winder, he stood up and spoke to the General.

"You'll hear from us in a day or two. Keep this pass well bottled, General."

"It will be done" Azavedo promised. He smiled and put his hand on my shoulder. "Go with God, *mi caballero*."

Sergeant McGuire had the horses waiting and he was sober, which seemed to surprise father somewhat. The camp festivities were going full blast and the sounds swelled louder than ever. The dancing went on, stimulated by countless bottles of wine.

The night was clear and dark, illuminated by a million lidless stars. A cool wind eased across the scorched face of the land and father led us at the trot. There was no talk and no stopping and at last I could see the bright pin-points that were our squad fires.

Sergeant Haukbauer had sentries out, and they challenged us, then passed us in. McGuire turned the horses over to Trooper Murphy for picketing.

Father stripped off his gauntlets. "Three hours here, Sergeant." His watch came out again. "We'll leave at one-thirty." He looked at me and smiled. "In case your mother asks, and she usually does, you went to bed at seven-thirty."

"Yes, sir," I said.

Wade Hastings' brows wrinkled. "Sir, will Ludke have enough time to get here?"

"Yes, he'll take a more direct route than we did."

Sergeant McGuire's lined face was grave, his voice deep and concerned. "Sor, I've got that god-awful feelin' again in me stomach." He looked around the camp. The troopers must have shared it for they had all moved their blankets back from the fire, away from the light, closer to the sheltering darkness.

Father wiped a hand across the back of his neck. "I can't understand the telegraph being down. If Ludke fails to show in the morning, I'll send out a patrol to find the broken wire."

"Or cut, Colonel," Hastings said. "Azavedo could have let Diablito get away and been ashamed to admit it. That Apache could be in Arizona right now."

"That thought has occurred to me," father said. "Well, get some sleep. We'll pull out quietly at one-thirty."

"That's the way I like it when there's Apaches about," McGuire said. "Nice and quiet."

"Don't build ghosts," father said. "We don't know yet."

"There's no ghost in me stomach," McGuire said. "And no booze either—it's as dry as a waterhole in August." He turned to his own blankets.

Father chuckled, but I knew he wasn't laughing at Mc-

Guire. He spoke quietly to Hastings. "The general has been camped near the pass for a week. Perhaps our coon *has* escaped in the dark."

"I don't like to think of that, sir," Hastings said. "There's a lot of land out there for him to hide in."

"Wade, we'll try not to get ahead of ourselves," father said. "My first concern is the telegraph line. If Mr. Ludke arrives shortly after midnight, then I have proven that there is a line down between Fort Starke and a point where we turned to go south. If Mr. Ludke does not arrive, new possibilities have presented themselves. The station itself could be out of order, or the lines in both directions have been cut."

"Isolating Fort Starke," Hastings said. "We're the nearest to the pass. It could be a good way for Diablito to cover his border jumping—isolate us, so we can't spread an alarm."

"If you're suggesting that Diablito would attack Fort Starke with twenty-some men, I'd say you'd been drinking."

Hastings blew out his breath. He was a worried man and didn't care who knew it. "Who says Diablito has only twenty in his party, sir? As you said, the Apaches are strong in Mexico. Azavedo wouldn't know how many have filtered across —and he couldn't stop them."

"We'll not knock the general," father said firmly. He realized that I was still standing there. "I thought you went to bed at seven-thirty. Get!"

I hurried over to where Trooper Heggen had my blankets spread. When I sat down to take off my boots, Heggen said, "Your old man can get on a man's back and paw, can't he?"

"Not often enough to hurt," I said, and settled down, pulling the blankets tight about me.

I listened to the small sounds of the troopers shifting about, and against the vast silence of the land these small disturbances were magnified. Sleep came easy for me and Sergeant McGuire's hand on my shoulder was a rude shock.

"Time, lad," he said and moved on to the next man.

The wind was down. Nothing seemed to stir and it was an odd sensation, this grave quiet. While I pulled on my boots the troopers made ready. There was no talking; McGuire saw to that, and in fifteen minutes we were standing to horse.

Yet father seemed reluctant to leave. He and Wade Hastings stood together, vague shapes in the night. Father was saying, "I'll give them another fifteen minutes."

"Ludke could be having trouble finding our bivouac," Hastings said. "He's new out here, Colonel."

"Every Academy man can read a map, even by matchlight." He waved his arm to the single squad fire. "On the

37

desert that will be visible for miles. No, if Mr. Ludke does not arrive in fifteen minutes we must assume that Fort Starke did not receive the message from Frontieras."

Hastings was hard to convince. "A lot could have happened, sir. I mean, perhaps the message got shelved some place."

"Hardly likely," father said. "Wade, in Mexico, the army is the authority, and this message was backed by a general's rank. No, the message was sent—I'll bet on it."

Time dragged and every man had his ears tuned to the north, but there was no sign or sound of Lieutenant Ludke's detail approaching. Finally father gave the quiet order that sent us into our saddles, and we moved out.

McGuire rode on my left and finally he turned to me. "The night is unholy quiet without the wind, eh, lad?"

I swallowed so the lie wouldn't show. "It don't bother me."

To prove that my nerves were relaxed, I kept turning in the saddle, looking back, looking to each flank, for there was something awesome about the desert at night. A man can be but a few miles from town and yet feel utterly alone in the world; so great is the illusion of emptiness. Never in my life have I recaptured that sense of complete isolation as I knew it on the Arizona desert.

The march back to Fort Starke was the short way, the way Ludke would have taken, but there was no sign of him, and father searched as best he could in the darkness. Most of the troopers slept in the saddle but I was never horseman enough to try that. The sky was streaked with the first of the false dawn when we approached the palisade gates. They opened, and we filed onto the parade ground, there dismounting.

To McGuire, father said, "Find the signal sergeant and the officer-of-the-day. I'll see them in headquarters in ten minutes."

"Yes, sor." McGuire trotted to the guardhouse.

"Do I have to go home now?" I asked.

"You can wait," father said and I walked with him to headquarters. Wade Hastings lighted a lamp although the dawn was getting brighter by the moment. Father sat at his desk and unwrapped a fresh cigar.

A moment later Lieutenant Reindollar came in. He was a very small man and always reminded me of a blooded fighting cock eager to bare his spurs. Reindollar came to the point. "Didn't you contact Mr. Ludke's detail, sir? I didn't see him come in with you."

Father's eyes came up steady and slow and I realized this

was what he had been afraid of hearing. "The message came through?"

"Yes, sir." Reindollar paused as the signal sergeant came in, saluting.

"What time?" father asked.

"Nine-fourteen, sir," the sergeant said. "Savage relayed it from Frontieras."

Father put his cigar aside as though the taste was unpleasant.

Hastings said, "What could have happened to Ludke, sir? Lost?"

"Fourteen miles from the post?" Father's voice was sharp. "Sergeant, have you tried to get through to Fort Savage since last night?"

"Yes, sir. The line's dead now, sir."

"You're positive that our telegraphic equipment is working?"

"We acknowledged last night's message, sir. It worked then."

Father sat for a moment, fingering his mustache. "That'll be all, Sergeant. And thank you."

"Will you need me, sir?" Reindollar asked.

"No. No, go ahead," father said absently. After Reindollar went out, father said, "Wade, I think we've closed the door after the coon escaped in the darkness. Diablito was in Arizona when we left Fort Starke yesterday. Azavedo must have known it."

"We don't know that, sir. Not definitely."

"But do we dare to guess otherwise?" Father stood up and he seemed very tired. "Tell Sergeant McGuire I'd like to see him in my quarters." He got up, checked his cigars, then started for the door.

"Yes, sir," Hastings said. I went to the door and waited for father. When he paused there, Hastings said, "Ludke could show up, sir. Diablito would have no reason to attack Ludke."

"Do you really believe that, Wade? Or did I send Ludke and his detail out to die so I could determine whether or not the damned telegraph worked?" He pushed me gently ahead of him, and we went outside. Together we walked slowly toward the two-story house on the other side of the parade. All the other quarters on the post were connected, but my father's sat by itself.

As we approached, he stopped and looked down at me. "If I were you, Mel, I'd say nothing to your mother about the man we met."

39

"You mean the general, sir?"

"I mean Gentry. He's not a man your mother likes to talk about, and she'd be put out if she knew you'd met him."

"All right," I said.

"And we'll not speak of Mr. Ludke either," father said. "There's no need to get her upset."

"This is Army business, I guess, sir."

"That's right. It's Army business."

There was a light in the kitchen, and my mother turned quickly when I opened the door. She smiled at father and went to him. He put his arms around her and kissed her, not one of those pecks on the cheek, but on the lips, a long kiss, the kind that made me feel warm because I lived here with two people in love.

Then he released her, and she raised a hand to his cheek. "You need a shave, Jim."

"And some of your coffee," he said, then added: "I've had my cigar."

Mother laughed and she was young again. This was a joke between them, about the cigar. She never spoke to him on matters of importance unless he was in the proper humor, and that was always after his morning cigar. That was the way it was between them, a lot of little things, all of which came back to me now—things I really didn't understand at the time, but knew to be part of their life and their love, and so a part of me.

She went to the cupboard for dishes. Father said, "Mel was the guest of a Mexican general."

"That was nice," mother said and carried the coffeepot to the table.

"There were a lot of women in their camp," I said. "You should have seen the way they carried on, dancing and whooping it up."

"Well," mother said, a little primly, "your father'll be taking you into the pool halls next."

"Oh, I've been in Brohammer's," I said. "The last time we was in—"

Father cleared his throat. "Ah—I hardly think your mother would be interested."

Mother shot him a grim look and went to the stove. "Go wash your hands if you want to eat."

I sighed to let her know I would do it, but under protest. It seemed that every time she wanted me out of the way so she could talk with father, I had to go wash my hands. There were days when I had to wash three or four times.

While I was drying, Sergeant McGuire came in. Reed and

40

Paul ran down the stairs and climbed on father's lap. I thought this was a little silly; they were getting too old for that, but father didn't mind, and mother smiled. She fussed about, getting them seated at the table.

Reed said, "Can I go along the next time, sir? Can I?"

"You're too young," mother said. Her glance brushed father, and I thought I detected amusement in it. "He knows too many sinful places to take you."

"Now, Cora," father began, but mother had the reins and wouldn't let go. Fleas scratched at the back door and mother let him in. He looked like a different dog, for he had been bathed—the mortification was still in his eyes as he went to father for sympathy.

"What was he doing outside?" father asked.

"He slept there," mother said.

Father seemed amazed. "How did you manage that?"

"A firm hand," mother told him. "Once he understood his place, he was all right."

"He howled all night," Paul said.

Father tipped his head forward and laughed while mother went to the stove, finding a dozen tasks there. Sergeant McGuire opened his mouth to speak, but father shook his head, holding the sergeant to silence.

Without warning, mother turned to me and asked, "What time did you get to bed last night, Melvin?"

"Ten, I think," and I looked quickly up at my father.

"I swear, Jim—he's not a soldier, you know!" Then she turned to McGuire. "If you want coffee, then get your own. And the next time your thirst gets too much, *ask* for the cooking sherry—don't snitch it."

"Ma'am—" McGuire began.

"I gave it to the Mexican general," father said. He turned to McGuire, who was getting a cup from the cupboard. "I want an ambulance ready in an hour and a half. Have the bugler sound officers' call after reveille."

McGuire's face was serious. "Yes, sor. A detail, sor?"

"Twelve men," father said. "Carbines and pistols. And take along anything else you think we'll need."

"Aye, sor." McGuire knew what father meant, and I could guess.

I looked at mother but she was fixing breakfast. Father's face was smoothly unreadable. Mother said, "Where are you off to now?"

"Tucson, to see Miles," father said. He poked me with his finger. "You can come along. I'll buy you your first drink of

41

whiskey." He was joking, we all knew that, but the idea nevertheless shocked mother.

"He needs sleep," mother protested. "Besides, he shouldn't be chasing all over the country with you."

Father smiled and I cannot recall a time when that smile failed to melt mother's resistance. "He needs to live a little."

Sergeant McGuire said, "I'd best be tendin' to things, sor." He went to the door and there paused. Strange as it seems, I can't bring myself to think of Terry McGuire as an enlisted man; he was a man who felt a near paternal responsibility toward my father. "Don't you be worryin' now, sor. Not about a thing."

Father spoke softly. "Plenty of time for that. Now get out of here, Terry. I've been home a half hour and haven't yet told this wonderful woman I love her."

"Take your brothers outside and play, Mel," mother said. She was looking at father and smiling, her eyes bright.

"We're not through eating," Reed complained. "Besides, it's just getting light out."

"Don't argue," she said. I urged Reed and Paul out the door. They ran toward Captain Hanson's quarters, Fleas at their heels, barking in his booming voice. Then I opened the door, but turned back. Father and mother were standing, and he was holding her. Her arms were tight about him, and I could see his face, and his thought: What happened to Mr. Ludke?

I turned and ran across the parade corner to the infirmary. There was a lamp lighted in Doctor Bickerstaff's office. In the center of the parade the regimental bugler was blowing reveille, golden ribbons of sound. And this made me stop and think of young Mr. Ludke, who was awaiting his fiancée. Perhaps, out on the desert, someone should have been blowing taps.

5

Doctor Ludwig Bickerstaff's office was a haven to me when I was troubled, or when I was thirsty for knowledge. I liked the doctor and I liked his books. But I believe I liked best his collection of specimens, all neatly bottled and labeled, and the many charts he had. And Doctor Bickerstaff always made me feel welcome, giving me free rein, never tiring of my endless questions, never failing to send me away with a new book, or—more important—a new thought.

He was a fat little man and spoke with a broad accent. He had a round, florid face, and thick glasses over which he peered at his patients. I knew he was a good surgeon, but he was a better doctor of medicine, a facet of the science frowned upon by the army at that time. Bickerstaff was a constant experimenter—his laboratory was as complete as every cent of his salary could make it.

He turned, gave me an over-the-glasses glance, then said, "How is der biology, boy?"

"I'm finished, sir."

"Den ve must haf der examination," he said. He waved his fat hands. "Look at der bottles—I'm busy now."

So I studied the specimens—diseased livers, a diabetic pancreas. Without raising his attention from his experiment, Bickerstaff said, "To learn, you must take notes. The mind vill not retain without notes."

I got paper and pencil and began to study the most fascinating specimen in his collection, the unborn fetus crouched in the quart of formaldehyde. Many times I had looked carefully at this mite of humanity who never lived and many times I had wished to take the jar off the shelf and examine it more closely.

Doctor Bickerstaff knew this. He said, "Before, you vas just a curious boy. Now you have read der biology. You've studied Liebig, Henle, and Virchow—you may now take it to der table."

I did, with trembling hands. For better than a half hour I made observations and tried to organize some notes, but nothing came out right. My mind kept wandering to Mr. Ludke somewhere out on the desert with his detail.

Doctor Bickerstaff left his work to join me. When he saw me idle, he clucked. "Vat's dis? Ver is der eyes, boy?"

"I can't think," I said. "I'm sorry, sir."

Bickerstaff's brows bunched. "Troubles?"

I would have told him, in spite of what my father said, but I was saved when mother opened the door and stepped inside. I don't know why I did it, but I put the jar containing the fetus under the table.

She took off her shawl. "I thought I'd find you here, Mel." She smiled at Bickerstaff. "Good morning, Doctor. If he bothers you, just send him home."

43

"No bother," Bickerstaff said.

"Melvin," she said, "I want to talk to you about your father. Something is worrying him—I've lived too long with him not to know."

"Yes, ma'am?"

She frowned and canted her head. "I recognize that tone too. You're going to be evasive."

And when I got evasive, mother usually got persuasive, something I had never been able to withstand. Another five minutes and she'd have the whole story; father was usually quite pliable in her hands and I wondered by what ruse he had escaped. I was certainly going to need an out.

Then my foot touched the jar, and I had it. I stood, making sure I knocked the jar over. It rolled from beneath the table and stopped near her feet.

She gave it a glance, then said, "Melvin Luns—" Then she stopped and looked down again, staring this time, her eyes large and sort of hypnotized. She backed up quickly. "Melvin Lunsford!"

This was a command and a reprimand all rolled into one.

I quickly put the jar back on the shelf. Mother swung her anger to Doctor Bickerstaff. "How could you show a thing like that to a boy?"

"He is a student, *Frau*—"

"Student, my foot! He's a boy who ought to be thinking of other things besides—" She paused. "Whose child is that?" Then she whipped her shawl over her head. "I'll find out. Now you come home, Melvin. Your father will want to talk to you about this."

She went out, slamming the door. I looked at Doctor Bickerstaff, feeling somewhat ashamed, but he smiled and took the fetus from the shelf, wrapping it in an old newspaper. Then he pressed the jar into my hand.

"Vimmen don't understand des t'ings. Take it home. Put it in a goot place. Ven you need another to study, come back."

"I don't know how to thank you, sir," I said, and I really didn't. I didn't know how I was going to get this into my room either, but that was a problem best kept to myself.

"Go like der mama says," Bickerstaff advised. "But make der notes."

"Yes, sir." I went out and across the parade. Knowing mother, I figured she'd be in the kitchen, so I skirted the house and used the front door. My guess was good for as I pounded up the stairs, her voice followed me.

"Mel, come down here!"

"In a minute."

"Come down now!" She wasn't fooling, and I looked desperately for a safe place to store the specimen. The closet was too risky. The bureau was out of the question. So I placed it under the bed, a place so obvious no one would look there.

Then I went downstairs. She said. "Go to headquarters and wait for your father. Tell him to come home as soon as he's free."

"Aw, you're not going to tell him?"

"I most certainly am. The idea, a boy your age looking at such things. It isn't—decent." She saw I was going to argue and would have none of it. She pushed me out the back door. "Go on and do as I tell you."

"Yes, ma'am." I crossed the parade, my boots scuffing dirt at each step. The bugler came out of headquarters, wet his mouthpiece and ripped into officers' call. I went into father's office as the last noted faded.

He glanced up. "I thought you were home."

"Mother wants you to come as soon as you're finished here, sir."

An eyebrow was raised. "What did you do now?"

"She'll tell you, sir."

"All right," he said. "Now sit over there and wait."

I took a chair near the wall and Major Miles Regan came in, a hefty man with an unsmiling manner. He sat down and immediately two other officers came in. The last one closed the door. Wade Hastings winked at me and took the chair next to mine.

Second Lieutenant Barney Reindollar leaned against the far wall.

Mr. Ludke should have been in this room too, but he was not, and we all felt his absence.

"Gentlemen," father began, "we may be facing a trying period. We're severely cut in strength—I should have three captains and six more lieutenants in this command, not to mention four more troops of cavalry. But we'll do until I can get more. We'll have to do."

He then explained about our expected departure from Arizona, as soon as Miles cut the orders. He also covered the talks with General Azavedo.

Then he came to Second Lieutenant Ludke and the missing detail.

"Major Regan, you will be in command while I am absent from the post. I have a detail ready to go in search of Mr. Ludke."

"It's possible that he's lost," Major Regan said. "Have you considered that, Colonel?"

"Considered it? Major, I've been praying that it's so. But I'm afraid our disrupted communication system and Mr. Ludke's disappearance are far too serious to be coincidental."

"Do you think this Apache has actually come across the border?" Reindollar asked.

"Is it safe now to assume otherwise?" father asked. He blew out a long breath and put a match to his cigar. "Then again, I'm faced with the problem of restoring our telegraph system. Major, I want two platoons dispatched within the hour, each traveling in opposite directions until they find the breaks and repair them." Father gnawed at his lip for a moment. "On the Redoubt road, the break is undoubtedly between here and a point fourteen miles out. I can only guess at the Fort Savage line, but I'll bet it's close in."

"Why do you say that?" Regan asked. He was a man who liked full explanations.

"Let's assume that Diablito is definitely in Arizona and that he cut our lines. He would have to drive west to cut the Fort Savage line and still get back in time to ambush Ludke. Consequently, he must have cut it close to the post."

"Aren't you assuming a lot?" Regan asked. He liked to point out the flaws in others, probably because he had more than his share and felt them less when he saw weaknesses that were not his own.

"I'm assuming only what it's safe to assume," father pointed out. "I want the line breaks found and repaired, then signal detachments set up in both directions. If there is any hostile activity in this vicinity, I want the other posts advised of it."

"Putting out detachments will spread our men pretty thin," Regan pointed out.

"I can't help that," father said. "The job has to be done."

"Do we have that many men who can signal?" Reindollar asked.

"I think so," father said. "Make these platoons from D Troop—they are mostly unmarried men."

"Which leaves Troops C, A, and F," Major Regan said.

The major was beginning to exasperate father, but he pushed his feelings down by puffing on his cigar. "We've always been shorthanded, yet we have managed to campaign successfully. Reindollar, I want you to leave in the morning with A Troop. Patrol the border between here and a point fifteen miles east."

"One troop doesn't cover much, sir."

"Split into three platoons," father said. "Sergeants Maxey and Lovering are capable. They can each command a section."

"That's hardly more strength than Ludke had," Regan said. "And he was ambushed."

"Now who's supposing?" Father said. Regan flushed, then looked at his dusty boots. "The difference, Major, is that Ludke was a green officer who wouldn't know an Apache from a bunch of *sacaton* grass. Sergeants Lovering and Maxey do." He looked from man to man. "Any questions?"

Regan had one; you could count on it. "Am I to understand, sir, that only one troop is to remain in defense of Fort Starke? There are thirty-five women and children here. Captain Henson and the other four officers are without tactical experience—they would be useless in defending the fort."

Father said, with tight-drawn patience, "Fort Starke is a solid post and Diablito's strength is unguessable. If there are no more questions, you are dismissed." Until now he had not spoken at all to Wade Hastings, but as Regan and Reindollar turned to the door, father said, "Please remain, Wade."

Reindollar closed the door and father offered Hastings one of his cigars.

Hastings said, "Regan's a damned old woman!" That was his way, to speak his mind quickly and I could remember the times when he regretted it.

"He's also a major in the United States Army. You ought to watch yourself, Wade—you're a disrespectful cuss."

Hastings laughed and leaned back in his chair. He puffed a cloud of cigar smoke around his head. "Good Havanas, Colonel, but they spoil me for Moonshine Crooks." His tastes ran to the best in everything and sometimes I had the feeling that he resented the limits of a lieutenant's pay.

"I've been thinking," father said, "that taking a detail off the post now may be an unwise course. If we assume that Mr. Ludke's detail ran afoul of the Apaches, then we can also assume that he is dead and haste may only get us into trouble. However, if he is lost—although that seems unlikely—a few hours' delay may pay us dividends, should Ludke return."

"That makes sense," Hastings said.

"I want to avoid making a quick decision for which I might have to apologize to the general. It's my intention to go to Tucson and ask Miles for more troops. I want you along, Wade. We'll scout for Mr. Ludke on the way."

"Any time you say, sir," Hastings said. He stood up and went to the door, there pausing. "Mel, you're growing too fast. Stay young, boy—it's the happiest time in your whole life."

After he went out, father cleared his desk of papers, locked the drawers, then stuffed a half dozen cigars in his shirt pocket. "Now, let's hear your mother's complaint," he said, and we went out.

Mother was cleaning the parlor when we entered the house. Reed and Paul were at Lieutenant Biers' quartermaster office absorbing fractions. Mother put the feather duster aside.

"James, I have a serious matter to discuss with you."

"I gathered that," father said. He sat down on the horsehair sofa. "Don't get upset, Cora."

"Well, I am upset. Leave the room, Melvin."

"Why?" I asked. "Gosh, don't I get a chance to—"

"If Mel's done something, it's only fair that he should be given a chance to defend himself."

"I'm not going to get anywhere with you," mother said stiffly. "He's your first-born. Naturally you'd lie and he'd swear to it."

"That's not quite true—"

"But true enough," mother said. "Something's going on around here." She stopped, realizing that she was getting off the point. She flushed and wrung her hands. "Doctor Bickerstaff has a heathenish collection of specimens—things in bottles." She looked at me and I could see her choosing words. "This morning, when I went to the dispensary after Melvin, I found him with one of the horrible things."

"It was an unborn baby," I said.

Mother gasped, and father tipped his head forward to study the tip of his cigar. Finally mother said, "Jim, you've got to make Bickerstaff get rid of it. Why, there's no telling whose it is. There've been stillbirths on this post, and he's got one in a bottle. It's simply not Christian!"

"It's science," I said quickly. "Science can't be bound by sentiment, mother. If we're to learn—"

"I'll learn you with a hairbrush!" Mother looked about to cry. "There are some things you'll do well never to learn. How can you look at a—a child like that and think of anything but the tears that were shed and the shattered dreams?" She put her apron to her face. "How can you?"

"Gosh, I—"

Father shook his head and I fell silent. He drew mother to the couch. "Did Bickerstaff say whose child it was?" Mother shook her head. "Then I'll speak to Bickerstaff about it." He stood up, motioning me into the kitchen ahead of him. Then he closed the kitchen door.

"Mel, you've done a cruel thing."

I stared at him. "I didn't mean to, sir. She was going to worm it out of me—you know, about Mr. Ludke. I didn't know—"

"That's all right," father said. "Mel, six years ago your mother was very sick—do you remember?"

"Yes, sir."

"We were planning on another child, but it wasn't to be. I think your mother's first thought was a natural one. She thought the child might have been hers."

"But it isn't, sir. Doctor Bickerstaff says the mother was Papago." I hesitated, sorry now that I had brought the fetus home. Mother would find it, and there would be more of this. "I have it in my room now, sir. Under the bed."

Father stared. "You've got to get it out of there!"

"But if I explained to mother—"

"There are some things that can't be explained to a woman," he said. "You get upstairs. Wrap it and take it back to Bickerstaff. Use the front door. I'll get her into the kitchen."

"Yes, sir," I turned to leave.

"Mel." I turned back. "Mel, in the future, do that kind of studying in Bickerstaff's office."

"Yes, sir."

Passing mother, I felt compelled to stop. "I'm sorry," I said lamely.

Her anger was easily melted, and she hugged me to her quickly. "Melvin," she said, "do you really have to study—things like that?"

"Yes, ma'am."

"Doesn't it bother you? I mean—"

"No, ma'am. Doctor Bickerstaff says a doctor has to think of treatment as a problem, and that he has to train until his hands and mind function without emotional interference."

"I see," she said quietly.

I ran up the stairs while father called her into the kitchen. Lifting the quilts, I took the jar and hurriedly wrapped it. I went down the stairs a lot slower and quieter than I'd gone up. I even remembered not to slam the front door.

The doctor's office was empty when I went in, so I put the fetus back on the shelf and ran across the parade. Stupidly I used the back door and mother looked around startled. "I thought you were upstairs."

"I—I came down," I stuttered.

"That's obvious," mother said. "I suppose you're hungry."

The kitchen clock ticked loudly. Father said, "If we could eat at eleven, Cora. We're departing at noon."

"Bring me back some needles," mother said. "Reed's pants are out at the knees."

"Nothing else, Cora?"

"No. I'll wait until I leave before I think of a new dress. Jim, a man puts on a coat to keep himself warm. A woman wears a dress so people can see it. There's no one around here I want to impress."

Then she asked it, the question. "Why didn't Mr. Ludke come back with you this morning?"

Father sat quietly for a moment. "My troop didn't meet Ludke. He's missing."

"And you're going to look for him?"

"Yes," he said. "We'll search until dark tonight. Then I'm going on to Tucson." He knew her. Knew that she wanted answers. "Cora, what can I tell you? My suspicions? Wait until I know what happened."

"All right," she said.

We ate at eleven. Then McGuire came in, perspiration slick on his face. He went to the coffeepot and found it empty and for a moment mother let him stew. Finally she produced a pitcher of lemonade.

Father sat at the table, puffing his cigar. I perched on the back step where I could hear everything. Fleas lay at my feet, and I combed his thick hair.

When McGuire finished his lemonade, mother said, "Want another glass?"

"Ah—no thanks, ma'am. But it was mighty fine."

To father, he said, "Everything's ready, sor."

"The shovels? In case there's need of a burying detail." McGuire shot a quick glance at mother, but father added, "You can't keep anything from a woman. Foolish to try."

"We've shovels," McGuire said.

"Get Hastings, and we'll leave," father said.

6

THERE WAS an army ambulance and a fifteen-man detail waiting for father in front of headquarters, and not since 1886, the year Geronimo surrendered, had I seen troopers so heavily armed. Each man wore double belts of ammunition, and each man had something else, something that made the heavy load seem natural—each man had a stone-firm face. Beneath the tugged-down hat brims, lead-serious eyes peered. And the men waited, not with their usual restlessness and turning in the saddle, but with a reined patience men show when there is killing to be done, and they are eager to get at it.

I climbed into the ambulance, carefully, so as not to crush the pocketful of cookies mother had given me. Father came out of headquarters. He placed a .45-70 Winchester repeating rifle in the box and mounted without a word. McGuire and Lieutenant Hastings waited while he lifted the reins, then raised their hands in the signal to move.

Near the warehouse, Captain Hanson, the ordnance officer, watched us drive from the post. Everyone seemed tense, including Haggerty, the blacksmith, whose whole world was the farrier's yard. But now the gong-like strokes of his hammer were stilled. Everyone was thinking of Mr. Ludke and what we might find out there on the desert.

While there was fighting, death became common fare and men learned to live with its threat. But four years of peace had lulled their habits and their thinking, and they found changing back difficult.

The palisade gates opened and closed and once more the vast land claimed us with its almost unbearable silence. The sun bore down, a flaming weight. We turned southeast, along the route Mr. Ludke might logically have taken. For better than an hour we traced the switching course of a dry wash. Father took the ambulance into the rocky bed while the detail split into flankers on the rims. I kept looking up at the troopers; they were alert, riding with their carbines at ready, butt resting on the thigh, hammers at half cock.

51

No wind stirred the gagging heat. I sat with my mouth open, drawing air painfully. Father rode with the Winchester across his lap; he had already worked the lever, feeding a cartridge into the chamber.

The dry wash finally petered out, breaking into the flats. The command, fanned out for the search, began to gather in single file behind the ambulance.

Then I saw movement, not on the ground, but in the air. I touched father's arm, drawing his attention, and he hurriedly unlimbered his field glasses.

"Hastings! McGuire!"

They rode forward immediately. "Can I look?" I asked and he handed me the glasses. Under magnification I could see them, the buzzards circling, but staying high. When Wade Hastings came up I had to relinquish the glasses. He had his look.

"Mr. Ludke, sir?"

"I don't know," father said. He looked through the glasses again, this time scanning the desert. "I don't see anything. But look at the way they're circling, as though something were frightening them."

I had noticed that too. Buzzards are cowards, and they circle high, dropping lower and lower as long as nothing moves. But these birds stayed aloft, circling, crying in rage.

"Could be a wounded animal," Hastings said. He had his eyes squinted against the smashing heat glare.

"Put out the flankers," father said, lifting the reins.

We put the dry wash behind us and edged out onto the flats. But the flats sank away to a depression in the desert floor, and father stopped, swearing softly to himself. Then I could see Mr. Ludke's detail—small, miserably huddled shapes a hundred yards ahead. The horses were gone; the Apaches took horses. Then I saw movement. One of the detail was alive. We all saw him working, digging.

Father put the ambulance into a run and the detail surged forward. We closed rapidly and the man who had been digging, stopped, reversing his shovel, only it wasn't a shovel, but a rifle. He recognized us as Army and put the rifle down. We were close enough now to see that he was not a soldier.

He was a young civilian in a sweat-stained white shirt. And beneath each armpit, in shoulder holsters, pearl butts protruded along with the blued, impersonal metal of guns.

Father stopped the ambulance and jumped down. McQuire dismounted the detail.

As I scrambled off the high seat I saw that two of Ludke's men were already buried.

"Get the shovels," father said and Hastings promptly went to work. "Find Mr. Ludke and place him in the ambulance." He took me by the arm and pushed me toward the ambulance. "This is nothing for you to see."

I agreed. I had already seen enough to make my stomach queasy. The Apaches had stripped every man and mutilation made identification difficult. Rifles and all ammunition had been taken; the Apaches were always hard-pressed for those things.

Father walked over to the young man who waited by two fresh mounds. He was blond and mild-mannered, not a big man, but the guns made him big. He wore flat-heeled shoes and dark trousers, now gray with dust.

"You took a chance," father said, "being alone."

"I've taken chances before," the man said. He nodded toward the dead soldiers. "I came on them over an hour ago. Part of your troops?"

"Yes," father said. "Would you care to give me your name, so I can thank you properly?"

The young man thought about it for a moment, then shrugged. "Bob Van Orden." He said it as though he expected a chill to follow, and I guess in some quarters it would have. His name was well enough known and so were his guns.

"It was Christian of you to stop and bury these men," father said. "Have you drawn any conclusions as to how this happened?"

Van Orden paused a moment. "I'd say they cat-footed through that dry wash and were caught here in this hollow. There wasn't much of a fight; I didn't see a sign of downed Apaches." He took a hunting case watch from his coat and popped the lids. After a quick glance at it, he put it back. "I'll say goodbye now, Colonel. The soldiers are with their own."

"Is there a hurry?" father asked.

"Unless you want another dead man," Van Orden said. "There's a gent behind me; you'll recognize him on a sorrel stud. I don't want to meet him."

"I see," father said, but I could tell from his manner that he didn't. He was simply willing to let Van Orden's story stand without further explanation. He offered his hand and Van Orden hesitated, as though he were unaccustomed to any display of friendship.

They shook briefly and father asked, "Are you going to Tucson, Mr. Van Orden?"

"Likely. I could use a crowd to lose myself in. A man's too easy to find out here."

"Then give us a moment," father said. He beckoned for Wade Hastings, who came over on the double. "Mr. Hastings, I can see now that my going to Tucson is out of the question—I'll be needed at Fort Starke. However, I want you to go. Take the detail and Sergeant McGuire. Mr. Van Orden will accompany you. I'll take Mr. Ludke's body back to the post."

"Can I go with Mr. Hastings, sir?"

Father frowned. He weighed carefully the risks involved and decided that I would be safer with Hastings and the troopers than with him alone in the ambulance.

"All right," he said. "But you mind what he tells you."

"Yes, sir."

"Fetch my dispatch case," father said to Hastings. "I'll write a report and you can plead my case with General Miles."

Hastings brought the case and for fifteen minutes father wrote furiously. Bob Van Orden kept looking east, his eyes squinted. He moved around considerably, clearly wanting to leave. The troopers were finishing up the burying, for the ground was sandy and the digging went quickly. Each man was wrapped in a blanket and Sergeant McGuire made the proper final entries in his book.

Father finished his report, sealed it and gave it to Hastings. "Be alert, Wade. Diablito's moving around this section, and he wants war." Then, as an afterthought, he added, "And, Wade, if you can locate Mr. Ludke's fiancée, inform her of this tragedy. See that she gets on a stage heading east."

"I'll attend to it, sir," Hastings promised.

Van Orden stopped his pacing long enough to say, "Can't we be moving, Colonel? I wasn't more than two or three hours ahead of this fellow when I left Fort Redoubt."

"Ahead of whom?" Hastings asked.

"It doesn't matter," father said. He put his hand on my head and gave it a shake. "Your mother's going to raise holy Ned because I didn't bring you back with me, but you'll be safer with Wade and fifteen good soldiers behind you."

In a subtle way he was seeking reassurance, it had never occurred to me before that he ever needed it.

I said, "Don't worry about me, sir. I can take care of myself."

"Yes," he said, "I believe you can." He got into the ambulance. "Don't waste time in Tucson, Wade. You'll be needed at Starke." He lifted the reins and made a U-turn, driving across the flats at a good clip.

"Column of twos," Hastings said, stepping into the saddle. He looked at Bob Van Orden. "Where's your horse, mister?"

"In a draw over there," Van Orden said, pointing. "I'll get him." He trotted away and a moment later disappeared from view. And just as quickly he returned, mounted on a roan gelding with a blaze face. Since I had ridden out in the ambulance, I was without a horse. Before McGuire or Hastings could say anything, Bob Van Orden took my hand and in one swoop put me behind him.

He smiled and said, "I'm good company."

His eyes were the color of clear ice and I could guess what they would be like when he was angry. But at that moment his smile was quick, and I found that I could easily forget the guns in the shoulder holsters, and what they usually stood for.

Wade Hastings waved his hand forward, and we turned north toward Tucson, a good four and a half hour ride.

At first I kept turning to look back at the fast diminishing plume of dust, and finally I could no longer make it out at all. Bob Van Orden must have understood my feelings, for he said, "He'll be all right, bub. The colonel will be a hard one to do in—he's got the eyes of a stayer."

"He's my father," I said, feeling proud.

"Why, sure," Van Orden said. "His mark's all over you."

At the hour Hastings had the detail dismount and lead. Bob Van Orden swung his leg over the pommel and slid to the ground. "When in Rome," he said and smiled. I would have dismounted too, but he shook his head. "Take the sit down while you can."

This drew a sharp glance from Wade Hastings. "He's Army —he does what the Army does."

Wade's voice was sharp and defensive, and I wondered why. Bob Van Orden must have wondered, too, for his head came around and he was suddenly all raw nerve ends, a cocked gun ready to go off. "Since the horse is mine," he said, "I say he can ride." He spoke softly, but there was an undercurrent in his voice declaring that he didn't like to be pushed, and the hint of how dangerous it could become if someone did push him too far.

Wade Hastings stared for a moment, then waved his hand as if to say, forget it, but I kept watching Wade and I could see the smoldering resentment in his stiff-set cheeks, and I knew he would never forget it. Somehow this was no different from the time he had faced Gentry in Azavedo's tent —Wade was determined to prove something. I didn't know what.

55

They mounted again and, later, walked. That was the way the Army moved: mount, dismount and lead, trot, walk the horses; everything by the book, but of course I'd lived by it so long that any other way was alien to me.

At six o'clock Wade Hastings halted the detail and ordered cold rations all around. Bob Van Orden had a can of peaches in his saddlebag and insisted on sharing them with me. The heat had turned them warm and over-soft, but they were a king's treat to me. When the can was empty, Van Orden sailed it out and it landed near a dried-up *chemise* clump.

"Ever shoot a six-gun?" he asked.

"No, sir. Just a rifle."

He smiled again, the way I liked, a warm and friendly smile. "Care to take a shot at the can?" He pulled his left hand gun free of the holster and the spring popped.

Wade Hastings said, "You don't have to prove anything to me, mister."

Bob Van Orden's expression was genuinely puzzled. "I wasn't trying." He handed the pearl-handled Colt to me. "Know how to work it, bub?"

"Yes, sir." The gun felt strangely light, but beautifully balanced. With the four and three-quarter inch barrel it lacked the muzzle heaviness of the cavalry pistol. I cocked it with my left hand, sighted carefully and squeezed. The trigger pull was exceptionally light—the gun bellowed and re-coiled against my palm. The bullet kicked up a shower of sand three feet to the left of the can.

"Golly!" I said.

"Not bad for a first try with a strange gun," he said, easing himself to his feet. I tipped my head back to look at him, I saw him draw—and yet I guess I didn't really. He was too fast to follow, even when you were concentrating on it. His hand whipped across his chest, there was a flash of blued metal, then the explosion. The can jumped into the air, landing six feet away.

Wade Hastings watched with an expressionless face. Sergeant McGuire chewed on his mustache while Van Orden rocked open the loading gate, punched out the spent cartridge, then slipped a fresh one into the chamber.

"Let's mount up," Wade said and Van Orden holstered both his pistols.

He swung up, pulled me up behind him and Hastings gave us the signal to move. The tag end of the ride was rapid and silent. Between Hastings and Van Orden lay an enmity that I didn't understand, for the seeds seemed planted in

56

Hastings. Somehow, I felt that if any existed, it should have been the other way around.

Yet there was nothing in Van Orden's manner that indicated he was aware of Wade's dislike. The situation filled me with a nameless anxiety, for I wanted Wade to be big and tolerant and suddenly I knew that he was not. Van Orden grew talkative and, before we reached Tucson, taught me the words to a Mexican song, leaving out some of the Americanized stanzas that were hardly fit to repeat, even in the barracks.

Since Tucson was quite a distance from Fort Starke, my visits were few and far between, but I had been coming to this town off and on for ten years, and every time I saw it I had to stop and reorient myself—its rapid progress. Spanish Tucson was fast fading; the rest of the town was moving away. New buildings flanked the streets, and there were new streets to accommodate the new buildings.

Wade Hastings took the detail down the main drag, sitting as straight as a general. He pulled up in front of Lord and Williams Store and there dismounted. McGuire started to swing a leg over.

Hastings said, "I gave no order. We're not farmers, Sergeant."

This stung McGuire and belittled him in the eyes of the troopers, something no noncommissioned officer liked. Even Bob Van Orden, who shouldn't have cared much either way, frowned.

His look was sharp and his voice sharper, when he asked, "Lieutenant, is it all right if I dismount?"

Now it was Hastings' turn to color. He bawled, "Detail! Disss—MOUNT!"

No one was caught napping this time. The men swung down and stood to horse, at attention. Wade Hastings stripped off his gauntlets, speaking to Sergeant McGuire. "The detail is your responsibility; I want them here and cold sober when I return."

"Yes, sor."

Van Orden was getting ready to leave. I didn't want him to go without some kind of goodbye. So I offered to shake hands.

He said, "This must run in the family."

"Goodbye, sir, and thank you for burying the troopers."

He was touched, though he was a man who never allowed himself the luxury of sentiment. "You're all right," he said. Then he turned and ducked under the hitchrail, crossing the walk to enter the store.

Wade Hastings was impatient. "Come along, Mel. Remember what your father said about wasting time."

I honestly couldn't see how I was holding anyone back, but Wade was the commander and, being army, I never argued with commanders. We walked two blocks south to Mr. Neugass' Palace. When important people came to Tucson, they stayed at the Palace. General Nelson A. Miles would be there.

The clerk was polite and gave us the number of Miles' suite. We went up the carpeted stairs and going down the hall I turned and walked backwards so I could see the imprint left in the thick material by my boots.

Miles' orderly answered the door. Wade gave his name and we were admitted. Miles was seated in a deep chair. The flavor of his cigar was thick in the room.

When Wade Hastings came to a stiff attention, Miles said, "At ease, Lieutenant."

General Miles was not a big man, but he was impressive, especially his eyes. Sergeant McGuire, who had served under Miles on the frontier and during the War between the States, said that when Miles turned those eyes on a balky quartermaster mule, the animal rolled over and died. Of course I understood that this was one of McGuire's little exaggerations, but I had noticed that when Miles spoke, no one ever contradicted him.

"I have a dispatch from Colonel Lunsford, sir," Hastings said. He handed it over, then stood quietly while the general read. Finally Miles folded it and laid it on a small table near the arm of his chair.

"So Diablito is in Arizona?"

"Yes, sir," Hastings said. "Colonel Lunsford respectfully requests more troops, sir."

Nelson Miles frowned. "How many troops, Lieutenant?"

"Three, sir. And additional officers."

Miles stood up and crossed to the sideboard. He poured a glass of water and stood with it in his hand. He spoke without turning. "Where does Colonel Lunsford think I'll get these troops? Lieutenant, I've ordered Fort Apache nearly vacated. Bowie began to move out last week—there's a troop and a half there now. Camp Lowell is down to cadre strength, as are McDowell and Camp Grant." He drank his water, put down the glass, then turned around. "Lieutenant, I don't have troops available. Please inform Colonel Lunsford that I gave my orders before my departure from Starke. He'll have to catch Diablito the best way he can."

"Yes, sir."

Then Miles' glance touched me, a soft, paternal glance. "Don't stand there hating me with your eyes, boy. The Army is run by the book. I can't run it any other way."

"I know that, sir."

"Then you know I'll try to organize a relief column, but it will take time. Maybe a week." The general gently puffed his cigar. "Stop thinking of Mr. Ludke, boy—soldiers die, but ultimately they also win battles. Diablito will be caught, and I know your father will capture him."

"Yes, sir."

Miles smiled. "I see you're enough of a soldier to take orders." He spoke to Wade Hastings. "Come back before you leave for Starke. I'll have new orders for you to take to Colonel Lunsford."

"Very good, sir." Hastings saluted the general and did an about-face, which is to say, in the army, we were leaving. The orderly let us out and, once in the hall, Hastings said, "Generals make me nervous. Too damned much rank."

We went down the stairs and into the street, there pausing. "Are you going to look for Mr. Ludke's fiancée, sir?"

Wade Hastings snapped his fingers. "By Jupiter, I forgot all about her." He jerked his head toward the hotel lobby. "Go ask the clerk if she has a room here."

I didn't figure this was my place, but I went anyway. The clerk was not too responsive to me; grown-ups have a subtle way of ignoring young folk. "I beg your pardon, sir," I said, and he opened his eyes a little. Perhaps it was the manners; they have a certain shock value among those unaccustomed to them. "Do you have a Miss Lilith Shipley registered here?"

"I do." He eyed me oddly. "Friend?"

"I have a message for her," I said. "At least, Lieutenant Hastings has." I looked toward the front door. Hastings was peering inside, and he came in when I beckoned. "Mr. Hastings, she's here."

"What room?" Hastings asked the clerk.

"Eleven. At the head of the hall."

"I'll find it," Wade said and turned again toward the stairs. I followed, knowing that I shouldn't. He glanced at me once, and I thought he was going to tell me to go back, but he didn't.

We found room eleven and Wade Hastings knocked. A moment later the door opened, and a tall, serious-faced young woman said, "Yes?"

Lieutenant Hastings took off his hat, but I beat him. "I'm

59

Lieutenant Wade Hastings, ma'am. Mr. Ludke was second in command in my troop."

"Oh." She said it pleasantly, surprised, as though Hastings brought with him a touch of home. "Won't you come in?" She looked at me, a question in her eyes. Hastings supplied the answer.

"This is Melvin Lunsford, Colonel Lunsford's son."

The name was unfamiliar to her, but she didn't ask a lot of questions. Her thought was of Willie Ludke, as was mine.

"Do you bring word from Mr. Ludke? Or did you come for me in his place? He was expecting me, you know."

"I know," Wade said. "May I sit down? Thank you." He twirled his hat in his hands, so ill at ease a blind man would have noticed. But not Lilith Shipley. She was in her early twenties, dark-haired, dark-eyed. Not a beautiful woman, but attractive—she had the kind of looks a man seeks when shopping for a wife.

"I've been on edge all day," Lilieth Shipley said. "I haven't seen Mr. Ludke for nearly six weeks." She smiled and I liked it. "Six weeks can be a very long time when you're in love, Lieutenant."

"That's never been my pleasure," Wade Hastings said. He licked his lips and glanced at me as though I could help him. I could only feel sorry that he was the one who had to say the words. He waved his hand toward the other chair. "Won't you sit down, ma'am?"

She did, her smooth brow wrinkled. "Is there something wrong, Lieutenant?" Wade Hastings nodded. "Something concerning Mr. Ludke? He's not ill? He never was very strong, you know."

"I'm sorry," Hastings said. "I wish I could say that he is only sick, but I can't. There was a patrol the other night—we expected nothing. Routine. What I mean is—Mr. Ludke had the bad luck—Colonel Lunsford and I found the patrol this morning, ma'am. The colonel took Mr. Ludke back to the fort in the ambulance. I came on to Tucson."

Her face was curd white, and her eyes were dark raisins. "Mr. Ludke's been injured?"

"Mr. Ludke is dead," Hastings said softly.

His words struck her motionless, speechless. Sparkling tears crowded against her bottom lids, spilling over, making twin runnels of brightness down her cheeks. Her mouth opened, and she began a low moaning that went on and on to increase in pitch until it was a shriek.

Hastings' complexion blanched, then he struck her sharply on the face with the flat of his hand. I jumped involuntarily and the shrieking stopped as suddenly as though someone had shut it off.

"You were hysterical, Miss Shipley," Wade Hastings said. He kept his voice conversational. Lilith Shipley stared at him for an instant—then her expression broke like slowly melting wax and her crying was full of grief, an understandable sound. And Wade Hastings let her cry. All this made me nervous, and I wished I were somewhere else, but I made myself sit still. Finally the crying was checked, and she sat red-eyed and forlorn.

"I'm truly sorry," Wade Hastings was saying. "If there is anything I can do—"

She shook her head dully. "Nothing. There's nothing. Everything is beyond repair now."

"I don't understand," Wade said uncomfortably. "Can I get you anything? Arrange for your passage back East?"

She looked at him and it was as though her ears had come unstopped, and she was hearing him for the first time. "No. No, I don't want to go back."

"Tucson is a rough—"

"I don't care about Tucson!" She stood up and walked around the room, wringing her hands, biting her lip. "Let me think. I've got to think!" Finally she stopped, turning to face Hastings. "Why did he have to die? Can you tell me that?"

"It never should have happened," Wade said. "If you're looking to put the blame on someone, there just isn't anyone."

"The colonel—what's his name—couldn't he have warned him that there'd be danger? Didn't he have a chance at all?"

"None of us can read the future," Wade said. He looked at me, nodded slightly, then stood up, ready to leave.

"No," Lilith said softly. "None of us can. I had everything all planned out. Everything was going to work out just fine. But it hasn't. The colonel gives an order, and Mr. Ludke is dead, and suddenly I'm alone with my troubles—there's no answer now."

"Ma'am, I don't understand."

"I'm sure you don't," she said, with new composure. "And it wouldn't matter much if you could. Willie Ludke was the only person on earth who could have helped me, but he's out of my reach now."

"Please," Hastings said. "If you'd let me get someone to stay with you. The shock—"

"I don't want anyone," she said quickly. "Please go now, Lieutenant."

"Goodnight," Hastings said and moved me ahead of him to

61

the door. In the hall he paused, puzzled by Lilith Shipley's calmness.

"What's wrong with her, sir?" I asked.

"Huh? Oh! I don't know, Mel. Can't figure it. She cried natural enough—then she went dead inside. Women need watching when they do that."

"Maybe we ought to get someone anyway, sir."

"And maybe we ought to mind our own business," Hastings said. "She'll probably break down again and cry herself to sleep. Tomorrow she'll get better and go on home."

We went downstairs and through the lobby. Down the street three troopers stood by the horses, all tied along one rail. The rest of the detail was inside somewhere, and knowing McGuire, I guessed a saloon, although I knew he was broke. Maybe he was spinning a story and cadging one off anyone sucker enough to buy.

I said, "McGuire may be drinking, sir."

"If he does I'll bust him to private."

The way he said it brought my attention up sharp. It was as though Wade had held this in for a long time and now let it go.

"Father says—"

"Your father's not running this—I am," Wade said. Then he smiled, I suppose to soften the rest. "Mel, don't tell me how to soldier. One Lunsford doing that is enough."

He peeled the wrapper from a Moonshine Crook and touched a match to it, his face harsh and angular in the brief light. Then he whipped out the match and for a moment studied the traffic on the street.

Farther down I made out Bob Van Orden's horse; he was in one of the saloons, but I didn't have him down in my mind as a drinking man. Probably bending over a faro layout or a game of cards—he was the kind who took a chance without a second thought.

The town traffic was picking up. A few buggies moved past, side lanterns flinging light. A wagon rumbled in from the east, pulled by a pair of heavy mules. It passed along the out-flung light of stores and as it drew abreast, Wade Hastings stiffened, his cigar forgotten.

Then I recognized the man driving. It was Gentry. He sat hunched over on the seat, the reins laxly held. His long rifle was on the seat beside him, and he looked neither left nor right, driving on to the Spanish part of town.

"Well, now," Wade said, trouble thick in his voice, "this is my night after all." He flung his cigar in the dust and started down the street. Then he turned back. "Come on."

"You better leave him alone, sir. Father wouldn't like—"

"I'll cross that bridge when I come to it," Wade said. "Your father's always stepped between us when I wanted to call Gentry, but this time he can't. I want you along, Mel. He won't shoot a boy, and he won't dare to back-shoot me in front of you. This is going to be my way."

I didn't like the way this trouble was shaping up. We had enough to worry us without asking for more. But there would be a hiding waiting for me unless I minded Wade Hastings. So I walked down the street with him, keeping well behind Gentry's wagon and hating every step I had to take.

7

As I followed Wade Hastings down Tucson's dark street, I had the distinct feeling that I was following a stranger. I didn't know this man, nor understand the things that pushed him. But a person can't think like that, not about the people they call friends, so I tried to reason it away, telling myself that it didn't matter what kind of man Wade was off post, as long as he was a good soldier.

We passed the crowded market sections, and the noisy *cantinas,* moving on past the Catholic Church to some out-fringe shops. There Wade Hastings stopped, sweeping me against a dark wall with his hand. He held me there, and I could see why.

Gentry had stopped the wagon across the plaza and was getting down.

"Keep quiet," Hastings said softly. "We'll see what he's up to."

There was not much light, and it was difficult to see what kind of business Gentry patronized. A hanging lantern diffused a soft glow over a large doorway, and then Gentry worked the wagon tail-end to for loading. For better than a half hour we stood there watching as Gentry and a Mexican rigged an A-frame with block and tackle, then hoisted three heavy stones to the wagon.

I said, "We'd better get back, sir."

"Shut up," Hastings said. "I may never get another chance like this."

"Chance at what?"

He touched me lightly on the shoulder. "You don't understand how it is with men, Mel. Someday you will. This is something I have to do."

Finally the loading was finished and Gentry handed the Mexican a sack of money, for the clink was unmistakable even across the plaza. Then Gentry loaded the A-frame into the wagon and drove slowly away. I thought we were going to follow, but Hastings crossed the plaza. As we approached I could see that this was a stonecutter's shop; various samples of the man's work were stacked around the small yard.

The Mexican looked up quickly as Hastings stopped in the doorway. He was surprised and a little wary and tried not to show it. "Yes, *señores?*"

The man who just drove away gave you a sack of money," Wade said. "I want to see it."

The Mexican didn't try to hide his fear now. "*Señor,* the pesos are mine. Many years I worked for them."

This was wrong. Wade had no right to meddle here, but one look at his face, set and determined, was enough to tell me I wouldn't dare interfere.

"I'm not going to take it," Wade said. "How much did he give you?"

The Mexican swallowed heavily. "Three thousand pesos, *señor.*"

"Blood money! You know how he gets it!"

"I am only a stonecutter," the man said. "The pesos are no different from other pesos."

Hastings laughed softly. "All right, all right. Where did he go?"

"I do not know, *señor.*" The Mexican smiled nervously. "Why not ask him?"

Hastings let this slide by, for it was an invitation to get killed. "What was the money for? I want a straight answer."

"For my work," the stonecutter said. "I have done much work for *Señor* Gentry. Tonight he has paid for the last of it and taken it away in his wagon."

"*Gracias,*" Hastings said, turning. He acted as though he had forgotten I was along. He hurried through the narrow streets, and I trailed close behind. When we got to the edge of Spanish town we stopped. Gentry's wagon was moving off down the main street, in no particular hurry, and after a look at Wade Hastings' face, I rather wished Gentry would go faster, for trouble was thick enough to cut.

"Get the horses," Wade said, "and don't waste time about it."

"But, sir—"

"I won't tell you again." There was a snap to Wade's words. I trotted down the street, got our mounts from the hitch-rail and brought them back. Wade swung up and we eased out of town at a walk.

I didn't like any of this, our following Gentry and leaving Sergeant McGuire to whoop it up in some saloon. Wade knew McGuire's weakness and was deliberately ignoring it because of something personal.

The night was dark, but not one of those inky, blind nights, and Wade had no difficulty following Gentry's wagon. Time passed slowly, and I lost track of it, yet Hastings gave no indication of turning back. Poor horseman or not, I slept in the saddle, waking often and dozing off immediately. We did not stop—at least I don't remember stopping—but the dawn woke me, still moving along at a walk.

With the coming light, the distance between ourselves and Gentry was lengthened until he became a very small speck against the gray smudge of horizon. Wade Hastings had not slept at all; his eyes were red-rimmed and he needed a shave. We were approaching the river—a dark line of cottonwoods was visible, and into these Gentry disappeared with his wagon.

Hastings cut his pace, and stopped often. An hour later we approached the fringe of trees, and at the river stopped to splash water over our faces. The wagon tracks were easy to find, running into the trees and winding upward to the crown of a low hill.

"Stay behind me," Hastings said and led out.

For awhile we saw nothing. The trees were growing too close for a view—then they thinned, and I saw the wagon. The A-frame was rigged and Gentry was stripped to the waist, unloading the stones. He saw us, or heard us—some animal instinct warned him of intruders, for he covered us with his rifle as we came on.

When we were within speaking distance, Gentry said, "You just couldn't leave it alone, could you?"

"I've always been curious," Wade said, stepping from the saddle. "You stay put," he said to me, and I did.

From where I sat, I could see the stones, headstones, finely carved. The largest one had an angel in marble. The two smaller ones were decorated with elaborate floral wreaths. There was writing on all three.

Wade Hastings ignored the rifle in Gentry's hands. He

65

stepped around the tall man and read. I was reading too and a lot of things suddenly fell into place for me, especially what Gentry had done with the scalp money.

On the largest stone was written:

NANCY GATES GENTRY
BORN JULY, 1861
DIED MAY, 1884
. . . REST IN GOD'S ARMS . . .

The other two stones were for children, both girls, both under four, and the date of death was also May, 1884. No one had to tell me that they were victims of Apache raiders —Gentry had already told me this with his undying hate.

"She liked the trees," Gentry said. "There weren't any where we lived. So that night I brought them here where there were trees." He set the rifle aside, but I hardly noticed. I was watching his eyes, and they were no longer emotionless. He said no more, for there was nothing left to say. All his love and his life were buried in this place.

Wade Hastings stood still, sure now that he was butting in where he had no right to be, and I suspected that he knew regret that he had followed Gentry. Yet I knew Hastings would not back up or indicate that he was sorry; these virtues weren't in the man, and I felt a flood of shame.

Gentry's expression settled, and he looked for a moment upon Wade Hastings, the intruder. "You couldn't let it go once you put your mind on it, could you?"

"I'm not the only man who's wondered about you," Hastings said. He shifted his feet and looked at me. Somehow he didn't seem so brave or so right, or even determined.

"You and I've got to mix it up," Gentry said soberly. "That's in the cards."

"Suits me," Hastings said stiffly. "It's been a long time in the making."

"Your making," Gentry pointed out, and I was certain that he was right. He stepped forward, his face bland and without anxiety. Without anger, too, I couldn't help but notice. Hastings' cheeks were frozen, and he was mentally working himself up to the fight. Gentry did not have to. He was as cool as a butcher about to dissect a side of beef into choice cuts.

When he struck Hastings, the suddenness was shocking. The sound was flat and solid. Hastings stumbled back and half fell, his lips bright with blood. He wiped his hand across his mouth as if he couldn't believe it, then growled deep in his chest and charged Gentry.

When Gentry leaped aside at the last instant and clubbed Wade across the back of the neck, driving him to his knees, I knew how it was going to be, and how it was going to end. Gentry stepped back and waited. He could afford this, for he fought without malice, without hate. This was a job to do, and he would do it well.

Wade Hastings was shaking in the legs when he came erect. He stepped forward, and Gentry met him head on. Hastings struck Gentry on the cheek, ripping open the flesh, but Gentry did not feel this—I doubt he knew he had been touched. He hammered Wade in the stomach and across the mouth, making Wade's nose bleed freely.

Then he struck him under the heart, and Wade's mouth flew open in a windless cry. He back-pedaled against the wagon and gripped the sideboard to support himself. Gentry struck him a precise ax-blow, and Wade's eyes grew dim. He would have fallen had not Gentry supported him with his left hand.

With his right, he began to flail Wade Hastings in the face, not with a clenched fist, but with his open palm. The sound of this was clear and sharp, and I bit my lips as Gentry's horny palm ripped Hastings' face.

Gentry hit him this way a dozen times, then stepped back and let him fall.

I stepped down from the horse and Gentry turned to me, his eyes calm and flat-looking. "He wouldn't give, boy. A man's got to learn that."

I didn't want to defend Wade, but he was still my friend. "You don't give. Why blame him?"

"That's right," Gentry said softly. "I don't. But there's no hope for me." He looked at the tombstones. "I'll have these set by noon. Then I'm leaving the country. Say goodbye for me to your pa."

Wade was coming around, but he couldn't stand. He was a sick man and would be for several days. This started a small alarm in my mind; we now had a detail without a capable officer. Gentry lifted Hastings to his horse, and Wade sagged forward with his face on the horse's neck.

"Get him out of here," Gentry said. "Can you find your way back to Tucson all right?"

"Yes, sir."

Gentry's eyes narrowed. "I showed him up, and I guess he was kind of special to you. Do you hate me for it?"

"I don't know," I admitted.

"I did you a favor," Gentry said. I mounted and leading Wade's horse, left the cottonwood grove. Wade was in no condition for fast traveling and the pace I set was none too easy on him, but he was in too much misery to complain about it.

On the way back to Tucson I stopped for cold rations. Wade just rested his head on the horse's neck. His face was hot to the touch and I knew he was beginning to develop a fever, a natural state after the body has undergone shock.

The nearer I got to Tucson, the more worried I became, and when I reached the end of the main street, the worry became a real problem, full-blown. Sergeant Terry McGuire was in front of Tully, Ochoa and DeLong's store, waving his arms and reeling back and forth across the sidewalk. He had four troopers with him and from the way they sang, I knew that Tucson's citizens had been good to them.

I pulled up in front of the store and slid down, tying both horses. McGuire leaned against the store front and tried to identify me through eyes that could hardly focus. "Well, well," he said, smiling, "watcha been doin', son?" He saw Lieutenant Hastings' face and appeared deeply shocked. "Shame, shame, hittin' an ossif—osstif—officer." Then he laughed, as though this were an uproarious joke.

A crowd was beginning to gather, a situation I disliked, for there is nothing more harmful to the service than a soldier making a spectacle of himself. I tried to take McGuire by the arm, but he pushed me away. A voice in the crowd asked, "That your old man, kid?"

The laughter rippled, and others had remarks to make. I took a step toward McGuire, not at all sure what I was going to do, but before I could decide, a firm hand came down on my shoulder. I looked around quickly, into Bob Van Orden's serious young face.

"What do you want to do, bub?" The voice was easy and sure.

"Get them off the street. Please!"

"Will do," he said and stepped past me. He had brushed his dark suit and wore a clean shirt. A fawn-colored hat sat squarely on his head, casting a shadow over the upper part of his face.

Terry McGuire stared at Van Orden.

"Do as the boy says." Van Orden spoke quietly, the way he must have spoken a thousand times in Santa Fe, and El Paso, and Dallas, when he had a star on his shirt front and the law behind him.

McGuire growled something, indicating resistance, and

Bob Van Orden didn't wait to see it take shape. He grabbed McGuire by the arm, spun him into the hitchrail and dumped him face first into Tucson's dusty street. "Off the street," he repeated and there was no argument this time. McGuire and his four friends went south toward the stable.

Then Van Orden turned to the crowd. "Don't you have business?" he asked. The way he said it, and the way they moved on, told me everything there was to know about this man's reputation, his deadly talents. When the crowd thinned, he took me by the arm, moving toward Hastings, who was still too sick to care whether school kept or not. "What happened to him?"

"Gentry," I said, and Bob Van Orden grunted.

"The man can leave his mark." He glanced at me. "Leaves you in a spot, don't it?"

"Yes, sir."

"Figured out what you're going to do?"

"General Miles has a message for father. Wade was supposed to pick it up."

Van Orden shook his head. "The general rode out of town this morning. I saw him. He took the Fort Lowell road."

This was a relief, and at the same time a tragedy. A relief because I had been afraid the general would see Wade or McGuire. I didn't want my father to have to answer for their conduct, and he certainly would have to if this ever came to the attention of the general. Yet it was a tragedy because I had no one to turn to, no one to supply the answers, or function in a command capacity.

"He could have left something for you at the hotel," Van Orden suggested.

"I'll ask," I said, starting across the street.

"Wait!" I turned back. "Is there anything I can do?" He smiled. "Why don't you let me round up your outfit? I'll have them waiting at the stable. Maybe I can sober up that sergeant enough to where he can take over."

He didn't want thanks for it—I saw that. So I went across and down to the Palace. The clerk was reading the Tombstone Epitaph and he seemed annoyed when I palmed the bell for his attention.

"Did General Nelson A. Miles leave an envelope for Lieutenant Hastings?"

The clerk searched through the pigeon holes. "He did. Send Hastings in, and I'll give it to him."

"Mr. Hastings is at the stables getting ready to leave, sir. He sent me for it."

"You'll have to sign," the clerk said and passed pen and

69

paper over. I signed, took the letter, and went out. Bob Van Orden was leading Wade Hastings' horse toward the stable. I trotted down the street after them.

Bob Van Orden was an efficient man. He got Hastings off the horse and laid out on some hay. Then he turned his attention on Terry McGuire, who was sullen and getting sick. Van Orden marched McGuire to the horse trough and pitched him in. McGuire went in with a splash and a curse, and when he tried to get out, Van Orden kept shoving him back in.

Finally McGuire said, "Goddammit, I've had enough!"

He wasn't sober enough for duty, but he could stand straighter. Van Orden then dunked the four troopers until he seemed satisfied that they could ride.

"You'd better fetch a doctor for him," Van Orden said, nodding toward Wade Hastings. "There's one over DeLong's."

Doctor Leeman turned out to be a typical frontier surgeon, rough as a cat's tongue, and as straightforward as barrel whiskey. He squatted, made an examination of Wade Hastings' battered face, then said, "Put him in a wagon and he'll be all right. He's too sick to ride." He looked at Van Orden. "How far's he going?"

"Fort Starke."

"He needs a wagon," Leeman said again, his first judgment strengthened.

"We don't have a wagon, sir," I said. "How long before he can sit his horse?"

Doctor Leeman pursed his lips. "Today's Wednesday. The fever ought to be down by tomorrow. Saturday, I'd say."

"Can you wait that long, bub?" Van Orden was leaving it up to me, but behind his words lay his willingness to help, should I ask.

"Gosh, no!" I said.

"Then get a wagon," Leeman said, closing his bag. He walked away, coat flapping.

Bob Van Orden watched him for a moment, then said, "Looks like you've got your command a little earlier than you thought. Of course you could ride to Fort Lowell and ask some officer to take the detail back."

"I couldn't do that!" The idea was unthinkable. This was one story I didn't want circulated in the army.

"I can't go to Starke with you," Van Orden said. "It wouldn't be smart. The gent who's been following me is liable to be traveling that road. I don't want to meet him."

"You've done enough," I said. "My father'll thank you for it."

70

"I did it because I like you, bub," Bob Van Orden said. He mussed my hair and left the stable. Sergeant McGuire stirred and followed him with his eyes.

McGuire was not a well man and I knew it would be another six or eight hours before he would be cold sober, and then he would have such a headache as to render him useless. But most of all I knew McGuire's limitations. He was a detail man, not a commander. If the trip went smoothly, then he'd do, but Diablito was loose in Arizona, and I didn't want to meet him with McGuire in command.

Until you're alone, you never stop to think of how it is, but I was alone then, and I had plenty of time to think about it. I considered Wade Hastings. The man was in trouble for he had committed an error in judgment that bordered on the inexcusable. He had deserted his command for personal reasons. McGuire might end up in the guardhouse this time. I could see no way out for him, and at that moment I didn't much care.

Nine men out of the fifteen were sober, or sober enough to know what was going on. They stood at the rear of the stable, talking among themselves. They left me alone, and I was glad of it. This was the code—a man could always ask for help and get it, but afterwards he was always a little less a man for having asked.

Around one o'clock, Lilith Shipley came to the stable arch and timidly peered inside. She saw me and a frown marred the smoothness of her forehead.

"Where can I rent a buggy?" she asked.

"Here, I guess," I said. "Wouldn't it be better to take the stage, ma'am?"

"They told me the stage was no longer running," she said. "There's a paymaster's stage due in day after tomorrow, but I don't want to wait."

This didn't make sense to me. "Are you going back East?"

"I'm going to Fort Starke, if I can rent a buggy and find someone to take me there."

Here was my answer. Father would hit the ceiling when I brought Lieutenant Ludke's fiancée to the post, but I didn't care about that. My immediate concern was to get home and get there as quick as I could.

"Ma'am, we're returning to Fort Starke, and we'd be happy to escort you providing Lieutenant Hastings can rest in the back of the buggy."

She turned her head and looked at Hastings. He wasn't too pretty and I guess Lilith Shipley was not accustomed to seeing men who had been beaten, for she turned her head quickly away.

"All right," she agreed. "Where is the proprietor?"

"At the Shoo Fly," I said. "He'll be back any time."

"I'll go to the hotel and have my satchels brought here," she said. She lifted her skirts and walked back toward the center of town.

I fidgeted until Mr. Laudmacher came down the street, a toothpick protruding from his bushy whiskers. He wasn't delighted to find the Army bunking in his stable, but he brightened when I told him Miss Shipley wanted to rent a buggy, and that the army would pay for it. He made out the bill, and Wade Hastings came out of his stupor long enough to initial it.

Mr. Laudmacher hitched the team and had the buggy waiting. I told the troopers to mount up after we stowed Wade Hastings on a straw bed. McGuire had difficulty sitting his horse, as did some of the others, but I didn't worry about this. A cavalryman can ride, drunk or sober, and sometimes better when drunk.

The boy from the hotel loaded Lilith Shipley's baggage and I drove. She wasn't too keen about this, but before we were free of Tucson, she was convinced that I knew how to handle a team.

Until then I was feeling pretty good about it all, my slick business with the buggy and solving the problem of what to do with Wade Hastings. But with the town behind me and four hours of open country ahead, I got scared. Real scared.

For all I knew, Diablito could be waiting behind the next clump of *chemise*.

8

BEFORE WE had traveled five miles I knew that we had started too late in the afternoon—it would be dark by the time we reached Fort Starke. I kept turning in the seat, looking back at the double file of troopers. McGuire was taking punishment, and right then I felt that he deserved it.

Lilith Shipley was inclined to silence, which suited me,

for I was too worried to make polite conversation. Wade Hastings' fever was not diminishing—I could tell because he moaned and tossed about.

The habits of "the book" were too strong in me to ignore and at the end of the second hour I called for a rest stop. The sun was sliding down but the heat was intense, blinding to look at and insufferable when one's back was turned to it. Lilith Shipley suffered in silence. Her shoulders were rounded in misery and perspiration darkened her dress.

Yet the heat was doing some good—it soaked the poison out of McGuire. Wade Hastings tried to sit up, but was too sick to make it. I was ready to go on when McGuire approached with a downcast mien.

"Are you hatin' me, lad?"

I guessed, when he put it that way, I didn't, but it wouldn't hurt him to wonder about it awhile. "You've disgraced yourself," I said, "Father will bust you to private for this."

"Ah," McGuire said, smiling, "lad, it's the devil that gets hold of a man."

"I can't help that," I said. "When I needed you most, you were drunk."

It was entirely possible that he saw Hastings for the first time, at least since he came out of the whiskey bottle. McGuire swore heartily, then blushed when he realized he had slipped in front of a woman, something the roughest soldier would never do. "What the divil happened, laddie? His face is a mess, that's sure."

"He fought with Gentry," I said. "I'm mad at him too."

"There's goin' to be the devil to pay when your father hears of this," McGuire said. "You'll not be tellin' on an old trooper, now will you?"

"I'll have to," I said.

"Aye," McGuire said sadly. "Now it's me time to pay the piper—yet she was a merry tune, lad. T'was a day I'll carry to me grave. The whiskey was free, and there was no officer to stay me hand."

"If you're able," I said, "take charge of the second section."

"Aye," McGuire said, giving me a mock salute. "It's your father I hear speakin' now. It's a doctor you may want to be, but it's a soldier you are first."

This kind of talk rankled, and I slapped the team with the reins, urging them into motion. Some of the worry eased away, for McGuire, even half-drunk, was soldier enough to keep his eyes open. And he had fought Apaches long enough to know their tricks.

Lilith Shipley braced herself on the seat, for the road was poor and I was dead-set on making time. The livery pair was a good span of trotters, and they got a good workout.

The sun finally sank out of sight, but the light remained, dimming gradually. Lilith Shipley took off her wide bonnet and loosened her hair.

"A wind will come up soon," I said.

"That's nice."

"Well," I said, hating to disillusion her, "it cools things down all right, but it blows sand into everything."

"The sand will be a relief," she said and smiled. I was glad to see her relaxing, for grief is something a person ought to let go of as soon as he can. I could not help but think of Gentry and what it had done to him.

"What do you want to do at Fort Starke?" I asked.

"Talk to your father about Mr. Ludke. Perhaps I'll be in time for the funeral."

I shook my head. "They don't keep in this heat. We try to get them in the ground right away."

As soon as I had said it I realized how coldly brutal that sounded and wished I had been more tactful, but she didn't seem offended.

"I've reconciled myself to the fact that he's gone," she said. "Gone beyond my ever reaching him."

"I didn't know him very well," I told her. "None of us did; Mr. Ludke was new to the post."

"Yes," she said softly. "He was new. New at everything."

"He—he spoke of you often, ma'am."

This brought her attention around quickly, and she seemed intensely interested, even gripping my arm in her excitement. "Oh, did he? Tell me about it. Please. It's important to me."

Now that she had me cornered, I wasn't sure where to begin. "He wanted father to send a telegram to you," I said. "Only the telegraph line was down. He was worried about you alone in Tucson."

"Then he really wanted me to come? Did he say that?"

"I heard him talk of the time you'd arrive. Yes, he was looking forward to it."

She settled back on the seat, her eyes closed, and there were tears against her tight-pressed lids. Finally she said, "Thank you. I needed to know that he still wanted me. That all I hoped and dreamed were not only my dreams but his as well."

I didn't understand her and said so. But she just smiled evasively and shook her head.

From the back of the wagon, Wade Hastings said, "Got to get on my horse! Can't go to the commander in a damned wagon!"

He was trying to sit up and almost making it. I stopped the team quickly, afraid he'd fall out and have one of the wheels run over him. He was trying to get out now that we had halted.

"McGuire!" he bellowed. "You drunken Irishman, put me on my horse! By God, I'm going to ride on the post, not be carried."

McGuire looked at me, and I nodded. A trooper brought up Wade's horse and with help he made the saddle, although the effort left him weak and gagging. He still lacked most of his faculties, for he said, "Damn you, McGuire, getting drunk. It's all right, Sergeant. Made a mistake myself. I won't tell on you. You won't tell on me."

"Let's go," I said. "Try to keep from falling off."

I kicked the team into motion, and we rode into the last of the daylight. Ahead, nearly five miles, was Fort Starke, now nothing more than an indistinct smudge.

Wade Hastings, like a fool, drove his horse into a gallop, and I was forced to storm after him, the detail pounding along behind. He stayed ahead of me; I could see him bobbing in the saddle, ready to spill off at any minute.

At the end of a mile I entertained a small hope that he was not going to lose his seat. He was out of his head, yelling, even drawing his saber and waving it. Sergeant McGuire rode with set jaw, his headache unimproved by the pace.

Finally it happened. Hastings cascaded from his horse and tumbled end over end. He would have had to stop soon anyway; two miles at his pace was killing the horses. I sawed the team to a halt and jumped down. The half-darkness of early evening closed in rapidly; another few minutes and it would be dark.

The way Wade was sprawled, I feared he was dead, but three troopers lifted him and flopped him in the back of the buggy.

"He's all right," O'Casey said. "Just a broken arm."

Lilith Shipley gasped and turned quickly to look at Hastings. I made my own fumbling examination and O'Casey was right. Hastings' left arm was fractured a few inches above the wrist. A simple fracture—I knew enough to determine this. It would have to wait until we reached Fort Starke.

We moved out, at a more sedate pace this time, and McGuire put out close flankers until we hailed the palisade gate. The unaccounted presence of the buggy made the guards suspicious, but they opened the gates and covered us with carbines as we filed in.

Someone brought a lantern, shining it in the wagon. Father came charging across the parade from headquarters as I stepped down, tired enough to sleep on the spot and relieved enough to cry, although I dared to do neither.

A trooper helped Miss Shipley down and father got her out of the way by saying, "Escort her to my quarters, Fitz. My wife will look after her."

Wade Hastings was being helped from the wagon. Father had his look. "Get Doctor Bickerstaff. Take Mr. Hastings to my office." His face was like thunder and I knew a storm was about to descend. "Melvin, what the blue blazes happened here?" He whipped his head around. "Sergeant McGuire!"

The last thing McGuire wanted was to get close to father and have his breath give him away, but father had gone through this before; he knew the signs. "Sergeant," he said, "dismiss the detail, if you're sober enough to give the command. Then report to my office."

"Yes, sor." McGuire sounded cold sober. I guess the thought of what was coming did it.

The buggy was being led away, and father put his arm around my shoulders. "Come along. I want to talk to you. Perhaps you can give me the straight of this."

Doctor Bickerstaff was in father's office, tending Hastings' arm. He was applying a splint and a snug wrapping. There was little he could do for Wade's face, except cleanse it and apply ointment to the abrasions.

Father waited until Bickerstaff left, then said, "Perhaps I could have a report, Wade?" There was frost in his voice.

When father was angry he didn't try to hide it. Experience had taught me to remain silent at these times, but I felt compelled to defend Wade in his present condition. "Couldn't Mr. Hastings go to bed, sir? I was with him all the time. I can tell you what went on." This was a weak plea and I knew it, but for old times' sake I couldn't let Wade down. Not while he was sick.

Hastings looked at me, and I met his eyes. Father put a match to a cigar and let this calm him. "All right, Mel. Report."

"Mr. Hastings spoke to General Miles. He has no troops available, sir."

This must have been the answer father expected, for he said, "I'm not surprised. But I had to ask."

"He left this for you." I withdrew the letter and handed it to him. Wade Hastings frowned, and then I remembered that he knew nothing of this. I explained, "After Mr. Hastings fell from his horse, I took the letter, afraid that it might be lost."

Father's glance to Wade was sharp. "What's the matter? Can't you sit a horse any more?"

"It was an accident," I said quickly. "The horse stumbled while we were galloping."

"And I suppose McGuire fell into a vat of whiskey!" He slapped the desk with his palm. "When I send out a detail I expect it to come back led by an officer, not by a sixteen-year-old boy." He blew out his breath and ripped open Nelson Miles' new order. I watched him as he read. Father put his cigar down carefully and read every word. When he was through the anger was gone.

He said, "Go to your quarters, Wade. Try to get some rest. We'll talk about this when you're feeling better."

"Yes, sir," Hastings said. He got unsteadily to his feet, his face gray with pain. To me he said, "Thanks for everything, Mel. You're a real soldier."

I wished that he hadn't said that. It was bad enough to have to lie to cover for him—I didn't want to be congratulated for it.

After he went out, father said, "I expected you back before noon, Mel. What delayed you? And who is that woman?"

"Mr. Ludke's fiancée, sir."

"What the devil did you bring her here for?" He puffed on his cigar. "Forget it now. You're dead-tired and your mother's worried sick. Go on home. I'll be along in a minute." He picked up Miles' orders and began reading them again.

"Is there something wrong, sir?"

His original intention was to say no, but he told me the truth. He handed the orders to me and let me read them for myself.

Tucson, Arizona Territory
July 19, 1890

Lieutenant-Colonel James G. Lunsford,
Commanding
Fort Starke, Arizona Territory

Dear Sir:

Pursuant to the authority granted me by

77

the Congress of the United States and the War Department, I hereby appoint you commanding officer of all military detachments remaining in Arizona Territory after August 1, 1890. In accordance with this increased responsibility, you are, of this date, promoted to the rank of colonel, with all due pay and allowances.

Signed: Nelson A. Miles
Major-General,
Commanding.

I put down the orders and stared. "Does that mean we're not leaving?"

He nodded, got up and walked to the dark window. He stood there, his back to me. "I'll have to tell your mother, but how can I?" He turned back to me. "Mel, you're old enough for responsibilities now. Say nothing of this."

"I won't, sir."

He smiled, a tired smile with defeat in it. "Go on home, son. Your mother's waiting."

As I turned, McGuire rattled the door with his heavy hand. I opened it and stepped back. He was all soldier now, coming to a heel-clacking attention, his salute as smart as any Academy man's. "Reporting, sor. I expect the lad's given you the details. I'll not be blamin' him, sor—he's only doin' his duty."

Father opened his mouth to speak, then merely murmured, "Yes. Yes, he did. But I'd like to hear it from you, Sergeant."

"Well, sor, it's a fact that I did have a bit to drink." He paused as if wondering how far he dared stretch the truth. "And it's a fact that I was drunk when Mr. Hasting's returned, sor."

Father's eyes grew veiled and secretive. "Returned? Explain it to me, Sergeant. Clarify for me exactly where Mr. Hastings was while you were tying one on."

"I've got to go," I said and started out the door.

"You'd better stay," father said, and I heard the trap snap shut. I came back and sat down.

"Well, sor," McGuire was saying, "I'd not snitch on an officer to save me own skin, you know that. But since the cat's out, what's the harm in speakin'?" He licked his lips, sweat bold on his forehead. "When Mr. Hastings took out after Gentry there was nothin' on me hands but time. And the drinks were free, sor—an Irishman can never resist a free nip. I've got me punishment comin', I'll not deny it, sor."

Father looked at me, then at McGuire. "You're dismissed, Private McGuire."

"Aye," McGuire said, sighing, "I thought it would be like that, sor."

He went out, a downcast man. I would have liked to follow him, but I knew father had a few things to say. "Why did you cover for him, Mel? Is Wade Hastings that much of a hero?"

Then I told him the whole story, all of it. When I finished father sat in silence, cigar smoke drifting in ribbons across his face. "I'll have to reprimand Wade. You know that, don't you?"

"Yes, sir."

"This was something that had to come out, Mel," father said. "Understand that—it had to be told."

"Just like you're going to have to tell mother we're not leaving Arizona?"

That was a pretty bold thing for me to say, but he let it pass. "Yes," he said. "Even that has to come out."

I left headquarters, cutting across the dark parade. Mother was in the kitchen and when I came in she put her arms around me quickly. Had I come in at noon she would have had a scolding waiting, but long ago I learned to be very late if I was going to be late at all—her relief then overrode her anger, and I was spared the lecture.

She whisked off my hat and brushed back my hair. "I've got a hot supper waiting for you. My goodness, I'll bet you haven't eaten a good meal since you left." She slapped the dust from my clothes and seated me at the table, fussing with the plate and silverware. She heaped my plate with roast and potatoes and poured a full glass of milk.

"I baked a pie," she said. "You may have a piece after you've finished that." Then she sat down across from me, her hands folded in her lap. "Who is this woman you brought home, Mel? Heavens, Fitz brought her here, and I showed her to the spare room, and she closed the door. Not one word from her since."

"Her name's Miss Shipley."

Mother made aggravated sounds with her lips. "I know that. It isn't what I asked you."

"Mr. Ludke's fiancée."

"Poor Mr. Ludke," mother said, and she was genuinely sorry. "But what does she expect to find here, Melvin? Her place is back East with her folks. It isn't as if she were Army already."

"She wants to talk to father," I said around a mouthful of

79

food. At any other time mother would have upbraided me for this, but she was in a forgiving mood.

"About Mr. Ludke?"

"I guess," I said. "I was so busy I didn't care what she wanted." Then, since the story was out, I told about Wade Hastings' trouble with Gentry.

Mother listened, brittle-cheeked; she was shocked that I had witnessed such a thing. "The idea!" she said, when I was through. "I'll give Wade Hastings a piece of my mind."

"I was glad to bring Miss Shipley along because Wade was too sick to ride a horse, and I needed her buggy," I said. "McGuire got drunk too."

"He did what?"

"Got drunk in Tucson. Father just busted him to private for it."

"Oh!" Mother said, and she was really burning. I hoped that McGuire had enough sense to stay away, at least for a day or two until she cooled off.

Then I had to top it all with a kid's dumb brag. "I brought the detail back all by myself. We didn't see any Apaches, though I wasn't scared."

But mother was. Angry and scared. Her maternal mind began working overtime, dreaming up countless dangers that I would never have thought of. "What you've been through," she said. "Mel, you're still a boy." She unfolded her hands. "I'll have a word or two to say to your father about this. From now on you're not leaving the post—I've put my foot down." Then she added: "That is, until we leave for good."

There was so much of her dreams in her voice that I couldn't bear to look at her. I bent my head forward and stared at my food.

"Are you sick?" she asked. "You're acting strange."

"It's—it's nothing," I said.

"Nothing? Look at me, Melvin."

I did. I had to when she spoke in that tone.

"What's bothering you? I want the truth."

Several things were bothering me, so I told her about one of them. "It's Mr. Gentry."

"We don't speak of him in this house," mother said. "He was once welcome here, but that was before he turned savage."

"He had three gravestones," I said. "For his wife and two little girls. Did you ever meet them, mother?"

She bit her lip and twisted her apron. "Yes. Sweet things too. I suppose I should tell you—you'll worm it out some way if I don't. Gentry was once a good man; he was your father's best friend."

"Did the Apaches kill his family?"

"No," mother said. "That is, no one knows for sure. There were Apache tracks in the yard. His team was killed, and there was a dead fire where they had eaten. As near as anyone can tell, Gentry's wife killed the children, then herself. Gentry nearly went out of his mind when he found them."

"He sure beat Mr. Hastings," I said, "and he had it coming, too. Gentry didn't want anyone butting in, and Mr. Hastings did."

Mother took my empty plate to the sink, bringing back a piece of pie. "A boy's loyalty is like a weathervane. I don't want you thinking Gentry is a hero. He's a lost man whom nobody wants."

"He's going away—he said so."

"Then it's good riddance," mother said. "I don't mean to sound cruel, Mel, but you've got to understand that a man can put himself beyond redemption by his acts. Gentry has done just that."

Father's footsteps sounded on the porch, and he came in, closing the door gently. "I thought you'd be in bed, Mel."

"He's going as soon as he finishes his pie and has a bath," mother said. "I put Miss Shipley in the spare room. Do you have any idea how long she's going to stay?"

"No," father said. "I had no opportunity to talk to her when she arrived. There was Hastings and McGuire to attend to. McGuire is now a private. I'll see Hastings in the morning." He hung up his hat and pistol belt, then sat down, facing me. "How's the pie?"

"Cinnamon and soda crackers," I said, "but with the sugar you can't tell it from apple."

"Your mothers a clever woman," father said softly. "Whatever the problem, she finds a way to lick it."

I wondered if father was searching for the courage to tell mother of Miles' orders, then I decided he was just being a good soldier and reconnoitering, feeling out the opposition's strength.

But there wasn't much that went by mother. She turned to face him. "What's that supposed to be, a compliment?"

"Flattery," father said.

"I need that like a toad needs a pocket," she said. "If you're through, Melvin, you can march into the pantry and get ready for your bath. I'll bring in the hot water in a minute."

For once I appreciated the soothing comfort of the tub. I wasted a half hour just soaking, then dried off and went upstairs to bed. The room was dark but I didn't bother with a

81

light. I can never recall a time when the bed felt better, or when I was so glad to be in it.

There was talk going on downstairs, but it seemed far away and indistinct. Soon I was asleep and there were no more sounds, not even dreams. For all I cared, Diablito could have been on a distant star. I even forgot about father's new orders and what mother's reaction would be when he told her. In her mind she had already packed for moving and unpacking is always unpleasant.

9

WHEN I opened my eyes, darkness was solid in the room and I lay for a moment wondering what had awakened me. The house was quiet, too quiet. Then I heard mother downstairs, and Lilith Shipley's voice. I got up and dressed, then went down the stairs.

Mother stopped talking when I entered the parlor. "Did you get enough sleep, Mel?"

"What time is it?'

She consulted the watch pinned to her bodice. "Quarter to nine."

I was ready to turn around and go back upstairs to bed. "Gosh, I woke up. What woke me?"

"It's time you were awake," mother said. "You just slept the clock around." She stood up. "I'll fix you something to eat."

The mention of food reminded me of hunger. I went into the kitchen and Lilith Shipley followed. She had changed to a simple pale yellow dress, and her hair was done up sort of loose and wavy.

Your father's over at headquarters," mother said. "Mr. Reindollar's patrol is overdue." She dropped three eggs into the hot skillet. "There has been no report from him since late yesterday afternoon."

"I hope he fares better than Willie Ludke," Lilith said.

Mother gave her a sharp glance, and I expected her to say something, because we don't say things like that in the Army, even when we're thinking them.

"You're looking for someone to blame for Mr. Ludke's death," mother said. "That's foolish. There's no one responsible."

"Your husband sent him," Lilith said. "That makes him responsible." She closed her mouth firmly, the way a person does when he has made up his mind about something.

Mother put the eggs on a plate, along with three slices of bread, and I ate hurriedly.

When I was through, I asked, "Can I go to headquarters?"

"If you don't bother your father," she said, and I left quickly.

The night was velvet and cool. I could hear the rattle of carbines, the clack of closed breechblocks clear across the parade. Father stepped to the headquarters porch, lamplight strong behind him. As I walked toward him he stripped a wrapper from a cigar. I could see his face briefly in the match flare, then he whipped it out and sniffed the cigar's bouquet.

The guard detail was changing, the old palisade watch being relieved. Father's attention was on this routine when I came onto the porch.

"You got slept out?"

"Yes, sir. Any word from Mr. Reindollar?"

Father took the cigar from his mouth. "So you know." He shook his head. "Reindollar had a troop behind him, and he's a long way from being a fool. I can't bring myself to believe he's in serious trouble."

Across the brief interval of the parade, Major Miles Regan came from his quarters. His boots thumped on the solidly packed earth as he walked toward headquarters, but the lamplight streaming from father's open doorway seemed to make him uneasy for he stopped just out of its reach.

"Waiting gets on my nerves," Regan said. "Has the telegrapher been able to raise Fort Savage yet?"

"No," father said evenly.

"Damn it, I repaired the line!"

"Yesterday," father said. "Twenty-four hours can be a long time. The line has been cut again."

Regan cursed, unmindful of me. "I suppose I'll have to find the break again?"

"If we expect to raise Fort Savage," father said. "I've given up on Fort Redoubt—it's been nearly five days since we've heard from them, or got a message through."

Regan frowned, not liking the idea of taking another patrol into the field. "You never know where that devil, Diablito, will pop up next. I repair the wire and he cuts it again."

Father said, "War, so I'm told, is hell."

"You call this war? The way Ludke died? Ambushed? Is that what you call war, Colonel?"

"I haven't called it anything," father said.

"I call it murder!"

"Let's not call it anything yet," father said. "Diablito is after something. Right now I don't know what it is, but I do know Apaches and I know they raid for women and horses, but as of now Diablito seems most interested in the Army." Father turned. "Come into my office, Major."

Regan squinted at the light. He had a fighter's blocky face. His hair was prematurely thin, and he kept running his fingers through it, then lowering his hand to brush his full mustache.

Father drew paper and pen toward him. "Major, let's assemble the facts as we know them." Regan frowned as father made three column heads: Facts, Supposition, and a question mark.

"Under facts," father said, "we will list Diablito's regular haunts: Mexico. Why, Major? There has to be a reason for Apaches to stay in one place."

"Because we ran them out of Arizona," Regan said. "That's obvious."

"It's also obvious that we haven't. Diablito's here now, but for a reason." He paused to draw on his cigar. "Diablito has enemies, Major, and I'm not talking about the Mexican army."

This puzzled Regan. He wrinkled his brows. "Gentry?"

"Ah," father said. "The thought occurred to you too."

Now it was my turn to wonder. Father snuffed out his cigar and made an entry under the second column. "Gentry has killed more Apaches than the Mexican army. It's my theory that wherever Gentry is, Apaches will be found. The hunter and the hunted—it would be difficult to tell them apart."

"The raid on Frontieras—do you think Gentry was in that country?"

Father shrugged and said, "I'd like to ask him. Yes, I think he was. And Gentry crossed the border the same night as Diablito. I believe the Apache is trying to trap Gentry and kill him."

"Fantastic theory," Regan said. "But it does explain Ludke's death, sir. He simply bumped into the Apaches."

And the reason Reindollar has not returned," father said softly.

"And the telegraph line being cut," I said.

That was the picture, and Regan thought it over. "I've always been amazed at the counter-intelligence of the Apaches.

They seemed to be aware of troop movements the moment they're happening. I suppose they know the Army's getting thin in Arizona."

"Yes," father said. "And they know Gentry's in this district. I believe that's why they're trying to isolate Starke—Gentry has come here before. He may come here again." Father turned around in his chair and faced the darkened window. "That's why it is of the utmost importance that telegraph communication be established with Fort Savage. In the morning I want you to depart with a full troop. Find the line and repair it."

Regan was scared, and I didn't blame him. Under the circumstances, any man would have been shaken by the prospect of patrol.

"Sir, do you still want me to depart if Mr. Reindollar fails to return?"

"Especially if Mr. Reindollar fails to return," father said.

Regan stood up and left. I didn't say anything, just watched father who sat staring out the window.

Finally he said, "Command is rotten, Mel. Be glad you've decided on a medical career."

"What's going to happen, sir?"

Father shook his head. "There's no telling. The Apache is a strange man, and he moves in strange ways." He pointed to the wall map. I saw the three small flags indicating Fort Starke in the middle, and Fort Savage and Fort Redoubt on either side. "Gentry," he said, "is in or near Tucson. You say he's leaving. East or west? Diablito doesn't know either, so he's going to cut off the escape in both directions. Gentry won't go south into Mexico, and Diablito will see to it that he can't go north."

"All that for one man, sir?"

"Gentry is more than one man," father said. "He is the big medicine against the Apaches. He knows them better than they know themselves—that's why they have never caught him. This isn't hate on Diablito's part, Mel. It's his religion, his medicine."

"I sent Ludke out blind," father said. "The factors for tragedy were all there, and I failed to compute them properly. So Willie Ludke died because of my error in judgment—that's the way it will have to go into the record."

"But it wasn't your fault, sir, and no one will every say that it was!"

"The Army will never say that it was," father amended. "To them, my decision was correct, but it's not the Army I'm thinking of now. Miss Shipley loved Ludke, and now

85

he's dead. She didn't come here to see Fort Starke, Mel. She came here to see me, to ask the questions for which I have no answers." He slapped his hands against the arms of his chair. "But Reindollar is different; I knew what I faced when I sent him out. And if he's dead, the Army will want to know why." He paused, eaten by concern. "What could have happened to the man? His troop outnumbered Diablito two to one, and Reindollar's been here long enough to have picked up a few Apache tricks. He's smart enough to avoid them."

He turned in his chair so that he faced me. "Mel, you're growing up. I'm glad, and yet I'm sad, for it opens up the door to trouble that all men must pass through." He was trying to say something he knew would be unpleasant. "Wade Hastings has been more than just a friend, hasn't he, Mel?"

"I liked him better than most, sir."

Father gnawed at his lip. "I had a talk with him this afternoon, a bitter talk. I think you'd better stay away from him for a few days."

"Why, sir?"

My father swiveled his chair back to stare out the window. "Some men like to shift blame—it makes their own weaknesses easier to bear. Wade is ignoring the fact that he made an error in judgment. All he's concerned about is you, Mel."

"Me?"

"He believes you told on him."

"Sergeant McGuire told, sir!"

Father smiled. "Son, when a man's angry, it doesn't matter what the truth is—he'll believe what he wants to believe. Wade Hastings believes you put him on the carpet. Nothing I could say would change his mind."

"Can I speak to him, sir?"

"I advise against it," father said. "But you're at a point where you ought to make your own decisions and stick by them. If you think there's anything between you and Wade that needs patching, go ahead and try."

Now that I had his permission, doubts began to form and I could think of several good reasons for not seeing Wade. Yet a boy's loyalty is strong, and there were many wonderful times I remembered, when Wade and I had shared laughter and a feeling of comradeship I had known with no other man, not even father. I suppose, thinking about it, this was because Wade preferred no real emotional ties to anyone. He liked having fun as long as it was free; then he would go his way and I mine, until the next time. He wished to live with as few responsibilities as possible, yet I had never before had occasion to hold this against him.

"I've got to see Wade," I said. "You understand, sir."

"Sure," father said. "A good friend is hard to forget, even after he's through with you. It's happened to me." He turned to look at me. "Did you see Miss Shipley when you left the house?"

"Yes, sir." I decided to be bluntly honest. "She doesn't like any of us, sir. I don't think she'd ever be Army."

Father pursed his lips and was silent for a moment. "No, she's not Army. Some women never are, even after spending years with the service. She's thinking of Ludke, Mel. And every time she thinks of him, she thinks of me, for I gave the order that sent him out to die. I'm the commanding officer, and responsible for everything that takes place in my command." He smiled and I saw how tired he was, with the new lines of worry etched in his face. "Miss Shipley will have to be faced, Mel. Just as Wade will have to be faced. You'd better run along. And stop in to see Bickerstaff—he's been asking about you."

I went out because I knew he wanted to be alone with his thoughts. The post was strangely quiet, and it wasn't hard to guess why. Soldiers can smell trouble, and years before, when Geronimo had roamed free, I could remember them acting this way, quiet and watchful. The barracks seemed vacated as I crossed the parade, but as I walked by the long buildings I could see the troopers against the walls, holding their conversation to low tones.

The easy way would have been for me to see Bickerstaff and forget all about Wade Hastings, but my father's lessons were all explicit—a man has to face his problem squarely or go under.

So I proceeded along the officers' picket row, passing Captain Hanson's quarters. Reed and Paul were inside. I could hear them laughing with Henson's two children, but I resisted the temptation to stop. There was a light in Wade Hastings' quarters. I knocked. I heard a chair scrape, then the door opened. Hastings looked down at me, his face settled and unfriendly. I could see that his arm was causing him considerable pain and that didn't improve his disposition.

"You come to rub my nose in something?"

"No, sir. I came to set something straight." I looked past him, into the room. "Can I come in?"

He shrugged and turned away from the door. I closed it, then stood there with my hat in my hands. Hastings rolled a cigarette awkwardly, since one arm was useless. He gave all his attention to the act. Finally he licked the paper and struck a match.

"Your old man threw the book at me. Thanks to you."

"I didn't tell him," I said.

Hastings turned his head quickly and his eyes were sharp as drills. "You're a poor liar, Mel. McGuire is too much a soldier to shoot off his mouth. He knows how miserable life can get when an officer is down on him."

"I didn't tell," I repeated. Wade looked at me for a long moment, then snorted through his nose and turned away, puffing on his cigarette.

Finally he whirled back, angry, whether at me or himself I couldn't tell. "You expect me to believe you? Why should I?"

"Because we're friends," I said. There was a lot more I wanted to say, about how I had never judged him before, right or wrong—but I didn't know how to begin, and most important, I wasn't sure now that he would understand. As each minute dragged by, I felt that I knew him less and less, and what I had known before was all a lie.

He ground his cigarette out under his heel. He held out his hand in an appeal. "What was it to you, Mel? What difference did it make to you whether or not I hated Gentry?"

"You left your command," I said.

"Is that why you told?"

"I didn't tell, sir."

My insistence irked him—the stiffness of his cheeks told me this, yet I faced him. I had to. Fort Starke—yes, even the whole army—was too small for me to run from this.

"I guess you're going to stick with that lie," he said. "What the hell difference does it make now?" He smiled, no longer angry. He put his hand on my shoulder and gave me a little shake. "Forget it, Mel. We're still friends. You did what you had to do."

"But, sir, I didn't—"

He shook his head. "Let's not go over it anymore, shall we. It's all right, I tell you. You're just a kid—there are things you don't understand yet." He turned me and opened the door. "Now go on, get out of here. I want to be alone."

There was no argument to this. He had me pushed outside and the door closed before I could object. I stood there a moment, wondering what I could do to bring our relationship back to the way it had been before, for I was at that age where I wanted nothing to change. I didn't know it at the time, but I was never to feel that way again about any man, and it was well that the future was hidden for, knowing what was to come, I doubt that I could have looked forward with any degree of hope.

Angling across the parade to the infirmary, I was again aware of the silence. Even the palisade guards traveled their measured posts with more serious regard to duty than ordinarily.

Doctor Bickerstaff was in his office. Indeed, he was seldom absent, for he liked his work and had few close friends on the post. He was at his desk, writing another lengthy article for some medical journal. When I entered, he raised his head quickly, briefly annoyed at the interruption, but his irritation vanished almost immediately.

I said, "If you're busy, sir, I can come back."

"Nien, nien," he said quickly, putting aside his pen. Sit down." He swung his chair away from the desk and began to polish his thick glasses. "Didn't I tell you der mama would come around? *Ja,* I know vimmen, boy."

"Sir?" I didn't know what he was talking about, but this was nothing new for Doctor Bickerstaff often started a conversation in the middle.

"Der mama! Ver' is der eye? You didn't see vat she done for you?"

"No, sir. What did she do for me?"

Bickerstaff puffed his cheeks and peered at me over the rims of his glasses. "You haf not been in your room since you come back?"

"Sure, but what's in my room?"

He slapped his thighs. "Fool! *Dummkoff!* So blind you vill never make a doctor, not even of horses!" He waved his hands. "Go—I haf no time for the blind!"

I went out, perplexed by Bickerstaff's words, for in spite of his linguistic handicaps, he had always made sense to me before. But since the answer lay in my room, I recrossed the parade. Mother was in the parlor, sewing.

She raised her head when I came in. "I suppose you're too slept out to go to bed?"

"I'm not tired," I said. "I think I'll go to my room and read."

"Doctor Bickerstaff brought over two boxes of books," she said. "Did you see them?"

So that was it. I should have guessed. "Ah—yes," I said, hoping I didn't sound too vague. "Good night, mother." I bent, kissed her briefly. As I went up the stairs, I noticed her puzzled glance following me.

Once in my room I fumbled for the lamp, then spent a moment adjusting it. Bickerstaff had brought me some books, but that wasn't all. To my amazement, mother had had shelves built near my small desk—shelves now holding a solid row of medical textbooks, and another shelf containing bottled specimens, all gifts from Bickerstaff's collection. And on the far end sat the fetus—this must have been difficult for mother to tolerate, and I could accurately gauge her feelings, for she had made a cloth cover that hid it effectively.

For a moment an overwhelming wonder pushed all else from my mind, then I was puzzled as to how I could have missed seeing the shelves before. Thinking back, I recalled that the room had been dark when I went to sleep, and I hadn't bothered to light the lamp. Neither had I lit one when I got up.

I went back down the stairs. Mother looked up from her sewing when I sat down in father's easy chair. She said, "If your father finds you there, he'll declare war, Melvin— you know he prefers that chair." Her tone, the forced unconcern in her manner told me that she knew what I wanted to say.

"How can I thank you?" I asked.

She wrinkled her nose as she always did when someone crowded her into showing emotion. "Mel, I didn't do it for thanks. I want you to learn, to amount to something. If you have to study those—things, then study them at home, not behind my back. People always draw away from each other when they have to do things in secret."

"Does father know?"

"Not yet." She turned her head and when she did this I listened for his footfalls. She seemed able to make out his step long before anyone else.

Father came onto the back porch and the rear door banged. When he stopped in the parlor archway, I left his chair while he removed his pistol belt, hanging it on the halltree. He sat down immediately.

"Any word from Mr. Reindollar?" mother asked.

"Nothing," father said softly. "I'm running out of troops, fighting an enemy I haven't yet seen." He sighed. "Fetch me a cigar, Mel. Take one for yourself." Mother gave him a mock scowl. Father said, "When Regan leaves in the morning I'll have fifty-three regulars inside the palisade walls. If this keeps up, there won't be anyone left to leave Fort Starke when moving orders arrive."

An upstairs door opened and closed. Father took the cigar from me, and leaned forward to accept the light I offered. Through a cloud of smoke, he said, "Is Miss Shipley all right?"

"She stays in her room," mother said. "An odd girl. I can't make her out."

I kept one ear tuned to the conversation and the other to the steps overhead. After you live in a house a while you can distinguish movement from the subtle sounds of loose planking. I distinctly heard her cross the upper hall and enter my room.

"I think I'll go and read," I said.

Father waved his hand and mother went on with her sewing. I took the stairs two at a time and made sure I didn't make a lot of noise. My door was closed and when I took hold of the knob, I did so easily, and opened it slowly.

Lilith Shipley was wearing one of mother's robes, and she was standing before my new shelf, looking at the books. My first impulse was to speak, but she took the cover off the fetus and lifted the bottle. Then I was afraid to say anything for fear that she would start and drop it. Having it in a bottle might have just been barely tolerable to mother, but cleaning it off the floor was out of the question.

So I waited, the door partially open, and when she set the jar back on the shelf, I rattled the lock. She did start, and I stepped inside, closing the door behind me.

"You must think I'm a terrible snoop," she said. Then she had the grace to blush. "I guess I am." She motioned to the shelves. "What is all this for?"

"I'm studying to be a doctor. Those are textbooks and specimens."

"Yes," she said. "I saw the one on the end." Her eyes wandered over the small room. "May I sit down?"

Hurriedly I swept some clothes from a chair, shoving them under the bed. I didn't understand this woman, and I told myself this was because of her background—she was from a social sphere completely alien to me. Her clothes were expensive, and her manner poised, yet from the very first moment I saw her, I knew that she was deeply troubled, and not entirely from the shock of Mr. Ludke's death.

"Perhaps I could get you something, ma'am?"

"No, nothing. I was hungry for talk. Do you mind, Melvin?"

This was both flattering and embarrassing. I perched uncomfortably on my bed, unsure of what to say, for at sixteen girls of all ages left me on edge. I had no confidence in their presence. "Have you talked with father yet?"

Her eyes flickered oddly. "No," she said. "There's really very little to talk about now." Her glance moved again to my shelf of books. "How long have you been studying?"

"Dr. Bickerstaff has been helping me for two years. I've been able to assist him a little this past year.

"Then you must know a lot."

I couldn't decide whether or not she was serious, so I chose an answer to take care of either event. "Compared to the average man, I guess I do know a lot about medicine, but compared to Doctor Bickerstaff, I know almost nothing." Then a very strange possibility pushed into my mind and I asked the question before thinking. "Are you ill, ma'am?"

She gave a start; then her face smoothed and her voice became absolutely calm. "No. No, I'm quite all right." Her eyes narrowed as though she had raised a guard, but in a moment she smiled, a warm, intimate smile, which would disarm any man. "You're a very serious boy, Melvin, and manly. I noticed that immediately when you came to my hotel with that officer. You stood so straight, so completely sure of yourself."

I blushed like a fool, and her smile deepened. The shine in her eyes brightened. Later, thinking about it, it struck me as odd that a man on the run never knows it until the run is over, and the woman has had her way.

She was still talking. ". . . you're gallant; I think that's what impressed me so. So young in years, yet so much a man." Her voice sank to a soft, almost breathless pitch. "Melvin, a woman feels that she can trust a gallant man. I suppose that's why I came here tonight, dared to speak to you in confidence, because I know how gallant and brave you are. You would never cause me to regret my trust."

I felt foolish, like an actor in some love drama, but I was excited too, newly aware of the alien chemistry of women and now mortified because I had the ball and didn't know which way to run with it.

"What—what can I do for you?" I managed to stammer.

"My heart told me that I could count on you," Lilith Shipley said. "Melvin, there is no one for me to turn to but you. No one I can trust completely except you."

"I'll—do anything I can," I said, all at once terribly in earnest, and determined not to disappoint this fine woman. And I think that I was just as quickly, unreasonably in love with her because she was so kind and understanding. Never before had I felt so protective.

"Since Mr. Ludke's death, I've felt terribly alone. I can't sleep. I can't eat. I can't go on, restless like this. I need to go —riding. Would you come with me? I know that getting away, even for a little while, would help me."

"Father wouldn't let us off the post," I said quickly. "Not with the trouble about."

"Do you always do everything your father wants you to?"

She reached out and touched my hand, giving it a small pressure. "Besides, does your father have to know?" Never before had a girl held my hand and in embarrassment I tried to pull away, but Lilith Shipley clung to me. I stood up. She stood with me and now everything was worse, for she was too close. "You're not afraid, Melvin. I know you're brave. Only a brave man could have brought the detail back from Tucson."

"This—this is different," I stammered. "The whole thing is out of the question, Miss Shipley."

"You may call me Lilith." Her lips drew into a slight pout. "Please, don't make me think I've misjudged you, Melvin."

Such a thing was unthinkable, especially with her so close and my heart pounding. "I'll—I'll have to think about it, Miss—Lilith."

"Don't think," she urged. "Tomorrow morning, when the air's cool, we'll go for a ride. We could be back by the time the bugle blows and no one would be the wiser." Her free hand touched my shoulder, then my face. "Melvin, you'd do this for me, wouldn't you?" She knew I was afraid, knew it and used her knowledge against me. "Perhaps your father would storm a little, but we'd be back safe, and he couldn't punish you without looking a little silly. Now, could he?"

"I—I suppose not."

Her smile warmed me. "You *are* brave. I knew you were, from the start." Seemingly on impulse, she leaned forward and kissed me, a brief, moist-lipped kiss, that left me trembling in a fog of bewildered embarrassment—and desire. "I knew I could turn to you, Melvin—you're so understanding."

At sixteen a man can be fantastically foolish. Impossible visions clouded my mind, visions of Lilith Shipley and me together, and I was making her forget all about Willie Ludke. We were walking together, in love, and I was ten feet tall, a full-blown hero.

"All right," I agreed. "I'll take you riding. Anything you want, Lilith. Damn father's rules."

She was happy, intensely happy. "In the morning, before anyone else is up. Just you and me, Melvin. Alone, so you can help me forget my heartache."

"Yes," I said, a bit feverishly. "Yes, I'll make you forget everything." I grew bold and put my arm around the softness of her waist, and she permitted this liberty.

"I'll be waiting," she said. "This is between us, Melvin. A secret."

"Anything," I said.

I wanted to kiss her again—she knew this and expertly

parried my impulse before it assumed shape. Her hand brushed my cheek and her eyes held many promises. It was the kind of glance that allows a man to take his pick.

"I must go now," she said, moving away from me. I stood there, and watched her slip out. When I heard her step on the stairs, I opened my door a crack. From there I could see down the stairs and into part of the parlor. Father left his chair and remained standing until Lilith Shipley sat down.

I could hear father's voice. "Regretfully, my duties have prevented me from having a talk with you, Miss Shipley. I hope I can set that right without delay."

"I'm sure we can," Lilith Shipley said, the run of her voice soft and satisfied. I wondered if she were thinking of me, and that brief moment when our lips touched—what else could she be thinking about? I could think of nothing else. In a detached way I heard Reed and Paul come into the house by the back way; they chattered in the kitchen, getting cookies and milk.

Lilith was saying, "You have a delightful family, Colonel. Mr. Ludke liked children."

A heavy silence followed in which father took refuge in his cigar. Finally he said, "I wish I could express my regrets, Miss Shipley, but there seems to be no way to compensate you for your loss. Believe me when I say that I understand your grief."

"Do you really, Colonel? I've been robbed of the most precious thing in my life. Can you really understand that?"

"Perhaps not in the sense you mean," father said. "My family is together and in good health. But there are things that can happen for which no blame can be levied. Were Mr. Ludke to speak now, I believe he would agree."

"But he's dead," she said. "What can change that, Colonel?"

"Nothing," father said. "Cora, why don't you make us some coffee?"

When I heard mother go into the kitchen, I closed my door softly and undressed for bed. Propped against my pillows, I tried to get interested in Hebenstreit and intestinal disorders, but the learned German was too dull to crowd out my thoughts of Lilith Shipley.

Then I heard Reed and Paul on the stairs and pretended to read so they wouldn't pester me. As usual, they made a big thing of getting ready for bed, and when they settled, I snuffed out the lamp.

The house was quiet at last and I lay listening to the cottonpacked silence. I liked silence, the absence of sounds, but now I felt that everything was too quiet, a troubled silence. And when I dropped off to sleep I carried that feeling with me into my dreams.

10

I AWOKE suddenly, chilled through, although the wind was down and the night was mild. Reed and Paul were asleep, their breathing loud and regular. Carefully, so as not to wake them, I swung my feet to the floor and fumbled for my trousers. I could only guess at the time, and I placed it somewhere near four o'clock.

While I was tugging on my boots, the door eased open and Lilith Shipley stepped inside. She saw me, a vague shape in the darkness and groped for me with her hand.

Putting my lips close to her ear, I whispered, "Be quiet. Reed is a light sleeper."

"Then I'll see you outside," she said. Her hand brushed my cheek. "You haven't changed your mind, have you?"

"Never," I said and wanted to say a lot more, foolish things about how I would always be near her with my strength, and my modest devotion. Thinking back, it is fantastic to what heights of idiocy men can be driven by a woman's smile, or a quick, promising kiss.

When she turned to the door, I noticed she wore a divided riding skirt and a short jacket. After she stepped out, I held back until I was positive she had cleared the stairs. Father's and mother's room was across the hall and I took pains to be quiet. As I passed through the parlor, I saw father's pistol belt hanging on the hall tree, and on an impulse calculated to impress Lilith Shipley, I unflapped the holster, withdrew the gun and slipped it in my waistband, covering it with my corduroy coat.

Lilith was waiting by the back porch. She whispered, "Are you sure you can get the horses?"

"I think so, but if we get caught, father will throw the book at us."

The parade was graveyard-still and deserted when we crossed it and entered the stable yard. A little care and timing put us in the horse barn without the stable guard seeing us. Lilith Shipley paced back and forth in the dark, while I quietly saddled two of A Troop's mounts. She assured me she could ride like a man, so we led the horses along the back wall until we came to the water gate. A guard walked by but he failed to see us. Four o'clock is a sleepy time and men naturally become less alert. One part of my mind kept reminding me of the risks I invited by being here. A guard might shoot first and identify us later. But Lilith Shipley seemed to sense my melting resolve, and then she would touch me, or stand close, urging me on with those silent, inflexible pressures of a mature woman in full command of her powers.

I found a discarded horseshoe behind the farrier's shed and pitched it over. When it hit, one of the guards said, "Who goes there?" in a loud, demanding voice. The guard near the water gate left his post to see what was going on.

"Let's go," I said, and while the guards were busy, we slipped out. There was no way to lock the gate behind us, so I just closed it and hoped no one would see the dropped bar until we were well away from the post. Lilith Shipley started to step into the saddle, then changed her mind and leaned against the horse, drawing breath through her open mouth.

"What's the matter?" I whispered. "We can't stay here."

"I'm sick," she said and groaned softly. And she *was* sick. "Get—me up," she whispered, and I gave her a hand into the saddle. She sagged forward, her face starch-white in the coming grayness of dawn.

"Maybe we'd better go back," I suggested and would have been glad to do so.

"We'll go—on as we—planned." She urged her horse into motion and there was little I could do but follow. I don't believe I took a decent breath until we were well clear of the palisade walls. But before we had traveled a mile I knew we were in for a time. Lilith Shipley was so ill she could hardly sit the horse, and twice I had to dismount and hold her to keep her from falling off.

Time was against us. The sky was getting light and if we remained where we were, the palisade guards would soon spot us. Lilith must have realized this for as soon as she could control herself she pushed east, away from the post. She rode erect now, her illness having inexplicably passed.

For twenty minutes we followed the telegraph poles while I looked to the back and both sides, my nervousness increasing to a point where only the hard feel of father's pistol under my coat could calm me.

"We'd better not ride far," I said, hoping there would be nothing in my voice to betray my uneasiness, or destroy her opinion of my courage.

"I want to ride far," she said, her voice sounding unpleasantly stubborn. "What's out there?" She pointed down the dim line of telegraph poles.

"A lot of desert."

"Let's ride that way," she said. Quickly she looked at me, her face strangely white and determined in the mounting light. "You're not going to disappoint me now, are you, Melvin?"

I shook my head, not trusting my voice, and she smiled. She seemed cool, almost aloof, as though she no longer cared one way or another about me. But this was impossible to believe, recalling her earlier warmth, her intimate touch.

So we rode east along the line of poles. For a time she remained silent. I thought she was ill again.

"How do you feel?"

"All right now. Don't bother to diagnose."

Her voice was spiteful and contemptuous; I realized it suddenly, and with the realization came a sick knowledge that I had been used for a fool. What her purpose could be I didn't even consider. She had never cared about me and such a discovery is always a shock to a man's vanity. For a time I rode along, trying to find the proper, stinging words with which to accuse her, but I only got madder at myself.

The flatness seemed to stretch as the dawn grew—we could see nearly a mile ahead now. A fringe of pink started to spread along the distant horizon and in another ten minutes the sun's glare would be dead on and blinding. Riding into such light was uncomfortable at any time, but with Apaches about, there was an additional deadly risk.

"We ought to turn north," I said. "Toward Douglas. The sun's going to be smack in our eyes."

"I like the sun," Lilith said. "Do you think that's strange?"

I thought a lot was strange, but I couldn't figure any of it out. "We ought to turn. There may be Apaches out here."

She smiled. "I'm not afraid. Was this the route Mr. Ludke took when he was murdered?"

"Yes."

"Then we'll ride on," Lilith said.

At last it dawned on me just what we were doing, and I didn't like it one bit, but saying so wasn't going to do any good.

"Your father's a nice man," Lilith went on. She wore no hat and now that the flaming rim of the sun was coming up, she squinted her eyes against the glare. "You're his favorite son, Melvin. Did you know that?" She gave me a quick, appraising glance. "He's very proud of you. I could tell by the way he spoke."

Lilith acted like she was talking to herself, and none of it made sense to me. I pulled my hat brim down, for the sun was dazzling. In an hour the heat would be like a furnace.

"I've noticed," she said, "how we gather about us the things that are most precious. Willie Ludke was precious to me, Melvin. I hope you understand and forgive me."

"For making a fool of me? For using me?" I was angry and let her know it.

Her smile mocked me. "You're just a boy, Melvin. I gave my love to a man. What made you think I could ever accept less?"

I could hate her and hate myself, but never strongly enough to forget where we were and the attending dangers. I figured that we were three miles from the post and with Apaches about, that was three miles too far, I meant to put my personal feelings aside and tell her of these dangers, but one look at her locked expression told me she wouldn't listen. She rode with her head back, her body straight, looking ahead as though she could see her destiny and was restraining her eagerness to arrive.

Finally I had to ask, "What the devil are we riding here for?"

She gave a look that said I was stupid, which, in view of my recent performance, was an opinion that had some merit. Her expression was sweetly controlled and noncommittal. "I'm going to meet someone."

That was the sort of answer I gave mother when I wanted to keep a secret, yet didn't feel up to defying parental authority. Being on the receiving end was disturbing. I kept looking around at the gullies and, as far as I was concerned, they were full of Apaches.

When my nerves would no longer take the strain, I said, "We'll turn back here." I hoped my voice held enough authority to forestall an argument.

"I'm going on," she said. "Alone, or with you." She gave me a knowing smile. "If you left me here, your father would be furious."

"That's why we're turning back now," I said. I halted and I thought she was going to make good her threat for she rode on a dozen yards before pulling up.

"Will your father be up by now, Melvin?"

Of all the questions! "Yes, he's always up by dawn."

"Good," Lilith Shipley said, and there was exquisite pleasure in the word, as though she had just received some rare award. "Melvin, has your life been happy?"

"Yes, very."

"And if you had to leave it now, would you be sad?"

"You mean, die?"

"Yes, die. Would that be too bad?"

A chill wind began to blow through me. "I've never thought about it. It's always seemed a long way off."

"It's very near now," Lilith said. "When we least expect it, that's when death comes." She let the silence run for a moment. "I believe you when you said there was danger out here. I wanted danger. I want the Apaches to find us. We're not going back to Fort Starke, Melvin. Not ever going back."

For a moment the enormity of her insane plan held me speechless. Lilith Shipley laughed softly, and I knew she had gone mad. "Don't hate me, Melvin. It's too late for hate now. The sun's out and the Apaches will find us."

"What do you want to kill me for? What have I done to you?"

"Nothing," she said. "You were unlucky enough to be your father's favorite son, that's all. It could have been Reed or Paul, but it wasn't. It was you. I left a note for your father on the kitchen table. He took my man, my love. Now I'm taking his."

"You'll die too," I said. "Did you think of that?"

"I have nothing to live for," she said.

Then she wheeled her horse and kicked it into a run. There was nothing I could do but follow her, and I cursed her each step of the way.

For nearly a mile we ran at breakneck speed, and although I flayed my horse, I could gain only a few yards. Running on the desert could be dangerous, for there were many dog holes for a horse to stumble into, but luck was with us both, the devil's luck.

My horse was beginning to blow badly; hers was no better. Finally she was forced to pull up, and then I caught her. Fright and anger drove me and I made a grab for her reins. She struck out at me and I took the blow on the shoulder, nearly spilling out of saddle. I roweled the horse, knocking her neatly to the ground.

Her horse ran off before I could grab the reins, and there was nothing I could do to stop him. I cursed this luck, for if there were Apaches about, they would soon find the horse, and a short time later, the rider.

Lilith was on all fours, coughing, trying to get her breath.

I dismounted quickly. "You can ride double with me. But we're going back. Now!"

When mother wept, I always felt like a misbehaving monster, but when the tears rolled down Lilith's cheeks, I found myself cool and unemotional. She stood up, her riding dress dusty. I took her arm and tried to steer her toward my horse, but she broke free. Before I could catch her arm again she whirled and struck me in the mouth with her fist. I fell back, tasting blood, and this gave her time to lash my horse and send it off, running.

With this done, the fight left her and she stood serene and sweet-smiling. "Now we're helpless. We have only to wait."

The thought of being alone and afoot made me feel ill, and my heart threatened to pound its way through my chest. With an effort I forced myself to think, to calculate our chances of getting back to Starke alive, and I honestly thought only of myself.

The gullies would offer concealment for the moment, and I seized her arm, turning her toward them. But she twisted away again, only this time I didn't wait. I slapped her across the face as hard as I could, at least hard enough to knock her down.

Then I said, "Get into that gully."

No matter how much she deserved it, hitting a woman can make a man feel like a dog. I felt like one, but I wasn't going to let on to her. She got up, the side of her face flame-red and clearly marked. Her eyes never left me and in that moment she must have realized that from here on in this was my show. Obediently she walked ahead, perhaps twenty yards. When we reached the lip of the wash, I said, "Jump," and she did, landing on hands and knees. I followed her.

"What—what are you going to do?"

"Fight to stay alive, if I have to," I said.

She laughed at me. "What can a little boy do?"

"I can pull a trigger as well as a man," I said and showed her my father's Colt. This was my ace in the hole, and her eyes widened.

She sank back, afraid of me now, and I relished the feeling of power, of having her on the run. But I couldn't afford to waste time. The day was turning into a scorcher and we had no water. Seven or eight miles doesn't sound far when you're telling about it at the officers' club with a drink in your hand, but on the desert it can be a distance so great you may never reach its end. I calculated the time, and the temperature, and tried to guess the kind of terrain stretching between us and Fort Starke. I could count on the gullies for at least a mile of cover, although walking in zigzag course to take advantage of it would double the distance. Then the country broke into nearly smooth flats, with only a few depressions where a man could hide.

"Let's go," I said.

"Go where? There's no place—you said so yourself. The Apaches will find us and then we'll die."

"Please get on your feet." When she continued to sit and stare, I cocked the pistol and pointed it at her, a foolish thing to do, but desperation drove me. Then I discovered a strange thing. I discovered it when fear came into her eyes, and she scrambled to her feet.

Lilith Shipley really didn't want to die, not when the possibility got close enough to touch.

"Put—put—put that thing down!"

"It's not heavy. Just walk ahead of me and keep quiet."

She did, and I uncocked the gun with my left hand, being very careful not to let the hammer slip. The empty chamber was to the right now and I had to half-cock the revolver, rotate the cylinder all the way around until the empty came under the hammer again.

Lilith Shipley stumbled as she walked, and the clicks behind her must have raised hob with her nerves, for she said, "For God's sake, put that down before you kill me!"

"I thought you wanted to die?" I couldn't resist rubbing her nose in that.

The gully was man-high, enough to screen our movement, and for an hour we followed the switching course. Without visible landmarks to guide me, I used the molten sun, keeping it at our backs as much as possible.

Finally the gully emptied onto the flats, as I knew it would. Sweat soaked my shirt and made the shoulders of Lilith's dress a ruin. Dust caked our faces and I would have given my place in heaven for a drink of water.

"We'll rest here," I said and Lilith sank gratefully to the ground. There was no shade at all and the sun boiled down.

I found that a fellow can get so frightened that he actually steps outside himself, one part of his mind crystal clear. And I guess this was the part I used. I wondered if father would take the remaining troops out to search for us, then I decided that he would not, for he could not leave the post unmanned to save two people, even his own son. Once this firmed up in my mind, I knew that I was really on my own, a thing I had always dreamed of, but not exactly like this.

"Time to move," I said.

She looked at me, her face as expressionless as a stone. Only when I pressed the muzzle of the revolver against her breast did she stir, and then she cried again.

"Walk ahead," I told her and we started out across the flats.

This was the dangerous part—I knew it but could not avoid it. Diablito could be a mile away, or fifty, but the distance did little to diminish the risk, for the gamble was the same, equally hard on nerves.

Through the early part of the morning we moved in a westerly direction. Lilith wanted, in quick succession to stop, a drink of water, for me to shoot her and get it over with, to leave her, to save her, and a dozen other things. I made her keep a pebble in her mouth to help fight her thirst and once when she got angry and spat it out, I slapped her again. After that she obeyed without protest.

I found a shallow depression in the desert floor and there we rested again, not that we could spare the time, but because I was going to need cover shortly and was unsure just where the next lay.

Living with the Army and some Indian trouble made watching the back trail almost second nature, and twice in the last half hour I had spotted movement.

That meant Apaches.

Lilith Shipley said, "I don't want to stay here."

She was, I decided, just a contrary bitch, determined to get her own selfish way. The seven years in age that separated us faded, and I was sorely tempted to take her over my knee and spank her.

"Did you hear me? I said I didn't want to stay here."

"Shut up!" This was impolite, but effective.

I braced myself near the shallow rim of the depression and had a careful look. Ten minutes before the Apaches had been a mile behind, but Apaches are great runners, capable of chasing horses afoot, and they had gained considerable ground. They had cast aside all pretense of concealment and ran in the open.

Two I could see—perhaps there were others I didn't know about. I was surprisingly calm, or better, was so frightened I couldn't shake. But then I guess most men can be coolheaded when they know the game is for keeps and the last card is about to be turned face up.

There was a chance, although a mighty slim one, that the Apaches would bypass the depression. I cocked the pistol and waited.

Lilith Shipley, who watched as though fascinated, said, "What are you doing? What do you see?"

"Just keep down." The two Apaches were splitting, cutting to the left and right, crossing and recrossing their own trail, or the one Lilith and I had left. The nearest was still a hundred yards away.

Lilith stirred, and before I could stop her, rose head and shoulders out of the depression. I made a grab for her, to push her down, but she saw the two Apaches and screamed, a long, pulled-out wail of pure terror.

Had the Apaches been handed a map, they couldn't have found us any quicker. They broke into a run and I saw that one carried a pistol, the other a bow. Lilith stood up and tried to run. One swipe with my pistol barrel put her down, limp and rolling. Then I turned my attention to the two Apaches.

They were close enough now for me to see them clearly, naked, a broad streak of vermilion across their chests. One had painted a circle on each kneecap while the other had a white handprint on the side of his face.

The one with the pistol worried me, but the bowman really made me sweat for he could shoot with rifle accuracy up to a hundred yards. I hunkered down and waited, my breathing quick and heavy. A glance at Lilith Shipley told me I hadn't hit her hard enough—she was moaning and trying to sit up.

The Apache with the pistol cut to his left, trying to flank us. The bowman came on, an arrow notched for me. I lifted the Colt, held it with both hands and tried to draw a bead. A couple of deep breaths calmed me and I held the front sight blade high on the painted chest, slowly squeezing. The .45 recoiled and black powder smoke drifted back in my face but, to my surprise, the Apache was gone. I looked for him, then saw him, twitching, trying to drag himself—at last he lay completely still.

Lilith was crouched in an uncomfortable position, rocking back and forth with her hands clasped, her eyes closed, crying. And I suppose she was praying too—I didn't have time for it. The crack I had given her with the pistol had cut her scalp and blood streamed across one cheek. Quickly I turned, trying to find the Apache with the pistol. He was off to my right, and at least sixty yards away, but closing the distance as fast as he could sprint.

I tried a shot and missed, then forced myself to wait.

Lilith Shipley's crying began to tear at my nerves, and she kept mumbling, "Save me. God, save me."

Then she tried to grab my pistol. I slapped her, hard, and pushed her back, and barely in time, for the Apache closed in like a deer breaking for shelter. I shot and missed, realizing then that I had to steady down. So I stood erect, arm extended and sighted father's big Colt as though I were at the Fort Starke pistol butts. I let the front sight settle while he yelled and fired a wild shot that kicked sand over my boots. Then I let go and watched him roll up. His legs thrashed when he hit, and the pistol flew from his hand. It was an old cap and ball Starr double-action and it fell near my feet—he had been that close.

Then, for the first time, both Lilith and I did the natural thing—she fainted, and I got sick.

Fortunately I recovered first, and she never knew. By the time she was able to stand I had the Starr tucked in my waistband and a burning urge to leave the immediate vicinity.

Lilith was reluctant to move. "I'm sick," she said.

"Start moving," I told her. "Start, or I'll boot you all the way back to Fort Starke."

She got up and began walking.

Three miles, that was my guess, and I set an hour aside from the passing time in which to travel that distance. After awhile I could see the walled fort and the sight cheered me. The heat was making me lightheaded and sundogs danced endlessly, Lilith Shipley, hatless, was suffering, so I gave her my light coat to throw over her head. Had this been three in the afternoon we would both have been prone and clawing at the sand.

When the post was still a mile away, I took the Apache's pistol and fired and remaining loads into the air. For a moment I thought I had wasted the ammunition, then there were answering shots from the palisade wall—in the clear air I thought I saw the powder smoke dissipating. A bugle blew. The call was somewhat distorted, but it was father's call.

That was, quite easily, the longest mile I ever walked, and I still am unable to decide whether or not I blamed my father for not coming to meet us with a detail. But he was waiting by the main gate, the ever-present cigar sending ribbons of smoke in front of his face, disguising his worry.

He took one look at Lilith's near exhaustion, then spoke to Haukbauer. "Take her to Bickerstaff and have him look her over."

To me, he said, "I'll take back my pistol now, if you're through with your walk."

Had he shouted, or remained silent, I could have taken it,

but this sarcasm cut like a whip. I couldn't face up to him as I handed over the pistol. He examined the spent loads, then ejected them without saying a word.

I offered the Starr and his eyes narrowed. "Where did you get that?"

One of the troopers offered a canteen, then took it away from me when I tried to drink it all. I wiped the back of my hand across my mouth. Father was waiting for his answer.

"I killed two Apaches, sir." I hoped my voice sounded right, without brag, although I wanted to boast—anything to relieve the tension.

"Where?"

I pointed. "About three miles from the post, sir." He watched me as I spoke, his eyes narrowed, and behind his anger I thought I read a deep-seated approval—and pride.

"It's a good day for hunting," he said. Then he turned to a nearby trooper. "Tell Mrs. Lunsford that Melvin came back safe." He nodded to me. "Come with me."

He was angry, the kind of anger I didn't like, the very calm kind that promised real trouble. The gates were closed, and the troopers returned to their duty. I followed father across the scalded parade to the infirmary. Father didn't say anything and I was glad of the silence.

Doctor Bickerstaff was not in the outer office, so father took a seat to wait for him. "Sit down," he said, puffing on his cigar. "What made you do it, Mel?"

"I don't know, sir."

"Don't know, or won't tell?"

"It's mixed up, sir. I don't have the straight of it myself."

Father nodded. 'When you do, I want to hear it. Did you lose the two horses?"

"Yes, sir."

"Well, we'll consider them a trade for the Apaches." I believe he knew I acted bravely, but he made no allusion to it.

Finally Bickerstaff came out of his examining room. He peered at father over his spectacles. "Dis is a complicated situation, colonel." He sat down at his desk and laced his fingers across his round stomach. "It is plain to see v'y der *fraulein* vanted to take her life. A mother she is going to be."

"No!" Father seemed stunned. And me too, I guess, but it placed the pieces in the proper places, building a picture of her that I could understand, and no longer hate her for what she tried to do.

"She is resting," Bickerstaff said. "Better to leave her here for a few days. Dere may be complications."

"All right," father said. He stood up. "Can I speak to her?"

"*Ja.*" Bickerstaff opened the door. "But only a moment."

"Come along, Mel."

Lilith Shipley was in bed, a sheet pulled up to her chin. She looked at me, then at father, and the tears began again. Bickerstaff had bandaged her head, and now I was ashamed that I had cracked her with such complete enjoyment.

Father said, "Miss Shipley, I'm going to be very brief with you. You tried to kill my son for a wrong you fancy I've done. You're a very immature person, Miss Shipley—there is no place at Fort Starke for you. The paymaster's stage will be her in a few days. I'll put you on it."

"Where can I go?" she asked in a dull voice. "I have no secrets now."

"That's your concern," father said. "Miss Shipley, grow up and accept the responsibility of your own acts. Stop trying to blame them on innocent people."

"You detest me," she said. "Is that why you're so hard now?"

"Too many people have helped you," father said flatly. "The kindest thing I can do for you is to throw you out on your own, bag and baggage." Father stepped outside, and I followed.

As soon as we got to headquarters, he said, "Close the door." I could guess what I was in for.

He sat down behind his desk. I sat facing him. He dropped his cigar into the cuspidor and stripped the wrapper from a fresh one. "I believe you've just completed a fair growing-up process, Mel. Did you fancy yourself in love with Miss Shipley?"

"Yes, sir."

Father didn't smile, and I blessed him for it. "Mel, when I was thirteen, I was in love with my teacher. But she married a clerk in the barrel factory, so I ran away to a town twenty miles away. My father came after me in the buggy."

"Did he lick you, sir?" I figured this might afford me a clue as to my immediate future.

"As a matter of fact," father said, "he didn't. It seems that he had had a similar experience, only with the county librarian." He drew on his cigar a moment, his eyes veiled by down-pulled lids. "It's strange how a boy can do something, something simple like making a fool of himself over an older woman, and have it reach out so far and touch so many peo-

106

ple. I guess you figured that this was a personal thing, and you would be the only one who'd get hurt?"

"Yes, sir."

"Well," father sad, "that's not exactly so. Are you wondering why I didn't come after you?"

"I guess you couldn't risk the troops for just two of us."

"That's right. You could have died out there, Mel, and I would have had to stand here, helpless. That was the choice you forced me to make. A choice you had no right to inflict on me."

"I'm sorry."

"Being sorry is not enough," father said. "Your mother and I have been married many years, but this morning she moved in with Captain and Mrs. Hanson. She took Reed and Paul with her."

This stunned me. "Why, sir?"

"Because you forced her to make a decision she didn't want to make, Mel. She wanted me to take the troop and go after you. You're her first-born and her feeling for you is pretty strong. You're my son too, but I had to think of Fort Starke. I refused to go. We had words. Finally she gave me her choice; I couldn't accept. So she moved out."

"Sir—" I couldn't finish. I would have wept had I tried.

"You'd better go to her," father said in a flat, controlled voice. "You owe her that."

I got up, turning to the door. "Won't she come back to the big house, sir? Can't you make her come home?"

"Yes," he said. "I could make her, but what would that be? Mel, a woman can stand poverty, or even a man who drinks, but when he fails her, as your mother believes I've failed her, then she rebels."

And I had failed them both, failed the worst of all. I went out and hurried across the parade to Captain Hanson's quarters. Mrs. Hanson was a thin, graying woman, long accustomed to frontier discomfort. She opened the door, then motioned me inside.

"Your mother's lying down. You'd better go in."

"Yes'm."

At the door I wondered should I knock or not, then decided not. Mother had her head turned away, but when she heard the lock click shut, she looked around. For a moment she just looked, then she began to cry. I dropped my hat on the floor and knelt by the bed. She cradled me against her, and I didn't feel sixteen or an Apache fighter. I felt exactly the same as I felt when I was five and came home with a black eye.

"You're all right?" When I nodded, she added, "No thanks to your father. His heart turned to stone."

"He couldn't come after me," I said. "Can't you see how he couldn't?"

"No, I can't," she said. She sat up and brushed her eyes with her fingertips. "Mel, I begged him to go, but he refused. I never thought I could hate him, but I hated him then, enough to have killed him."

"You don't mean that."

"I do mean it," she said. "I know your father too well to think he sent you here to plead for him. We've had our say and it's all over, and I'm not happy about it because I still love him." She brushed my hair away from my forehead in that way she always had, half tidying up, half caressing. "When the paymaster's stage arrives, I'm going to leave on it. Reed and Paul are coming with me."

"No!"

She shook her head. "There's no other way, Melvin. I've thought it out. Your father and I have talked it dry."

"You can't leave him! He needs you. We all do."

"How can I stay?" She tried a smile and half carried it off. "It was God's will alone that saved you out there. But he was ready to stand by while you died and as long as I see him I'll think of that moment when he said he would not take a detail off the post. But I want you to stay with him, Melvin—he'll be lonely, and he needs looking after. Besides, there's Doctor Bickerstaff and your studies. I want you to finish."

The way she said it, the way she had it all figured out, all for us and nothing for herself, broke my resolve and I found I could cry without shame. In front of father this would never have happened, but tears, even a man's, are something all women understand. I suppose it is because grief is more commonplace in their lives.

But crying was not the answer. Somehow, in my foolishness, I had pulled asunder the lives I cherished most. Now I had to pull them back together again, and I didn't know where to begin.

11

THROUGHOUT THE afternoon I slept and when I awoke the sun was low and a heavy, withering heat lay over the post. During the first moments of awakening I slipped back into the old feeling I had about my bed, and this room in the big house, a feeling of sanctuary and belonging—then remembrance came flooding back, and I rose and dressed hurriedly.

The house was like a tomb when I went downstairs, then I heard the stove lid clatter in the kitchen, and my first thought was that mother had returned. But she hadn't. Father was fixing a cup of coffee. He glanced at me as I sat down at the table.

His face seemed drawn, older. When the coffee was ready, he poured a cup and brought it to the table.

"How do you feel, son?"

"Fine, sir. A little stiff."

He sipped his coffee, his face inscrutable. Finally he got up, took the pot to the sink and dumped it. "I never could make a cup of coffee that didn't taste like swill." He stood there, a troubled man full of problems, with no ready solutions for any of them.

He consulted his watch, and a moment later looked at it again. Then he came back to the table and sat down. He glanced at me briefly. "How is your mother?"

"Not very happy, sir."

"That makes two of us," he said. "I never thought the day would come when—" He stopped talking as the signal sergeant came onto the back porch.

"Pardon me, sir. Message from Major Regan."

Father nearly knocked his chair over getting up. He read the message aloud:

Fort Starke Signal Det.

Located line break eight miles west Ft. Starke. Repairs being made. No sign hostile activity. Please acknow—

Father looked up quickly. "Is that all, Sergeant?"

"Yes, sir. The message just broke off there."

"Have you tried to get back to them? They probably had a man on the pole."

"We tried, sir, but there was no answer. The line is dead again."

Father's expression was one of despair. "Carry on, Sergeant. There's nothing we can do but wait for further word."

The sergeant returned to his duty and father stood by the door, his hands clasped behind him. He could see across the parade, and as I watched him, his head came up, his attention sharpening. By moving slightly, I could see out the window, and then I understood his alertness. Mother and Fleas were walking toward the house.

When mother stepped onto the back porch, father opened the door for her. "My it's hot out," she said, then turned and snapped her fingers. "Come in, Fleas."

The dog came in and went to father. Fleas' tail scrubbed the floor and he looked up, his eyes large and adoring. "He's unhappy with us," mother said. "He's always been your dog, Jim."

"And are you happy, Cora?"

Mother's lips pulled together slightly. "No, I'm not, but it doesn't change anything." She looked at me, then quickly away. "It isn't my wish to split a family this way, Jim. Your first duty is to your son."

"Arguing about that will get us nowhere," father said. "But try to understand and come back, Cora. Nothing is right without you."

She shook her head. "You know I can't, Jim. I'm leaving on the paymaster's stage. Perhaps when you get your new assignment, somewhere else where it's civilized, then we can talk. Until then, I can't promise you a thing, Jim."

Father struck a match to his cigar. "Is that what it will take, Cora? A safe assignment? Somewhere where this will never come up again?"

"Yes. Where another decision like that will be impossible."

Father nodded slightly. "Twenty-one years ago this June I told you I loved you. Twenty-one years haven't changed me, Cora. I still love you. Doesn't that mean anything? Has it no weight in my favor?"

"Yes, but it's not enough." She turned to the door, but stopped when father spoke.

"Then we might as well finish it now, Cora. I already have my assignment. Mel brought it back from Tucson. Miles has

110

ordered me to remain in Arizona. I've been promoted to full colonel in command of the department."

Mother's eyes got round and a little desperate, and then I knew how much she had been counting on our leaving. Counting on it because it gave her a way to bring the family together again without either of them backing down. I knew without thinking about it, that this wouldn't work, for this was a matter in which one had to give in to the other. Give in and never look back on the decision, or regret it later.

Yet neither seemed ready to give, and that is usually the case when the battle becomes one of principle. No one had to tell me how stubborn mother could get, and I knew well father's pride, his feeling of mastery over his family. And no one had to tell me that the more they talked, the more determined each would become.

"Then there's little hope for us," mother said. "I can't stay here, Jim. I've thought about going too long now. The yearning is too strong to put down."

"I see," father said softly. "It's too bad you couldn't find contentment here."

"Fort Starke, or Arizona, means nothing to me," she said. "To you it does, but to me it's just a hot, dusty place I'll be happy to leave." Then she opened the door and went out, walking rapidly toward Captain Hanson's quarters.

Father watched her until she went inside, then he sighed and said, "It's terrible to disagree when both parties are right."

"Will she really leave, sir?"

"She's a headstrong woman," he said. "And she said she would leave. Her pride will force her to make good that threat, even when her good sense tells her she's acting foolishly." Then he paused. "But she hasn't gone yet, and the way things look, she might not."

"Sir?"

"It's possible the paymaster's stage will never arrive," father said dismally. "Mr. Reindollar is missing and Major Regan could be in trouble. Diablito is tightening his grip on Fort Starke, and I can no longer predict what tomorrow will have to offer."

When you are sixteen, you like reasons for everything, and I guess what made life difficult was that for some things there weren't any. "Why is Diablito doing this, sir?"

"I'm not sure now," father said. "Awhile back I thought he was cutting off our communication to get Gentry, but the man's gone by now, and Diablito should be chasing him." He puffed his cigar, letting smoke dribble from his lips. "The

Apaches are a dying race, Mel. They're hunted in Mexico and here, too, by men like Gentry who can't forget the Apache wars are over. Diablito believes he's fighting for his life, all the while knowing he can't possibly win. In the end he'll be killed or die in prison."

"Then why does he fight?"

Father showed his irritation. "Because there're some things that are hard to give up!" He lowered his voice. "Why don't you go play with your brothers?"

He was telling me to leave him alone and I did. Reed and Paul were playing with Captain Hanson's boys and after an hour of tolerating their antics, I left them and went to headquarters. Father was in his quarters, and when I sat down he didn't order me to leave.

Later, the bugler blew mess call, but father didn't answer it. Instead, he sent a trooper for two trays, and we ate in the office as the shadows grew long.

"Where's Terry McGuire?" I asked.

"He has his duty with the troop," father said. "Being a private deprives him of certain privileges."

"Are you still mad at him, sir?"

Father put down his fork. "I'm not mad at McGuire, Mel. What gave you that notion?"

"You busted him."

"Because I discipline a man doesn't mean I'm angry," father said. "If I broke him, then remained angry, I'd be punishing him continually for one offense."

"You're mad at us when you use the razor strap," I said.

Father smiled faintly. "Mel, the only time a man can strike his own children is when he's angry. How could he be so cold-blooded as to do it otherwise?"

We finished our supper, and it wasn't the kind mother fixed. The trooper took away the trays and father said, "Give my respects to Mr. Hastings and ask him to report here."

Father enjoyed his cigar while I stood by the window, watching night darken the parade. I saw Wade leave his quarters and walk along the porch. When he came in I turned away from the window.

"Sit down, Wade," father said. "Do I have to explain our situation?"

"No. You've lost all your command except one troop."

This drew a frown. "That's one way of putting it. I'd like to count on you again, if I may." Father put his cigar aside and folded his hands. "I don't like to place an officer under arrest. Especially a capable officer."

112

"Thank you," Wade said. "You didn't think I was so capable in Tucson."

"I've tried to understand that," father said.

"What's there to understand? You like Gentry, and I hate him."

"Why?"

"Because he's no good." Hastings looked at me as though he wanted me to leave, then decided it didn't matter. "I've run into Gentrys all my life, Colonel. They break every rule in the book, then end up with all the money, most of the friends, and the prettiest women. Men like me, who live with the book, end up small."

Father pursed his lips and ran a hand over his cheek. He needed a shave and the whiskers made a soft, scuffing sound in the silence. "Wade, can't you see Gentry at all? He's a good man if you stop judging him by the rules society holds so pure."

"I judge him by the rules I'm judged by," Hastings said.

"If that were true," father said, "you'd still be in arrest of quarters, and I'd have a report written. The only way to judge a man is by his own code. That's the way I judge you, Wade."

"That's not a compliment."

Father shrugged. "Wade, you're not as big a man as Gentry, and the knowledge must hurt like blazes. I think you were trying to prove otherwise when you tackled him. It seems important to you to prove you are better."

"I *am* better!" He rose half out of the chair when he said it. Then he settled back. "Anyway, I'm not fool enough to argue with a colonel over it." He rubbed his hands together; backing up was difficult for Wade Hastings. "I thank you for giving me my command, sir."

"I'll tell the orderly to make the proper notations in the record," father said. He stood up and pulled the wall map down. He had inserted some colored pins at various points around Fort Starke. "Please note," he said, pointing to the spot where Willie Ludke had been ambushed, "that the Apaches have been making a sweep around Starke." His finger traveled to the west. "Here is where Regan found the wire cut the first time, and here is where Regan sent his message a few hours ago. From this I conclude that part of Diablito's force flanked west." There was another pin mark to the east, close in. "Here is where Mel killed the two Apaches early this morning. Probably an advance guard for Diablito, and may indicate that he is closing in."

"We have nothing here he wants," Hastings said.

113

"We have a troop left," father pointed out. "Without that in his way he could raid Douglas and even as far north as Tucson."

"Damned unpleasant picture," Hastings admitted.

"I want the water detail to work until tattoo," father said. "In the event we're bottled here, I want sufficient water inside the walls to carry the post for at least ten days."

"I'll attend to it," Hastings said. "Will that be all, sir?"

"At the moment," father said. Hastings went out and father sat for a moment, his eyes thoughtful. "Melvin, see how Miss Shipley is doing. I want her to be able to leave if the stage arrives."

From headquarters porch I could see Bickerstaff's light and cut toward it. Before I opened the door I detected the rank odor of cooked sauerkraut. The doctor looked around when I entered and a wide smile broke the moon shape of his face. "Vill you eat?" When I shook my head his smile dimmed. "V'y not? You like sauerkraut. Sit down, I fix you a plate."

"I only came over to ask how Miss Shipley was, sir?"

"Tomorrow she vill be up," Bickerstaff said. He wound sauerkraut on his fork and raised it steaming to his mouth. "It is too bad, *nicht wahr?* Such a piggle to leave a woman in."

"Father wants to know whether she can leave on the stage or not?"

Bickerstaff shrugged. "Haf you forgotten? The Apaches may keep the stage from coming."

I left him then, returning to the big house and my room to read. The house was strange and empty without mother there, and I hurried up the stairs and slammed the door as though this would shut out all the unpleasantness, or the memory of what had once been very pleasant. The house was, I suppose, like an island, but I could find no safety or security there.

From time to time the hall clock chimed, and I kept an ear open for father's step, but at eleven I gave up, closed the book and settled down to sleep.

When I woke in the morning, father had eaten and left the house. The sink contained a dirty plate and silverware. I tried to fry an egg and burned it around the edges. When I left I had added somewhat to the pile of dirty dishes.

A sharp wind was blowing when I stepped outside, and the brassy sun was hidden behind a far layer of thin clouds. One glance around the post was enough; something was wrong, for along the palisade ramp, guards stood no more

114

than ten feet apart. And the way they stood, hunkered down so as not to expose themselves too much, told me there was more than sand and sage out there.

I raced across the parade to headquarters. Father was there, talking to Wade Hastings. "There's no denying their intention now, Mr. Hastings. Keep an alert guard for its only a matter of time before they try to breach the wall."

"In broad daylight, sir?"

"It's possible," father said, "that Diablito will want to show his strength—Apaches are vain devils. And there's always an Apache looking for glory."

"What could one man do once he got inside?"

"Kill a soldier," father said bluntly. "Face it now, Wade— we have fifty-three men and Diablito has many times that."

"That many?" I'd been taught to keep quiet when someone else was talking, but this just came out.

I think father noticed for the first time that I was there. He glanced at me and said, "We can guess why Diablito has been playing his sniping game, Mel. He was expecting reinforcements from Mexico and wanted to make sure we were without communication to either Miles or Azavedo." His glance swung to Wade Hastings. "I dislike being at the whim of this savage, but he'll have to make the first move now before I can do anything."

"Colonel," Wade said, "I'm a soldier who takes orders, but isn't there some chance to gather the women, children and all and break through?"

"Like Ludke, Reindollar, and Regan did?"

This was the question Hastings didn't like to hear. He gave father a quick salute and wheeled away.

"Does Diablito really have us cut off, sir?" I found this hard to believe, probably because I was still child enough to think my father would never allow harm to come to any of us. Such being the picture children carry of their parents' powers.

"We are until General Miles arrives with a column," father said. He smiled. "The news will get around quickly enough, so don't say anything to your mother to worry her. This is Army business, Mel. We can hold the Apaches back for a day or two and then Miles will be here. It's been nearly a week since you talked to him."

"What if he doesn't get here?"

"He'll get here," father said. "You can count on Miles."

This was what I wanted to believe, and I felt better because of the assurance. I left and walked around the palisade wall, looking up. I found Terry McGuire at one of the corner stations. Dark, unfaded spots indicated his missing hooks, and he smiled, but nodded to Sergeant Haukbauer, who walked toward him, checking on the men. I took the hint and left before McGuire got into more trouble.

At Captain Hanson's quarters I found Reed and Paul on the back steps, whittling on sticks. "What are you making?"

"Spears," Paul said. "In case the Apaches try to get in."

"That's silly," I said, but they didn't seem to think so. Reed was a serious boy—at times he puzzled me, for he was a lot like mother—quiet, thoughtful, and headstrong. He had a placid face, mild brown eyes, and a shock of unruly hair.

Paul was different, seemingly careless about everything. He laughed a lot and talked silly, and liked to sleep.

"Ma's made some lemonade," Paul said.

I went inside.

"How's your father?" mother asked right off, as I was hoping she would. She was peeling potatoes and perspiration made bright beads on her forehead.

"Why don't Reed and Paul do that?" I asked.

"Boys should play."

"Let me," I said, taking potatoes and knife from her. I hated this kind of work, but I hated worse to see her sweat over it. I couldn't help asking. "Are you scared, ma?"

She was rinsing her hands, and she turned her head quickly. "Yes. I'd be lying if I said I wasn't. But your father's a capable officer. He'll stop them from coming over the walls."

It struck me as odd that she would have so much faith in his military judgment, yet be estranged now because of it. Yet I had enough sense not to bring up the subject.

"I suppose there're dirty dishes in the sink," mother said. "He never could clean up after himself." She took the pan of potatoes I had peeled. "Did he have a good breakfast?"

"I guess."

"He'd go without if he wasn't reminded to eat," she said.

Reed came in, banging the back door. "Ma, can I go on the wall?"

"You'll get in the soldiers' way," mother said.

"Can I go if Mel takes me?" He waited for her reaction and when she hesitated, said, "I'd be safe with Mel, wouldn't I?"

"I suppose," mother said in a preoccupied way. "But don't stay long."

There were other things I wanted to do with my time but Reed was out the door before I could object. He kept running ahead of me all the way and had scrambled up one of the corner ladders before I could stop him.

McGuire caught him as he charged down the walkway. I came up then and McGuire turned him loose. "Keep a rein on him, lad. You father's liable to paddle you both for this."

"I want to look out and see the Apaches," Reed said, and this reminded me of myself in '84, when I too, had little knowledge of what Indian war meant, thinking only of the excitement. Reed was like that now, hardly realizing how serious was the predicament of Fort Starke.

"Ah, now, there's nothin' to see," McGuire said. "Apaches are a careful bunch. They don't show themselves much."

"I want to see anyway," Reed insisted.

Sergeant Haukbauer came down the ramp, his boots striking hard. "I think you lads had better go," McGuire said, knowing trouble when he saw it.

Father chose that time to come from headquarters, and he saw us. "Haukbauer! Get those two down from there!"

Heads turned all along the walkways, and Reed and I dashed for the ladder. Then father shouted again, and I stopped, but he wasn't shouting at us. His attention was lifted to a corner post, a confined shelter where a lookout stood in cramped discomfort. The sentry was standing erect, his back turned to the land beyond, and I believe he was straining to hear what father was yelling.

Below the wall, on the outside, a bowstring thrummed and there was a sodden thunk a heartbeat later. The guard dropped his carbine with an echo-raising clatter, then bent forward over the low guard-rail like a candle going limp on a shelf. His kepi came off and fluttered down, and he followed it, falling the eighteen feet to the parade below.

Father swore loudly as he flung his cigar into the dust and ran toward the downed man. Reed and I scampered down the ladder as the dust began to settle around the trooper.

"The wall!" father shouted. "Watch the wall!"

His shout brought the soldiers out of shock, and they turned as a naked Apache came over, screeching, shooting, his copper body hideously painted.

He stood erect on the palisade wall, like a diver about to plunge, and carbine fire cannonaded raggedly, catching him there, flinging him back to the hostile desert.

Reed began to cry, then ran for the Hansons'. A crowd was gathering around the fallen trooper, and father had to push his way through this forming ring. The women of the post were all standing on their porches, eyes shading their faces, viewing this tragedy from a respectful distance.

117

Sergeant Haukbauer came on the run, battering his way through. He stepped around father, bent down and tugged at the unadorned Apache arrow that was a savage flag planted in the bloody field of the trooper's back.

"I gave definite orders," father said, "for all gaurds to stand clear of the outer wall." He was angry, not at Haukbauer, or the dead man, but angry at stupidity, at thoughtlessness, the small things that always cost a man his life when a mistake is made.

Haukbauer came erect, and his voice contained the nearest thing to an apology I had ever heard him make. "The man was a ree-cruit, sir. He forgot."

The troopers who had been off duty and resting stood in a slack-faced circle, for it is rare that death occurs when men have time to observe it leisurely.

To Haukbauer, father said, "Burial detail after mess tonight. Dismiss these men to their barracks or duty."

"Yes, sir."

"You come with me," he said and walked rapidly to headquarters. Once inside, he said, "What the devil were you doing on the wall, Mel?"

"Reed wanted to see, sir."

"You ought to have better sense," he said. "And I ought to strap both of you." He slapped the desk with the flat of his hand. "That's not a game being played out there. And until you're old enough to pick up a rifle and fight the Apache way, stay out of it."

"Yes, sir."

"Now get out of here and stay out of mischief."

I went to the porch and watched the sky curdle. The sun was gone and a sharp wind whisked dust across the parade. Farther west a storm was building, and tonight we might catch it, an hour of smothering rain. Or it might pass us— the weather in Arizona was notoriously fickle.

Near the quartermaster warehouse, Captain Hanson came out and detailed the carpenter to construct a crude coffin. Then Hanson came on toward headquarters. He was a man in his forties, and walked bent over, as though the years crouched over quartermaster records had left an indelible stamp on his posture. He gave me a brief smile in passing, then went inside. I could hear him in father's office.

"Colonel, is there anything I can do? I feel damned useless trying to straighten out the records. Seems a little foolish at this time."

"Just what do you propose, Captain?"

"To let my duty go to hell." Hanson said. "Colonel, for

118

sixteen years now I've fought my campaigns in procurement and supply. I have two officers and eighteen men. We haven't fired a carbine in five years, but we'd like to take our tour on the wall."

"Permission denied," father said bluntly, and I was shocked, for he was not like this.

"We have families," Hanson said. "Think of them, sir."

"I thought of them before I denied your request," father said. "Captain, you won't be any good to them dead, and you'll soon be dead if you try to fight the Apaches on their terms." Father turned to the window and stood there for a time, looking out. "The sky smudging up for rain. Maybe we can get a little sleep if it turns off cool."

Hanson's hand was exploring his thinning hair, his drooping mustache. "I haven't been able to sleep at all."

"I'm not going to change my mind," father said. "Return to your duty, please."

Hanson saluted and came out. He didn't smile at me this time. I watched him recross the parade to the quartermaster building, his shoulders curved, his boots scuffing dust, and for the first time I saw a difference between soldiers. Before, they had all been fighters, the cavalry, but now I considered those men who remained behind, making the army go, never seeing the enemy, but feeling the strain of battle nevertheless. And when I considered men like Hanson, I found a new brand of courage, the kind that stood well under weight, and lasted while other men rode forth to fight.

A few minutes later father came out and stood on the porch. "Looks like rain," he said. "Mel, which would you say was the stoutest building here?"

"The infirmary, sir. It's adobe and the walls are three feet thick."

"Go tell Bickerstaff I want to see him right away," father said. He looked at his watch. "If we start moving immediately, I believe we can have all the women and children billeted in the infirmary by nightfall." He smiled. "Then Captain Hanson and his men can forsake their mundane duties and guard the place."

"Sir," I said, feeling a cool wind of apprehension, "are the Apaches likely to come over the wall?"

"They'll try," father said. "Most surely, they'll try."

12

NIGHTFALL BROUGHT rain, slanting sheets of it, pushed by a strong wind. The women and children of Fort Starke were now safely billeted in the infirmary. Bickerstaff retained four of the rooms, two for his own quarters and two for patients.

Captain Hanson took his new duties seriously, as did the men in his detachment, and by eight o'clock had the infirmary as well fortified as the palisade walls.

I ran across the slick parade to the big house for my yellow slicker, then went to headquarters, where I found father in conference with Wade Hastings and Sergeant Haukbauer. Father sat at his desk, the shaded lamps casting his face in shadow. Wade went out almost immediately, but Haukbauer remained.

"You sure you have that?" father asked. "Hastings will remain in command. I want twenty good men, Sergeant. Pick them carefully."

"Yes, sir. But there's one thing, sir."

"What's that?"

"It's me, sir. I'd like to be busted in McGuire's place and him restored to my duty."

Father had been lighting a cigar, and now he took it from his mouth, leaving the lips in an irregular *O*. "I don't understand, Haukbauer."

The sergeant shifted his feet, pulling the words out. "I'm a good enough detail man, sir, but what you propose is a little big—I might not handle it too well. And if I can't, you'd find it out at a poor time. There's no getting around it, sir— McGuire's a better soldier. I'll take a bust if you'll give him my hooks, sir."

For a moment father remained silent. "Haukbauer, it took a big man to get that out. Keep your rank—Hastings will need an able man here. And send McGuire to me."

"Thank you, sir," Haukbauer said and wheeled out.

"What's going on, sir?" I asked.

Father gave me a half-amused glance. "Mel, I'm going to take a little fight to Diablito. These one-sided games gall me a little."

"Go off the post?"

"Well, it's raining," father said, "and the Apaches won't expect us. I imagine we can take a little trouble to Diablito before the night gets much older."

"Golly, sir—" I was afraid, and showing it.

Father opened his mouth to speak but McGuire came in with Haukbauer, and whatever he meant to say always remained with him. McGuire came to a heel-snapping attention. Father discarded his cigar and placed his forearms flat on the desk.

"Terry, you've never liked Haukbauer, have you?"

"Well, sor, I can't really say's I have. But I don't hate him either, sor."

"Tell me why you don't like him," father invited.

McGuire knew better than to evade. "Well, sor, he's a good detail man, but he'll never make a top soldier. It's me opinion that Haukbauer's got a job he can't handle."

"It may interest you to know," father said, "that Haukbauer offered to have himself busted so you could be given his hooks. He admitted to me that you were the only man capable of handling this night's work."

"Ah," McGuire said, "that makes me out pretty small, don't it, sor?"

"Not quite yet," father said. "But it can."

McGuire glanced at Haukbauer, an ashamed glance. "I'd like to speak," McGuire said.

"Granted."

The words were hard-pulled from McGuire, but he got them out, and he met Haukbauer's level glance when he spoke. "Man, for eleven years I've not offered me hand in friendship, nor invited you to a tot of the sutler's best, so if you refuse to accept me apology now, I'll be understandin'. I've spoke out against you and it's me dyin' shame I'm showin' you now. It's a fit soldier you are, Matthew Haukbauer, and it's only me small Irish soul that kept me from admittin' it long ago." He offered his hand. "If you belt me in the mouth, I'll have it comin'."

For a moment the taciturn Haukbauer teetered. Then he smiled. He shook McGuire's hand.

"Well, now," father said, smiling, "I think, for the first time, that we might kick the hell out of the Apaches. McGuire, you're sergeant-major again, but remember how easy those hooks come off."

"Aye, sor, you've impressed me to me dyin' day."

"Haukbauer, give McGuire all your assistance in readying the detail. Have the men form on the parade in twenty minutes. Pistols and sabers. And get all the cotton wadding the quartermaster sergeant can spare. He has coal oil in gallon tins. Each man will carry one, and plenty of dry matches."

"Aye, sor," McGuire said, a smile slashing his homely face. "We'll do that, sor." He let Haukbauer go out first, then tromped off the porch, once again the top soldier of Starke. When he sent his bellow ahead of him across the parade, every soldier heard it and knew that his rank had been restored.

Father asked, "Are you going back to the big house?"

"No, sir," I said. I wanted to explain how empty it was, but I guess he knew.

"I feel the same way about it," he said. "If you see your mother, tell her—well, never mind. I've already told her." He scrubbed a hand across his face, then brushed his mustache with his finger. "I want to get off the post before she finds out about it. Then stay with her, Mel."

He began to gather his gear, his poncho, pistol, and saber. I wanted to ask questions, where he was going and what he hoped to do when he got there, but I knew better. Father always explained the things he wanted me to know. But I wasn't sure this man would, for war made him different—at times almost a stranger.

Sergeant Haukbauer came back with a roll of cotton. Father wrapped the blade of his saber with it and tied it with cord. He checked his pockets for matches, then went outside in the rain.

I followed as far as the porch.

Wade Hastings was standing near the assembled detail. He and father had a short, heated discussion, but the sound of rain drowned it so that I couldn't hear. Then father swung up and turned toward the main gate, his men behind him.

Suddenly I began to shake, and it became terribly important that I be with mother. I ran as fast as I could across the parade. Doctor Bickerstaff had assigned the rooms on the second floor to the enlisted men's wives—the bottom was reserved for the officers'. Mother's room was off the main entrance. Her door was open and I charged in, ready to blurt out that father was riding off to get killed.

She looked around, startled, then I got a grip on myself. "For heaven's sake, don't make so much noise. Reed and Paul are asleep." There was a small wood stove in the corner and she turned to it. "I've made some coffee. I expect you're sick of your father's by now."

This was a milestone, but I didn't care about that now. I knew that father would be clear of the post by now, but I decided to wait anyway.

"Won't you stay here tonight?" mother asked. "The big house will be cold."

I shook my head. "I don't want to leave it, even if it is empty."

Suddenly mother turned her head away, tears in her eyes. "I don't know what's happening, Mel. I just don't know. You've grown up, out of reach of me, almost overnight. And I've put your father away from me—that was a sinful thing to do. I need him and can't swallow my words and go to him." She brushed at her eyes. "What kind of a woman am I? Not a good woman." She took a deep breath, and this seemed to steady her. "I don't mean to blame your father, but where are our dreams, Mel? Everything we hoped for is gone."

I loved her and blamed her and was sorry because I felt that way. My secure world of childhood was so suddenly shaken. I was unsure of her, and of myself. Too many perfect people had shown themselves to be less than I had believed—my feelings were undergoing a constant overhauling.

But I believe she understood, for she said, "Sixteen is a terrible age, Melvin. So many dreams are shattered when we are sixteen."

Suddenly, over the rumble of rain, came a shout from the wall.

"What was that?" mother asked.

"Father left the post," I said and bolted for the door.

"What?" She nearly screamed this after me. "Oh, God!"

Then I was running for the wall and the first ramp ladder I came to. The soldiers were all peering out into the rain-smeared night. I could see bobbing pinpoints of light, and flashes from gun muzzles, but no sounds. Then the rapidly moving flares would go out and the shooting would stop, only to start up again somewhere else. For nearly thirty minutes I watched, then time stretched into an hour, and two. Toward the end there were a few less intermittent flares, and much less firing. Finally there was none.

I stood near the wall, chilled, water leaking past my collar. There was nothing but the sound of rain and the troopers patrolling in silent dejection. I saw Haukbauer and wanted to ask him about father, but the sergeant's expression pushed aside my inclination.

Another hour dragged by, and the rain slacked a bit. Then a guard over the gate yelled, "Detail approaching!"

The gates swung open and father reentered the post, only he had nine men missing. The remainder dismounted at McGuire's word. I hurried down the ladder.

Their sabers were blackened where the oil-soaked cotton had heated them, and very little of their pistol ammunition remained unspent. Two of the troopers were wounded—McGuire had them taken to the dispensary.

Wade Hastings trotted up and he seemed amazed that any of them got back. "Well," father said, "I think Diablito will need quite a few new recruits."

"You damn fool," Hastings said, but there was admiration in his voice.

Father went into headquarters with Hastings, telling him all about it, how the Apaches fired at the burning cotton skewered on the sabers, while the troopers cut up the Apaches with pistol fire.

I turned away and walked to the house that was so dark and forlorn. Without lighting any of the lamps, I went up the stairs, listening to the hollow rattle of my own boots. In my room I shed my clothes and crawled between the cold sheets. The bed felt damp and lumpy and strange, and I felt uncomfortable, as though I had stumbled into someone else's house by mistake. This odd sensation remained with me until I fell asleep, and then it reappeared in my dreams.

The bugler woke me at reveille and I dressed, then went across the parade to the officers' mess where I talked Sergeant Gleason out of a meal. The rain was a drizzle, one of those pestering rains without wind behind it, yet it seemed to go right through a slicker.

I made a nuisance of myself until noon, then went to headquarters. Father was there and cigar smoke was thick enough to cut.

"Is your mother all right?" he asked.

"You ought to go see for yourself."

His eyes fastened on me, surprised, and somewhat sharp. "Is that the kind of answer I get?"

Trouble loomed, but I was getting used to it. "You're always talking about big men, sir. Why don't you be big and tell her you're sorry?"

"That's enough out of you." He was getting angry.

I ploughed ahead stubbornly. "You went off last night without speaking to her. You could have got killed, but you didn't care how she felt."

Father studied me for a moment, then blew out a long breath. "Mel, I think you've reached a point in life where you're too big to lick. Since you've made up your mind about this, why don't you let me run my own business, and you run yours. A man can't be dictated to by a woman's whim, even when she's right."

124

"If you feel that way, you never will make up with her."

"See here, young man—" A knock broke off father's speech.

Trooper Mulvaney stood in the office doorway. "McGuire said you wanted a volunteer, sor."

"Ah, yes. Come in." Father took a leather dispatch case from the desk. "Tonight, I want you to go over the wall and see if you can get through." He glanced at his watch. "You can sleep the rest of the day. If you find Apaches joining Diablito, go on to Camp Bowie. General Miles will be there now, and we'll try to stay alive until he reaches us. Any questions?"

"No, sir."

"Then rest up. We'll try to go out again tonight to create a diversion."

After Mulvaney left, father said, "We were talking about you, I believe, and the fact that you've outgrown you pants."

"Why don't you go see her?" I asked. "She has that coming, the way you left last night."

Father slapped the desk. "Dammit, I'm trying to save my command! Can't anyone understand that?" He calmed himself. "All right, I'll go see her, if that's what you want."

"Are you going to argue who's right and who's wrong?"

"Mel, you don't understand. There's a principle involved here."

"I don't care about your old principles!" I shouted. "If I ever have a wife I won't fight with her over who's right!" I jumped to my feet. "McGuire's a bigger man than you! He could at least apologize when he was wrong!" Because I didn't want him to see me cry, I rushed out.

His voice followed me. "Mel! Come back, Mel!"

But I didn't go back. I ran blindly for the big house and, once in my room, locked the door. With this privacy I could let go my fears and try to pull together the emotions torn apart because the two people I loved most had to be right and wrong at the same time.

A little later father came in and up the stairs. He tried my door, and finding it locked, said, "Mel, open the door so I can talk to you." He rattled the knob. "Mel, that's no answer, son."

"What's your answer?" I asked and in a moment he went down the stairs. The front door slammed and I was really alone.

At ten o'clock the layer of clouds split and the rain

stopped. The sun touched the wetness everywhere, shining and hot. In a few moments steam began to rise, swirling and gauzelike.

The post was unusually quiet, so quiet I could hear the troop horses in the stables a hundred yards away. I left the big house, but did not go to headquarters—I didn't want to see father or talk to him, not this man, not this stranger I hardly knew. Instead I went on the ramp and stood there watching the sunlight build steam from the wet earth.

Sergeant McGuire was near the main gate and he studied the distance with field glasses.

Finally he turned to a trooper and said, "Fetch the colonel."

The trooper went down the ladder and McGuire turned back to his study.

Almost immediately father came splashing across the muddy parade. He gave me a glance, then took the field glasses from McGuire and threw their power at the shimmering distance.

"It's the paymaster's stage from Fort Redoubt," father said, his voice puzzled.

I could barely make it out, a six-up span lunging against the harness. They approached Diablito's lines and I held my breath until the shooting began. The driver crouched down, and the man beside him handled his pistols while the team came on at a dead run. The sounds of gunfire were only faintly discernible, but I could see the puffs of powder smoke, both from the Apache's rifles and the pistols of the guard. Two Apaches dashed forth, trying to catch the lead horses, but the guard shot them.

The driver held a true course for the main gate and when he drew alarmingly close, father yelled, "Throw it open!"

The heavy bar was wrestled out of the hooks and the gates pulled open in time for the mudwagon to race through. The driver was half-lifted from the high seat, his foot teetering on the brake—the hind wheels slid and flung mud. To check the team, troopers ran out, and grabbed the lead horses, pulling them to a blowing halt.

As we hurried from the ramp, the driver threw down the reins and stepped down. He was a big man, wide-eyed now and trying not to show his fear. But I was not watching him. I ran around the coach as Bob Van Orden got down.

He stood there, punching empty brass from his six-shooters, and when he spoke, his voice was quite controlled. "Thought I wouldn't see you again, bub."

He smiled, and I felt fine; I trusted this man.

When Van Orden went around the coach to father's side, I followed. It was like finding an acquaintance in a strange town; the first impulse is to cling like a shadow for a place is less lonely with a friend.

"I hardly expected to find you here," father said.

"Hardly expected it myself," Bob Van Orden said. "I don't know yet how Pollard here got through."

Reese Pollard looked up, his eyes round and surprised and still afraid. "By God, Jim, I don't know myself! I was in 'em before I knew it and there wasn't no turnin' back."

"Where's the paymaster?"

Pollard bit off a chew of cut plug and worked it to the corner of his jaw. "Redoubt. He wouldn't take the ride." He nodded to the boot. "I brought his goods though, thirty thousand."

Troopers were unhitching the span and leading them into the stable yard. The stage sat tongue-down and useless by the flagpole. Reese Pollard took a bottle of Taos Lightning from his pocket, upped it briefly, then wrinkled his brow. Then he went to the rear boot and brought out a broken guidon with the remnants of a flag hanging from it.

Father accepted it with defeat in his eyes. "Reindollar's troop. Where did you find this?"

"I found it," Bob Van Orden said. "Between here and Redoubt. The Apaches left it sticking in the road." He rolled a cigarette. "It seems that every time we meet, I bring you trouble. This is the last stage from Redoubt." He paused as though uncertain as to how to finish. "I picked Pollard up on the last rise this side of Redoubt. It never rained over there, Colonel—you could see the smoke for ten miles."

"Burned out? Good God!" He tried to understand how this could have happened, and he did. We all did. With the uniforms taken from Reindollar's patrol clothing Apache warriors, entrance to Fort Redoubt would be easy and assured. And once inside, there were only forty men, an easy number for Apaches.

"It's hard to see a post die," Father said softly. "Very hard. I had friends at Redoubt—we all did."

His voice, his numbed expression made me see that I was not alone. Father's world was being shaken too. And I had never dreamed that such a thing was possible; he had always seemed so indomitable to me. Yet he wasn't—he was a man afraid, no different from Pollard, or anyone. The sudden tarnish on the image I had carried so long was almost unbearable. I turned away, and then Bob Van Orden flung one arm around my shoulders and led me to the watering trough, where he removed his coat to wash.

"You can worry a man, bub. After you left Tucson I wasn't sure you'd make it." He smiled. "Did that sergeant ever sober up?"

"Yes, sir, but Mr. Hastings fell off his horse and broke his arm."

"Too bad it wasn't his neck," Van Orden said and plunged his hands into the water. Father came over, his face grave but composed.

"I've much to thank you for—the courtesy you extended my son, and the return of Reindollar's standard."

Van Orden looked up, water dripping off his face. He dried his face with a handkerchief, then slipped into his coat. He watched father with the care a man develops when trouble has the habit of singling him out.

"If you're worrying about me," he said, "then don't."

"I have troubles enough," father said. "Don't add to them."

"That wasn't my intention," Van Orden said. "When I left Tucson I made it plain that I was heading for Fort Savage. My trouble's there and with the Apaches blocking the road, it will likely stay there." He smiled, gave me a punch on the shoulder and moved on to the sutler's porch.

Father watched him for a moment, then when I started to leave, said, "Mel, the next time I'm talking to you, don't run off." I gave him a bland, unreadable glance, and he frowned. "Mel, don't shut me out like that."

"Why not?" I asked. "I don't know you anymore."

"Mel, I haven't changed. Can't you see that I haven't?" He raised his hand, then let it drop. "What can I say? You're growing up, learning. Some of the things we learn aren't pretty."

"You don't have to tell me," I said. I turned but he caught me by the arm.

"Mel, I'm human—we all are. And we're not perfect. We have to live with that, son." I was blocking my ears, and he knew it. He sighed, a sad, defeated dullness in his eyes. "All right, Mel. Run along."

13

I TRIED to go it alone for an hour or two in the big house, but the stillness was so depressing that I had to leave. My first thought was to go to the Hansons' and see mother, but she would want to talk about father, and I didn't want to listen. The feeling of being cast adrift made me turn to a safe haven, or one I thought was safe—Bob Van Orden. I went to his quarters and knocked.

He turned around quickly and said, "Hello there, bub." I came in, and he went back to cleaning the mud from his shoes. His coat and gun harness were on the bed, and he pushed these aside so I could sit.

"Heard you fought the Apaches singlehanded."

"Just two," I said, not sure that he wasn't teasing.

He drew his lips together. "That's better than most men could do and live to tell about it. I like you, bub. You're salty."

"What's that?"

"An expression. It means you're all right and not scared."

"I was scared stiff," I said before he got the wrong impression.

"Sure, but you held your ground." He slapped me on the shoulder. "That makes you salty." He frowned briefly then returned to the scraping of his shoes. "You and your dad on the outs?"

I shook my head—I couldn't answer.

"Your dad's a good soldier. He expects you to be one, too." He put his hand on my shoulder and gave me a little shake. "If you got troubles it might help to tell someone."

"Talking won't help," I said.

"You're not going to be one of those fellas who keeps remembering, are you? You know the kind I mean. They keep little things around to remind them not to forget. I knew a man once who kept a cannon ball that had killed the horse he'd been riding. Another in Sante Fe had a bullet some doctor had dug out of him. Those fellas keep those things as though not remembering would be more sinful than for-

129

getting." He shook his head. "If you think your dad's done you wrong, face him, but forget the words that was said. You got to understand that a man takes a few knocks just living."

Van Orden rolled a cigarette, raking a match across the underside of the bed. He sat hunched over for many minutes, motionless while ribbons of smoke rose past his face to the ceiling. If there hadn't ever been guns in his life, I wondered what kind of man he would have been, then decided, not much different.

I'll never be able to explain why, but I took Bob Van Orden to see my mother. I found her alone, sitting at the table. Bob Van Orden made a deep bow when I introduced him.

"I'll fix some tea," mother said and turned to the stove. "I expect your father's well." She turned to look at me. "Today I intend to bake a cake. I want you to take him a piece."

"All right."

She looked sharp. "Are you sick?"

"I'm fine."

"When was the last time you had a bath?"

"Ah—the other morning."

"Scrub tonight," she said. "Mr. Van Orden, are you married?"

"No, ma'am." He smiled and scratched behind his ear. "I—ah—don't expect such will ever come to pass."

Mother considered this ridiculous. "Good heavens, what a thing to say! Why not?"

"My occupation is against it," he said.

"Just what is your line of work, Mr. Van Orden?"

He glanced at me and winked. "The hardware business would describe it best."

"That's a good steady business," mother said. "I was once engaged to a hardware merchant, but of course that was before I met the colonel."

"Tell me," Van Orden said, "have there ever been any regrets?"

Mother snorted and poured the tea. "Certainly there have been regrets. There have been times when we've hated each other. Mr. Van Orden, if a man held a woman to everything she promised, or she made him keep his, they'd end up killing one another before the second year was out." She gave Van Orden a shrewd glance. "I can see that a certain young man has been talking family business."

"He's said nothing to me," Van Orden said solemnly. "It was just a passing curiosity on my part."

130

"But we were talking about you and the hardware business," mother said. "You ought to have a wife—you could support one."

"Supporting isn't the problem," Van Orden said. "Madam, you're too gracious a lady for me to deceive. I'm a professional lawman. I believe the common term is gunfighter."

There was a moment of absolute silence in which mother stared. Then she raised her teacup as though nothing had been said, presenting to us those inflexible commandments of a gentlewoman. "I recall that you helped my son when he needed help badly," she said. "That is recommendation enough for me."

"Thank you," Bob Van Orden said, genuinely sincere. He finished his tea, then stood up, excusing himself. I went to the door with him, and when he walked away, returned to mother. She was gathering up the dishes.

"I want to talk to you about your father."

"Talk to him," I said.

She gave me a tightlipped look. "Don't you dare sass me, young man! You're not too old to have your britches warmed!"

"I don't want to get mixed up in your fights," I said.

"Wha—what do you mean, fight? This is a matter of principle and you know it."

"It's a fight! Just like Corporal Higgins and his wife have. Just because you didn't throw things don't make it any less a fight."

"I've had enough of your impudence," mother said. "Now you listen to me, Melvin Lunsford—"

"Don't want to listen," I said, racing for the back door. After it slammed shut, I shouted, "If you can't say you're sorry I don't care if you never make up!"

This was the biggest lie I ever told my mother, but it had a certain shock value, and I guess, the way I was feeling about it all, I couldn't have said anything else. As I ran across the slippery parade I could hear her calling for me to come back. I hoped she was angry enough to go to father with the problem. Once they got to talking again, even about me, I knew everything would work out.

But she didn't go to father, and I ate alone again in the big house. All I could find was oatmeal and soda crackers, but they were filling. Then I went to my room and read until dark. Fleas scratched at the back door, and I let him in. He prowled the house restlessly, and finally came in to lie on my bed, muddy feet and all.

Auenbrugger's Military Surgery failed to hold my interest

131

and around eight I left the house with Fleas tagging at my heels. Most of the troopers were on the wall, but I lacked the interest to climb up for a look. I wandered around a bit, and only when Sergeant McGuire sent his call for the commanding officer did I climb one of the ramp ladders.

There was a scatter of Apache fires—they had us circled, but I didn't care much. Father came onto the ramp, gave me one sharp glance, then turned to McGuire.

"You want we should throw a few rounds into them fires, sor?"

"You wouldn't hit anything." Father looked at the night sky. "Too bad it didn't muggy up. We could have given Diablito another slice of Army lead tonight."

"Aye," McGuire said, "that was a ball, sor."

One of the men guarding the gate, said, "Sarge, there's two riders approaching."

"What the divil—"

"Let them get close," father said, moving down.

I cocked my head around, listening for sounds of horses, but I heard nothing. But I saw them, vague shapes approaching at a walk. The rain-softened ground helped, and neither of the two men had a saddle to squeak.

"Hello the fort!" one of them called, not too loud, but loud enough for me to recognize him.

"Open the gate," father said, then went down the ladder.

When they were inside a trooper came up with a lantern and Gentry slipped off the horse, standing tall and severe. The other man dismounted, standing back, partly blocked by Gentry's tall shape.

McGuire said, "What does it take to scare you, Gentry? You came through Diablito's whole shebang."

"You want to know something?" Gentry said. "I'm scared now."

"I thought you left the country," father said.

"Couldn't get out," Gentry said. "The sign's thick to the east. So I rode west to Savage. Now that's closed."

Father nodded to the man standing behind Gentry. "Where did you find him?"

"Hidin' near the Fort Savage road," Gentry said. "Says his name's Brokaw."

Brokaw was a short man, stocky through the shoulders, and he wore a pistol butt forward on his left hip. "What's to drink around here?" he asked.

"There's water," father said, "and whiskey at the sutlers."

"Water's for a horse," Brokaw said and cut across the dark parade.

Watching him, father said, "You find strange friends, Gentry."

"No friend," Gentry said. "He was just goin' my way." He glanced around, saw me, and smiled. "Found your way home, I see."

"Yes, sir."

"I figured you would," Gentry said. His glance touched father's. "That lieutenant make out all right? Was it to happen all over, I guess I wouldn't light into him that way. I got a stone over her and the kids now and talking about it comes easier for me." He thumped his chest. "The pain's gone, Jim. Make sense to you?"

"Yes," father said. "Did you leave Fort Savage yesterday?"

"The day before, Jim. I've been holed up in the gullies." He shifted his enormous rifle to a more comfortable position. "You're sittin' alone, Jim. Not a comfortable position to be in."

"Alone?"

"Fort Savage is down," Gentry said. "Ran across some sign about ten miles out. Looked like the soldiers had a fight with Diablito's bunch."

"That was Major Regan's patrol," father said bleakly.

"I turned up eight dead, Jim. The sign said that Regan lit out north with the survivors."

Father's relief was immeasurable. His haggard expression vanished. "Then he'll telegraph Miles. And Miles will come."

"Better make it soon," Gentry said. "If Diablito knew I was here he'd come over the wall tonight."

"I've got a volunteer to put over the wall," father said. "Can he get through?"

"I got through," Gentry said, "but it's my business to get through Apache country. Through to where, Jim?"

"Bowie."

"Too far. You'll lose him if he goes." He paused to look around. "I don't like this, Jim. That rain we had will make the *mescal* beans ripen. When that happens, the Apaches will be brewin' *tiswin*. Once that starts, they ain't fit for nothin'. No war, no stealin', just drinkin'. Diablito knows that, and he won't go off to brew *tiswin* without settlin' up here first. So you watch the weather, Jim, and if she turns off hot the *mescal* will ripen. And when it ripens, get ready, because they'll come over the wall and burn you out like Savage."

14

THE NEWS of Gentry's arrival spread quickly, and because he had been a symbol of evil for so long a time uneasiness ran like a murmur through Fort Starke.

Before taps I found Reed on the wall again and took him home to mother, who gave him a scolding. She fixed a late meal for me and afterward I went to headquarters, but father was sleeping, and I left without disturbing him.

The sutler's place was wide open for business, but other than Brokaw and Gentry, he had none. Father had prudently placed the paymaster's gold under armed guard. He didn't like to have me go in the sutler's, but he seemed to have no objection to my looking in through the window. Brokaw was at the bar, a glass cradled between his hands. He needed a bath and a shave, but he must have needed a drink worse, for he had three while I watched. Gentry was alone at a table, his big rifle beside him.

He sat there, friendless, unwanted, even by Brokaw, who had traveled with him. From behind me, a man's step sounded on the duckboards and Bob Van Orden touched me on the shoulder.

"Looking at the elephant, bub?"

"Killing time," I said.

"Most men do it inside," he said. "You want to go in? Or has the sulter got it in for you?"

"This is all right, sir."

Bob Van Orden laughed and rolled a cigarette. His face, in the match flare, was relaxed and carefree. Then he turned and stepped in the doorway. I remembered Brokaw and that Van Orden had been standing on the blind side, where he couldn't see through the window, but it was too late. Brokaw turned from the bar and partially faced Van Orden, and this was warning enough. Gentry shifted gently in his chair; the legs scraped on the bare floor. The sutler sensed trouble and stood with both hands in sight.

Brokaw said, "Did you think you'd lost me, lawman?"

"This is the first time I've seen you face to face," Van

Orden said. He waited, relaxed and easy, as though he were asking directions of a passerby.

"I went to some trouble to find you," Brokaw said.

"Why? Am I supposed to know you?" Van Orden gently put out his hand and rested it on the edge of the bar. "Until now you've just been a shadow outside my hotel window, or a word dropped in a saloon. Who the hell are you?"

"Frank Brokaw." He shifted until he was free of the bar. "I'm Joe Bigelow's brother-in-law."

"So?"

"So you shoot a man and don't remember his name." Brokaw couldn't seem to understand how this could be.

"Or their faces," Van Orden said. "Leave this alone, Brokaw. I don't want to fight you, or anyone."

"You'd rather run?"

"I would now," Van Orden said. "You're not the first who's brought a quarrel to me this way. But you're the last."

"You're right there," Brokaw said and stabbed across his body after the pistol. Because I had seen Van Orden shoot, I watched him instead of Brokaw. Instead of reaching for his gun, Van Orden slapped upward with his hand, sending Brokaw's gun toward the ceiling. Then he drove into Brokaw with his shoulder, tripping him backward into the bar.

Brokaw's gun bellowed. The bullet puckered the sutler's ceiling. Van Orden had the gun now and he stepped back. Brokaw was propped against the base of the bar, wondering how it all happened.

"You're as clumsy as a drunk," Van Orden said. "Now don't push your luck again."

From the floor, Brokaw said, "This isn't finished."

"Yes, it is." Bob Van Orden took a deep breath; he was angry. "Listen Brokaw, I remember Bigelow, a drunk little man with a mouth all over his face. He shot three times before I got down the street, and I had to shoot him. He was firing into a crowd."

Feet pounded behind me, then father and Sergeant McGuire ran past me into the sutler's. In a glance father surveyed the situation and reached a decision. He took Brokaw's gun from Van Orden, then said, "Lock this in Mr. Biers' safe, Sergeant. This man—" he indicated Brokaw— "is to remain unarmed."

He turned and stomped out, McGuire following. He passed me and didn't even see me. Then Brokaw was picking himself off the floor. He found his hat jammed it on his head, and stalked out.

Gentry said, "Why didn't you dust him? He wanted it that way."

"But I didn't," Van Orden said. The sutler paused before Van Orden, expecting him to buy a drink, but he just shook his head.

"You going it alone now?" Gentry asked. "What happened to the marshal's job in Lordsburg?"

Van Orden blew out his breath slowly. "Man, you can go so far, then you can't go any farther."

"A smart man always gets out," Gentry said. "Even here."

Bob Van Orden frowned. "Is there a way out?"

"I can get out," Gentry admitted.

"How much to take someone along?"

Gentry smiled. "Are you that scared?"

"Take Mel Lunsford," Bob Van Orden said.

I don't know who was more surprised, Gentry or me. For a moment the tall man just stared. "I'll think on it," he said and turned to the door. He saw me standing by the window, for it was his lifetime habit to see everything, but he did not speak, just went along the walk.

A moment later Bob Van Orden came out. I knew he would, so I took the precaution of moving away from the window. I didn't want him to know I had heard his offer: there was no way I could express my feelings.

I leaned against one of the adobe walls and Bob Van Orden stopped. His fingers busily worked over a cigaret for a moment. "Looks like my running was all for fun. The trouble's caught up with me, bub."

"He can't hurt you without a gun," I declared. "And father won't let him have one."

"Killing him is just a waste," Van Orden said. "Too bad a man always learns that too late. My father found it out, near the end. You could see it in his eyes. They found him in an alley one morning, dead. All he left behind was a pair of forty-fives, a thirty-dollar railroad watch and a reputation for trouble." He dug into his pocket and palmed the watch. "It's stopped keeping good time."

What could I say? He had summed it up too well. I could understand, because I felt that way. What did anything mean now? My medical studies seemed like a project in the distant past. And since the big house was empty it seemed as though every root I had ever put down had been yanked up and left to wither.

The bugler blew tattoo, and Mulvaney readied himself for the trip over the wall. This was done quietly—he simply went up a rope that had been flung over the wall, then disappeared.

For awhile I had wondered why father would send Mulvaney when he knew that Major Regan had escaped the Apache trap. Then I decided that Regan's route and destination were too uncertain. There were too many uncalculated risks involved, while with Mulvaney, father's message stood more chance of delivery. Military decisions, I was discovering, were based on logic and mathematical odds, not a random supposition such as Gentry had made concerning Regan's possible route of escape.

Bob Van Orden went with me to the big house, and there I showed him the books I had been studying. He seemed very interested, and let me ramble on about how it had been when the family had lived here, all together. Then he found some eggs in the kitchen and fried them without blackening the outer edges; he was a man of many accomplishments and the answer to the vacancy on boyhood's highest throne of worship.

We were sitting at the kitchen table when Sergeant Haukbauer came onto the porch with Reed in tow. "Found him on the wall again. You know what the colonel said."

"I'll take him home."

"I figured it'd be better that way," Haukbauer said and left.

Taking Reed by the shoulders, I pushed him out the door ahead of me. "Come on, Reed. Mother'll be hopping mad at you."

Mother was in the infirmary, listening to Mrs. Biers, a fat, moonfaced woman who talked a lot and punctuated everything she said with waving hands. She stopped in the middle of a sentence when Reed and I came in.

"He was on the ramp again," I said. Mother scolded with her eyes.

"Aw," Reed said, "did you have to tell?"

"Father doesn't want you on the wall," I said.

"I like to see," Reed said. "There's nothing to do with those old Apaches out there. I can't even go out and play."

"It's way past your bedtime," mother said. She gave Reed a small slap across the rump to start him on his way. Then she excused herself to Mrs. Biers and took me outside. "Melvin, I worry about your father. I thought he'd call before this."

"Could you make up with him if he did?"

She took me by the arm and tried to shake me, but I had grown too big to shake. "Now I don't want your backtalk, Melvin!" She caught her lip between her teeth. "He—he needs me. It's my place to go to him. I'm his wife."

There was that moment, the first time I had ever been able to see clearly what was in an adult mind, and the revelation startled me and I stood there, dazed by my own cleverness. I could see clearly her need—pride made her twist it around so it sounded better. And this pride was something that I had to destroy, for as long as she felt it she would never be able to forget the words that had passed between them.

I said, "Well, you've run out on him so I guess you're even."

"What—what do you mean?" She was angry enough to stammer. "Melvin, I want an answer!"

"You're not so much," I said. "I guess we'd be better off without you."

She gasped. She looked at me with eyes as motionless as polished glass, and when tears spilled down her cheeks I could hardly keep from shouting how sorry I was and that I hadn't meant it and only wanted her to go to the big house and never leave, to go there and make it full again as it had once been. But I didn't shout. I turned and began running, as fast as I could.

When I got to the big house, Van Orden had gone. I was immeasurably relieved for I didn't want him to see me cry. I went up the stairs and into my room by feel and once there, locked the door and sat alone with the terrible thing I had done. Before, in my life, my acts had all been punishable and by punishment I gained absolution, but there could never be forgiveness for what I had said and done. The reason was no longer of importance.

The night was the most miserable I had ever spent, and in the morning I awoke feeling half-dead. The sky was turning pink in the east and there were no clouds. I dressed and went onto the parade, standing there a moment in the silence. Father came from headquarters, yawning and stretching, then headed for the nearest ramp ladder.

In the stillness I could hear him speak to McGuire. "Seems quiet out there. If I didn't know better, I'd say they had gone."

"Looks are deceivin', sor," McGuire said.

Father approached the wall and had his look at the flats. Then he craned his head and looked over the side and down. His swearing was immediate and clear. He pulled back quickly.

"Open the gate!"

He bolted for the ladder, used the first five rungs, then

jumped the rest of the way. Gentry and Brokaw were coming from the stable, and they started to run when the gates swung inward. I ran too, then halted dead in my tracks.

Trooper Mulvaney was hanging head down, feet and hands fire-blackened. But I think it was the hundred small knife cuts that had killed him.

Gentry and father surged forward. "Cut him down," father said hoarsely.

The troopers sliced the ropes binding his ankles, lowering him gently to the ground. McGuire was saying, "All right there, keep back now. There's nothin' to be done."

Gentry stood up slowly, his scarred face blunt and harsh. "I hate 'em, Jim."

One of the troopers picked up father's dispatch case, which had been returned with Mulvaney. Father threw it on the ground, then stood there, his face as ungiving as marble.

"Losin' your temper won't—" Gentry began.

"Shut up!" Father snapped. He whirled to McGuire. "How could this have happened? Were you asleep? Can you explain how they climbed the gate and tied him there without being heard?"

"They hooked their fingers between the poles," Gentry said, "and climbed like a rat going up a rope."

Father just shook his head from side to side. "McGuire, take Mulvaney away and see that a burying detail is organized." Then he swung to Gentry. "Come to the office. I want to talk to you."

"Talk here, Jim."

"This can best be said privately."

"Say it here."

"All right," father said. "I'll be to the point. How much to get through to Bowie?"

For a moment Gentry pondered this. "If this is a joke, Jim, it's a bad one."

"Set your price. I'm asking it."

"Why, Jim?" Gentry was genuinely puzzled. "You've never been licked before."

"I can't fight Diablito and win," father said. "The other night I took a detail off the post and cut him up a little, and I could do that again. But the cost in men is too high. While I whittle Diablito down to size, he's whittling on me, too, and I can't spare the trimmings."

"Well," Gentry said, "if I had my price, it would be gold, but when you paid it, I'd be too loaded down to get through. And I wouldn't want to leave it behind, seein' as how I had to take a big chance to earn it."

Father's face hardened. "Gentry, think of someone beside yourself for once. There are women and children here. I'm not pleading for the troops, but I want the others saved."

Watching my father plead with a man everyone despised was not easy, and for the first time in my life I was ashamed of him.

"You're making me say things I don't want to say, Jim," Gentry said. "I'm goin' to have to turn you down." He turned then and walked back to the long porch and stood there, a completely isolated man, impervious to the wall of dislike presented to him.

The tenor of Fort Starke's morale began to change after that. Fear came out in the open, and no one tried to hide it. The children were locked up, forbidden to play even near the infirmary. All the women on the post stayed together, guarded by Captain Hanson and his quartermaster detail.

There was little talk, and a lot of praying. I tried to see father, but he wouldn't talk to me. Sergeant McGuire made the excuses, saying father was too busy, but I knew otherwise—he was a brusque, sharp-voiced stranger.

At eleven a small firing-squad formed on the southeast corner of the parade and fired three volleys over Trooper Liam Mulvaney. Father read a brief prayer and made a short speech about Mulvaney, the man and the soldier. Gentry was there. He stood apart from the small crowd as though he was unclean and knew it.

After the service father waited until the others began to drift away, then spoke to Gentry. "He was a fine soldier. I don't suppose you care one way or another?"

"Would it make any difference?" Gentry shook his head. "Cuss me if you want, Jim. I used to cuss the wind and the weather when I needed to let it out." He shifted his .50-110 Winchester Express. "You want to see what I do about Apaches? I'll show you."

He shoved father aside and went up the nearest ladder. One of the troopers stepped aside while Gentry knelt, the barrel of his rifle over the palisade wall. He had the eyes, and the knowledge that told him which clump of brush was real, and which was an Apache's disguise. He settled down, squeezed off and the huge express rifle slammed back. Out on the flats a cry floated up.

Sergeant Haukbauer turned and said, "The devil! He hit one at three hundred yards!"

Gentry worked the lever and spun hot brass onto the ramp. Coolly, methodically, he set about doing what he did best, killing Apaches. Sweat ran down his cheeks and twice he paused to brush it from his eyes. Finally, when he had fired at least fifteen shots, he pulled the rifle back and came down the ladder, a vague worry on his scarred face.

"That's what it takes to back 'em up, Jim—a bullet in the right place."

"That was fine shooting," father admitted, puzzlement in his voice.

"I call it plain foolishness," Gentry said softly. "Diablito's heard this rifle before. Now he knows I'm here." He shook his head as a man will do when he's done something completely unaccountable, even to himself. "It's funny the damned-fool things a man's pride will make him do. You got under my skin, Jim. Been a long time since I've let a man do that to me." Then he turned and walked away. Father looked after him, his face smooth and thoughtful, his eyelids pulled nearly together, whether to keep out the sun or to screen his thoughts, I didn't know.

"Melvin," he said, without looking at me, "always judge a man by the code he keeps with himself. Gentry is the most honest man I have ever known. Because he's honest with himself. He asks nothing of any man, and because he expects nothing in return, is never disappointed like you and I." He put his hand on my shoulder and gave it a shake. "It's about time I faced myself. I'm going to see your mother. You wait for me in the office."

"Can't I go too, sir?" This was the victory I had hoped would come and I wanted to be there.

He smiled, an easy smile, free from strain. "I want to see her alone. Someday you'll understand how that is with the woman you love."

"You're going to bring her back to the big house, aren't you, sir?"

"Melvin," he said, "I'm going to try if I have to get on my knees to do it."

15

When Bob Van Orden finished his trick on the wall he stopped at headquarters and found me alone. He stood in the

141

doorway, his coat thrown over his arm. "Feeling ornery, bub?"

"Huh?"

"You look pretty pleased with yourself," Van Orden said. "Did you figure a way to put salt on Diablito's tail?"

"No, sir. Father's over to the infirmary, talking to mother."

Van Orden pursed his lips. "Heard there was a little mixup. This calls for a smile. I'm going over to the sutler's and I like company, especially a man I know isn't going to draw on me."

"Aw," I said, and picked up my hat. There were many things about this man I liked, for he was gallant, and smiling, and quick with his pistols, a combination sure to attract a large following of young admirers. But I liked him best because he was around when I needed someone; I would always be in his debt.

Walking across the parade corner, I was tempted to ask him if he really meant it when he had offered to pay Gentry to take me out of here, but I knew this was something we would never talk about.

Van Orden entered the sutler's first; he held me back with his arm while he had his quick look. Then we stepped deeper into the room. Brokaw was standing at the end of the bar. His glance was long on Bob Van Orden, but he maintained a strict silence. Gentry was in a corner, his chair back-tilted against the wall.

Brokaw turned his head as Van Orden and I passed him, then said, "Just a minute, shooter."

Van Orden whipped his head around, then revolved on his heel. I stood rooted, watching Brokaw brush back his coat. In his waistband was Gentry's pistol.

"You're about to do something fatal," Bob Van Orden said.

"I'm not going to let you get close this time," Brokaw said flatly.

"What are you trying to prove? That you're brave?" He watched the man, judged him, and through some subtle sign, divined the precise instant when Brokaw would draw. Van Orden's left hand flipped open his coat while his right whipped out his pistol. Brokaw's gun was coming up when Van Orden's bullet flung him into the bar. Brokaw shot into the floor then he sagged down, his eyes fixed and glassy.

For a moment, Bob Van Orden stood with his gun at arm's length along his leg. Then he bent and picked up Gentry's pistol.

His head came around to Gentry and spots of anger

142

darkened his cheeks. "Why did you give him this?"

Gentry tipped his chair forward and came up, taking the gun. After slipping it into his holster, he said, "He told me he only wanted to fire it once. I didn't think it would hurt it any."

"Did you want to see him killed? Was that it?"

"He'd have got killed anyway," Gentry said. "If you got out of here he'd still be after you. It was better this way. He got what he wanted."

Someone was coming on the run, father probably—I could hear the scrubbing run of boots on the walk. But it was Wade Hastings. He glanced at Brokaw and said, "Who gave him the gun?"

"I loaned him mine," Gentry admitted.

"Get to the palisade wall and stay there until you're relieved!"

I couldn't recall Wade in a nastier mood.

Gentry's easy manner fled. "You givin' me orders?"

"Yes, and if you want to dispute them here and now, just say so!" I watched Wade, for he was not angry this time. Somehow the situation had come around again to Gentry and Wade, only this time Wade meant to fight coldly, logically.

Gentry knew it, and backed down.

"I'll go," he said and stepped outside.

Wade let out a relieved breath. "Van Orden, I'll have to make a report of this." His voice was coldly civil, for Van Orden was in that league with the Gentrys as far as Wade was concerned, and he would never be able to forget it for a moment.

"Sure," Van Orden said. "You make your report." Hastings went out and Van Orden put his pistol away. I stepped near him, but he waved his hand. "Not now, bub. Do you mind?"

"I understand, sir," I said and hurried away, a little hurt because he refused to accept anything from me, even understanding.

The hour was late, at least past my bedtime, yet I felt a deep reluctance to go to the big house. The post was dark and every trooper was at his duty along the wall. I walked around for awhile, finally ending up at the infirmary. Paul was sitting on the steps with Fleas. This was odd for he liked to go to bed early and wake up late.

"Reed's on the wall," he said. "He sneaked off when father came."

"I'll get him," I said, starting off. Then I turned back. "Don't say anything about this, Paul."

143

"I won't. Reed gave me his jackknife not to tell."

Taking the first ladder I came to, I began to cruise the four ramps. He was not on the west wall, nor the south either. Near the northeast corner I found Sergeant Haukbauer. "Have you seen Reed, sir? Paul says he's on the wall."

"The devil! What's got into these kids? I chased four off already tonight." He stood up. "We'd best find him before the colonel does."

Along the east wall came the sounds of a sudden scuffle. And then the shout, "Scalers! Over here!"

A gunblast rocked the silence, then another, the deeper boom of a military carbine. Then it seemed that everyone was shooting at once, for a dozen Apaches streamed over the wall. This was a fantasy, a macabre moment of terror where friend and foe blended, indistinguishable. A bullet slapped the wall by my head—I have no idea who fired it. Several soldiers and Indians fell to the parade, locked together, seeking supremacy or death.

The full surge of the fighting lasted no more than a minute, and the Apaches were driven back into the hostile night. But the dead lay haphazardly scattered.

Then Gentry's bull voice shattered the aftermath of quiet. "For God's sake, get the doctor here! The kid's hit!"

I nearly knocked Haukbauer down getting around him, and in my haste I tripped twice. Gentry and another soldier supported Reed; the other troopers were guarding the wall in case there was a second wave.

"Get him down," I said quickly.

The soldier lifted Reed and carried him to the ladder where he was handed down gently to waiting arms. Father came running from the infirmary in answer to the shooting and Gentry's frantic plea for Bickerstaff.

I had no thought but for Reed, and to stop the terrible bleeding. A trooper gave me his neckerchief, and I tried to make a compress of this. Then Doctor Bickerstaff was there, his voice soothing, commanding. Father battered his way to my side and in the lantern light his expression was stricken. He saw the blood and Reed's chalk complexion and tears ran down his cheeks, unchecked, unashamed.

Bickerstaff was bearing Reed to the infirmary and father ran on ahead, for mother was coming toward us. Father caught her and held her, crying and fighting, trying to get to her son.

To me, Bickerstaff said, "I vill need you."

A soldier ran ahead, lighting the surgical lamps in the doctor's operating room, then stood by the door, blocking it to all others, except mother and father. Mother stood with her hands over her mouth, pressing back her sobs. Father had his arms around her, speaking softly, reassuringly. But over her head his eyes were black with fear.

Bickerstaff was cutting Reed's shirt away. He bent forward, sponge in hand. "Adjust lights," he said and I did as I was told.

The bullet was a ricochet; I could tell by the ragged entrance hole. It must have struck the adobe parapet, then glanced upward, striking Reed in the clavicle. The wound was wicked and bled freely.

The shock was wearing off and awareness returning. Tears built up in my eyes, and Bickerstaff slapped me across the face. "You are der doctor! No time for tears!"

There was a murmur of talk in the hall, and then Gentry stepped in, his blunt face tight and concerned. He stood behind father, not speaking, just looking at Reed, who barely seemed to breathe.

"Ve vill haff to get der bullet out," Bickerstaff said. "It is a pressure against the vindpipe." His glance came up to mine, daring me to weaken, to fail him in this moment of great need. "Wash your hands."

I turned to the sink and the hot water on the stove. There wasn't time to roll sleeves; I ripped off my shirt and scrubbed as I had been told to do. Bickerstaff prepared his surgical instruments and set out an ether cone. Mother was moaning and crying and finally Bickerstaff said, "Colonel, take her out."

She didn't want to go. She began fighting, but Gentry stepped in, lifted her off her feet and carried her out. A moment later Gentry came back in alone. He closed the door and stood with his back to it.

"The women are taking care of her," he said, to no one in particular.

The next half hour was brutal for me. I gave Reed the ether and kept a check on his pulse. Bickerstaff's knife was working, but I did not observe his technique. The knife could well have been going into me—the pain was the same.

The doctor's commands were terse and my response was quick.

"Water." After Gentry understood, he kept us supplied with hot water.

Then the knife again, always the knife—I learned to hate that word, yet the knife could heal.

Father's breathing was a loud sawing while we worked. I

145

wanted to look at him, but feared to remove my attention from the operation. An hour finally dragged by—I was told this later for I had lost track of time.

Bickerstaff's chubby hands moved with fantastic dexterity. I kept ether on the cone and was nearly sick from it.

"Pulse?" Bickerstaff asked.

"Weak, sir."

He brushed me aside quickly. He stood there, watch in one hand, finger on Reed's neck. Then he snatched a mirror from the surgical table and held it near my brother's lips. There was not the slightest trace of fog. Bickerstaff slowly straightened, his face dull. He drew up the sheet until it completely covered Reed. I let go with a rush, sitting on the floor to cry.

"Mel," father said, and I had never heard so lost a voice. He lifted me, and I flung my arms around him, forgetting all about how to be dispassionate and coldly scientific. His big hands stroked my head.

"It vas hopeless from der beginning, colonel, but ve had to try."

"I know you gave your best," father said in a bare whisper.

Someone knocked. Bickerstaff opened the door. Bob Van Orden stepped quickly inside, hat in hand. "I just heard." He looked at father. "Damn, Colonel—I'm sorry."

"Will you stay with Mel? My wife needs me."

"I sure will," Van Orden said softly. Father went out, his shoulders pulled in as though he were carrying an intolerable weight.

Van Orden said, "Let's take a walk, bub."

We used the side door and walked to the stable yard. On the parade, troopers moved back and forth, taking care of those wounded in the fight, and those who had died. Yet the post was very quiet. The mudwagon had been wheeled into the stable yard and Van Orden sat down on the dropped tongue. I sat beside him while he rolled a cigarette.

"That old man of yours is pretty great," he said. "Most men would just fold under the weight he carries around." He drew on his smoke. "I guess it don't make much sense to you—the boy dying. A thing like that don't make much sense anyway you look at it. But I don't want to see you driving yourself crazy looking for reasons, like Gentry did. We get older, a day at a time, but we get smarter by jumps."

"He was told to stay off the wall," I said, trying to pin responsibility on something. At sixteen there has to be someone or something to blame.

"That didn't make the difference," Van Orden said. "You

can't blame anyone, bub, not even the Apache who scaled the wall and pulled the trigger." He put his hand on my shoulder and shook me gently. "You don't believe me, and I don't blame you, but someday you'll find out what I mean."

"What's going to happen to ma? She hated this place before. Now she'll—"

"That's something your ma's going to have to work out for herself." He dropped the cigaret and put his heel on it. "We got to work out our own problems, bub—there isn't much anyone else can do to help you."

He was right. I could see what he meant. But growing up is difficult and painful; there is always regret attached to that time when parents can no longer heal personal hurt. From this day forward I would have to handle my own problems in my own way. I wondered if I could.

"You want to go back?" Van Orden asked.

"I—I guess."

"Bub, when you go back, remember that the crying's over."

"Yes, sir."

"Go on then. I'm going to sit awhile."

When I went past the infirmary, I found that I couldn't look at Doctor Bickerstaff's office, and I wondered if I would ever be able to go there again without thinking of Reed. When I was six, I had a fuzzy-haired dog who used to sleep under the sutler's wagon. One day the sutler ran over him, and it was several years before I could bring myself to pass the store—I'd walk clear around the parade to avoid it.

I don't know why I went to Gentry, probably because he had been with Reed when he had been shot. Gentry was in his room cleaning the bore of his rifle. I knocked lightly, and he looked up quickly.

"Come in, kid. You want to sit down?"

"No, sir."

"Suit yourself. A man does what he wants anyway. You want to talk about something?"

"I don't know."

He pulled the wiping stick from the barrel, then fed long cartridges through the loading gate. "When you was a little shaver I used to hold you on my knee. I expect you don't recall that."

"No, sir."

"That was before I had a family of my own," Gentry said. He set his rifle aside. "Things was different then. Things was—"

The shout from the wall made us both jump. "Corporal of the guard! Summon the commanding officer!"

147

With a grunt, Gentry pushed me aside and ran across the parade. I ran after him but he was up the ladder and onto the ramp by the time I began to climb. Father was coming up another ladder. He met Gentry near the gate.

The light was poor, but I could see father's face, older, and showing a definite strain. We all had our look, and one of the troopers swore, cocking his carbine. A dozen yards from the gate stood an Apache. He was a small man, well muscled, and naked except for leggings and breechclout. In his right hand he had a military carbine, and tied to the barrel, a white rag. At father's order, two lanterns were lowered on lines, and in this yellow glare I could see that the Apache wore no paint.

He had a bold face, very flat, and his eyes were two pieces of chocolate in a face only a shade lighter. Gentry said, "Man, you got the big one. Diablito himself."

"Ask him what he wants," father said. He turned to the trooper with the cocked carbine. "Don't fire that! He's under a flag."

"What does that mean to an Apache?"

"That was an order! Ask him, Gentry."

I kept watching Diablito, and found him less frightening in the flesh than he had been in my imagination. I don't know what I imagined he would be like, but at least seven feet tall and breathing fire. Hell, he looked skinny enough to be blown away by a stiff wind.

"*Ne-ju-bee, Shis-Inday,*" Gentry said. "*Nu-estch-shee.*"

"*Shis-Inday to-dah ya-dah!*"

Gentry grunted and spoke softly to father. "I invited him in, but he won't have any of it." He leaned over the wall. "*Aat-sos-ni!*"

Then, most surprising, came the answer in English. "White-eyes leader, you have one we seek, the killer of Apaches. I am Diablito, leader of the Mescaleros. My heart is big. Give this man to me, and we will leave you in peace. Give him to me before the sun sets tomorrow, or you will all die."

"Let me take a shot," Gentry said. "That's all I need, Jim."

"If he's shot, they'll swarm us," father said, then, in a voice loud enough for all to hear, "The first man who fires will be shot by McGuire or Haukbauer. Is that understood?" He looked at Gentry. "I could make a trade. You know that."

"I know it, but you won't trade, Jim."

Bob Van Orden had come up the ladder in time to hear Diablito's offer. He took father's arm and tried to pull him around. "For God's sake, give him to the Apaches. Think of the women and children."

"That's enough!" Father studied the insolent bronze face. "You've got to hand it to him—he's got guts. He knows every man here would like to shoot him." He paused to wipe a hand across his mouth. He acted like a man wrestling mightily with temptation. "McGuire, put a round at the Apache's feet. That's an answer he'll understand."

"Yes, sor!" McGuire took a carbine from a near trooper and blew dust across Diablito's hide moccasins. Instantly the Apache whirled and vanished, throwing threats over his shoulder.

Father let out his breath easy and slow, like a man will when he's made a decision and now wonders whether it will hold or not under the strain. He went down the ladder and crossed to headquarters. I hung back a moment, then followed him.

When I came onto the porch he was sitting with his head pillowed in his hands. He didn't bother to look up when I stepped inside. "Is—mother all right?"

"Right?" He said it as though the word were new to him, and without meaning. "I don't think it will ever be right again."

He sat in silence after that. I stared at the knots in the plank floor. Neither of us had the inclination or the words for communication.

Finally Sergeant McGuire came through the outer office.

"What is it?" father asked.

"The men are uneasy, sor. Lieutenant Hastings is with 'em now."

"Uneasy?" Father's laugh was hollow and without humor. "I think that is commendable, their being uneasy. I'm damned scared."

McGuire shifted his feet. "The colonel fails to get me meanin', sor. They don't like your decision to keep Gentry."

"Rebellion, Sergeant?" The way he said it, easy-like, promised a lot of trouble for someone if there was.

"I couldn't be sayin', sor. But there's a lot of ill-feelin'. They don't think it's right we should all get killed over a no-good like Gentry."

"Sergeant, return to the men and tell them that the first man opens his mouth to speak mutiny will be stood up against the palisade wall and shot."

"Yes, sor."

"And, Sergeant, tell them I intend to hold my command together whatever the cost. That includes locking them all up and fighting Diablito myself."

"I'll repeat what you said." McGuire turned to the door.

After the sergeant had gone, father sat looking at his hands, his bitter thoughts etched in his expression. Understandably, a boy believes his father is better than other men, but this is a childish notion, soon destroyed. Observing my father now I was aware that my boyish beliefs were not merely remnants of hero-worship—he was great, a man of tremendous strength and character.

I think, for the first time, I actually faced up to the fact that we were about to die, and that nothing in our power could change it. And with this knowledge came no very overpowering regrets. I felt that I must follow the example and not break from the all explicit discipline of father's teaching—a soldier is a soldier to the end. And he fights, because that is his sole, primary function, until he can fight no more.

Twice father consulted his stem-winder, and when a half hour dragged by he got up and crossed to the door.

An hour later father called Bob Van Orden, Gentry, and Terry McGuire to his office. They came in one by one, Gentry last, and he stood in a corner, alone, still the red-headed stepchild everyone was stuck with and no one wanted.

"I can't ask for another volunteer," father said. "Not with Mulvaney being sent back the way he was. So we'll draw lots."

"That suits me," Van Orden said. He looked at Gentry. "That suits you too."

Gentry smiled withour humor. "Are you telling me?"

"Very plain," Van Orden said.

"All right," Gentry said. "You've told me."

"I've put four pieces of paper in the cigar box," father said. "On one piece is an X. The man who gets it goes over the wall tonight."

"That's fair enough," Van Orden said.

"Stand on the desk, Mel, and hold the cigar box over our heads. By virtue of rank, I'll draw first."

I made him reach. He held the paper still folded in his hand. "We'll all draw," he said, "before any of us look. Van Orden, you're next, then Sergeant McGuire."

Bob Van Orden took his slip, then Gentry drew his bone-handled revolver and chuckled. Everyone turned to stare at him.

"Now ain't you a bunch of heroes," he said. "Take a look at yourselves. How long do you think you'd last out there? This is my business, and I'll do it and have no arguments."

Father said, "Put up the gun, Gentry. We all agreed."

"I've changed my mind," Gentry said, backing toward the door. "This is my department, Jim. It's too bad about us—we were once pretty good friends." He looked briefly at Van Orden. "If you ever get nerve enough to put up those guns, you might live to be thirty."

"How would you know?"

"I see things," Gentry said. "The trouble is, I can never talk about them. That's my failing." He caught the edge of the door and slammed it shut, throwing the outside bolt. Father lunged at it with his shoulder, then started to call. A moment later a trooper unlocked the door.

"Where is he?" father asked. "Where did he go?"

"Who, sir?"

"Gentry, you idiot! He put a gun on us and skipped."

A sentry on the wall yelled, "Someone dropped over, sir!"

"McGuire, shut that man up." Father spoke again, more softly. "If he's over, then give him a chance by not telling Diablito." He turned back inside.

Bob Van Orden sagged against the door frame, his fingers manipulating paper and tobacco into a cigarette. "You ought to be glad, Colonel. We wouldn't have stood much of a chance."

"I know that." Father offered him a cigar before he noticed Van Orden's cigaret. "I was hoping he'd get the slip with the X. He's the only man who could make it."

"Then be glad he did it his way," Van Orden said. "Who did get the X?"

"I don't know," father said. He still held his paper in his hand and opened it. There was a pencil marked X in the center.

Van Orden shook his head. "It's too bad none of us liked Gentry."

"I liked him in spite of what he was," father said. "A long time ago we were as close as two men can be. I liked him, Van Orden. Liked him because he was more man than any I've ever known." He stretched. "Let's get back to the wall. Diablito might not wait until tomorrow night."

There was a moon, a round, polished silver dollar. Van Orden looked at it, then at the silver-dusted land. "That will hold the Apaches back, Colonel. We'll be able to spot movement." He wiped the back of his hand across his mouth. "I keep thinking about the *mescal*. If tomorrow is another hot day, someone will start to brew *tiswin*. The waiting's going to be rough."

"They'll come in before they cook *tiswin*," father said. He fell quiet for several minutes, then turned his head and looked at Bob Van Orden. "You look a lot like your father. I met him once. A fine man."

"Dodge City?"

"Yes, I was fresh from the Academy then. He was on the Peace Commission with Wyatt Earp, Neal Brown and Bat Masterson. That was nearly eighteen years ago."

"A long time," Van Orden said. "Where did it all go?"

"Down the drain, minute by minute. Just like it's going now."

16

THAT NIGHT I went to the big house to sleep—but every man on the post bedded down on the palisade ramp. The house was stuffy from being closed during the day's heat, and I opened all the windows downstairs to air it out, to whisk away this strange deadness.

When I went to my room, the room I had shared with Reed and Paul, I found it unbearable and went downstairs to sit in the kitchen. The house was too silent for me—the stillness was almost a pressure on the ears. I kept listening for the wind to start, but even it was silent.

Finally I left the kitchen and went back to my room. There was an empty trunk in the closet, and I began to pack Reed's things. There wasn't much beside his clothes—toys were hard to come by, and it seemed that children outgrew them quicker then than they do now. There was his sailboat that he had never sailed—an uncle in Chicago had given him that when he was two, thinking we were near water. And a little wooden dog, articulated so it wiggled when pulled across the floor. Item by item, I packed away forever the brief residue of my brother's life.

But at last I was through with packing. I put the trunk back in the closet and undressed. Sleep, when it came, blotted out everything, and there were no dreams to disturb me.

The streaming sun woke me, and ten minutes later I was dressed and standing on the back porch while the day's new heat began to climb steadily.

At nine o'clock Mr. Biers came from the infirmary, dressed in his parade uniform. Slowly, the others started to assemble at the small plot on the corner of the parade.

152

I never liked funerals. I think all children hate them because sadness is an alien emotion to a child—he doesn't understand it. The quartermaster sergeant had constructed a small coffin, and this was carried gently to the graveside. There was a delay while mother came from the infirmary, weeping, supported on each arm by Mrs. Biers and Mrs. Hanson.

Mr. Biers read the sermon. Afterwards, we all went to the wall and stood there in the smashing sunlight, waiting for the *mescal* beans to ripen.

That night we saw a fire, a far-off cell of light. Father thought it was Apache signals, but Bob Van Orden didn't think so. We were tense and on the alert, for this was the time Diablito promised to come in and get Gentry, but he failed to show up. We watched and waited—when I armed myself with a carbine father offered no objection.

There was little talk of Gentry. I guess we were afraid to talk for fear one of us would say that he didn't get through. The waiting was bad and the night long. I slept in patches and did my two-on, four-off trick on the wall the same as everyone else.

In the morning a profound silence greeted us.

Bob Van Orden said, "She's going to be another scorcher, Colonel. If I close my eyes I can see those *mescal* beans ripening."

Father was unshaven, and his eyes were red-rimmed; I think he stayed awake all night. He looked at the land for a long time. "They're well hidden. On their bellies, and we won't see them until they're ready to storm the wall."

"Are the women and kids all right?" Van Orden asked.

"The infirmary's sound," father said. "When the Apaches start to scale, a detachment will fall back and defend the infirmary."

"Figured out what that fire was?"

"No," father said, "and likely I never will."

McGuire turned his head. "What time is it, sor?"

Father looked at his stem-winder. "Stopped."

"It don't make much difference," McGuire said. Then he wrinkled his nose and sniffed. "Do you smell anythin', sor? Like rags burnin'?"

"No," father said. Then he sniffed. "Yes, I believe I do!"

Along the four walls soldiers began to test the breeze.

"What the devil is it?" Van Orden asked.

"I don't know," father admitted. "You, Terry?"

"Smells like th' Pittsburgh city dump." He looked left and right. "Any of you men know?"

They all shook their heads.

Mr. Biers hastened from the infirmary. He stood at the base of the ramp ladder, looking up, a bookish sort of man with a round stomach and thick glasses. "Colonel, sir. The ladies would like to know what's burning."

Father turned. "We don't know, Mr. Biers. It's something on the wind. Reassure the ladies, please."

All that day we could smell rags burning. Father toyed with the idea of taking a small detail out to investigate, but the risks were too great; too few would be left to defend the post.

And that night there was another signal fire burning brightly in the hills to the south, toward Mexico. Every man watched that pinpoint of light and every man wondered.

Terry McGuire finally said it. "Gentry, sor?"

"I'm afraid to guess," father said.

"What would he be doing there?" Van Orden asked.

"You find the answer and tell me," father said.

McGuire was sniffing the air like a dog. "No more rags burnin', sor. What do you make of that?"

"I'm of the mind where I don't make anything of it," father said. "See that all men stay on the wall, Sergeant."

"Aye, sor."

Father walked wearily to headquarters, and I tried to find a soft plank on which to bed down. I must have found one, for the next thing I remember was sitting upright, the echo of a carbine shot ringing in my ears.

A few feet away a trooper was hastily reloading, and shouting, "I got one, sir! By God, I got one!"

A look over the wall assured me that he had indeed got one. The Apache was near the main gate, face down, and very dead. Father came storming from headquarters, signaling to have the gates opened. I leaned over the wall and watched as father went out, rolled the Apache off his rifle, then came back inside with it.

He climbed the ladder, his face leaden, and then I saw why. He was carrying Gentry's rifle!

Every trooper on that wall saw it, and passed the word quickly to those on the other three walls. Hope died suddenly and completely—you could almost see it let down.

"He must be dead," Bob Van Orden said softly. "Gentry never let that rifle out of his sight. Hell, he took it to the table with him."

"And Diablito sent it back to let us know," father said. "They must have caught him last night, but I can't understand it. He should have been to Bowie by now."

"That could have been Gentry's fire we saw to the south."

"Impossible! Gentry would never advertise the fact that he was out there. Diablito's been trying to catch him for six years."

"And now he has," Van Orden said, turning away.

At noon the temperature rose to 112 in the shade, and there was no shade on the wall. Fort Starke was at a standstill. The officers' mess was closed, as was the sutler's. A three-man stable guard remained in the farrier's yard, but everyone else was on duty on the wall. Even Reese Pollard stood his trick, his jaws gently working on a cheekful of Wedding Cake. Pollard's stage sat in the farrier's yard and, looking at it, I wondered if it would ever leave Fort Starke.

The waiting and watching went on until three o'clock. Then one of the troopers spotted dust on the northeast horizon. His shout alerted every man, and we tried to make it out.

Father called for his fieldglasses and I raced to headquarters after them. He took them from me and scanned along the base of the dust. Then he put the glasses down. "It is," he said in a choked voice, "a column of cavalry. No less than six troops."

The men nearby heard and passed it on. Someone cheered and twenty voices took it up. "The relief!" they shouted and everyone waved their arms and pounded each other on the back.

"Shut up there!" McGuire yelled.

"Let them sound off," father said. "Terry, inform Captain Hanson and Lieutenant Biers that the siege has been lifted."

"Aye, sor!" McGuire scampered down the ladder.

"Where are the Apaches?" Bob Van Orden asked.

"Gone," father said as though he couldn't believe it. "I find it hard to believe, but they are gone."

The column was close enough now to distinguish the general's flag at the head. The bugle's voice came to us, sparkling and clear.

Reese Pollard jumped down, shouting, "Hitch 'er up, boys! I'm damned far behind on schedule now! We pull out in ten minutes!"

Father spoke to Sergeant Haukbauer. "See that all but ten men are dismissed, Matthew. Then prepare the post to receive the relief column."

"Yes, sir!"

Bob Van Orden watched the cavalry approach. He turned

155

to father and started down the ladder. "This is where I say goodbye, Colonel."

"What for?" father asked. "Man, you don't have to go."

"My kind never stays long in one place," he said. He reached out and grabbed me by the ankle. "We've been friends, bub. We'll meet again." Then he dropped to the ground and trotted toward the stable.

Father looked at me and smiled. "If you want to go after him—"

I shook my head. Suddenly I understood that Bob Van Orden was a man who moved alone, not only because of his trade, but because of his thinking. He had said his goodbye to me once—he wouldn't want to repeat it.

Father went down the ladder and crossed rapidly to headquarters. When he returned, Pollard's mudwagon was being hitched and Lilith Shipley was standing by the off wheel, seeing that her satchels were properly stowed in the boot. She saw father walking toward her and hurriedly got inside, closing the door.

He came up, kepi in hand. "Miss Shipley, may I say goodbye?"

"Goodbye," she said.

Father withdrew an envelope from his blouse pocket. "I have here a document, perfectly legal, attesting to your marriage." Lilith's expression turned to one of amazement. Father smiled faintly. "In the excitement, perhaps I am off a day or two in regard to the dates, but only you and I know that, Miss Shipley. And we'll never meet again to contradict each other."

"Why—why should you do this?" she asked.

"Because people are morally stuffy," father said. "And because I've learned that we really never face nor solve our problems alone." He gave her a casual salute. "Goodbye, Miss Shipley, and may I offer you my best wishes."

He turned away quickly because the main gate was being opened and the column was no more than a mile away on the flats. Bob Van Orden rode from the stable and trotted across the parade.

At the gate he paused. "Is there a rush?" father asked.

"Just tell General Miles that I don't like people." He smiled.

"We know better," father said.

"Then keep it quiet, Colonel. A thing like that can ruin a man's reputation." He bent from the saddle and mussed my hair. "Write me a letter, bub. I'll be at the Palace Hotel in Denver."

Then he jabbed the horse with his heels and rode away.

156

Reese Pollard was ready to leave; he was on the high seat, impatiently threading the reins through his fingers. I saw mother and Paul come from the infirmary, and suddenly I couldn't look at them. I couldn't stand there and watch them get on Pollard's stage. And I guess father couldn't either for he stared out at the column as though he found it utterly fascinating. Never once did he remove his attention.

General Nelson A. Miles was halting his relief outside the post—a cloud of dust drifted in on the wan breeze. Reese Pollard's shout caused the team to fill their harness and he made a sliding U turn around the flag pole. The stage rocked past us and through the main gate, leaving behind a banner of choking dust. Father and I watched it swing west on the Fort Savage road.

Then he put his arm around my shoulder and pulled me to him. We stood this way when Miles entered the post with his color-bearers and staff officers. He dismounted with a deep grunt and strolled up, peeling off his fringed gauntlets. Father dropped his arm and came to attention.

"At ease, sir." Miles had his look around. "You've had a rough scare, sir." Then he saw a cigar in father's pocket. "May I, sir? I haven't had a decent sit-down or a cigar since yesterday." Father offered him a light and Miles spoke between puffs. "Chased the—goddamn Apaches—clear to—the border." He sighed. "Damn good cigar there. Havana, isn't it? Yes, the Mexican army was waiting. We pushed that drunken bunch of Apaches through the pass, and you could hear the shooting for three miles."

"You chased them?" Father's voice said he didn't believe it.

And Miles caught it, too. He frowned. "That's what I said, sir. Chased them. Who was that rider who just left the post?"

"Bob Van Orden, sir."

"The gunfighter?" General Miles snorted. "Good riddance there." I opened my mouth to call him a liar, but father's touch warned me in time. Miles was looking past us, a wide smile suddenly softening his expression. He removed his hat. "Ah, madam, you're pale. It's small wonder, what you've been through."

Father and I both did a quick about-face. Mother was walking toward us, slowly, even a bit unsteadily. She had a shawl over her head to ward off the scalding sun. Father stepped forward quickly, his arms outstretched. "Cora," he said, and she stood beside him, the way she always stood, as though nothing could ever separate them.

General Miles was speaking. "I was gathering relief troops

157

when your telegram arrived, sir. I had no idea the situation was so grave."

"Telegram? General, the line's been down for a week." Then he stopped, a complete and terrible understanding coming to him. "Gentry! He tied in where the wires had been cut and sent the message."

It was Miles' turn to appear surprised. "Gentry? You had that scoundrel on the post, sir? By God, you have had a time." Then he chuckled. "Of course I should have guessed it when I smelled the *tiswin* cooking. That drew Diablito like filings to a magnet. You can't hold Apaches when there's *tiswin* cooking, and I have it on good authority that Gentry brews nothing but the best."

Father eyes were sad. "General, Gentry is dead. I guess this was a big joke to him, helping us when we couldn't help ourselves, then making us go through life hating ourselves because we hated him. There were too many things in the man that we all saw too late."

General Nelson A. Miles was a busy man and not particularly interested in father's opinion concerning a man all Arizona detested. "A part of your command is at Fort Yuma, Colonel—my office received a dispatch from Major Regan. He wanted to know whether I would grant him a transfer." Miles carefully knocked the ash from his cigar. "Strange behavior for a field-grade officer. Some action ought to be taken. Well, I have my command to see to, sir. We'll bivouac on the flats tonight and discuss the details in the morning." He chuckled around his cigar. "Damn that Azavedo. Likely he'll be a hero in Mexico City for this."

Father gave mother a quick, searching glance, then cleared his throat. "General, there's a matter that I feel deserves your immediate attention."

"Eh?" Miles showed a faint annoyance. "Can't it wait, sir? I need a bath."

"I lost a son, General; he was killed when Diablito tried to breach the wall. This has been a severe trial to my wife and—"

"You want leave? Granted, sir. Go east for a few months."

"Not leave, sir."

"James," mother said gently, "we can talk about it tomorrow."

"We'll talk about it now," father said flatly. "I'm not going to question the miracle of your being here instead of on Pollard's stage. But this issue must be settled now."

General Miles was looking from one to the other, feeling more strongly that he was about to arbitrate a family dispute.

"Then I will settle it," mother said, her voice quite controlled and quite inflexible. "Jim, I've a son in the ground now, a part of me that's dead and gone. How can I leave now and go to another place, when I've given so much?" She tipped her head forward and looked at her tightly laced fingers. "We belong together, Jim. Together and here. I'm too much Army to think differently now."

"Cora—I—"

"Not now," she said, smiling. "You were never very graceful at apologies and I don't want one. General, you must have had a hard trip indeed. Let me fix you a cup of tea."

Then we turned, together once more, and slowly walked to the big house.

FIRST COMMAND

1

This was Lieutenant Jefferson Travis' third jolting day on the westbound stage and he was weary of traveling, weary of the dust and the oppressive heat and the miserable food served at the way stations. He was also disgusted with the company in which he traveled, two elderly officers, both first lieutenants at an age when they should have been majors. This told Jefferson Travis all he wanted to know about them: they were careless in their personal habits, lax in their duty, and now soured because promotion had passed them by. One was a quartermaster's assistant and the other a contract surgeon returning from leave. Since Travis was a cavalry officer, his commission barely ninety days old, he felt that he had no common thread of conversation to weave with these men.

A merciless sun beat down on the coach, and inside the temperature was a stifling hundred degrees, yet the leather curtains were drawn on the windward side to keep out the thick dust raised by the wheels. As far as Travis was concerned, this was a useless precaution. His uniform was unduly hot, for it was new and the sizing had yet to be laundered out. His tight-fitting collar, layered with abrasive dust, rubbed his neck raw, and his kepi, squared almost to the edge of his eyebrows, trapped sweat and allowed it to trickle down his temples, making runnels in his dust-powdered cheeks.

The contract surgeon and the quartermaster's assistant sat in their shirtsleeves, unshaven, collars open, and now and then they drank from a common bottle. At first Travis hoped they would not offer him a drink, then he hoped they would, so he might remind them of certain rules of deportment dealing with an officer drinking on a public conveyance.

He told himself that the heat was making him peckish, but he knew that wasn't all of it. Behind him were years of hard study; his commission hadn't come easily, and he was proud of his achievement, but no one else seemed to be. His father, even at the train, had gone on calling him "son," and the conductor, all the way to St. Louis had called him "young fella." Then when he got on the stage at Dodge City, the contract surgeon had said, "You can have that seat all to yourself, sonny."

Those were the only words said to him.

Jefferson Travis was twenty, but unfortunately he did not show his age. He was lanky, not yet filled out, and his hair was blond and fine, so that his beard, what there was of it, was little more than a lint on his chin and upper lip. He sat on the slick horsehair seat, arms outstretched, hands braced against the window frames to keep from sliding about. Some of his luggage lay between his feet; the rest was lashed on top.

The contract surgeon produced cigars and they lit them, adding an acrid bite to the dust swirling about the coach. They didn't offer one to Travis and he hadn't expected they would; they probably thought he was too young to smoke.

His saber lay beside him on the seat, and he kept the scabbard under his thigh to keep it from falling to the floor. Not a very good saber, but it was a gift from his father and the best he could afford, for he was a workingman whose wages had never been high. The pistol he wore had been bought in a New York moneylender's shop, a used .44 Smith & Wesson American, and Travis considered it a bargain at sixteen dollars. The two officers across from him wore no weapons and somehow this pleased him; they were nontactical, while he wore the cavalry yellow along his trouser leg and in the bandanna around his neck.

For the past hour he had been turning conversational openers over in his mind, such as: "Are you stationed at Fort Winthrop?" "This is my first tour of duty; I hope we become friends." "I haven't seen any Indians; they must be quiet this year."

He rejected the first as too ridiculous; of course they were going to Fort Winthrop, or else why would they be on the stage. The second was obvious; anyone who looked at him put him down as being fresh off the drill field. And

164

the last was just plain stupid; he had never seen an Indian and wouldn't know a quiet one if he saw one.

Lieutenant Jefferson Travis was not a man overly impressed with himself; he knew that he didn't know much, but what he knew had been well learned. He supposed this was from growing up poor and hustling for everything that came your way. It wasn't a painful memory to recall that several winters he had spent his afternoons along the railroad tracks with a bucket of rocks, and when a train came by, he'd pelt the locomotive and the firemen would get mad and throw coal back. He'd pick this up, carry it home, and enjoy a warm house that night.

In school, when the knees of his pants were threadbare, he'd get the best marks, and then it didn't matter how poor you were; you were smart and polite and people liked smart, polite people. And later, when he discovered the charming company of girls, he had developed a ready wit to amuse them; it cost a lot less than taking them to the nickelodeon or to an ice-cream parlor.

But he was not at his best with strangers, and he wasn't much of a conversational opener. His forte was to wait and then comment; to let others act, then react. In his youth, and during the years at the Academy, he had brushed against a relatively unkind, unforgiving world without losing his sensitivity or his humor, and some of the time he thought he knew what he was doing, and part of the time he was sure, and with what remained he neither cared nor worried.

Yet he disliked being shut out of anything; he was a man who liked to participate, in a joke, a fight, anything. But there wasn't an opening here, and he didn't know how to make one for himself.

So he sat in stony silence and endured the miles that rumbled away beneath the iron-shod wheels.

In mid-afternoon the driver of the stage shouted and the contract surgeon put his head out the window and yelled jubilantly at a rider who was bearing rapidly down on them. The quartermaster's assistant crowded against the surgeon so he too could see. Then the rider pulled alongside and without breaking stride, yelled, "How was Chicago, lieutenant?"

"Damned good! Climb aboard; I'll tell you about it!"

Travis then observed a creditable feat of horsemanship,

for the rider, a grizzled cavalry sergeant, left his saddle and jumped to the rocking coach without missing his grip or releasing the horse's reins. The door was opened and he came in, then tied his horse so that it could run alongside.

His glance touched Travis briefly, and he said, "If you move your feet there, son, I'll be able to get by." He sat down then and ignored Travis. "Case, you didn't get married in Chicago, did you?"

"Hell no," the surgeon said. "But she sure treated me like we were." He gleefully pounded a cloud of dust from the sergeant's shoulders, then offered him the bottle.

The sergeant upended it, swallowed heavily, smacked his lips and handed it back. "My, that's good. Cheap, but good." He glanced at Leiutenant Jefferson Travis' saber. "Do you find it necessary to take all the seat?" He wiped sweat from his face. "Your first tour of duty, huh? Well, I'll give you six months. Seen a lot of 'em come out, and a lot go back."

"I don't intend to go back, sergeant," Travis said.

"That's what most of them say, but they either resign or get a transfer." He looked at the two officers across from Travis. "I'll see you at Fort Winthrop." He opened the door and stood half in, half out.

The quartermaster officer said, "Take the bottle, Ben. You're welcome to it."

He laughed. "I'm closer to a full one than you are. Thanks anyway." He looked again at Travis and smiled, then made the saddle in one dangerous jump. A moment later he pulled ahead and was out of their line of vision.

"Who was that?" Jefferson Travis asked; he didn't care which one of them answered.

The contract surgeon said, "The best damned sergeant in the army. And the toughest, sonny. And he was being real generous when he gave you six months. But if you get to soldier with him, count yourself lucky."

On the frontier, where a soldier's year was recalled as a procession of monotonous days, it took but little to elevate one post above another, and Fort Winthrop's only real claim to this distinction was the river; the back gate was only a pistol shot from it, which meant that even a buck private got his bath every Saturday night. One lonely road cut across the prairie in two directions, and each Wednesday a stage came through, using the fort as a relay station, and in exchange for this service the line carried dispatches to the far towns where details from Fort Winthrop established military order.

The fort's buildings and the encircling walls were adobe; there was nothing on the flat land to tease the eye except stunted sage and short grass and the limp scrub cottonwoods along the river. When it rained, the earth turned to gumbo mud, which then dried quickly and assumed the characteristics of iron; there was little change in between, for an hour after a rain the ground was already drying from a relentless sun. If there was one thing that Fort Winthrop had plenty of it was wind; it whistled in from the south, carrying the tantalizing flavors of the gulf waters as well as pecks of sand that sifted under collars and into the food. The sun also touched Fort Winthrop each day, very early in the morning, and by eleven o'clock a trooper could lay out a shovel and fry an egg on it thirty minutes later. This would have made field cooking quite simple, if they had ever had eggs along to fry.

Normally, the fort held three companies of cavalry, one company of infantry, a quartermaster detail of seventy men, and a substantial hospital staff. Time, circumstance, and a feeble appropriation from Washington had reduced this force to thirty-six men, nineteen of whom were nontactical. The remainder were scattered along the north Texas-Indian Territory border in piddling outposts, and concerned with keeping the reservation-bound Indians in one place and the buffalo hunters from intruding, and the settlers from antagonizing both.

The government had a strong interest in this part of the country, for by putting the Indians on reservation they could not only make some effort to wean them from warlike habits, but also keep an eye on them so that settlers could move in. But this was accomplished at great expense, for agents and agencies had to be established and maintained and the Indians had to be fed; they were quick to understand the advantages of free handouts.

Yet in spite of its barren surroundings, the fort was a landmark and once every three months Sergeant Ben Arness saw it as he made his journey from Spanish Spring, sixty-odd miles to the northeast. Sixty miles of unchanging

167

flats, buffalo wallows and dust and hell-heat in the summer, yet Arness always rode it in one fell swoop, stopping only twice, at the twenty- and forty-mile stage relay stations to change lathered horses. There was no reason for him to make this ride in such rapid fashion except that some men had to do things bang-rattle-clatter, and Arness was such a man. Some who knew him said he didn't care about anything, but he did. Some said he was born reckless, but that wasn't true; time and times had made him so. He always arrived near sundown, and as soon as he was admitted through the main gate, he rode directly to the stable.

He flung off there, then staggered to the watering trough while a stable private ran up with a bucket. Arness filled this, then slowly poured it over his head, letting it rinse away the grime and the ache of so much traveling. Then he climbed onto the low stable roof and stood there looking out on the eye-aching sweep of land as though he found it hard to believe he had come so far so fast. The sun was burning in a wood-smoke haze against the far horizon, turning it an orange-red with a hint of deeper purple. Every grass shadow was long and brush clumps appeared larger then normal, dark and thorny and spare-limbed. Grayness seemed to rise from the land, building darkness like an early morning tule fog builds a cloud, and when the sun was only a faint orange smudge below the earth, Arness came down the ladder to the ground.

The stable sergeant came over, rubbing his round, first-in-the-chowline stomach. "What was your time this trip, Ben?"

"Nine hours and—" He paused to consult a large key-winder watch, "—forty-one minutes."

"I don't think you'll ever do it in nine hours flat," the sergeant said, as though he considered it a beastly shame. "Ben, how come you never count the time at the gate? It's always after you come down from the roof."

"The look is part of the ride I miss," Arness said. "You ever watch a sunset, Gurney?"

"Mess call at that time," the sergeant said, and went back into the stable working a toothpick between his teeth.

"I guess there's something in this world for everybody," Arness said half to himself. He took off his cavalry yellow

168

neckerchief, and then his shirt, and wrung both dry before putting them on again. He was a stumpy man, about five-foot eight or nine, with short legs and arms like oak boles. His age was thirty-seven, yet he looked older, for his hair was graying and lines made a cracked-mud mottle of his weathered skin. At seventeen he had stood in an Iowa cornfield and watched a squad of soldiers march by and the feeling had taken hold of him all of a sudden. He had left the plow standing there and with bare feet padding the Spring earth, he had followed them and signed his name before the recruiting officer. Of course his father had come after him, but it was too late; he had a contract to fulfill with the United States Army, and later Arness decided his father hadn't minded him joining. It was just that he hated to lose an able-bodied farm hand. In the years that followed there were many places to go, and he went, fought when he had to, and somehow survived it all. During the Civil War he made corporal, and afterward, he thought about getting out, but the army was pretty well rubbed into him by then and after eighteen years he got his sergeant's hooks.

He was a man of rugged competence, blocky-faced, blunt-mannered and without a blemish on his record; not one day of guardhouse time chalked up against him. Ben Arness did his job and waited, secure in the knowledge that promotion was slow and that a lot of officers were crowding fifty before they made captain, so he could wait for that last grade that would make him a sergeant-major, a top soldier.

Dusted, hair wetted down, he straightened his hat and neckerchief and walked across the parade ground, stamping his feet to ease the burning cramps of a saddle-borne sixty miles. His heels rattled the loose boards on the headquarters porch and he went into the orderly room.

"Sergeant Arness reporting," he said. "If you'll tell the major I'm here—"

"I think he's about ready to go to mess," the corporal said.

Arness' voice rose to a parade-field bellow. "If you'll tell the major I've ridden sixty miles without my supper—"

An inner door banged open and Major Deacon snapped, "Shut up that ox-calling and get in here!" Arness whipped off his hat and clicked his heels as he came to attention;

169

then he went in. "Close the damned door," Deacon said. "Sit down." He pushed a chair away from his desk and offered Arness a drink of whiskey and a good cigar, in that order. "Sergeant, just once couldn't you arrive, say, before mess, or a little after it?"

With the whiskey building a warm fire in his stomach, and the cigar fragrant between his teeth, Ben Arness found a smile. "You're the best officer I've ever served under, major."

"Now don't start buttering me up," Deacon said. He was a very tall man, and very thin, looking as though he had never fully recovered from some . wasting illness. "Let's go out on the porch. The westbound stage is due in."

"I know. I caught up with it. Pickering and Case are on it. And a new lieutenant."

Deacon smiled. "That's *your* new lieutenant, and I don't want to hear any arguments about it."

Ben Arness groaned. "Aw, sir, did you have to?"

"Now you know someone has to take these new officers in hand and teach them the army. Here, put a few of these cigars in your pocket."

Arness grinned. "As long as you're bribing me, major, couldn't I take that bottle of whiskey too?"

A guard signaled that the stage was approaching and they went out to stand on the porch. It came rattling and careening across the flats and bucketed through the main gate, sawing to a rocking halt by the flagpole. The officer of the day stood by with a lantern as the passengers got down. Pickering went to his quarters and Case walked to the infirmary. Lieutenant Travis took a handkerchief from his pocket and wiped the grime from his shoulder boards.

Deacon, watching this, said, "If you say a word, Ben, you'll never see that bottle."

"Now, I wouldn't say anything, sir."

"You can even quit thinking it." The officer of the day came over and Deacon said, "Bring that new officer to my office. Come on, sergeant."

They went inside again and Deacon took his seat. A moment later a slightly hesitant step sounded in the orderly room; then Lieutenant Travis knocked, although the door was open.

"Come in," Deacon said.

Travis came to attention, saluted, and introduced himself, and when Deacon gave him "at ease," he looked at Ben Arness, a flicker of recognition in his eyes.

"Did you find your full bottle, sergeant?"

"I will in time, sir," Arness said.

In the lamplight Deacon could see Travis clearly, a week of peach down on his chin and upper lip. Travis' uniform showed hard use; he had slept in it since St. Louis and he itched with Dodge City lice. Now he stood before his commanding officer with the full realization that he was making an untidy impression. Travis had a spare, rather angular face with a thin, sensitive mouth. His eyes were pale dabs of brightness in deep sockets.

"Please sit down, Mr. Travis," Deacon said. "I believe you met Sergeant Arness on the stage."

"He asked me to move my feet," Travis said pleasantly. "But we didn't exchange names."

Major Deacon cleared his throat and shuffled some papers on his desk. "Mr. Travis, I never coddle a new officer. The quicker he gets to his duty, the quicker he finds his place in the service. I'm sure Sergeant Arness will agree with that."

"Yes, sir," Travis said. "I'm sure the sergeant would never disagree with the major."

Deacon frowned and his eyebrows drew together. "Did you two have words on the stage?" He glanced from Travis to Arness, then back again.

"It was a most pleasant conversation," Travis said, smiling. "Wouldn't you say so, sergeant?"

Arness squirmed a bit in his chair. "Yes, sir, most pleasant."

"Well," Deacon said, rubbing his hands together. "There's no reason why you can't go with Sergeant Arness in the morning then. Your luggage can accompany you by pack horse. I don't imagine you brought too much."

"No, sir, just a small trunk and a satchel." His glance touched Ben Arness again. "Not much to bring, not much to take with me when I go. Wouldn't you say that was right, sergeant?"

Arness frowned and studied his blunt fingers. "Whatever the lieutenant says, sir."

"What's going on here?" Deacon asked. "Who's leaving?"

Travis' expression was innocent. "No one, sir. I believe you were about to explain my duties."

"Yes, I was," Deacon said. Again his glance flicked from one to the other. Then he leaned back in his chair, resting one hand on the edge of his desk, his arm straight and still. "Your detail is billeted at Spanish Spring, a small town sixty miles northeast of here. North, across the river, is the Indian reservation. Of course some of it has been opened up to settlers, and farther north, the buffalo hunters make their yearly migrations with the herds. Mr. Travis, I'm not going to lie and tell you that your duty will be easy. The situation there is peculiar, but I suppose we are living in peculiar times. Recruitments are down and the frontier posts are at less than a quarter strength, with no hope of getting more men in the immediate future. Of course, officers in Washington are trying to get us more money, but like it or not, the military is ultimately controlled by the civilians, the politicians who vote us the money on which we operate. However, we face a situation worse than no money or troops. The Department of Interior controls the Indians; they expect the army to help keep them on reservation. Yet the Interior Department is highly critical of military policy; they blame much of the Indian unrest on past military campaigns against Indians. You'll have to work with the Indian agent, but I'm afraid without much cooperation."

"I'm sure I'll manage diplomatically, sir."

"Yes," Deacon said doubtfully. "There's something else too, Mr. Travis. Strong political forces in Washington feel that the Indians have no right to the land, and have pushed through legislation authorizing settlers to farm certain choice sections of the reservation. Needless to say, the Interior Department is unhappy, the Indian Agent is unhappy, and the Indians are making war talk. You will, of course, assume the responsibility for the settlers' safety, but be sure not to antagonize the Indian agent when you do it."

"I believe I understand," Jefferson Travis said dryly. "Sort of like grabbing oneself by the nape of the neck and holding oneself out at arm's length."

"Well, I wouldn't put it quite that way," Deacon said. "There is a third matter that needs airing, Mr. Travis. Colonel Dodge has been largely instrumental in opening the plains country; Dodge City, new and brawling as it is, bears his name, and he has considerable influence in Washington. Colonel Dodge feels that the Indians *and* the settlers ought to get the hell out and leave the country open to the buffalo hunters. He has, in some way, made it an army responsibility to see that there is no trouble between settlers, Indians, and his buffalo hunters. Dodge City is their headquarters, you know."

"Yes, I passed through there," Travis said. He wiped his thin lips with his fingers. "Let me see if I have this straight, sir. The Indians hate the army, the settlers, and the buffalo hunters. And the settlers hate the army, the Indians, and the buffalo hunters. Of course it stands to reason that the buffalo hunters hate the Indians and the settlers." His face was perfectly straight.

The major threw Travis an oblique glance, not quite sure of what was happening.

"It's not as impossible as it sounds," Deacon said uneasily. "Army policy is to maintain a reasonable vigilance. I just don't want to forward reports that will force my superiors to battle political factions. Conduct a one-eye-open policy, Mr. Travis."

"Wouldn't you say, sir, that it was more of a both-eyes-closed policy?" His amused eyes touched Ben Arness. "I'm sure you agree with me, sergeant."

"The matter is not for debate," Deacon said flatly, sure now that he was being gently ribbed. "We do the best we can, Mr. Travis. And don't call for additional troops; I don't have a man to spare. Given some trouble right now, I couldn't muster enough men to load the quartermaster wagons."

"Do you mean, sir, that I have only one company of cavalry at Spanish Spring?"

Deacon stared at him. "One company, hell! You have fourteen men." He tapped his fingers on his desk and pursed his thin lips. "Mr. Travis, you have a very honest face. I'm going to be quite truthful with you. Sergeant Arness has been at Spanish Spring three years, and in that time, two junior officers have requested relief from their duty and reassignment."

"Because of the duty or Sergeant Arness, sir?"

"Ah, so you did have words on the stage!" He shook his bony finger at each of them. "You two are going to get along, is that understood? Mr. Travis is not going to get a transfer, and you, Ben, are going to behave yourself." This seemed to settle the matter as far as Deacon was concerned. "Now I imagine you'd like a bath and a clean bed, Mr. Travis. Just take any empty quarters you find across the parade; the officers' picket row is nearly vacant, that's how far under strength I am."

"Thank you," Travis said, rising. "I'd like to see you before tattoo, sergeant."

"Yes, sir," Arness said glumly. After Travis went out, Arness helped himself to another of Deacon's cigars. "Why did you assign him to me, sir?"

"Now he's a nice boy, you can see that. Give him a chance, Ben."

"He's not army," Arness said sourly. "His father wasn't army either. You can tell, sir, just by looking at 'em. A second-hand pistol and a cheap saber, and you've got another civilian in uniform ready to put in a tour so he can resign his commission and get a soft job back East. I give him six months, sir."

"It's easier to get sergeants," Deacon said, "than Academy graduates. It may pay you to remember that. But I like him. Like the cut of him. At least he's got a sense of humor, even if he's so new he doesn't know the buckskin bottom of his breeches from an adobe brick." He tipped his chair back and smiled gently. "In a way he reminds me of myself on my first assignment. My father was a schoolteacher, sergeant. He wanted me to be one too, and I don't think he ever forgave me for entering the Academy. So I know how Mr. Travis feels, without the 'proper' background. Every officer and twenty-year sergeant will try to break his back just to see if it's brittle. And if he survives it and is lucky enough to find a woman who can stand the life, he might have a son who'll find it easier, because he comes from an 'army family.' God damn it, Ben, the army isn't some kind of a religion, you know!"

"It is to me, sir," Arness said flatly. "It's my whole life; I'd rather die than retire." He puffed on the cigar a moment, then laughed. "I can get along with Mr. Travis, sir, because he won't last. He's still a kid, and he'll find out it isn't his kind of army; no parades and gay cotillions. And when he gets on that stage to go back East, I'll be watching him, because it *is* my kind of army."

174

Major Deacon studied Ben Arness carefully before speaking. "You're a hard, unbending man, Ben. A long time ago you made up your mind and nothing's going to change it. All right, so a good many Academy men resign after their first tour. What about the rest, men like me?" He saw that he wasn't going to change Arness' mind, so he waved his hand. "Go on, Ben, get out of here and let me eat a cold supper."

Arness always took a room in the bachelor officers' row, although it was not permitted by regulations; he seemed to find satisfaction in this sort of thing, as though he waged some constant war with the commissioned ranks, trying to establish himself on an equal basis with them.

He filled two water buckets for his bath, then undressed and got in the tub and scrubbed clean. Afterward he dressed in clean blues and went to find Lieutenant Travis, not that he wanted to, but because he knew a green second lieutenant could get a sergeant in as much trouble as a colonel.

Travis was not difficult to find; he was sitting on his bunk, dubbing his boots when Ben Arness stopped in the open doorway.

"Come in, sergeant. Sit down." He put dubbing and cloth aside. Then Arness took a chair, balancing his felt campaign hat on his knee. Travis studied Arness, trying to decide what to say; he knew he had to say something, even the wrong thing. "Sergeant, you've spent more time in the army than I have years in my life. But I don't think that entitles you to special privileges. No one came up to me and handed me this rank. I studied for it, and because I'm not the smartest man in the world, I had to study hard."

"Yes, sir."

"It's amazing how much disrespect you can get into a 'sir,' isn't it?" He smiled. "All right, sergeant, so we're not going to be friends. But I'll tell you one thing, we're both in the same army, and we'll work for the army. What was your reason for riding here?"

"To make a report to Major Deacon and pick up the payroll."

"I'll take charge of the payroll in the morning," Travis said. "What is it about me that rubs you so raw, sergeant? My age? Or the gold bars and the age combined?"

"Do you really want to know, sir?"

"I asked you, didn't I?"

"Let me ask you something, sir. What made you choose the army?"

"Because it was a chance to get an education," Travis said. "An officer's folks do not necessarily have money, sergeant."

"Are you going to stay in the army, sir?"

"I don't know," Travis said frankly. "I'll know after I've been here awhile. Why? Does it matter to you?"

"Yes, sir, it does," Arness said. "It means I've got to put my life, and the lives of my men in a greenhorn's hands while you make up your mind whether you're going to soldier or just mark time."

"I see," Travis said softly. "What do you want? A man to be born an old soldier?" He picked up his key-winder watch and tightened the spring. "I'll expect to leave at six in the morning. Have the horses ready."

"Yes, sir," Arness said and went out, his footfalls heavy on the duckboards. Travis waited a moment, then blew out the lamp and settled in his bunk, a deep sense of depression dogging him.

2

Before dawn, Lieutenant Travis breakfasted alone, then gathered his luggage and carried it to the stable where Ben Arness was readying a pack horse. Arness nodded coolly and Travis didn't bother to speak; he felt no compulsion to carry on a conversation with this man.

While Arness went to the sutler's place, probably to get a bottle, Travis woke the paymaster and signed for the payroll he was to take for the Spanish Spring detail. He stowed this in his saddlebag and joined the sergeant by the flagpole in the center of the parade ground.

"You want to follow the stage road, sir?" Arness asked.

"Whichever is the shortest distance between the two points," Travis said. His voice had not yet attained the full manly resonance that he wanted. At the Academy he had practiced many hours before a mirror, trying to develop a commanding manner, but he could never quite bring it off. Some men were born with piercing eyes and a deep voice; he hadn't been. So he always chose his words carefully, hoping they were strong enough to carry the conviction his manner couldn't.

Be firm, be brief, be final; he tried to live by these edicts.

"Cross-country it is then," Arness said and stepped into the saddle.

A four-man detail came on the post, tired from an all-night search for two lost horses. Travis and Arness passed this detail while going through the main gate, just as the sun began to blush redly on the horizon; Travis rode a few feet behind Arness, letting him establish the direction and pace. The sun didn't take long to get hot. By nine o'clock they were both sweating and squinting, and at eleven the heat bounced a-shimmer off the parched land and made their eyeballs ache from the glare of it. They rode in an endless sea of stunted grass and withered brush, a land of unspeakable monotony, unbelievably barren. Far to the north a smudge marked some low buildings and Lieutenant Travis said, "Is that a shack, sergeant?"

"A shack and a waterhole. Somebody's trying to ranch a little."

"You're joking," Travis said. "Sergeant, a jack rabbit couldn't subsist out here."

"Well, people try anyway, sir. A man can make it if he learns to eat out of a scoop shovel and live in a hole in the ground." He waved his hand in the direction they were traveling. "They come and go, sir, just like second lieutenants. Some leave a mark on the earth, and some don't." He looked at Travis, a flat speculation in his eyes, as though he waited to see whether or not he was going to get away with this. But he knew he would. They were alone and he could say what he wanted to; there were no witnesses.

He wants me to argue with him, Travis thought. He wants me to steam a little and get mad at him and pull my rank on him so he can tell himself that he was right, that here is another second lieutenant who can't survive a man-to-man relationship but who has to hide behind his congressionally appointed rank.

"When I came through Kansas I sat for hours looking out the train window at the flatness of the land," Travis said. "Where are the hills, sergeant?"

"We got hills, not very high though." Then he looked at Travis and grinned. "You want me to give you the fifty-cent tour, sir? I always give new lieutenants the fifty-cent tour. I answer all the questions, about Indians, the country, the buffalo, and what you ought to know about the army."

"I'm sure you're a gold mine of information," Travis said. "So when recruitment picks up, I'll see that you get a few men to impress."

Color came into Ben Arness' sun-darkened cheeks. "You don't insult very easy, do you, sir?"

"I'm sure I do, sergeant, but I've learned to ignore the complaints of the mentally retarded, immature children, and crotchety old sergeants. While you lull yourself into believing that you won't have to put up with me for very long, I rest secure, believing that you'll retire from active service and sit on some saloon porch and tell everyone how you ran the army."

Ben Arness quickly wheeled his horse around so that he faced Travis, who pulled his horse to a stop. They looked at each other, anger and open resentment in Arness' eyes, and a cool-headed watchfulness in Jefferson Travis'. Then Arness whipped off his hat and smashed it against his leg, and again turned his horse and resumed his pace, so angry that he could not speak.

Indistinct in the distance was another group of buildings, another settler trying to scratch out an existence. Travis and Arness rode toward it and later Travis looked back toward the other place they had seen, but it was blended into the heat-smeared horizon. Arness rode with his felt campaign hat tipped low over his eyes to shield them from the merciless sun.

"Rink's place," he said. "I never stop anymore. They're an unfriendly bunch."

"Let's stop this time," Travis said. He rather enjoyed being contrary with Ben Arness. He watched Arness' mouth compress and the cheeks draw flat against the bones, and his neck go stiff while he stared fixedly ahead.

178

Travis could now see Rink's place quite clearly: a low sod house, a corral, and middling-sized barn. As they approached, two men came out of the soddy; they carried rifles. A woman eased past them, a hand to her forehead to shield her eyes. Then she turned and went back in while the two men came forward to meet Travis and Arness.

"Hidy," one said. He was a gaunt man, with a full mustache and dark eyes rather closely spaced. He wore knee-length boots, ragged-kneed jeans, and no shirt at all; his once red underwear was now a pale pink, grimy at the collar and worn through at the elbows.

These men were brothers; Travis could see the common whelping stamped on them. Ben Arness said, "This is Pete Rink. His brother, Oney."

"Hidy," the other one said.

"The woman is their wife," Arness said. "Name's Esther."

"*Their* wife?" Travis said.

"She be," Oney Rink said. "Pete and me shared the same breast as little yonkers. Somehow we never lost the habit of sharin'." He looked at Travis as though he expected him to make something out of it, because others had. "Wimmen is scarce out here. Esther's satisfied. So're we. If you don't like it, ride on. Got no use for the army anyway."

"Me neither," Pete Rink said.

They still carried their rifles, brass-receivered Henrys, and Travis wished they'd point them somewhere else. "You can put the rifles down," Travis said pleasantly. "We don't intend you any harm."

"I sleep with my gun," Oney Rink said.

"Me too," Pete Rink said.

Travis looked at him, then at his brother. "Doesn't he ever say anything except 'me neither' and 'me too'?"

"Got an agreement," Oney Rink said. "I do the talkin', he does the listenin'. Never quarrel that way. If you got no more business here, I'd oblige you to get."

"Well, we'd be grateful to eat in the shade of your barn," Travis said. "If that isn't asking too much."

"Don't allow anyone near the barn," Oney stated flatly. "That includes army. I said my hidy, now I'll say goodbye."

Ben Arness was ready to let the whole thing go at that,

179

but Jefferson Travis didn't want to. He'd met a few irascible people in his life, but the Rinks were a breed apart. He could understand that their stark existence on this land made them suspicious and mistrustful, but he felt that the army, like a policeman, was just something everyone should trust.

Travis stepped down from his horse and handed the reins to Ben Arness. "I'll fill the canteens from the seep, sergeant. You'd better get the horses in the shade." He looked at Oney Rink. "We're not going to hurt your barn, mister. It's just blasted hot in this sun."

"I said my say," Oney Rink declared. "I start shooting next."

Travis frowned and smiled at the same time. "What?" His voice was incredulous. Clearly he found this hard to believe.

"Be careful now," Ben Arness warned softly.

"I've had enough of this nonsense," Travis said flatly. "By golly, I'm going to have my rations in the shade!" He waved his hand at Arness and turned his back on the Rinks. "Go fill the canteens, sergeant."

He turned toward the barn and took three steps when Ben Arness yelled, then a rifle went off with a sharp crack and Jefferson Travis felt a tug on his forearm heavy enough to spin him half around. He fell to one knee, his hand jerking at the leather holster flap.

Ben Arness jabbed spurs into his horse and rode Oney Rink down. The man screamed and thrashed on the ground, his hands clutching his crushed chest; then Travis was running back, his revolver in his hand. He jabbed the muzzle into Pete Rink's rib cage and said, "Drop it! God damn it, I said, drop that rifle!" This sudden flare of reasonless violence shocked him numb, but he forced himself to function, to maintain control of his emotions.

Arness was dismounting and the woman ran out of the soddy and stared at Oney Rink. She was of an indefinable age, young, but hard-used by the country. Her body was round, but her breasts beneath her cotton sack dress were flat and formless. She stood there silent, brushing strands of hair from her homely face. Pete Rink did not move while Arness knelt by the dead man.

Blood ran down Travis' arm and into his glove, and he took it off and held it under his arm while he rolled his sleeve to examine the wound. The bullet had caught him below the elbow, in the muscle, and ripped out a respectable amount of flesh, making it ugly but not serious.

"Is he dead?" Travis asked, still trying to believe it had happened so suddenly.

"Yes, sir. When the horse reared, he caught him with both front hooves."

"Go take a look in that barn," Travis said. Voicing the command helped him to maintain his self-control.

Arness stood up, then looked at the blood dripping from Travis' fingers. "That serious, sir?"

"Just a pink. I've had worse in saber drill. Go on with it now."

Arness looked at Pete Rink for a moment, then trotted toward the barn. The woman scratched her breast and pushed nervously at her hair, still staring at the dead man.

"What's the matter with him?" Travis asked, nodding toward Pete Rink. "Doesn't he know he's dead?"

"I guess he's been told what to do for so long, he can't think or do for himself." She stepped away from Travis, then looked back at him. "Did you have to kill him, mister?" She didn't wait for his answer, but took Pete Rink by the arm and turned him toward the house. He wore the expression of a man who is hopelessly lost, and the woman patted his arm, speaking soft, soothing words to him. "He ain't all there in the head, mister." With this explanation, she led him away to the soddy.

Ben Arness came back from the barn, leading two horses. "Army," he said. "They didn't want us to see 'em, I guess." He took off his hat and then wiped his mouth with the back of his hand. "I guess they found the horses and figured to sell them for thirty-forty dollars apiece. It may be hard for you to understand, but the horses are more important to these people than the man who was killed over 'em. Eighty dollars, sir, would have fed them for a year and bought some seed, new clothes, and a jug of whiskey. That's a lot of comfort to people like them. Probably more'n they ever saw in their lives. They'd kill to get less than that." He looked at Travis' arm, still bleeding. "You ought to put something on that." He hesitated, then added, "I've got a bottle of whiskey." Clearly he implied that it was a rotten shame to waste it on a thing like this, but he got it and uncorked it, then poured some on the wound. The young man's face went white and he caught his breath sharply. "Prance around a little, if it'll make you feel any better, sir."

"Thank you, sergeant. I believe I will." He stamped his feet in a small circle, waving his arm like he was trying to snap something sticky off the fingertips. Then he took off his neckerchief and wrapped it around the wound. "For a minute there, sergeant, we were on the same team. Any regrets?"

"Well, sir, I pitched in because I just didn't think I could explain to Major Deacon how I lost an officer five hours out of Fort Winthrop." He shook his head. "I told you to go easy, sir. People out here mean it when they say they're going to shoot." He blew out a breath of long duration. "I expect you want to take the damned horses along, huh?"

"They're army property, aren't they? Better see if you can find a shovel. We'll help with the burial." He turned then and walked into the soddy. Some packing crates had been fashioned into a table and two benches. An old cast-iron stove sat in one corner, and a brass double bed across the room. Buffalo chips were piled behind the stove, and litter lay around on the dirt floor where it had been flung.

The woman was brewing some chickory coffee, and Pete Rink sat at the table, staring at nothing. Suddenly he turned and looked at Jefferson Travis.

"I guess you're going to take the horses too," he said defeatedly. He spread his hands and laid them flat on the table. "Oney, he just meant to nick you a little, scare you off, that's all."

"We'll help you with the burial," Travis said. "I'm really sorry it turned out this way."

"Nothin' turns out good for us," Pete Rink said softly. "And I'll bury him, mister. It's my place."

"Why don't you just go, like Oney asked, mister?" Esther asked. Her voice was curiously toneless and devoid of emotion. "Ain't it bad enough we got to lose without havin' someone watch us?"

"I'm— very sorry," Jefferson Travis said and went out. Arness had found a rusty shovel, but he threw it aside when Travis stepped into the saddle. Arness fastened the lead ropes of the recovered horses to the pack horse, then gathered the reins of his own mount.

Pete Rink came out of the soddy and Arness left his horse and picked up the two rifles, levering the cartridges out of the magazines. He dropped these in his pocket and mounted; they turned silently out of the yard and when they were a few hundred yards out, Jefferson Travis turned his head and looked back. Pete Rink had taken off his brother's boots and was putting them on, and the sight of him, sitting there in the dust, trying to salvage something, hit Travis like a cold clod in the stomach.

"Don't they feel anything, sergeant?"

Arness looked at him, then shook his head. He reached into his pocket and brought out two cigars, offering one to Travis. "Here, sir, second lieutenants are old enough to smoke." He furnished the light, and after his was going, he said, "I seen kids die of the fever out here. I've seen their folks bury 'em in the morning, and go back to the plowin' an hour later. If they didn't, they'd be that much farther set back. You got to have *time* to cry, sir. Got to have time for grief. And they got no time at all. There's just so much luck in the world, sir. A man can't make it and he can't destroy it. Now when a man comes into some luck, he ought to stop and think a minute, because someone else has just lost a little. These people, they've lost it all, sir. They lost it all so long ago that they don't know a bad thing when it happens, because what's bad to some is just normal for them." He pointed to the prairie ahead. "There's some buffalo wallows about a mile or so. We can eat there and rest the horses."

Travis had never seen a wallow, but as they neared one, he found that the prairie around it was littered with buffalo droppings. The wallow was a large depression in the earth, well trampled, with a dried mud bottom. They dismounted and broke out cold rations. Travis took off his kepi and placed a wet handkerchief over his head, then put the kepi back on to keep the sun off his neck.

"What causes these wallows, sergeant?"

"No one really knows," Arness said. "I guess it starts with a little hollow in the ground that collects water. The buffalo wallow around in it and make it a little deeper. After a hundred years, it gets like this." He took a long pull from his canteen. "Maybe it takes a thousand years. One's pretty much like the other out here."

"Or six months, sergeant?"

Ben Arness looked at him, then laughed. "You go pokin' your nose in people's barns, sir, and it won't be six months. No horses are worth it." Then he shrugged. "Well, you've got to write the report, I don't."

Travis regarded him solemnly. "What made you join the army, sergeant?"

"Because there was nothing for me on the outside," Arness said. "I was a farm boy, and it was poor land. Just a lot of hard work and nothing to look forward to. My father was fifty before the land became his. He'd have to die before I got it." His beefy shoulders rose and fell. "All I know is the army. Put me out and I wouldn't know where to go, what to do. But you wouldn't understand. It's not your life."

"What is my life then?"

Arness shook his head. "A tour here, probably, then resign. Then a good job someplace, where you can wear a clean shirt and a celluloid collar and carry a cane. I've seen a hundred come and go, sir, and it's always as if they've taken something that's mine and used it and put some of it in their pocket so that I can't get it back."

"I see," Travis said softly. "And I really do see, sergeant. Any family?"

"No," Arness said. "Why?"

"I don't know. All this emptiness out here makes me think of home, and my family. My father's a bricklayer."

Arness frowned, and studied Travis. "Is that the truth? I never knew they'd take a bricklayer's kid into the Academy. Just a bricklayer, huh?"

"Just a bricklayer. He's never made more than ten dollars a week in his life." The sun dried out the handkerchief under his kepi, so he refreshed it from his canteen. "My brother, Paul, is a clerk in the barrel factory near my home. He makes fourteen dollars a week and someday he'll be manager." He leaned back until he was almost supine. "I chose the army, sergeant, just the way you did, and for quite possibly the same reasons. When I finished high school, I could have gone to work, maybe as a junior clerk in a law firm, or a brokerage house; my father wanted that. But I wanted to see something, a great big lot of something."

"Dust and scrub grass?"

"Well, that's *something,* isn't it? Sergeant, I stood on a

depot platform in Kansas and listened to a train whistle blow five miles away. Can you imagine that, five miles? That's how big and still it was. Back East it's so crowded and noisy such a thing would be impossible. And the life is so humdrum. You just go home every night on the same street and wear the same suit to church every Sunday." He chuckled softly. "And when I write home and tell them about all this, they aren't going to believe any of it."

Arness grunted, and then they were silent for a while. They mounted up and wore out the rest of the day at a walk, to save their animals, and that night they stopped for a fire and a hot meal, backfat and wheatcakes. Afterward they made coffee in the skillet and washed their tin plates in the dirt.

Travis' arm was paining him badly and he kept it against his stomach, his hand thrust into the waistband of his trousers. Thinking back about the things he had discussed with Arness, Travis wondered if his increased understanding of the man would allow them to work more amicably together. He hoped that this would be so, but he wondered about Ben Arness. The man was so entrenched in his ways that there was little hope of him changing.

They were resting, stretched out on the ground, and from the darkness, Ben Arness said, "The arm giving you hell, sir?"

"I'll get along with it," Travis said. "But I'd appreciate another cigar, if you have one."

Arness handed it over, then said quite frankly, "You're going to have to start buying your own."

After the cigar was ignited, Travis lay back again and looked at the sky. "That's the biggest, blackest sky I ever saw," he said. "And the brightest stars. It's easy to think that everyone's moved off the earth except yourself."

"I'll bet you wrote poetry to the girls," Arness said dryly.

"I did, sergeant, and it wasn't bad. You know, I've always had a flair for that sort of thing." Then he raised up and peered at Ben Arness. "Sergeant, you want to know something? You're not going to rile me. I'm going to see the day when you get blue in the face and run out of cuss words, and you're going to know then, sergeant, that you've

185

been out-soldiered. Now you put that in your pipe and smoke it, and I'll lay money that it's no worse than these rope cigars."

"Some people have no gratitude," Arness said sourly.

3

As he rode through the darkness with Ben Arness, breathing the dust raised by the dull thud of the horses' hooves and feeling it settle on his face, Jefferson Travis reflected on how little one person really learned about another through conversation. All you could glean were surface impressions; you had to dig deep for the truth. Arness had spoken of his youth on the farm, and why he had left it, but Jefferson Travis knew that the things that were left unsaid were often the more important aspects of a man's life. He knew because this was true of himself.

He had come from a genteel but very poor home, a proper home, one full of virtue and free of disgrace, except, of course, for Uncle Timothy, who drank. But nobody mentioned this. Just as nobody admitted the poorness of their circumstances. Jefferson as a boy had quickly learned that he could do practically anything to alleviate those circumstances, provided he did it unobtrusively, and provided it hurt no one. So he discovered the difference between hypocrisy and pride, and he never forgot the hard lessons that respectable penury taught. But there was a great longing in him to shed pretense of any kind, and he knew he could never do it at home. Indeed, although the Academy was a revered institution, his people had felt betrayed when he secured an appointment there and left their way of life. It was as though he hadn't really approved of them and wished to elevate himself out of their class. He hadn't been able to explain his real reasons, that he wanted only to become a man in his own right.

"There's lights ahead, sir," Arness said, snapping Travis away from his thoughts.

"Is that Spanish Spring?" He studied the faint sparkle of lights. The night was very clear with not a breath of wind stirring, but the lights winked like stationary fireflies.

"Yes, sir. About an hour now, sir."

In the cool of night it was difficult to recall how hot it had been during the day; Travis would have welcomed a jacket now. Had he been traveling alone, he would probably have stopped for the night and rolled into a blanket, but he had hesitated to suggest this lest Arness think him tender-bottomed.

They reached the edge of town and rode down the dark streets. It was a small town, laid out around the courthouse, an ugly, adobe building flanked by gnarled trees. The main street was a wide, dusty strip, bracketed by flat-fronted adobes, and only the saloon and hotel were still open.

The United States Cavalry detachment occupied what had once been a large trading post. It was surrounded by a low mud wall and the building was U-shaped, with a stable and wagon yard in back. They dismounted in front and Jefferson Travis stepped stiffly to the ground.

Ben Arness said, "The center part is an office, with mess and quarters on either end. The troopers' barracks is on the right, sir; we use the other wing for a storeroom."

"Take the horses around back, sergeant," Travis said. He turned and looked up and down the compound. "I don't see any guards."

"Well, sir, we haven't been posting any. With fourteen men, sir, it's every man to his duty, and the less extra he has to do——"

"I quite understand," Travis said. "We'll let it stay like that."

Arness was pleasantly surprised; he had been prepared to put up with guard duty and all the garrison foolishness that new officers liked so well. "Thank you, sir." He took the horses and led them around to the stables while Travis went inside.

He fumbled about until he found a lamp and put a match to it, adjusting the wick until the flame was bright, then he turned and surveyed the room with some distaste. There were a desk, a bookcase, four chairs and a brass spittoon, with some brightly colored Indian blankets adorning the walls. Dust and old papers lay about and this offended Travis' sense of order.

As soon as Sergeant Arness came back, Travis said, "Sergeant, is there a well nearby? Good! Fetch me about four pails of water, some soap, and a mop."

"You're going to scrub it out tonight?"

"I intend to open this office at reveille, sergeant, and I don't want anyone to mistake it for the stable." He stepped to an adjoining door and opened it; this was his quarters. Holding the lamp high, he looked at it critically and found it neat enough for occupancy. He turned back to Arness. "I asked for water, sergeant."

He worked until nearly daylight, scrubbing the floors, washing the windows, clearing out the rubbish and dust, and only a strong compulsion to do the job right kept him from lying down on his bunk and going to sleep.

Corporal Busik brought him his breakfast, and he met the rest of his detail afterward at roll call. Travis made no speech; they were all professional soldiers, with more guardhouse time than he had total time in the army. He tried to be crisp and to the point, merely stating that the army operated by rules, which he had memorized, and they were expected to follow them.

Sergeant Arness, whose duty it was to relay an officer's commands, went into the office and stood while Travis sat down behind his desk.

"Who are the legally constituted authorities in this town, sergeant?"

"The sheriff, sir, Owen Gates. And a judge."

"Send for the sheriff. I want to report on the trouble at the Rink's place. It wouldn't do for the local powers to be able to say that the army didn't cooperate."

"I don't think the sheriff's up yet, sir."

"Well damn it, get him up!" He took out his watch and popped the lid on it. "I'm going to bathe and shave. Shall we say, thirty minutes, sergeant?"

"Yes, sir." He shifted his feet on the plank floor and cleared his throat. "Lieutenant, that matter at Rinks—ah, you ought to talk to General Wrigley about it. I've always taken him into my confidence, sir."

"Who in blazes is General Wrigley?"

"Well, sir, he's the president of The Dixie Land Devel-

188

opment Company. Most of the settlers around here lease their land from the general, sir. When he hears about it, he'll come here anyway, and I guess it'd look better, sir, if you invited him."

"All right," Travis said.

Arness left and Travis took a pair of buckets around to the well for his bath water. He squatted in the tub as long as he dared, to soak some of the weariness out of his bones, then shaved carefully and brushed the dust from his uniform. He still hadn't found time to unpack his belongings; his satchel lay on his bunk, and the chest sat in one corner where he had shoved it with his foot.

While he waited, he looked out past the low walls at the town, now bathed in the bland early morning sunlight. Around in back, a detail of troopers curried the horses, and three others, under Corporal Busik's direction, diligently straightened out the storeroom, not knowing when the new officer would pull a surprise inspection.

Travis had written his first order and it was posted outside his office door: pay call would be held at four that afternoon. He knew that everyone had read it, but he let it stay up anyway.

Arness and another man came through the wagon gate and walked across the compound. Owen Gates was identifiable by the badge on his coat. He followed Arness one pace behind, in the manner of a man who has always had a subordinate role in life. He was middle-aged, rather thin and wan looking. Travis stepped aside so they could enter his office, and Arness introduced Gates, who shook hands half-heartedly, seeming embarrassed to be there at all. He had the uncertain manner of a man who hadn't made up his own mind in years.

"Ben told me all about the trouble," he said, sitting down. He wore a dense mustache that dripped past the ends of his mouth, and he kept brushing this with his forefinger as though it bothered him. His hat was balanced on his knees and he kept looking around the room and blowing out his breath between compressed lips. "I've been sheriff seven years now. Never had any trouble with settlers. Fact is, I never have trouble with anybody."

"Well," Travis said, "I'm just curious enough to want a look in a man's barn when he becomes overly obstinate about my not having a look in it." He regarded Owen

189

Gates steadily. "How many men do you have in jail now?"

"Why, I don't have anybody," Gates said, surprised. "As a law officer I got other duties besides throwing people in jail. Most of the time I'm busy serving papers for General Wrigley; he's got plenty of business for me to take care of."

A fringed-top buggy wheeled through the gate and came on across the yard, its brightly-painted wheels sparkling. An impressive-looking man dismounted and tied the horse, then came in the office. He wore an expensive dark suit and an embroidered vest accented by a heavy gold watch chain. Thomas C. Wrigley was sixty, but still as trim as a young sapling. He had a deeply lined face and hair that was almost white. A thick mustache hid his mouth completely; he was like an historical painting, vivid in every detail, with a noble brow and a stern, unforgiving jaw.

"Mr. Travis, I believe. General Thomas C. Wrigley, C.S.A." His handshake was firm, but very brief. Then he swept his coat-tails aside and sat down, seeming to dominate the room with his commanding presence. "I think we'd better get right to the matter, sir. Regrettable, but not beyond salvaging." This man obviously enjoyed his role of public benefactor. His every word and gesture were calculated to show that his life was dedicated to the public cause, regardless of any inconvenience to himself.

"You're referring to the death of Oney Rink, sir?" Travis asked politely.

Wrigley frowned as though annoyed. "Of course I'm referring to Oney Rink. What a tragedy! And they were doing quite well too. Another five years and they'd have been clear of debts."

"How, sir? By selling army horses?"

"I hardly think that's the case," Wrigley said, his voice edgy. "A mistake is a mistake. It need go no farther, sir." He spread his hands briefly. "I am willing to put the whole thing aside as an impetuous error on your part, sir. The last time I talked to Major Deacon he assured me that the army's position is one of protection toward the settlers. Not of enforcement. In the future, if you suspect irregularities, please report them to the sheriff and they will be duly investigated. He is employed to handle these matters."

Travis shook his head, "General, I get the distinct impression that you want this to be entirely my fault and that

190

you're looking for a tail to tie the can to." He pointed to Owen Gates. "Has he ever arrested anyone?" He watched the color come into Gates' face, then he laughed. "Never mind, general, you don't need to answer. I'm not really interested in your sheriff. But you intrigue me, sir. I understand that you are the president of The Dixie Land Development Company. I've never met a land speculator before."

"President and owner, sir," Wrigley said. "It's my dream, my ambition, to see the vast fertile prairie populated by hardy pioneer stock, Mr. Travis. I envision schools and churches and fine homes and waving fields of grain, and I—"

"It's not necessary to make a stump speech in my office," Jefferson Travis said quietly, then he watched the amazement turn to anger in Thomas C. Wrigley's eyes. "General, I've just ridden over some of your fertile prairie, if you are referring to that dry, dusty, heat-seared section of country running all the way into north Kansas. And I find your reference to hardy pioneer stock a little amusing, if you're holding up the Rinks as an example." Travis' boyish cheeks tightened against the bones and his jaw seemed to square somewhat; he placed his hands flat against the surface of the desk and hoped that he looked like an officer capable of making a decision. "I understand my duties quite well, sir. And I also understand that there are strong factions here pulling every dangling political string in favor of the settlers, the hunters, or the Indians. I trust, general, that there is nothing in your company that cannot bear looking into."

"You'll find everything legal, sir," Wrigley said stiffly. He glanced at Ben Arness as though he thought he were being betrayed and blew out an aggravated breath. "Bless me, Mr. Travis, I came here to make friends, not split hairs. I need cooperation, sir, not irascibility. If you're going to spend your time turning up rocks to see what's under them, why—" He left the rest unsaid and stood up. "Perhaps we can talk again, after you've been here awhile. After you get a true perspective of conditions here." He tapped Owen Gates on the arm. "Come along. I've got some papers I want you to serve."

Gates went out and got in Wrigley's buggy, and they turned out of the yard. Arness sighed and scratched his head. "Did you have to make him mad, sir? He's doing a lot for this country. He's a good man, once you get to know him."

"Has he put you in his pocket too?" Travis asked. He saw a stain of red flood the sergeant's neck, then Arness gave him a blunt, angry stare.

"No," Arness said quickly. "I just do my job, sir."

Travis continued to study him, wondering if Arness was telling the truth or not. Then he said, "How did Wrigley acquire the land to form his company, sergeant?"

"Squatters' rights, mostly," Arness said. "Wrigley used to range cattle there before the war, and he had a treaty-lease agreement with the Indians. When the settlers started coming in, they had to go to Wrigley. Some proved up on the land, but couldn't make a go of it, so he bought those out, five cents on the dollar. The rest he subleases. It's just good business, sir."

"Yes, from the cut of his clothes and the price of that rig he drives, I'd say that business was very good." He got up and put on his kepi. "Is there a doctor. in town? I think I'll have this arm dressed properly."

"Yes, sir. Doc Summers lives down the street."

"I'll write my report this afternoon, sergeant. How often does the Fort Winthrop stage come through?"

"Every Friday, sir. If you're not back by pay call, sir, shall I—"

"I'll be back," Travis said, and went out.

He wondered if he had made a hasty decision regarding General Wrigley, but he had seen at once that Wrigley wanted him "on his side," and Travis realized that would never do. The minute he started to play favorites, he was finished as a commander of a functioning unit, and on the way to being through as a man. He felt a sense of pride that he had had the acumen to appraise Wrigley as a favor-seeker, a man who lived and worked along that twilight fringe of legality, taking more from the people and land than he ever put back.

There was a sign hanging near Doctor Walter Summers' gate, and as Jefferson Travis passed through and went up the walk, he suspected that a woman lived there; the carefully nurtured flowers and shrubs were evidence of this, also the crisp curtains that hung at the parlor windows.

There was even a marble bird bath in the middle of the front lawn.

He knocked and heard a light step in the hall; then the door opened and a girl stood there, frankly examining him.

"I've never seen you before," she said. "Oh, you've been hurt! Come in. The doctor will be along in a minute." She took his good arm and tenderly led him down the hall, giving him the impression that she suspected he might faint at any moment. He opened his mouth to protest this solicitude, but she didn't give him a chance. "You're very young to be an officer. I suppose you've taken charge of the detail here. Have you been in the army long?" She made him sit down and then removed the crude bandage. "My, that's ugly, isn't it? I don't suppose you put anything on it. Men never think of such things, you know. Or else they put something smelly on like the Indians use."

He studied her while she chattered, for she was a charming girl. She was somewhere between eighteen and twenty; a delightful age where being exact about it really didn't matter. Her hair was dark and shiny and her eyes were large and expressive; he imagined that she wept easily, but rarely because of herself. She moved her delicate hands with quick grace, and when he smiled at her, she smiled back.

"The doctor will have to take some stitches in that, lieutenant. If the pain bothers you, I can let you have a drink of whiskey." He shook his head and she frowned. "Wouldn't you like a drink? Men usually do, you know. Doctor Summers says it's the first rule of medicine; give them a good drink and let nature take its course."

An elderly man stepped into the room, shrugging into his coat. He had a pipe locked between his teeth, and he puffed on it. After a glance at Travis' uniform and rank, he said, "Mmmm. Kind of messy, isn't it? Give you much trouble?" He prodded the flesh around the wound with his finger and Jefferson Travis gripped the arm of the chair tightly to keep from flinching. "Pretty tender. We'll wash it out with peroxide and close it."

"I'm Lieutenant Jefferson Travis, doctor."

Summers looked at him for a moment, as though wondering what the point was. "You get this from the Rinks?" He nodded toward the wound.

"News travels fast," Travis said. "Well, he shot me first."

Summers turned to the cabinet for a bottle, a swab, and a surgical sewing kit. "Fetch me a pan of water, Hope." He soaked the swab with peroxide and washed the wound carefully. "The Rinks are wild all right. They ran Ben Arness off once." He placed Travis' arm straight out. "This might hurt a little."

When the needle bit in, Travis realized what an understatement the doctor had made. He bit his lip and stiffened, and sweat popped out on his forehead, but he managed to keep his mouth shut. Hope wiped his face twice, then Summers was finished.

"Hope will bandage that," he said. "Shall I send the army the bill? It's only two dollars."

"I'll pay it," Travis said.

"Come back in a week and let me have a look at it," Summers said, and went out.

Hope wrapped his arm and he sat there and observed the play of sunlight on her cheeks and bare arms. "Is your name Hope Summers?"

"Hope Randall. Doctor Summers is my mother's brother." She finished with his arm and was going to make a sling for it, but he shook his head.

"I'm not going to baby this," he said, rolling down his sleeve. "Would you tell me something if I asked you?"

"You'd have to ask me first."

"I got the impression from Doctor Summers that I'm more to blame than the Rinks for what happened."

Her expression became serious for a moment. "Mr. Travis, it's hard for us to really blame those people for anything. They have nothing at all, and so little prospect of getting anything. So when they steal a horse or a buffalo hide, or a steer, we secretly hope they'll get away with it. Not that it's right to steal. But it's less than right to have so little, and we're always sorry, just a little bit, when they get caught. If being blamed bothers you, Mr. Travis, then you ought to get another assignment. You're always going to be blamed; that's what you're here for. There are cattlemen here who'll blame you for not killing all the Rinks, and General Wrigley's settlers will blame you for being in the pay of the cattlemen, or the Indian agent, or the buffalo hunters, who sometimes come this far south.

Do you understand how it is? You can't be fair. Ben Arness tried it, but he had to decide who he was for. Sooner or later, you'll have to swing over to one side or the other."

"And what if I don't?"

"You won't be able to help yourself," she said. Then she smiled. "Come back next Wednesday."

After pay call, Ben Arness walked to the edge of town and cut across a vacant lot, walking toward a scatter of adobes. The largest of these was four rooms with a porch running around all sides, and he went around to the rear patio. Strong poles had been set into the ground and ropes tightly strung, and from these hung enough washing to supply a regiment. A woman worked over a scrubboard, sweat coursing down her face and soaking the shoulders of her dress. A small girl helped her, folding clothes in a large basket while a boy of eleven stoked the fire, keeping the kettles of water hot. This was her living, at ten cents a bundle, and the work went on six days a week.

The girl saw Arness first and ran toward him; he scooped her up in his arms and carried her back. Grace Beaumont snapped her hands to fling off the soapsuds, then wiped them on her apron. She was a small woman, touching thirty, dark-haired and dark-eyed. Her face was round and ruddy from near-constant exposure to the sun, and her hands were always chapped from immersion in hot water and strong soap.

To the boy, Arness said, "Let the fire go for a while, son."

"What you got in the saddlebag?" the boy asked.

"Something," Arness said, and sat down on the porch step where there was a little shade. The girl climbed on his knee and Grace Beaumont shooed her off.

"Ben doesn't want you pestering him."

"It's all right," Arness said, and picked up his saddlebag. He produced a doll first and gave it to the girl, and she hugged him and kissed his cheek. Linsay Beaumont was disgusted at this feminine display and snorted through his nose. The girl went into the house with her doll, humming to it.

"That's the first pretty thing she's had in a long spell, Ben. And it was mighty thoughtful of you."

"Here's a jackknife for you," Arness said, handing it to the boy.

"Gosh!" He dashed off for a piece of wood.

Arness hesitated. "I bought you something and I want you to take it without any fuss now." He showed her a bolt of blue velveteen and she put both hands to her mouth and gasped. Then she shook her head.

"I can't take it, Ben. Lord knows, I want to, but I can't."

"Why?"

She smiled wistfully. "If I made a dress of it, people would see it and know I didn't buy it here. They'd guess where I got it. But it was a lovely thought, Ben. One I'll remember."

He took off his hat and sighed. "I see you scrub your knuckles raw to earn seven dollars a week, and you tell me you can't have something pretty? You keep it. Maybe you can't use it, but you keep it and look at it and feel it once in awhile, just to remind you there's other things in the world besides sweat and disappointment."

"All right, Ben." She caressed the cloth and smiled. "Someday I might make a dress of it." She studied him carefully, detecting a worry in his expression that hadn't been there before. "Ben, what's the matter? You look discouraged. Is there something wrong?"

He spoke softly. "That new lieutenant asked me a question a few hours ago. He asked me if General Wrigley had me in his pocket, and I said no. But I didn't want to lie to him, Grace." He slapped his leg angrily. "Twenty-seven years a soldier, and a kid makes me ashamed of myself."

"Ben, don't be so hard, so unbending. Isn't it time you gave it up?"

He looked at her. "Get out? No. No, I couldn't do that. I don't want to talk about it, Grace." He shook his head. "I'll see it through, because I've been in too long to throw it all away. Travis won't get a chance to bust me in rank. No fresh-faced kid's going to steal twenty-seven years from me, Grace."

"What makes you think he will, Ben?" Her voice was quiet.

He looked at her, suddenly embarrassed. "No reason,"

he mumbled, and added quickly, "Well, I'd better get back before I give him one. I'll see you soon." He turned and walked rapidly back to the barracks.

4

In making out his report, Jefferson Travis took the greatest care to be exact, relating every pertinent detail of the affair at the Rinks' soddy. He offered no excuses or apologies and made no special point about recovering the two horses, although he included a description of them, identifying them positively by the company and regiment number cut into the hooves.

Placing the report in a small dispatch pouch, he sent a trooper to the express office with it to see that it got into the Fort Winthrop mail pouch. He was bone-tired, so he slept for a while, had a late supper, then went out and sat on the porch, hoping that a night breeze would come up to cut the heat rising from the sun-soaked ground.

Sergeant Arness came into the compound; he did not see Travis sitting there to one side of the porch. But when Travis spoke, Arness came over and stood in the shaft of dull lamplight streaming out of the doorway.

"Sit down, sergeant," Travis said. "We'd better have a talk."

"What about, sir?"

"About your twenty-seven year contract with the army. It seems that your long service has given you the idea that you can run things to suit yourself. I'm not going to assume that you *knew* there were horses concealed in the Rinks' barn, sergeant, or that you were *willing* to pass up an opportunity to recover them. But at the same time, I'm going to have to take with a grain of salt all I've been told about you being such a good soldier. 'The best damned sergeant in the army,' as it was put to me. So far you've proved to be no more than a recalcitrant crank with a peckish grudge against anyone who doesn't believe the army is a great career. I don't feel that I have to put up with it. Do you understand?"

"Yes, sir. May I speak freely, lieutenant?"

"Go ahead. I'm not going to pull my rank on you."

Arness took off his hat and folded the brim back so that it was a roll of felt in his hands. "I've been running this detail without an officer and with no complaints from the major, sir. And no Academy-green officer can do any better. I'm not going to claim that I don't favor the home-steaders, because I do. But I do know what's good for this country and you don't. You keep on the way you're going and all the work I've done will be wasted. The buffalo hunters are guttin' the country, sir. And the Indians, they don't bring anything but misery; the sooner they're gone or held on reservation, the better off everyone will be. Wrigley's trying to open up the country, promote a rail-road, and get people to settle the land. I made up my mind some time ago as to who was doing the most good. You want to bust me, court-martial me for that, then you go right ahead."

"Hell, man, we're not talking about disciplinary action," Travis said. "If you'd stop for five minutes and forget that you're a twenty-seven year man, you might remember the job you're here to do." He fell silent for a moment, then said, "From the way Gates and Wrigley talked, I knew that you favored their action. Of course, nothing openly; you think too much of your stripes to run any risks. Now, you may consider that clever as hell, but I consider it much less. As far as I'm concerned you've never had nerve enough to take a stand for fear you'd lose your precious chevrons." He turned his head and looked at Ben Arness. "But the fence-straddling is over, sergeant. You realize that, don't you? I'm going to give it to you straight: you soldier with me, my way, or I'll send you back to Fort Winthrop. Make up your mind."

"What do you know about soldiering, sir? Hell, the creases ain't out of your uniform yet." He slapped his hat on his head. "All you know about the army is what you learned at the Academy out of a book. Well I learned mine first-hand, sir. The only way to learn. And there's a hell of a difference in what I already know and what you've got to learn."

198

"You're right," Travis said. "And I'll point out one of those differences right now, sergeant. You like to think of yourself as a first-class sergeant, a man who's always had his duty and done it. The truth is that you're as much a slacker as the worst recruit. You haven't done army duty for a long time, sergeant. You do duty for yourself, because you can't think of anything but your long record of faithful service. What do you want, a testimonial from the area commander? It's a big army and it was working fine long before you came along, and it'll do just as well after you're gone. Your army, sergeant?" He smiled and shook his head. "Ten days after your retirement retreat the army won't even remember your name." He got up and brushed off the seat of his pants. "I want the detail mounted and ready to leave at seven, sergeant. Rations for five days and regular ammunition issue."

He stood there while Arness walked away, and he wondered how wise it had been to lay it on the line that way. Whether he liked Arness or not, he needed him; an officer was nothing without his sergeant, next to helpless. Yet it made Travis angry when an enlisted man used that as a wedge to get his own way. Somehow, and he didn't know how, he would have to win Arness over. Or get rid of him entirely. But that would look bad, for himself and Arness; just because they didn't get along was no reason to blot his record.

The whole thing irritated and upset him; he hated a bad start, and this was not good. Well, it would take time and some thinking out. He had no intention of making a hasty decision.

He thought about going to bed, but it was too early, and he wouldn't be able to sleep anyway. Activity was what he needed, something to take his mind off his problems, and he thought about going to the Summers house. He could test the cordiality of his welcome, and if it was cool, he could say that his bandage was too tight and that he'd like it changed.

And if it wasn't cool? He found that possibility rather pleasant. He felt the need of something pleasant to take his mind off Arness.

As he walked along the dark street he told himself that he was being foolish going to the doctor's house on the off chance that he would see Hope Randall. But he'd always been pretty foolish where attractive girls were concerned, and he saw no reason to change now.

A lamp was lit in the parlor, though the rest of the house was dark. He thought of turning around and going back, but it wasn't in his nature to turn back from the things he started. As he stepped on the porch he realized that someone was sitting there.

"Doctor Summers?"

"He's at a cattlemen's meeting at the hotel," Hope said. "You can wait for him, if you like. I was just going to have some lemonade. You'd like some, wouldn't you?"

He was going to say that he would, but she got up and went into the house, returning a moment later with a pitcher and glasses. "It certainly was hot today, wasn't it? A hundred and three by the thermometer." She handed him a glass and he perched on the porch railing so he faced her. The light was faint here, just enough to break the solidness of night.

"The cattlemen called the meeting as soon as they heard you recovered those two horses from the Rinks."

"I don't get the connection," Travis said.

"Why, it's simple. You got the horses back, and it's been a long time since anything was recovered from the homesteaders. They steal all the time from the cattlemen, but with Owen Gates working for Wrigley, and Ben sympathizing—I suppose I shouldn't have said that." Then she shrugged. "But you're bright enough to have figured it out anyway. You can't blame Ben, Mr. Travis; he wants to marry Grace Beaumont."

"That's a reason?"

She laughed. "That did sound a little disjointed, didn't it? She and her husband tried dry-farming. Hard work killed him, then she came to town. It's natural for Ben to feel as he does, being in love with her. You certainly don't talk much, do you?"

"Not when it means interrupting," he said.

"All right," she said, laughing. "So I chatter. My mother chattered, and Aunt Clara did too. She lived with us, but she never married. And it was a shame too. She was a wonderful cook. But father said she would have talked a man into his grave. What's your first name?"

"Jeff," he said. "And you're never going to be an old maid, Hope."

She laughed musically. "Well, I'm glad to hear that. I guess it wouldn't matter anyway, but people make such a thing of it, as if it was some secret sin, and they spend all their time trying to figure out what's wrong with you that you couldn't get a man. What made you go into the army? Were you unhappy at home?"

He shook his head helplessly. "You make good lemonade, Hope. Where did you get the ice to cool it?"

"Oh, there isn't any ice," she said. "You wrap the pitcher in a cloth, set it in a pan, then saturate the cloth with ether. It evaporates so rapidly that it makes the pitcher cold."

"A scientist," he said, jokingly. "My respect increases by the moment." He raised his glass in salute. "To cool lemonade on the front porch. I grew up on a front porch, you know. It was just a straight line to the cookie jar, which mother always hid in the hall closet. Cookies were precious in my family. She never knew that I knew where it was."

"I'll make some cookies if you like."

He quickly put out his hand, as though expecting her to leap up and make them that very moment. She laughed and said, "I meant the day after tomorrow."

"Could you make it next week? I'm going to take a patrol to the reservation." He took out his watch and looked at it. "I've overstayed my welcome. Thank you for the talk. I'll be back for the cookies."

"Cinnamon or sugar?"

"Do you know how to make gingersnaps?"

"Yes." She offered her hand and he took it and bowed gallantly and touched his lips to it in a most courtly, continental manner.

He whistled softly as he walked back to the barracks, and when he took off his boots, getting ready for bed, he stopped and stared at the wall for a moment, then laughed and shook his head. He was still smiling when he turned out the lamp and squirmed to find a comfortable sleeping position.

Before ten o'clock Lieutenant Jefferson Travis, trailed by Sergeant Arness and fourteen troopers, splashed across the river north of Spanish Spring, and approached Regan's trading post, a low, log building nestled in a cottonwood grove. Regan heard their approach and came out as they dismounted in his yard. A trooper took charge of the horses while the detail rested.

Regan was a man of indeterminable age. His place was a catchall for trading with the Indians, and his store and yard as untidy as he was. Regan shaved when he thought about it, which wasn't often, and he made it a practice to wear his shirt and pants until they became too dirty even for him to bear, then he threw them away, about once a year, and put on new ones. It probably never occurred to him to bathe first. There was a wild varmint odor about him and the trading post, and Travis wrinkled his nose in distaste as he stepped inside.

"I guess you be the new officer," Regan said, smiling, offering his hand. "Howdy, Ben. Ain't seen you for a month. Whiskey inside, if you want it."

Travis glanced at Arness and found the man's face quite red. "No, Mr. Regan, the sergeant isn't accepting gratuities today. Let me see your government permit to operate this boar's nest."

This insulted Regan. "I ain't had any complaints. Ask the Indian agent."

"I will," Travis said. "Let's see the papers."

Regan could not immediately find his trading permit. He searched through old cigar boxes under the counter, then finally came up with it. Travis looked at it and found that the yearly endorsements were there, and that it had been signed by the commander at Fort Dodge.

"That satisfy you?" Regan asked. He was a wizened man, like an ancient piece of leather, toughened rather than weakened by age. His hair was long and he wore a pistol in a hip holster.

"Don't you ever clean this place up?" Travis asked.

"What for? The Injuns don't mind a little dirt." He squinted at Jefferson Travis. "For a kid, you're pecky as hell, ain't you? What you want to do, get promoted the first year?" He scrubbed a hand across his dirty face. "Goddamn, ain't it bad enough for a man to try to make an honest livin' without the army pokin' around? I got a gov'mint license, sonny. I'm as important as you."

"Do you keep records?" Travis asked.

"Sure I keep records. An officer from Fort Dodge

comes here every three months and checks 'em. What about it?"

"I'll take a look at them," Travis said and watched the contrariness come into Regan's face. "If you'd like, Mr. Regan, I can find them myself."

"Oh, hell, I'll get 'em," Regan said. He planked some books on the counter and looked sourly at Jefferson Travis. "But sonny, I'm sure going to write Fort Dodge about this; they'll have your ass for foolin' with me."

"Yes, you do that," Travis said. "Sergeant, would you see that a noon camp is established in the grove. Then come back in here."

"Yes, sir." He detected frost in Travis' voice and knew that he was responsible for its being there. Travis wasn't saying anything now, but Arness knew it would come later.

The complete account of Regan's trading was there, only Travis had another word for it: cheating. Two knives, some beads and a yard of cloth for one buffalo robe; he thought this was the most outrageous swindle he had ever heard of, yet that seemed to be the going rate. Regan's trading was not confined to Indians; he also bought horses from time to time, and cattle, and the name of every settler within a thirty-mile radius was listed there, and the price paid for the merchandise.

Travis was a little surprised at the clear picture the records painted. He was struck right away with the oddness of all the horses being described as fifteen hands high, solid-colored, gelding; this must be army stock, bought by Regan and sold through some Dodge City contact. And surely the officer who checked these books saw this, or was totally blind.

When Arness came back inside, Travis looked pointedly at Regan until the man moved away. Then he spoke quietly, "Sergeant, have you lost any horses this past year?"

"Yes, sir. Three." He looked steadily at Travis. "I made a report of it, and a search."

"With your eyes closed?" Travis pointed to the entries. "How much would you bet that those aren't army mounts, sergeant?" He snapped the ledger closed. "Haven't you seen anything, sergeant?"

"Now don't start blaming me, sir," Arness said. "Sure,

203

I knew Regan bought a few horses, but that never gave me the right to dispute the officers from Fort Dodge." He wiped his mouth with his hand and shifted his feet. "And if you've got any sense, you're not going to make a big fuss over this either. Major Griswald signed those ledgers, and there's one hell of a lot of difference in authority between a second lieutenant and a major." He reached out and tapped Lieutenant Travis on the chest. "Dodge is headquarters for the buffalo hunters. And the officers at Fort Dodge know what side their bread's buttered on. Ah, sir, you're going to get yourself busted right out of the army before you get started. What do you expect, sir, everybody to live by the Golden Rule? There ain't a man in a hundred miles who don't have an ax to grind. You'd better start sharpening your own, sir."

"Which faction would you suggest I join, sergeant? You seem to favor several."

"I've never seen a man so pigheaded," Arness snapped. "All right, do as you damned please. You will anyway."

"Thank you for seeing it," Travis said softly. "Get the detail mounted, sergeant. We're going on to the reservation headquarters."

Arness smiled with relief. "That's more like it, sir. Hell, what good would it do to make a fuss about Regan; they'd just put somebody else here as crooked as he is."

"That's true," Travis said. "That's why I'm going to padlock the place and confiscate the records. Will you see that Corporal Busik attends to it?"

Arness was too furious to answer; he stomped out and a moment later Regan came in, anger staining his dark cheeks.

"You can't close me!"

"I'll give you five minutes to gather your personal belongings," Travis told him. "You can make your complaints at Fort Dodge."

"And you can damned sure bet I will!" Regan shouted, and began to throw a bedroll together.

Travis went outside just as a trooper called from the river crossing, and he looked that way; four mounted men were splashing across. They came directly toward Regan's yard and this gave him a moment to study them. They were sun-browned men, and all of them wore suits and wide hats, spike-heeled boots with Mexican rowel spurs and pistols on their hips; the cattleman stamp was on them.

They drew up in a swirl of dust and dismounted. One of them said, "I'm Janeway, Circle T. This is Hodges, Rider, and Butram. We heard you pulled out early this morning and hoped we'd catch you."

"Well, you have, gentlemen," Travis said. Corporal Busik went around Regan's place, locking the doors while two other troopers nailed boards over the windows.

"You closing him?" Janeway asked. Then he laughed and slapped his side and turned to the others. "By God, it's about time, ain't it?" He looked again at Travis. "Well, I always said we'd get something done if an officer took over. Every damned year there's a hundred head of beef crossing that river with homesteaders right behind them. I'll bet we wrote a dozen letters to the army asking them to do something about those thieves, and it looks like we're finally getting results."

"I wasn't aware that you had written letters," Travis said. "And as far as closing Mr. Regan, I did so for military reasons."

Janeway looked disappointed and puzzled. "Well, now, wait a minute. From the way you handled the Rinks, we thought—" He looked at his friends. "I guess we were wrong."

"I haven't chosen a side," Travis said. "And gentlemen, I don't intend to. Why don't you try to get along with the settlers?"

"What?" Janeway reared back. "Sonny, every waterhole they squat around is a waterhole we can no longer use. By God, if it gets much worse we're going to get up a Winchester and hemp party!"

"If you do that, Mr. Janeway, the army will come after you and hang you."

"Let's get out of here," Hodges said. "We're wasting our time." They stepped into their saddles, and Hodges said, "I can see how it is, sonny. It figures that you'd be more ambitious than Ben. We could never count on him because of the Beaumont woman. Not that way with you though, is it? You'll side with the money, the buffalo hunters and the bunch at Fort Dodge."

"Good day, gentlemen," Travis said with careful civility.

Janeway snapped, "Well, you don't deny it. I give you

credit for that." He wheeled his horse then and headed for the crossing, the others right behind him.

Regan was saddling a horse when Travis mounted his detail and swung to the northwest toward the Indian reservation headquarters. On the hour they paused to dismount and walk the horses, and every two hours there was a fifteen minute halt for housekeeping. It was during this time that Jefferson Travis sat down beside Arness.

"I was too generous with you last night at the barracks, sergeant. I offered you a chance to get along. If I had any sense I'd send a dispatch to Fort Winthrop and have you recalled." He studied Arness. "And if you want to know the truth of it, sergeant, I wouldn't miss you a damned bit. It would be a relief to let some other officer wear you around his neck."

"I figured you'd duck behind that little gold bar when it got tough," Arness said softly, so that no one else heard.

"What did you do," Travis asked, "make a bet on it?" He got up and took off his neckerchief, throwing it on the ground. "No one has ever really taught you respect, sergeant. I'm not talking about respect for a man, but for rank. You've never admitted that Congress makes the officers, not Ben Arness." He slipped out of his shirt and dropped it to the ground, and a trooper saw him and nudged another, and this went on until they were all watching. Unbuckling his belt, Travis lowered pistol, saber, and bullet pouch to the ground. "Do you know what's eating you? You secretly detest all officers and wish the army could get along without them. Or perhaps you want to play the old army game of hiding behind your stripes. Enlisted men do that, sergeant. When they're alone with an officer, they get insulting with their mouths, and other times they just fool around on the fringe of insubordination, or get balky in the ranks. You know I could get court-martialed for offering to fight an enlisted man, but that would be better than listening to any more of your jibes." He pointed to his shirt. "The rank's there, sergeant. What are you going to do about it?"

One of the men said, "Why don't you take him, Ben? He's beggin' for it."

Travis wasn't sure whether this swung Arness or whether he'd decided before the man spoke; anyway he

206

began to peel off his shirt and sidearms. "Did you take boxing lessons at the Academy, sir? You'll need 'em."

"A little," Travis said. "But I was captain of the wrestling team for two years."

"That's nice," Arness said, and swung, and in the blow was all his resentment and pent-up hostility. Travis twisted and the fist bounced off his shoulder, then he chopped a blow to Arness' mouth and sent him staggering back, feet pawing the grass for purchase. Travis hadn't hit him hard, but he'd hit fast; the fist had just flicked out and found the target.

The first blood brought caution to Arness, then he whirled in, arms windmilling. Travis stood like a rooted tree until the last moment, then he whipped aside, blocked Arness' rush with an out-thrust foot and sent him sprawling.

He got up quickly and eyed Travis, then he came in low and bull-rushed the slender young man. He hooked Travis under the heart and in the face, knocking him to one side so that Travis had to stagger to catch his balance. He kicked and missed, then Travis got in close, his arms embracing Ben Arness. There was a flick of his hip and Arness sailed to the dust and rolled away.

Suddenly Travis altered his tactics and went for Arness as soon as he came erect. He caught an arm, twisted it, put his shoulder in place, and flipped Arness into the air. A bomb of dust arose when Arness struck, and he grunted as the breath was all but knocked from him. This time Travis fell on him and there was a moment of snake thrashing.

This stopped suddenly and Arness gave an agonized cry. Travis had one hand in his hair, cruelly pulling his head back. One of Arness' arms was brutally twisted behind his back, securely locked; he was held in a posture of pain, and quite calmly Jefferson Travis said, "We settle it now, sergeant. Twenty-seven years of mule stubbornness is going to go. Either I command or you do, and I know which it's going to be, but I want you to say it. I want you to know it and live with it."

He applied pressure and Arness groaned loudly, then between ragged breaths he said, "You do—sir."

He released Arness and turned to his clothes and started to put them on. The troopers were silent, and he fully understood why. They did not applaud his victory; rather they resented it, for he had taken a man they had admired and trusted and humbled him. And Arness could only genuinely hate him for it. The only one he had proved anything to was himself, and he wondered now if it had really been necessary. He really didn't need Ben Arness' scalp to be a man.

5

Travis' destination was the Indian reservation, and he made a slow night march toward it. He rode at the head of the column, jumping jack rabbits from the brush and startling small game. A wind came up which helped to blow the dust they raised away from them, and after three hours of this he ordered a two-hour rest.

Lieutenant Jefferson Travis then spent a great deal of time in soul-searching introspection. He knew that only time would correct his youth, but he could not always reconcile himself to patience. Since beginning his military career, he had tried only to obey the dictates of his conscience and the inflexible commandments of Army regulations, and in this respect he felt that he had done tolerably well. But his relationship with Sergeant Arness was badly awry, and he had succeeded in aggravating two of the factions wrestling for dominance in his district. None of this would set well with Major Deacon, but thinking about it, Travis decided he could not afford to feel concerned over this. To choose a side, a man had to feel that all the right was on one side and all the wrong on the other, but he couldn't see any such clear-cut division in this instance. He could not really blame the settlers for stealing since he knew how desperately poor they were, but still he recognized his responsibility to curtail this thievery.

As far as the sergeant and Major Deacon were concerned, he did not feel compelled to conform to their formula of a typical career officer, and perhaps, Travis reasoned, this was his biggest mistake. Perhaps he should try to attain this peculiar mental attitude, this state of aloof detachment which seemed to be necessary to get him through his first tour of duty with the least amount of unpleasantness, and if by such neglect he left behind certain loose ends, the next officer, who might be more seasoned, would take care of them.

The detail made an early morning approach to the agency headquarters, passing east of the sprawling Indian village. Nestled in a hollow, with trees and a spring, headquarters was a long adobe with a scattering of outbuildings. A flagpole marked the agent's office, and as Travis brought his detail closer he saw an army escort wagon and some cavalry mounts tied by the stable. A half-dozen soldiers lounged in the shade of the blacksmith shop, watching as Travis dismounted his troop and turned it over to Ben Arness.

Mr. Brewer, the agent, came out as Travis stepped to the porch. He was a short, scholarly man in his middle thirties, and in spite of the heat he wore a dark suit with a vest under the coat. His handshake was perfunctory; he presented only a surface politeness and from this Travis deducted that Mr. Brewer had no love for the army, which was natural since he represented the Interior Department. Now he said, apparently amiably, "Come inside. It's cooler there." From the man's manner, Travis suspected that he wasn't particularly well suited to this job, but that he tried to do what was expected of him, probably writing letters to Washington begging for more help, more money, and less army interference. And Travis saw with detached clarity what Mr. Brewer did not see at all: that he was a man destined to lose. The taxpayers would always accuse him of graft, the army would accuse him of ignorance, and his own superiors, bowing to the policy of the moment, would accuse him of incompetence. Meanwhile, the Indians would take his handouts as long as they lasted, and in the end desert him, for they wasted no loyalty on white men.

Travis looked around the pleasant room, thinking that Brewer had it nice. There were Mexican rugs on the floor, drapes at the windows, and substantial furniture, better than most colonels found in Quarters "A." There were many Indian artifacts. Evidently Brewer was a collector, taking pleasure in the primitive craft of the people around him.

"Major Griswald is here from Fort Dodge," Brewer said. "He's in my office. Would you care for some wine?" He opened a door and ushered Travis in ahead of him. Griswald was sorting through some papers; he looked around, saw Travis, then put the papers aside and stood up. He was a large man, with a rather flat face and a dense mustache, clipped short. His eyes were wide spaced and bland.

"Travis, from Spanish Spring?" Griswald asked. "This meeting is unexpected. I hope there's no trouble. Goes in the report, you know."

"Just getting familiar with the territory, sir." He offered his hand. "Glad to meet you, sir."

Mr. Brewer was closing his liquor cabinet; he had three glasses of wine on a small silver tray. "Won't you sit down, Mr. Travis." He folded his hands together and looked from one to the other. "Well," he said, "I don't usually have so much company."

"Mr. Travis," Griswald said, "I don't want you to think I'm infringing on your territory by being here. As it happened, Mr. Brewer and I met briefly last year in St. Louis, and every time I go south to Regan's crossing, I always stop and visit." He laughed softly. "You're obviously new to the army, Mr. Travis, but one thing we never do is to mind another officer's duty. I take it you crossed at Regan's."

"Yes, sir," Travis said. "However, I might save you the trouble of the ride. I imagine he's now headed for Fort Dodge, sir. You see, I closed his place because he was buying stolen army horses."

Major Andrew Griswald had been sipping his wine; he stopped but still held the glass to his lips. He looked at Jefferson Travis as though he had not really seen him before, then he put the glass aside. "Did I understand you correctly, Mr. Travis?"

"I'm sure you did, sir. The army has been losing horses from time to time, and everyone seems to be aware that the settlers are taking them to sell rather than returning them to the army. I recovered two horses myself before they could be sold, and I found entries in Regan's books showing that he'd bought six this past year. And so it will go in *my* report."

"By God," Griswald snapped, "you have a cool manner, I must say. I'm going to write to your commanding officer about this, Mr. Travis. As far as the army is concerned, Jack Regan is an honest man, and I consider your action in this matter quite impertinent." He slapped his hands together in exasperation. "Dammit, I've personally inspected his accounts and in my opinion they are quite legitimate. And I'm not going to alter my opinion, regardless of what you may think." He calmed himself by drinking the rest of his wine. "Mr. Travis, you're new to the army. Perhaps you didn't realize when you closed Regan that you would place the military in an embarrassing position."

"On the contrary, I gave it every consideration, major. In fact, sir, Regan threatened me at some length, claiming friends in high places." He glanced at Brewer. "This is good wine."

"Just one of the social graces I've tried to preserve," Brewer said wistfully. "It's difficult to remain civilized out here. And it's not often I entertain men who appreciate the good things." His anxious expression showed that he hoped his guests would find a more amiable topic.

"Hang your social fetishes, Brewer!" Griswald snapped ungraciously. He got up and walked around the room, then went to the window and stood there, looking into the yard, and beyond, to the Indian camp. "Mr. Travis, you seem to be a sensible young man. I don't want to have to write a report in rebuttal that will affect your future. Do you follow me?"

"Yes, sir," Travis said.

Griswald turned and looked with some irritation at Brewer. "Aren't you having a beef issue tomorrow? We don't want to detain you from your duties."

"Well, I have nothing—" Brewer stopped, then nodded. He was a gentle man, preferring to absorb rudeness rather than create more unpleasantness. "Of course, major. You'll stay for supper this evening, won't you, Mr. Travis?"

He went out and closed the door, and Griswald said, "Stupid ass! He'd be more at home serving tea in a parlor instead of beef to the Indians. God knows why the Department sends men like that out here." Then he turned to his chair and sat down. "Army business, Mr. Travis, is best talked over among army men." He brought out a cigar case and offered one. "Have you been fighting, Mr. Travis? There are several bruises on your face. Well, it's no matter. Not in my jurisdiction." He shook his finger at Travis. "That's a very important point, sir: jurisdiction. In spite of its proximity to Spanish Spring, Regan's trading post is in *my* jurisdiction, while the agency here is in yours. I suppose I could make sense of it, but I'm not being paid to. Ah, well, you'll hear your share of complaints, Mr. Travis. And be sure to note them very carefully, then forget them. There isn't a time that I come here when Brewer doesn't get on me about the buffalo hunters taking over the Indians' grassland and hunting ground. How can you argue with him? It's true, the Indians were pushed back, and some say it's unjust, but say what you will, *we* brought roads and towns. It's progress, Mr. Travis. Buffalo hides built Dodge City and they're paying for the railroad now." He tapped ash from his cigar. "What do the Indians pay for? Nothing! They cost money. And the sod-busters?" He chuckled. "Mr. Travis, if you went around and gathered up all the money they have, it wouldn't stake you to a good Dodge City poker game. Are you beginning to understand what I'm talking about, Mr. Travis?"

"Yes, sir," Travis said. "It's quite clear. The homesteaders have to go because they're poor, and the Indians because they're in the way. It's a very defined policy, sir. Hardly fair, but well defined."

Major Andrew Griswald frowned. "You have a damned blunt tongue, Mr. Travis. I'm sure the general wouldn't put it quite like that, even in the company of his closest associates. You apparently haven't learned how to get along in the army, and I advise you to correct that immediately." He shifted in his chair and crossed his legs. "I assume we can consider the matter of Jack Regan closed? I'll send him back and you can strike the lock off the door."

"Very well, sir," Travis said stiffly. "But if he buys another stolen horse, or a rustled steer, I'll have him thrown in jail."

Brewer came back into the room before the major could explode. Griswald clamped his cigar between his teeth and said, "I'll see you at supper, Travis." His boots thudded on the porch, then he crossed the yard to the spring.

"He's upset very easily," Brewer said, regretfully. "I'm afraid you've disturbed him, Mr. Travis." Then, evidently seeking a more pleasant topic, he said politely, "Will you stay for the beef issue tomorrow? It's quite a barbaric spectacle; the Indians like to turn it into a hunt."

"Where do you buy your beef?"

Brewer shrugged. "Where I can get it. The cattlemen around Spanish Spring mostly, when the price is reasonable. Some of the settlers bring in a few head now and then. Never more than four or five. I'm buying from them tomorrow."

"Stolen stock, Mr. Brewer?"

"I'm not very well informed on brands, Mr. Travis."

"I see. Well, I can hardly expect that you've required a bill of sale."

"You have quarters next to mine," Brewer said evasively. "I really would like to talk to you. It's damned lonely out here, with only a trunk full of books, and the memory of a pleasant life I'll likely never resume."

"Perhaps you should have a wife," Travis suggested.

"No decent woman could bear this life," he said. He pointed to a wall map with isolated pins thrust into it. "Those are settlers' places. I've been to a few. Do you know that some of them live in caves, Mr. Travis? I've never seen such poverty. I couldn't live that way. No, there are certain amenities a man must observe, or stop being a man."

Privately Travis doubted that Brewer would ever know the meaning of the word. He wondered what weird circumstances had brought this fussy wretch out to Kansas as Indian agent. Yet, Brewer was not really corrupt or venal. Within his own pathetic limitations he evidently tried to do the best job he could. Travis was conscious of feeling both pity and impatience. Embarrassed, he rose and put on his kepi.

"Well, I'd better be off, Mr. Brewer. Many thanks for the hospitality."

The agent ducked his head. "Supper's at eight. The sun's down then and the flies aren't so thick." He paused, then added, "And we always had supper at eight at home. A man mustn't forget those things, you know."

213

Lieutenant Travis made a polite sound of agreement and departed to conduct an impromptu inspection of his men and mounts. He found everything in order. Arness was not going to be caught that way. The sergeant spoke to him, but only when asked a question, and he limped a little, suffering from the aftereffects of the fight.

That evening, at supper, Travis tried to hold up his end of the conversation; Major Griswald was inclined to silence and excused himself early, saying that he wanted to start back to Dodge right away. His tone implied that this would have considerable significance for Jefferson Travis' future, but the young officer refused to show concern.

Brewer kept him up until nearly midnight, recounting his boyhood experiences in Pennsylvania, and his present ambitions. He wanted a career in politics, but listening to him, Travis knew that he was both too sincere and too ineffectual. Brewer's ambitions had the texture of impossible dreams. Finally, when the wine bottle was empty and the lamp nearly out of coal oil, Brewer was ready to retire. Travis was already half asleep.

Before dawn, Jefferson Travis woke to the husk of the wind and got up without lighting the lamp. The minute he stepped outside he smelled the rain and knew it wouldn't be long in coming. He supposed this was the kind of weather a man had to get used to in this country, dry as a week-old cake one day and a regular gully-buster the next. He turned back inside to finish dressing and by the time he was finnished the first blast hit the building.

The rain would turn the prairie into a morass, especially in the agency yard, where the dust was four inches thick. Today's beef issue would be a filthy business.

Travis ate breakfast with Brewer, then went out on the porch to watch the beef issue begin. In all, he estimated that there were five hundred Indians clustered about, away from the yard, most of them mounted and waiting with spears or bow and arrow. The women and children made a noisy knot apart from the men; they milled about calling to the children, and the dog pack, an integral part of Indian life, ran yipping among the gathered cattle, trying to spook them.

The agency employees had set up chair and tables and kept long lists of names handy. When a name was called out, a steer was released from the small herd, driven into a run, then chased and killed as buffalo were killed. The rain made a mess of the yard, and after the twentieth steer had been slaughtered the stench of blood and manure became almost unbearable. After each Indian made his kill, the women rushed out and began butchering on the spot, and soon the yard was dotted with kneeling women, covered with blood and mud, and the newly freed cattle were suffering for a place to run.

Now and then an Indian would dash through carelessly, bowling some woman over, and her man would get all steamed up about it, and then a fight would start.

Travis was paying more attention to the "cowboys" than the slaughter. Finally he stepped off the porch, splashed to the stable and got his horse. Mounted, his poncho spread about him, he rode over to where the herd was being held. As he approached, he noticed that the men moved away slightly as though he had some communicable disease and they were afraid of catching it. There was none of the "cattleman" look about them; they would have appeared more natural with hoes in their hands.

"I'm Lieutenant Travis, commanding the Spanish Spring detail," he said, facing two men. "Are these your cattle?"

"They be," one of them said. His open buckskin shirt revealed dirty underwear. Long hair fell to his shoulders in an unwashed, uncombed tangle, and one cheek was fat with a cud of tobacco. "I'm Bonner. Got a place out there." He pointed in a southeasterly direction. "Raised these cattle myself." He pawed at the rain running down his face.

Travis eased away from them and rode gingerly around the small bunch; there were no more than twenty-five steers left. He was not familiar with brands, or the art of blotting, but he could recognize crude work when he saw it. Some wore Janeway's brand; the Circle T was now in a slightly altered form. There were several other brands which he suspected belonged to Janeway's friends.

Returning to Bonner, who sat his horse, suspicious and sullen, Travis said, "Naturally you include a bill of sale with the cattle to prove ownership."

"Never have before," Bonner said flatly. "See no need

to now." He waved his hand and the other four men came over. "Sonny here don't think we own these steers."

They looked at each other and laughed, and Bonner stopped wiping his face long enough to bring a rifle from the saddle scabbard and mop water from the breech. This wasn't much of a threat by itself, but in light of what Travis had seen, it was strong enough.

"I'll tell you what I'm going to do," Jefferson Travis said. "I'm going to turn and ride back to the reservation building. And when I get there, Bonner, I'll expect you to come forward and present a bill of sale." He looked directly at the man, his expression flat, his smooth cheeks pulled tightly against the bones. "You know where you got the cattle, and I suspect I know too. But if you get the idea that a bullet in my back is going to solve anything, remember that I have fourteen men here who won't hesitate to kill you."

"What are you makin' such a fuss about?" Bonner demanded. "Jesus Christ, we've been sellin' cattle here for two years, and there ain't been any fuss." He pawed at his rain streaked face again. "All right, all right, we picked up the steers; they was strays. Now are you satisfied?"

"Branded strays, Bonner?" Travis wheeled his horse and rode back to the headquarters building. He saw Sergeant Ben Arness lounging there and snapped, "Mount the troop! You see those steers over there? I want them confiscated and driven back to Spanish Spring."

This time Arness offered no argument. "Yes, sir," he said resignedly, and left the porch to call for Corporal Busik, who was in the stable with the detail.

Brewer, who had heard Travis' order, detached himself from his helpers. "What are you going to do? What was that you said, Mr. Travis?"

"Brewer, you know some of these cattle are stolen, don't you?"

"I don't know anything," Brewer said, "except that the Indians have to be given a beef ration and I can't afford to pay Dodge City prices, and that's what those bandits around Spanish Spring want for their steers." He took Travis by the arm and his voice took on a pleading tone. "I'm asking you to be reasonable, Mr. Travis. These Indians won't understand why you are impounding the cattle. What are you trying to do to me? Destroy me? Put

216

an Indian uprising in my lap? In the name of heaven, man, these Indians have teen getting free meat for so long they've lost the ambition to do for themselves. Once a month they get a steer, they expect a steer, and if they don't get it——"

"For God's sake, stop pulling at my sleeve!" Travis snapped. Brewer jerked his hands away as though the sleeve had suddenly turned hot. "Why do you assume that I'm picking on you, Mr. Brewer? I'm not blaming you for doing the best you can, but there has to be a line drawn somewhere." He reached out and tapped Brewer on the chest. "Buy all the stolen beef you want, but get a signed bill of sale. That way, if a cattleman complains, you've put yourself in the clear, and some rustler's neck in a rope."

"Well, I'll do it next time!" Brewer protested. "I've got almost thirty families here waiting for their beef issue and now you tell me you're confiscating the herd!" He put his hand to his face and it was trembling. "What am I to do, Mr. Travis? What am I going to do with these people?" His voice was edged with pain.

"I'm sorry, Mr, Brewer," Travis said, and remounted; his detail was forming in the muddy yard and the Indians were beginning to grumble because the rationing had stopped.

"Form on me, a line abreast," Travis said. "Carbines at the ready."

They came up on him, a perfect formation, and he walked them across the muddy interval to where Bonner and his men waited. When Travis was still fifty yards away, Bonner made his decision and bolted; the others followed him and Travis motioned for Arness and the others to round up the stock with the blotted brands.

He wheeled about and returned to headquarters, where half a hundred Indians stood in the rain, yelling, shaking their fists at Brewer, who was arguing with hysterical futility, his yammering drowned in the angry shouting of the crowd. When Travis pushed boldly through and gained the porch, Brewer turned on him. "There! Here's the man who took your cattle! Talk to *him!* Tell *him* about it!"

The Indians had a leader; he stepped forward and announced that he was named Limping Deer. Someone had once mentioned to Travis that the fury in an Indian's face always centered in the eyes; he saw now that this was true. The man looked like a bronze casting ready to be placed in the hallway of a public library, the image of savage pride trampled.

"I will speak for my people," Limping Deer said. "What right have you to steal our cattle? You stole our land, made war on us. Now we will not see our food taken!" He waved his arms wildly. "All white men are liars, thieves! You will give us the cattle!"

"There will be more cattle," Travis said. "It will only be a few days, a week. You can wait. You won't starve."

"Limping Deer does not wait. He will have cattle today!"

"You will wait!" Travis said sternly. "I do not bargain with you, Limping Deer. It is the white man's law under which you must live, and it is my law you will obey now. These cattle are being returned to the men who own them. Other cattle will be brought to you. Now you will wait, and there will be no trouble over this!"

The Indian's face tightened while he raised his fist as though to strike. And suddenly Travis was mad with a blind anger at the whole impossibly tangled mess. He grabbed the Indian's wrist, twisted painfully, and threw him flat on his back. His voice was filled with fury as he said, "Now you listen to me, you stinking savage! You camp on the agency door so you won't miss anything that's free, but you earn none of it! You want the agent to feed you, to take care of you, and when he does not, you curse him! Now the United States Army has spoken and if you have any brains in your head you'll listen carefully! You take your shouting friends and go to your homes, and when more cattle come, you'll get them!" All the time he talked he kept his knee pressed against Limping Deer's throat, disgracing him before his people, humbling him as he had never been humbled before. Then Travis released him and turned his back on him. He took Brewer by the arm and pulled him to one side. "Now get this straight, Mr. Brewer, I'm going to Spanish Spring to talk to the cattlemen about a fair price for their beef, a price that you should pay." Brewer opened his mouth to say something, but Travis cut him off. "I'm going to find out how much a steer will bring in Dodge City, and how much it costs to drive there. That amount I think should be deducted by the cattlemen when they sell here. Now before you start crying that it's too high, it might pay you to remember that it won't be so easy to put leftover dollars in your pocket as it used to be. Good day, Mr. Brewer. I'll see you in about a week."

He turned away from the man, stepped off the porch and rammed his way through the angry Indians and went into the saddle. Without a backward look, he rode off in the pouring rain to catch up with his detail and the recovered cattle, now a mile away from the reservation.

6

The detail traveled southeastward in the slanting rain, pushing the small herd before them. In an hour the gray smudge of sky blotted out the reservation buildings, wiped them away as though erased from a blackboard. Even with the ponchos it was impossible to keep dry. Campaign hats funneled water down collars, and before they had traveled five miles, each man rode a soggy saddle and longed for a scorching sun to dry him out.

This came in the afternoon, when the clouds parted and steam began to rise from the sodden earth. There was considerable water running off; each depression held a rushing, muddy torrent, and the buffalo wallows filled rapidly.

Since the fight, Ben Arness had not spoken to Travis except when he had to, and on the march back he traded places with Corporal Busik, who now sided Travis at the head of the detail. Busik was a dark-complected man, a career soldier who did what he was told and never asked questions. He had a melon-shaped face and thick lips, and constantly chewed cut-plug tobacco.

Now he said conversationally, "In another twenty days, sir, the buffalo will be migrating. They move north and south every year, spring and fall." He made a sweeping gesture with his hand to include the whole prairie. "This time next week you'll see buffalo hunter camps all over. You think the slaughter at the agency was something, wait 'til you see the buffalo hunt. The prairie takes on a horrible stink; the hunters just take the hides and leave the carcasses to rot. The Indians go a little crazy then; they believe it's a sin to waste anything, even the bones. They hate the hunters and the hunters hate the Indians. You can smell trouble in the air like woodsmoke." He took off his hat and wiped his forehead, then put it back on again. "The Indians make war talk and the drums go all night and they put on paint, but what can they do? They know how far a buffalo rifle will shoot and that six hunters, holed up in a wallow, can hold off a hundred Indians. But a few always break away from the reservation and try their luck, sir. And they get killed and everyone raises hell. But how can you stop 'em?"

Jefferson Travis considered this for a while, then said, "When the hunters start killing buffalo, corporal, we'll be around."

Busik shrugged his heavy shoulders. "You can't stop much with fourteen men, sir."

"No, I suppose not, but we're going to try this year."

The cattle were turned into the barracks compound and a two-man guard was placed over them. Two more troopers were dispatched to notify the cattlemen and General Thomas C. Wrigley; Travis felt certain that the general would want to attend the meeting if only to defend the rights of his homesteaders.

With a few hours to kill before his invited guests gathered, Travis had his bath and shave and changed into clean clothes. He walked to the express office to see if any dispatches had arrived for him; there were none, and he was vastly relieved, for the best news right now was no news at all. When Major Deacon received all the threatened complaints about his new officer, he would be foaming at the mouth and penning a bitter letter, and Travis figured that until he saw it he could carry on in his own way, as he saw fit.

Janeway arrived first and came directly to Travis' office. He tied his horse in front and came across the porch, pausing in the open doorway. The daylight was fading and Travis was lighting the lamp; without turning to see who it was, he said, "Come in and sit down."

"Thank you," Janeway said. He unbuttoned his coat and shifted his pistol holster around to a more comfortable position. Travis looked at him for a moment and then Janeway said, "I guess I owe you an apology, lieutenant."

"You don't owe me a thing, Mr. Janeway," Travis said. "Where are your friends?"

"One of your soldiers stopped at my place and I came right on in," he said. "The others will be along. How many head did you save?"

"Twenty-five. The Indians got at least that many more."

"You haven't told me yet who was selling my cattle."

"No, I haven't," Travis said softly. "And all the steers aren't yours. There are other brands mixed in."

"Let's not split hairs—" He craned his neck and looked out the door as General Wrigley drove into the yard. "That's all we need, an unreconstructed Rebel. How the devil did he get wind of this?"

"I invited him," Travis said, and went out to greet Wrigley. "Come on inside, general. You're early, but I imagine we can find some way to pass the time."

Wrigley was in a peckish humor; he grunted something unintelligible to Travis and stomped inside. Then he saw Janeway sitting there and his mustache bristled as his lips settled in a disapproving line.

"I can wait outside," Wrigley snapped.

"Never mind," Janeway said, rising. *"I'll* wait outside."

"Why don't you both sit down?" Travis asked. "After all, you're here about a problem that concerns us all."

They sat down, on opposite sides of the room. Travis lit a cigar and studied them briefly. Wrigley kept fidgeting with his gold watch chain and casting oblique glances at Janeway, who crossed one leg over the other and studied the stitching in his boots.

Finally Wrigley said, "You have a gall, lieutenant, taking over those steers in such a peremptory manner."

"There was a question of ownership to be settled," Travis said, smiling. "If I'm satisfied that the homesteaders came into those steers honestly, I'll see that they're returned."

"They were rustled and you know it," Janeway snapped.

221

"He doesn't know any such thing!" Wrigley countered flatly.

"All right, all right, we'll save the bickering until the others get here," Travis said, and went on puffing on his cigar. He was beginning to develop a taste for tobacco; the first few cigars he had smoked had been for appearance. A cigar always made a man seem older, gave him a touch of maturity.

Hodges, Rider, and Butram arrived together; they tied their horses and came on in, smiling. This faded a little when they saw Wrigley sitting there. At Travis' invitation they sat down.

"I think we can begin now," Travis said.

"Where's Ben Arness?" Wrigley asked.

"The sergeant no longer dictates army policy in this district," Travis said. "He's where he belongs, with the enlisted men." Then he looked at each of them. "Gentlemen, I have under guard twenty-five steers. Eleven of them carry the Circle T; I believe that's your brand, Mr. Janeway." He consulted a sheet of paper. "Six are branded S on a Rail."

"That's mine," Hodges said.

"Three are Double O Bar."

"Mine," Rider said.

"The other five are Rocking Chair."

"That's me," Butram said. He looked at Wrigley and laughed. "Your damned thievin' bunch didn't get away with it this time, did they?"

"All right!" Travis said harshly as Wrigley started to rise. "General, the men who had possession of those steers claimed they found them on the prairie. Do you have anything to say about that?"

"If they said that, then it's so."

"They're lying," Rider said. "I keep closer tabs on my stock than that." He looked at Travis. "You haven't told us the names of the men who had them."

"I don't intend to," Travis said smoothly. "Gentlemen, let's be realistic about this. If I told you who they were, I'd find them hanging from a tree or a barn rafter. Right?"

"Naturally!" Butram snapped.

"That's why I won't say," Travis told them.

"I thought you were on our side," Janeway said sullenly. "God damn it, I almost apologized too."

222

"Just a moment!" Travis snapped. "Gentlemen, we're going to reach an agreement before we break up this meeting. Now you cattlemen have been holding out for high prices, and the agent can't stretch his budget that far. You have no call to charge a Dodge City price for your steers and get fat on the excess profit."

"We've got to charge high to make up for the rustling losses," Janeway said. "You get Wrigley and his crooked friends to stop putting their ropes on our steers and we'll meet the agent and establish a fair price."

"I'm sure the general will agree to that," Travis said, then looked at Wrigley.

"You're trying to chivvy me into a position that will suit you," Wrigley said angrily. "I'll agree to nothing."

Travis thought this over for a moment, then said, "General, I'm going to write a report tonight on this meeting, and I wouldn't like to have to say that you were uncooperative. I know your friends have to eat, and they steal a few steers to tide them over, but it all counts up, sir, and the cattlemen feel the pinch."

"Amen to that," Rider said. "Keep talkin' there, sonny."

"General," Travis said, "I find your attitude very unrealistic, in the face of a possible solution."

"What solution? You're discriminating against the homesteaders."

"Being poor, sir, does not entitle a man to steal." Travis slapped his hand on the desk. "I'm not going to mince words with you, general. I seek a solution to this, a just solution for the cattlemen, who have been rustled in the past, and a solution for the Indian agent, who must either pay high prices or buy stolen beef, and some just solution to the problems of your friends. Now, I've reached the cattlemen if I can put a halt to the rustling. You can help there. A word from you would do more than six companies of cavalry."

"Provided I gave that word," Wrigley said.

"I think you will, sir."

The general's eyebrow raised. "Will I?" He laughed cynically. "You're not only young, but foolish."

"General, unless you give it, I'll reveal the names of the men who were selling the steers. I venture to say they'll all be hanged within twenty-four hours." His glance touched the cattlemen. "Right, gentlemen?"

"Right!" they said in unison.

Wrigley's complexion faded. "You *wouldn't* do that! They'd blame me!"

"Only if you force me, general. Make no mistake, sir. I'm dead serious. And I won't give you long to make up your mind."

"It would cost you your commission, Mr. Travis."

"I'm not so sure of that. After all, it really is my *duty* to report their names."

"This is dirty blackmail," Wrigley said. "That's all it is. You've sold out to the cattlemen." He shook his head sadly. "All right, Mr. Travis. I'll do what I can."

"We are assuming," Travis said, "that it will be enough." He turned to Janeway. "I promised the agent some cattle. You'll have to drive a herd of about fifty right away."

"Are you running my business?"

Travis shook his head. "No, but I don't want Indian trouble and neither do you. As for your price, I believe the costs of a drive to Dodge should be deducted. The agent feels this is fair, and so do I."

Janeway stared at him for a moment, then shook his head and laughed. "Sonny, you beat the hell out of anything I ever saw. All right, since you've gone to so much trouble and brought some of our stolen stock back, we'll agree." He motioned to the others. "I speak for all."

"Then I believe the entire matter is settled," Travis said. "General, would you remain?"

The others filed out, mounted, and rode away. Wrigley looked at Travis for a moment, then said, "What could we possibly have to say to each other now, sir?"

"I don't enjoy the plight of your homesteaders," Travis said. "What I've seen of them, they're hog dirty and mouse poor. Isn't there anything that can be done for them? And I don't mean stealing army horses or Janeway's cattle."

Wrigley shook his head. "It's hard to get started when you have nothing."

"You look prosperous enough, general."

"Meaning?"

"That you're not leasing that land from the goodness

of your heart," Travis said. "The Indian agent showed me a map giving the location of every settler. I counted sixty-seven, all in my district. What do they pay you for a sublease?" He saw stubbornness come into Wrigley's eyes, and added, "I suppose I could get a court order to look at your books, general."

"That isn't necessary," Wrigley said. "They pay me two hundred and fifty dollars on signing, and a hundred dollars a year."

"Let's see now—that's roughly sixteen thousand dollars, and sixty-seven hundred dollars a year. Not bad. I don't think a United States Senator makes much more than that. It isn't difficult now to understand why you want these people to survive on the prairie. If they don't raise the lease money, they're out." He shrugged. "But I suppose that in itself isn't much of a tragedy. When one leaves, you can always re-lease the property, another two hundred and fifty, and a hundred a year. I don't see how you can lose."

Wrigley stared at Jefferson Travis. "You make it sound cold and mercenary, Mr. Travis."

"Well it is, isn't it?"

"It's a legitimate business, sir. Good night."

He went outside and got into his buggy, and after he wheeled out of the yard Travis left his office and walked the few blocks to Doctor Summer's house to have his arm dressed. It itched considerably, which indicated that it was healing well.

Hope Randall was sitting on the front porch, shelling peas, when he came up the walk. A shaft of lamplight filtering through the front screen door cast its golden glow about her. She lifted her head as he approached.

"My mother used to give me a nickel a gallon for that kind of work," Travis said.

"I pay off in gingersnaps. Sit down."

"Could I get the doctor to put a new dressing on my arm?"

"I'll do that," she said, and put the pan aside. She led the way into Summers' office and motioned for him to sit down. He rolled up his sleeve and she got out the salve and dressing. When she cut the old bandage away, she looked carefully at the wound. "It's healing very well. In another week it ought to close up."

"Well, it hasn't bothered me at all."

She gave him an amused look. "Jeff, I don't think anything really bothers you. You're one of those rare, self-sufficient men who never seems to need help with anything."

"Except myself." He smiled. "I just came from a meeting." He told her about it as she wrapped his arm and tied the bandage.

"Wrigley gave in? I've never heard of him doing a thing like that before."

"He wants to pretend that I didn't give him any choice," Travis said. "But it's not that, Hope. He just doesn't want to lose money."

"Is it wrong to want money?"

"Guess not," he said. "Of course, I've never had any, so I wouldn't know. Do you know how much a lieutenant makes a month?"

"Yes, but they seem to get along on it, don't they?"

"If they go light on whiskey and cards." He rolled his sleeve down. "I'll help you shell those peas. Anything for an excuse to sit and talk and look at you."

"It's dark on the porch."

He smiled. "Don't worry. I know what you look like; a little darkness won't make me forget. Hope, I——"

"Let's shell the peas," she said, and went outside.

He took a pan and sat on the steps near her feet, cracking husks and stripping peas into another small pan. "Do you feel a compulsion to do the right thing, Hope?"

"No. I don't worry about my mistakes. You shouldn't either."

"I've got a report to write," he said. "Should I confess all, how I maneuvered the general into doing what I wanted?"

She laughed. "Only fools confess all. Jeff, are you still trying to find the right and wrong of everything?"

"I suppose. But who is wrong?"

"All of us. We're all a little right too. Jeff, the Indians are right; they've been cheated and lied to all down the line. And the buffalo hunters are right; they're making money and spending it and towns are being built and railroads. The homesteaders are poor, but some make it and they're people; people are important to the land. And Janeway's got a point when he says that he was here first

226

and the politicians sold him short when they gave the waterholes to farmers. I think the homesteaders are more deserving, but then, ask anyone in Spanish Spring and I'm afraid you'll get four opinions." She set her pan aside.

"I'm beginning to see," he said, "Just why Major Deacon likes a neutral policy. It's not easy to takes sides." He looked at her. "Do you still think I will?"

"I still think you must, sooner or later, Jeff." She patted his arm and then let her hand rest there. "You're a very strait-laced man. By that I mean, you have a firm, almost profound sense of morality. And it's somehow misplaced out here." She frowned. "Do you see what I mean?" You want to apply this severe sense of justice that governs you to the homesteaders who don't understand it, and to the Indians who don't want it really, and to Janeway who would think it so much nonsense."

"Do you think it is, Hope?"

"No," she said softly. "I like it."

"Hope, did a man ever kiss you on the front porch?"

"Good heavens, no!"

"I am about to," Jefferson Travis said, and without giving her time to protest, he pulled her into his arms and pressed his lips on hers. He was surprised at the warmth of her, the fragileness, and strength.

When he released her, he said quietly, "I'm not going to apologize."

Doctor Summers, who was coming up the dark path, heard him and said, "I wouldn't either, Mr. Travis. And I hope you're not blushing." He took his bag into the house and came back out. "Any man who pursues such a bold course will be a general someday."

"Really, Doctor, I'm a man of sincere intentions and—"

"Will you stop explaining?" Summers asked. "Do you want to ruin it? I don't understand you young people, always explaining yourselves as though you were afraid someone wouldn't take you right."

"Doctor," Hope said, "why don't you wash for supper?"

"What? Oh!" He chuckled. "I never seem to know when I'm not wanted. Well, young man, come to supper sometime this week, if you haven't already been asked." He went into the house, humming to himself.

"I want to talk to you about something," Hope Randall said.

"About the kiss?"

She nodded. "If you were just trying to prove to yourself that you were a man, I'm going to be angry."

"It wasn't that at all," he said sincerely. "Hope, you're a chatterbox most of the time, but I like to listen to you. I think I'm falling in love with you. Do you mind?"

"No, I don't mind at all. Do you want to stay for supper?"

"Can't. I have to write that report."

"Be a little kinder to yourself, Jeff. Do you know what I mean?"

"Yes, but I have to be as honest about myself as with others," he said, then kissed her lightly and walked back to the barracks.

General Wrigley found Sergeant Ben Arness in the saloon, nursing a glass of whiskey. He sided Arness, wiggled his finger at the bartender for a good bottle, then took the sergeant to an isolated table. Business was light at this hour; there were a few men playing cards and a drunk sleeping it off in the corner.

Wrigley said, "I can't get used to dealing with that pink-faced kid instead of you, Ben. Somehow I just can't get along with him."

"Who can? I'm down on him. So's every man in the detail."

"Is that a fact? He must be a real son-of-a-bitch to get along with." He refilled Arness' glass. Almost on cue, Owen Gates came in, a toothpick probing the crevices between his teeth. He came over to their table and sat down.

"You're looking mighty glum, Ben," Gates said.

"Ben's getting a crawful of that kid lieutenant," Wrigley said. "You can't blame him, Owen. It's kids like him that give the army a bad name; always meddling, always stirring things up."

Arness squinted and shook his finger. "He just ain't army, general. You got to learn to soldier and it takes years. Why, I'll bet half of the men are ready to go over the hill right now. You know, he's been on patrol damned near ever since he got here?"

"I'd get out," Owen Gates said.

"After twenty-seven years?" Wrigley asked. "That's foolish, sheriff. Besides, if Ben retired now, half of the men would go with him."

"Yeah, I never thought of that," Gates said. "But you'll never trim him down to size as long as you're in the army, Ben." He tapped his shoulders. "Those little gold threads sewn there will beat you every time."

"Why don't you come and work for me?" Wrigley asked. "A hundred a month and the authority to back you up."

Arness looked at him. "What kind of authority?"

"Gates' badge," Wrigley said flatly. "Owen's going to give it up and I need a capable man in his place, a man I can trust, a man who sees my side. You know I'm in the right, Ben."

"You and Grace Beaumont could get married, Ben," Gates said. "It's what she wants, you know that." He thumped Ben Arness on the arm. "And then you can take a crack at that lieutenant, Ben, and the army can't do a thing about it."

"Think it over," Wrigley said. "Here, take the bottle with you, Ben. You let me know tomorrow, won't you?"

Arness nodded and stood up, the bottle under his arm. He walked unsteadily toward the swinging doors and then on down the street.

"Well?" Gates said. "What do you think?"

"He hates officers, and he loves authority," Wrigley said. "And then there's the woman pulling at him. That's something in our favor."

"Yes," Gates said wistfully. "But to give it all up after twenty-seven years——"

"I don't give a damn if he's got fifty years in the army," Wrigley said. "When I need a man, I need him, and that's all I think about." He turned in his chair and snapped his fingers for the bartender to bring him another bottle.

7

"It's for Ben's own good," Owen Gates said. He was standing in Grace Beaumont's doorway, hat in hand. The parlor lamp was turned up brightly, for she had been sewing; his knock had interrupted her. "Ben's at the barracks, Mrs. Beaumont. You want I should send him around?"

"I suppose," she said doubtfully. "It *is* for Ben's good, isn't it?" Then she sighed. "He's going to feel lost for a while. But he had to get out sometime. Thank you for coming around, Owen."

"Glad to do it," he said.

He left her house and walked to the barracks grounds. There was a lamp burning in Lieutenant Travis' office, and Gates knocked politely although the door was open. Travis put aside the letter he had been writing.

"What is it, sheriff?"

"Thought I'd better ask your permission first," Gates said, "but Mrs. Beaumont would like to see Ben Arness. Just thought I'd let him know."

"He isn't very sober," Travis said. Then he nodded toward the end where the enlisted men slept. "But go ahead. It's none of my business."

Gates turned to the door, then hesitated. He smiled pleasantly. "Making out your report card, lieutenant?"

"Yes, and I'm putting you down for a failure in effort."

Gates looked amused. "The general gave me my orders before you came, and he'll be giving them after you leave, which should be soon. It's too bad you have to find an answer for everything. Can't you just let things work themselves out?" He jammed his hands into his pockets. "But it's no use giving you advice. You go ahead and do what you have to do, sonny. It'll be a relief to all of us to see you leave."

Travis stared out the door after Gates left, then went on to finish the letter he was writing to his brother. He wanted to straighten him out on a lot of things, such as his notion that the west was a place where a man did what he wanted to do, and where he could pick up a fortune without raising a sweat. Travis wanted to assure him that it wasn't much different from back home, where everyone worked toward his own small dream, and if a man somehow got crowded out, no one really cared. He would have liked to write about his work, convincing them that it was important, but he couldn't very well boast about recovering two strayed army horses and twenty-five stolen cattle, and angering a lot of people in the process. Written down, that wouldn't sound very important at all, and Travis wondered if he could bring it into a truer perspective by going into detail about the geographic and economic structure of the country. He felt powerless to explain how important one poor homesteader became when the permanent population was less than ten per thousand square miles. And his brother would think the furor over a few horses ridiculous, for he had never owned one. He would find it hard to believe that the loss of a horse could cost a man his life on the plains. Each morning Paul got up and walked five blocks to work, his tin lunch pail in hand. And each evening he walked home. Now and then, when he wanted to go to Utica, a distance of twelve miles, he would take the train and stay overnight to rest up from the trip.

No, he wouldn't understand at all about towns being three to five days' ride from each other. So Jefferson Travis wrote about the Indians being troublesome by nature, and the settlers being inclined to thievery, and the cattlemen being prone to take the law into their own hands. He knew that Paul would believe these things, for they dovetailed so neatly with his own opinions: that the uneducated couldn't be trusted, the poor were all thieves, and the rich were always overbearing.

Since Sergeant Arness was away from the barracks, Travis went to see Corporal Busik. "General march order at dawn," Travis said. "Three weeks' rations; that'll mean pack horses. And double ammunition rations."

"Yes, sir," Busik said. "Shall I relay that to the sergeant when he comes back?"

"Yes, corporal," Travis said, "but I believe I'm capable of running this detail without Sergeant Arness."

Busik grinned. "Yes, sir, we've noticed that. Meaning no disrespect, sir, but we all put you down for a tough time at first. Not that any of us have it in for second lieutenants, sir, but generally they're long on regulations and short on horse sense."

"Thank you, corporal. I consider that a compliment."

Busik went back to his quarters and Travis turned in for the night, feeling warmed by the corporal's expression of confidence. *Someday,* he thought, *I may make a passable first lieutenant.*

He woke very early, breakfasted, and started packing his saddlebags. Sergeant Arness came to his room and knocked; Travis turned and saw him, then motioned him in.

"I'd like to have a word with you, sir," Arness said.

"All right. I hope we can bury the hatchet, sergeant."

"I don't change my mind easily, sir." He wiped a hand across his mouth. "If it's all the same with you, I'd like for you to write a letter for me." He waited a moment as though he wanted Travis to ask what about, and when the lieutenant said nothing, Arness said, "I want to retire, sir. Effective immediately."

Jefferson Travis sat down on his bunk, genuinely disturbed. "You want to throw away twenty-seven years, sergeant? Because of me? In the name of heaven, man, I'd rather transfer myself first." He spread his hands in an appeal. "Sergeant, this isn't a matter of who's right or wrong, or how you feel about officers. Twenty-seven years of service! A man just doesn't up and throw it——"

"Will you write the letter for me, sir? I want to be relieved immediately.'

Travis sighed. "I don't suppose there's anything I can say that would——"

"No, sir. My mind's made up." He jammed his hands into his pockets. "I've got a job right here in Spanish Spring; I don't need the army anymore."

"Very well, sergeant. I'll write the letter, but you understand that it will require Major Deacon's endorsement and it won't go out on the stage for another five days."

"That's all right," Arness said. "You just write the letter." He saluted stiffly and went out, and a few minutes later Corporal Busik came to the office, greatly agitated.

"Ben s packing his gear, says he's getting out. Is that true, sir?"

"You should be pleased, Busik. It's another stripe for you."

"Hang the stripe!" He shook his head. "God knows Arness has been hell to live with sometimes, but with three more years to go, and a top soldier's hooks just around the corner——"

"He made up his own mind," Travis said. "I'll endorse a letter promoting you to sergeant. Pick a good man to promote to corporal.'

"Trooper Ardmore, sir. He's reliable and he's army. Sixteen years in dirty-shirt blue."

"All right," Travis said.

He was a little crowded for time, with these letters to write, but he managed it and didn't hold up the detail to do it. Ben Arness' resignation had to be in triplicate, and there was a place for him to sign all three copies. The order promoting Busik and Ardmore was a simple letter; Travis intended to forward all of them when he returned.

With the detail mounted and putting Spanish Spring behind them, Travis felt that everything was all out of kilter without Arness riding behind him, with his ingrained prejudices and stony expression. This was his first awareness that it could actually be comforting to be disliked by someone.

At the crossing he noted that Regan's place was still locked up; the man must be on a drunk at Fort Dodge, he had had time to return by now. They stopped for a ten-minute rest, then went on, riding north toward the wide scatter of homesteader soddies.

Around noon they approached a place built of earth and sunk well into the ground, both for convenience of construction and safety from the twisters that now and then ripped through. A pack of naked children were gathering buffalo chips as the patrol drew near, then they ran for the soddy and an Indian woman came to the doorway to see what had disturbed them.

A man came out, armed with a repeating rifle, and Travis recognized him as Bonner, the man he had relieved

233

of the stolen cattle. He wore a buckskin shirt over filthy long underwear, and he was barefoot.

"Guess you've come to arrest me now," he said, putting up his rifle. "I can't fight you all."

"You're not under arrest," Travis said. "We'd like to fill our canteens from your spring." Bonner waved permission and Ardmore went around and gathered them up.

"Ain't been sleepin' much since I came back from the reservation," Bonner said. "Been expectin' to be hung."

"By cattlemen?" Travis shook his head. "They don't know who was selling their steers."

From Bonner's expression, Travis could see that he wanted to believe this, but didn't dare. "You wouldn't lie to me, would you, lieutenant?"

"Why should I?"

"Because I'm nuthin'. Most people don't reckon me worth wastin' the truth on." He laughed without humor. "Sonny, you don't know what it is to be nuthin'. Was I hung, it wouldn't mean anything to the men on the other end of the rope. My kind is just thrown away."

"Not by me," Travis said. "Bonner, I think I kept you from being hanged sooner or later; you're not smart enough to steal for long and get away with it." Ardmore came back with the filled canteens and passed them around before mounting. "Keep your rope off branded steers, Bonner."

"I surely will," Bonner said. "And much obliged for the favor."

Travis led them away from the soddy, cutting toward the Dodge City trail, an ill-defined, faint wearing in the grass, a jagged scar left on the earth by wagons. It ran in a faint curve, out of the vast flatlands to the south into the monotonous expanse to the north, where the horizon melted into the earth in a bluish mist and one could not be separated from the other.

The air was dry and oven hot, yet there was an unusual charge of electricity in everything; it set up static in the clothing when the seat of the britches rubbed the saddle. Near sundown, a purple-gray haze swallowed the sun, and not a breath of wind stirred.

Sergeant Busik sided Travis and spoke in a hushed voice. "I don't like this, sir. Look at the color of that sky. Like old lead." He jerked his head toward the column. "The animals are getting spooky too."

"What do you think is causing it? A storm coming?"

"Yeah, but a storm like you never seen before, sir. Winds strong enough to knock a horse down, carry him off even. We call it a twister, sir. She'll likely build all night, and tomorrow, when it gets hot, she'll let go." He waved his hand toward the distant horizon. "The sky turns black and a whirling cloud comes across the prairie, sir, like a funnel spinning on its end. It uproots trees, buildings, and everything in its path."

"Where's the nearest timber?" Travis asked.

Busik scratched his head. "Ash Creek, I guess. About four hours ride from here."

"Forced march?"

"No, sir. That way you could cut it to two and a half."

"All right, Busik. Lead out."

They made only short stops, alternating the trot with the walk, and arrived at Ash Creek well after dark. There were some trees on each side of the creek, and this slash in the earth's face was almost narrow enough to jump a horse across.

Travis dismounted the detail, had the horses picketed, and ordered Busik to have the hatchets broken out. He wanted trees felled across the creek to form a large shelter, and while six men chopped, others rigged rope harness and began to haul the downed timber into place.

They worked the night through, overlaying the logs with brush, then fresh earth, until they were heavily covered. It was an ideal spot for shelter, for the creek contained no water, just four inches of drying mud in the bottom.

Beneath the cover of logs and brush and earth, Travis ordered camp made and the horses brought in. He was on watch when daylight came, the most frightening dawn he had ever seen. The sky was like slate, and it was a chore to breathe the hot, humid air. To the southwest the sky was the color of oil smoke on a lamp chimney.

Suddenly a wind woke across the flats, husking dust before it, driving stinging particles of dirt against Travis' face. Busik came to stand beside him and said, "She's a twister, sir. Pretty soon you'll see her, like a black

235

whirling funnel. No tellin' where she'll hit or what her path will be. A man can only take cover and hope it's good enough."

Finally the leaden sky took on motion, a whirling torrent of lifted dust, and ferocious winds, running crookedly toward the ground, swelling, nearing. The wind increased to awesome proportions, a solid bursting roar of sound, and the earth seemed to tremble beneath their feet. For an hour it ripped its devastation across the prairie, the main funnel passing east of Travis' position, yet the force of the wind was enough to spin dirt and brush from the roof of his makeshift shelter. One or two logs were displaced and fell, but no one was injured. He watched the course of the twister and wondered how close it had come to Spanish Spring; it had seemed to come from that direction.

They did not leave the creek bed until late morning, when the wind had died and the twister was long gone. The air was still full of dust, blotting the sun from the sky as Travis mounted his detail; they were all tired from the night's hard work and the tension of waiting out the storm.

To Busik, Travis said, "Tell the men I'm sorry all the work was for nothing."

"They didn't mind, sir," Busik said.

"We'll push northeast and follow the twister's path," Travis said. "If anyone was in the way of it, they'll likely need help."

"If they were in the way, sir, they'll be beyond help."

"Nevertheless, we'll take a look," Travis said firmly.

He wished that he had a more detailed map, one marked with the location of the settlers. After seeing Brewer's wall map, Travis carried a section chart and meant to record this information the next time he touched agency headquarters.

Toward noon of a scalding day they rested in a buffalo wallow; it had six inches of mud in the center, so they squatted below the rim and ate cold rations. Sergeant Busik hunkered down near Travis to talk.

"I know of six or seven families who could have been caught in this thing," Busik said. He looked at the sky and the forming clouds. "Wouldn't surprise me if we got rain this evening, sir."

236

"We can stand something to break this heat," Travis said. "We'll rest here until the sun goes down. Tell everyone to get what sleep they can."

"No need to tell 'em that, sir," Busik said. He nodded and Travis looked; three of the men were already snoring.

Travis lay back with a handkerchief folded over his eyes and got some sleep; a cool wind woke him in total darkness and he sat up. Busik was near by and a touch brought him awake.

"We'd better be moving," Travis said.

A bright stab of lightning illuminated the prairie, and an instant later a thunderclap bounded across the sky. "Hope it comes down good," Busik said, and went to stir the others.

They were moving by the time the pelting rain began to fall, and they walked their horses, letting it beat against their ponchos and wash down their faces. Some time later they saw a blossom of yellow lamplight in the distance and rode toward it.

A barking dog ventured out, snapping at the horses' heels, and one of the troopers shied him away with a whipped rope end. A man was walking around his scattered soddy, carrying a lantern, his clothes soaked to the skin. He held the lantern high when Travis dismounted and walked up to him.

"You got hit bad," Travis said. "Anyone hurt?"

The man shook his head. "I live here alone." He peered at the soldiers. "I'm all right. Just digging out. Better go on north to the Pearl's place. They was likely in the path of it too."

Travis turned to his horse. "What's your name, in case they ask about you?"

"Riscoe. Say, you fellas wouldn't have some coffee to spare, would you? Found my pot, and there's no hole in it."

"Busik, fix him up with some bacon, flour, coffee and sugar. Better give him some dried beans too."

This was more than Riscoe had hoped for, and he said, "By golly, that's mighty decent of you. I guess I'm goin' to stay alive after all."

The way he said it, with an almost prayerful thankfulness, made Travis realize anew how thinly these people clung to the line of life. The twister had ripped up his buildings and killed his livestock; he had nothing left but his life, and Travis' native generosity had just renewed the lease on it.

"How far is it to the Pearls'?" Travis asked.

"Oh, sixteen miles or so," Riscoe said. "Say my howdy to 'em."

"We'll do that," Travis said and stepped into the saddle. The leather felt hard and uncomfortable and his leg muscles ached, yet he turned his detail out of the yard.

He had to conserve the horses so he kept them at a slow walk, and dismounted often to save them. The rain turned to a steady drizzle and the soft ground made walking a misery, yet they kept going, their boots sucking at the mud. Travis figured that he could spare the horses until he made his swing around to the reservation; two days there on stable feed would put life back into them.

They wore out a miserable night and when dawn came the drizzle slackened to a stinging mist, pushed by a sharp, thrusting wind. Through the gray light they could make out the rubble of buildings and a lean-to barn, and Travis decided this must be the Pearls' place.

When they rode into the yard and dismounted, Pearl came out, flanked by his strapping sons. He was a giant of a man, six foot four in his moccasins, and his chest was like the bole of an old tree, thick and immensely strong.

"Are you Mr. Pearl?" Travis asked.

"I be," he said. Then he looked at the tired troopers. "I thought the twister cleaned off the prairie. Where was you hidin'?"

"In a creek bed," Travis said. "It passed us by. Anyone hurt here?"

Pearl's face settled into sadness. "My girl, Nan." He pointed to a mound of fresh earth to one side of what had been his soddy. "We just finished the buryin'. Be you goin' near the reservation, you tell Brewer." He saw Travis' puzzlement, and added, "Brewer's stopped here a number of times, and he always looked on my little girl with a gentleman's favor. She never knew much politeness in her life, young fella, and she thought Brewer was somethin' special." His voice grew soft. "I guess he was, 'cause he saw woman in her, which pleased her. She was goin' to be eighteen come green up."

"I'm sorry," Travis said sincerely. "Is there anything I can do?"

The older boy's name was Kyle. He said, "Mister, you got a Bible?"

"I haven't, I'm sorry," Travis said.

Kyle shook his head as though he hadn't really expected one. "I wanted somethin' said over her, that's all. She knew only good thoughts, mister. Nary a word of meanness passed her lips, and bein' poor never bothered her much, never made her bitter toward no one."

Travis said softly, "Gentlemen, I believe I can quote a proper scripture from memory, if you'll permit me."

Pearl said, "We'd be in your debt."

Turning to Busik, Travis meant to give an order, but the man was already turning to the troopers. "Column of twos!" he said. "Dress it up there! Are you Tennessee farmers?" Then he pivoted and saluted. "Detail formed, sir."

"Thank you, sergeant."

They walked to the fresh mound and Travis stood at the head, with the Pearls about him, flanked by grimy, rain-soaked soldiers, all at attention, unmindful of the drizzle.

"Uncover," Travis said, and they were precise about it. He looked at the earth which covered a girl he had never seen. "I have never spoken at a graveside before; perhaps there are passages more suitable than the one I recall. According to Matthew, Christ went up into a mountain, and when his disciples came to him, and the multitudes gathered around, he spoke to them, saying: 'Blessed are the poor in spirit, for theirs is the kingdom of heaven. Blessed are they which do hunger and thirst after righteousness; for they shall be filled. Blessed are the meek; for they shall inherit the earth. Blessed are the pure in heart; for they shall see God.' Amen." He glanced at his men. "Cover. Sergeant Busik, mount the detail."

"Yes, sir. All right, you heard Mr. Travis."

Pearl was wiping his nose with the back of his hand. "That was mighty nice, mister."

"It seems so little to do, Mr. Pearl. If you need provisions——"

"No, no, we'll manage. Lost my wife two years ago. Bull buffalo got her, just over yonder." He pointed, then

239

rubbed his huge, hairy forearms. "My little Nan couldn't read a word or sign her name, but she knew about God and them things, mister. Some people just know, 'cause they're born gentle."

"Yes," Travis said. "I had almost forgotten there was such a thing out here." He turned quickly to his horse and went into the saddle. A wave of his hand got them going and he turned in the direction of the Indian reservation.

Busik rode a pace behind Travis, and the young man turned and looked at him before speaking. "These settlers—" he hesitated, "Damn it, Busik, how many starts does a man have to make in one lifetime?"

"Some never stop making them, sir. And it's a damned shame that they should have to, sir."

They rode on in silence and finally the rain stopped.

8

On the way to the reservation, Travis began to get a true picture of the twister's devastating effect; it had disturbed and littered a twenty-mile swath, uprooting the brush. When he drew in sight of the agency buildings and Indian camp, he saw damage there; roofs were torn off, lodges were down and scattered, and the horse corral was partially wrecked. He realized that their hastily made shelter had protected them only because they had been on the fringe of the twister's path, as had the agency, yet the winds had been forceful enough to cause damage.

When he dismounted, he gave Busik his orders. "Turn the mounts into the corral, then take a detail and make some emergency repairs. See what you can do to help straighten this up a little."

"Yes, sir."

"We'll remain here for a few days," Travis said. Then

he walked on to the headquarters building, where he met Brewer in the door.

"That was a real wind," Brewer said. "We didn't catch the full brunt of it though. Where were you?"

"In a creek bed," Travis said. He took Brewer's arm and led him inside. "We just came from the Pearls' place, Mr. Brewer. I'm sorry to have to tell you that Nan is dead."

Brewer looked at him for a moment, then he turned abruptly to the liquor cabinet, poured himself a drink and sat down.

"It's hard to believe," he said softly, and drained his glass; he refilled it immediately.

Travis cleared his throat, "We gave her a proper burial," he said, and then, searching to find something to say, he added, "Why didn't you tell me about Nan, Mr. Brewer?"

"Tell you? Tell you what, Mr. Travis? That I saw this girl, young, vibrant, pretty?" He shook his head. "Ah, she was a sight. Her hair was like flax, and her eyes reminded me of a still, spring sky in early morning before the sun burns the color from it. And when she spoke to me, the gentleness in her rushed out; her heart was full of fine things, Mr. Travis. I don't think she ever thought about being barefoot and having only one dress to her name." He paused to drink his whiskey. Travis again found himself embarrassed by the combination of sincerity in this man and the absurdity of his fulsome sentiments. For once, the lieutenant could not think of a suitable response. Fortunately, Brewer started up again, murmuring half to himself, "How can I know what drew me back to see her? Was it the yearning for love and gentility in her, reaching out to fill the void within me? Or did I find love in this loveless land after all?" He shook his head again and took out a handkerchief and blew his nose. "I'll never know the truth now, will I, Mr. Travis? For the rest of my life I'll carry with me the golden image of her, and wonder if I loved, really loved her." He picked up the whiskey bottle and held it on his lap. "Would you mind leaving me alone, Mr. Travis?"

Relieved, Travis said gently, "Of course," and left quickly.

He went out to the barn; three soldiers were on top,

hammers working to put part of the roof back in place. Corporal Ardmore had a detail repairing the corral, and Travis found many things to occupy him.

The Indians were trying to restore some order to their village; the wind had all but leveled it, and it was late evening before anyone found time to light a mess fire so they could enjoy a hot meal. As soon as they had eaten, the troopers found places to sleep and curled up in their blankets. Travis got out his leather-bound dispatch case and wrote his account of the twister and the damage he had observed. This would go through official channels and when Brewer put in for money to repair the agency, this account would substantiate his claim.

The lamp remained lit in Brewer's quarters, and the hour was growing late, which worried Jefferson Travis a little, for at such a time a man shouldn't be too long alone. Not a man like Brewer.

A glance at his watch told him that it was nearly eleven, and he wondered if Brewer would resent an intrusion. Perhaps the man was drunk and had passed out; if so, he needed someone to put him to bed. Or he might be cold sober, working on the riddle of his emotions, in which case he needed someone to talk to.

Travis was about to act on his decision when he heard a pistol go off inside the headquarters building. The sound was not loud, yet it brought Busik awake.

"What was that?"

"A pistol. Come on!" Travis said, and trotted across the muddy yard and bounded over the porch. The main office was dark, but a sliver of light appeared beneath the door to Brewer's quarters; Travis flung it open and stepped into the room, Busik right behind him.

The acrid odor of burnt black powder teased his nose, then he saw Brewer sprawled in his chair, a stain of blood spreading over his left breast.

"Gawd!" Busik said softly.

The pistol, a small .32 Smith & Wesson, lay on the floor beneath Brewer's dangling hand. The man was still alive; he rolled his eyes and looked at Travis and tried to smile, then his head dropped forward and rolled a little, tethered by the lax neck muscles.

"Funny place for a man to shoot himself," Busik said.

Travis looked at the sad figure of Brewer. "He pointed

the gun where he thought his trouble lay, sergeant. Well, I guess he found the answer."

"How's that, sir?"

"He told me earlier that he didn't know whether he was attracted to Nan Pearl because he was lonely, or because he loved her. I guess he made up his mind and decided that he couldn't live without her."

"It's a hell of a price to pay to find out, ain't it, sir?"

He looked at Busik. "Did you ever know any payment out here to be small? Brewer killed himself for a lot of reasons, Busik, but maybe he died easier because at least he could tell himself it was on account of the girl and not because he was a pathetic misfit. In the morning I want a burial detail made up. I suppose I'll have to take charge here until they send someone else." He sighed and waved his hand. "Go back to your blankets, sergeant. I'll stay the night out."

He got a blanket from Brewer's bedroom and covered him, then sat down in one of the leather chairs and smoked a cigar. The lamp needed refilling and he attended to this, then took off his boots and spurs and elevated his feet to a small table.

His stay at the reservation would have to be extended some; the property and Indians could not be left unattended, even for a week. The moment official representatives left, the Indians would break into the storehouse and gut it of provisions. That would really be something to answer for to Major Deacon.

By morning, he had reached his decision and called Busik into the office.

"Sergeant, on my desk at Spanish Spring there's a letter in triplicate, requesting Sergeant Arness' discharge to retirement status. It isn't effective as yet because Major Deacon hasn't signed it. I want you to take three men with you and bring Sergeant Arness here. But before you see him, tear up those three copies."

"Yes, sir," Busik said, a smile touching his lips. "You want me to tear up the other too, sir, the one making me and Ardmore——"

"This detail can stand two sergeants," Travis said. "Besides, Arness may object at coming and I wouldn't want a corporal hitting a sergeant."

243

"Oh, he's bound to object, sir. Maybe I'd better take four men."

"You can handle it," Travis assured him. "I don't care how you do it, sergeant. Tied hand and foot if necessary. But I'll expect you back in three days."

"Yes, sir." Then he laughed. "I can just see Ben now, sir, when I tell him. He doesn't like to be crossed, sir. Makes him contrary as hell."

"Busik, that man was born contrary. Now get on with it."

Ten minutes later, Busik and three troopers rode out and Travis set about the job of handling agency business. He had an inventory taken and signed by two witnesses, then talked to the four men who worked with Brewer. They told Travis what their routine was.

Burial was at one o'clock and the Indians gathered to watch. From a Bible found among Brewer's things, Travis read a brief service. Then, since Brewer was a government employee and because it would impress the Indians, Travis had a volley fired over the grave.

In the days that followed, he learned a great deal about the Indians; since there was a change in command, they assumed that he could be argued and wheedled out of extra provisions before he learned better.

Travis was young—there was no arguing that—but he was a long way from being gullible; the Indians didn't get a thing from him that wasn't their just due. He sent six men in six directions to contact homesteaders who had suffered property loss from the twister; he spotted them for the troopers on Brewer's map to save time. The soldiers were to inform them that if they needed anything to tide them over, they could draw from the agency stores.

This was hardly a procedure endorsed by regulations, but Travis figured that in such a time of emergency, the regulations could go out the window and they could argue about it later. All he thought about were the women and children living on the prairie who might be hungry and homeless; he intended to do something about that.

Some semblance of order had been restored to the agency; the buildings were repaired and the corral fixed. Then, from across the flats, Busik and his detail approached with Ben Arness in tow, although Arness seemed to be accompanying them without fuss. However, he was

244

not in uniform, Travis saw, as they rode into the yard. Arness wore a dark blue suit, a fawn-colored hat, and when he dismounted, the front of his coat parted to reveal a star pinned there.

He came toward Travis as though he meant to fight. "Damn it, you're going to explain this to me! What the hell's the idea going back on your word?" He thumped his chest. "I've got civic responsibilities now."

"The army needs you," Travis said calmly, "and until Major Deacon signs the papers, you're still army." He dismissed Busik and the others with a nod, and this disappointed them, for they wanted to hear how this would come out. "Come on inside," Travis said, and waved Arness in ahead of him. He poured a drink for him, then said. "How bad was the twister damage in Spanish Spring?"

"It leveled half the town," Arness said sourly. "Not many hurt though; they found cover in time. Where's Brewer?"

"Didn't Busik tell you?"

Arness laughed without humor. "Since he got those stripes, he's too important to talk."

"Brewer committed suicide," Travis said.

"Good God, why?"

Travis shrugged. "Does anyone ever really know why? This whole sorry mess was too much for him. If it hadn't been one thing, it would have been another. He left no message." He reached out and flipped open Arness' coat, exposing the badge. "You people are like sheep, sergeant. So Owen Gates docilely stepped down so you could step in. General Thomas C. Wrigley's flunky!" Then he shrugged. "Well, you're still a sergeant and I'm your commanding officer, like it or not. Since you sympathize with the homesteaders, I expect you know every one within a radius of seventy miles?"

"I do."

"Well, I saw what happened to two places that were in the twister's path, sergeant, and I suspect there's more. I've dispatched six men to pass the word that we'll distribute staples from the agency stores until they get going again. I want you to take charge of that detail, sergeant. You'll stay here and attend to the reservation duties until a new man is sent down from Fort Dodge."

Ben Arness stared dumbfounded at Lieutenant Travis. "You're going to give away government supplies? After all the fuss you made over—" He shook his head. "I don't understand you at all. And I can see why the general doesn't trust you; he doesn't understand you either."

Travis leaned forward and looked into Arness' eyes. "Sergeant, I don't like you, and I'm not going to pretend that I do. For my money, you're a 'sometime' soldier, when it suits you, but there's twenty-seven years of service experience behind you and I'm counting on that being stronger than your petty dislikes. This is a government post. Run it like one. And by God, if you don't, I'll personally drag you before a court-martial board. Do you understand that?"

"I understand—sir."

Travis grinned. "There, you sound like your small-minded, bigoted self again, sergeant. Be consistent. I can understand you better, and if I have to, I can even tolerate you. That really grates, doesn't it? You like to think that you tolerate me. Be honest with yourself, Arness. It isn't too late." He turned to the door and paused there. "I'll be gone ten days to two weeks. When I come back, you can do as you damned please."

Lieutenant Travis moved north with his men before sunup, and in the early afternoon they skirted a fair-sized buffalo herd; it took them half a day of traveling before the tail end of it was out of sight.

The next day they saw a hunters' camp in the distance, and, covering acres, skinned hides were pegged out to be fleshed; the flies were a thick torment, and the carcasses were beginning to stink. The skinners worked while the hunters, who were the aristocracy of this operation, lounged in the shade of the wagons, drinking whiskey, smoking, and telling lies. A few busied themselves with the task of reloading cartridges for the next day's shoot, or cleaned their long-barreled rifles.

As the cavalry approached, one man detached himself from the others and came forward as though he didn't want the army in his camp. He was a rangy, whiskered man, in his early thirties, and his eyes were as wary as an Indian's. He wore a brace of Colt cap-and-ball pistols on crossed belts, and a huge knife scabbard was sewn onto the leg of his leather breeches.

He nodded his greeting and went on chewing tobacco. Travis asked, "Have you seen any twister damage? Any homesteader's soddy in ruins?"

"Fella," the hunter said, "I stay clear of them places." He pointed to the northeast. "But I heard Luke Spears outfit came across somethin' interestin'. You might ask him."

"Where do I find Spears?"

"The last I heard he was skinnin' out near Ash Hollow. Eight, maybe nine miles from here."

Travis looked at the staked-out hides. "Looks like you did all right."

"Fair. Maybe seventy, eighty hides. The herds're just startin' to move now. Be better in another week or ten days." He looked sharply at Travis. "Hey, we ain't goin' to have no Injun trouble are we? I mean, with the army movin' around, I thought——"

"Everything is quiet on the reservation," Travis said. "And thank you for the information."

They rode off in the direction indicated, made a night camp, and got an early start in the morning. They found the site where Spears had camped; the ground was littered with rotting carcasses and scavenger birds hawked away as they rode near, protesting this interruption with loud cries.

Travis found the tracks made by Spears' wagons and they continued to follow them into the twilight. In the distance, the faint wink of a fire guided them and an hour later they came to the fringe of Spears' camp.

They were a wary, wild bunch, these hunters; there were a half-dozen rifles on Travis and his men when they came into the camp, and only after they were identified were the weapons put away.

Spears was a giant; bearded, loud-talking. "Can't be too careful," he said. "Been some bloody killin's over buff'lo hides." He laughed. "You fellas find a hole when the twister hit? It shook every building in Dodge and blew half the tents down, although it didn't come within thirty miles of the place."

Travis stripped off his gauntlets and stuffed them in his belt. "We stopped at another hunters' camp." He jerked his thumb in the direction they had traveled. "We asked if they'd seen any homesteaders in need of help, and the leader seemed to think you'd met up with some."

Spears' eyes flashed with a sudden anger. "That was Gadding, I'll bet. That son-of-a-bitch never could say nothin' good about a man. What'd he want to tell lies about me for?"

Spears was blustering and defensive without any obvious cause. Inwardly, Travis heaved a sigh. This looked like more trouble. He decided not to waste time on tact.

"You don't mind if we look around your camp, do you?" he asked.

"Hell, sure I mind!" Spears roared. "Do we have to be inspected or somethin'?"

The hunters had a huge fire going; it threw a wide circle of light, clear back to the wagons. Most of the men sprawled about watching the soldiers, while the skinners, who were not social equals, stayed farther back with the teamsters. Busik, who was standing near Travis' elbow, nudged him and pointed, singling Travis' attention on one hunter who lay half under a wagon; he appeared to be holding someone.

"Go take a look there, sergeant," Travis said. He watched Spears as he said it, and it seemed to be just like the Rinks all over again; Spears tried to draw his pistol and Travis beat him to it. He grabbed his wrist, pulled the giant's arm out straight, pivoted and slipped under it, then threw Spears over his shoulder to the ground. He hit with a dull thud and the hunters started to their feet, but carbines clicked in the silence and every man held his place.

Spears did not get up; he just lay there and looked at Travis as though he couldn't believe it had really happened. Travis said, "I don't want to turn this camp into a slaughter yard, so I'd suggest you all sit still until I see what's going on." He nodded to Busik. "Go have that look."

"As Busik skirted the fire, the man under the wagon yelped and a naked girl jumped up and ran for the grass away from the camp. Travis had only to snap his fingers and two troopers ran after her. To Busik he said, "Bring that man here!"

The hunter resisted, and Busik had to hit him several

times before he got him to cooperate. There was a struggle away from the camp, then the two soldiers came back, the reluctant girl between them. Out of consideration for her, they kept her away from the strong light of the fire, yet Travis could see that she was very young, fourteen or fifteen, not fully blossomed into womanhood.

One of the soldiers wrapped a blanket around her and she drew it tightly to her and huddled on the ground, crying, bent forward as though she suffered from intense cramps.

To Spears, Travis said, "Who is she?" Spears shrugged and remained silent. "All right," Travis said. "We'll do this properly. Busik, disarm this camp and if anyone gives you an argument, settle it any way you have to."

"Yes, sir."

It took a few minutes to gather up all the guns and knives, but the hunters offered no resistance; too many carbines were pointed at them and the troopers behind them all wore hard expressions.

"All right, Mr. Spears, I'll ask you again: who is she?" He turned and looked at a nearby trooper. "O'Donnell, if Mr. Spears does not answer, you may hit him on the head with the butt of your carbine until he does answer."

"Gladly, sir," he said grimly. He flipped it around and gripped the barrel, holding it like a baseball bat.

Spears held up his hands. "Oh, hell, she's some nester kid we found wandering on the prairie. The twister got the rest of her family, I guess. What difference does it make?"

"Who found her?" Travis asked flatly.

Spears hesitated, then nodded to the man Busik guarded. "He did." Then he made an appeal to Travis. "What the hell, lieutenant, she wasn't nothin' anyhow. They don't care what happens to 'em; one bed's as good as another."

The truth nearly made Travis sick, but he forced it down, forced himself to be coldly analytical. "How many of you raped this girl?"

One of the hunters in the background laughed and said, "Suppose we all give her a dollar apiece, then it ain't rape. That all right?"

"With your permission, sir," O'Donnell said in a hard voice. He handed his carbine to another soldier, walked

249

over to where the man lay, and kicked him flush in the face. A cavalryman's boots are heavy—graceless but sturdy—and O'Donnell made sure he put plenty of power into the blow. The man was flung back unconscious, and no one seemed to care. His face was a ruin; a lifetime disfiguration had taken place in an instant.

"Very good, O'Donnell," Travis said harshly. He looked at the hunters with a hatred born of outrage, and in his mind was the urge to punish the whole lot of them. Yet in spite of his anger, he knew that he must think clearly. Whatever his decision, he had to make it stick. He wasn't at all sure that violating a nester girl was a capital crime on the plains, or whether he was empowered to make charges; his position was somewhat undefined. But his shocked morality told him he must do something, arrest them, get them before a jury. The thought flashed through his mind that a jury in Dodge City would be comprised of buffalo hunters who would be unable to see the wrong of this at all, but it was a chance he had to take.

Travis spoke to Spears. "I want the names of the men who violated this child."

"Go to hell," Spears said, and was promptly knocked flat with the rifle butt. O'Donnell was somewhat of an expert. He hit hard, but only a glancing blow; enough to hurt Spears, yet not knock him out. The hunter lay back, blood dripping from his scalp. He looked at Travis and said, "Mister, if I told, I'd never be able to hire another man. When the girl was brought into camp, I said there'd be trouble over her. But whether my men are right or wrong, I've got to stick by 'em."

Travis understood this reasoning, yet he could not retreat from his own position. This was a tense moment, where the fate of military authority hung in the balance of a very young man's judgment. His enraged instincts told him to hang the lot of them, yet he knew that he must take a detached, unemotional stand, the stand that any good officer would take.

"Busik," he said. "Throw some water on that man over there, the one who shot off his mouth. Get him on his feet."

Busik found a slop pail and drenched the man, bringing him around. He had to help him up, and then hold him there.

"Can you hear me?" Travis asked. The man nodded feebly. "Then believe what I say. I want the name of the first man who violated this child. If you don't give it to me, I'm going to hang you from a wagon tongue."

This was completely unexpected to the hunters, and they stared incredulously at Jefferson Travis. They had expected a roughing up, and perhaps a week in the Fort Dodge guardhouse, but not a hanging. And they knew that he might do it, because other young officers had taken the law into their own hands, like the young lieutenant who had hanged the Apaches and started that Indian trouble in the Arizona Territory. Maybe he'd been wrong, and maybe he'd realized it later, but the men he'd hanged were dead just the same.

"He did," the man said, pointing to the hunter flanked by soldier guards. "He brought her in and got to her first." Then he shouted at the guilty man. "What did you expect, you son-of-a-bitch? That I'd hang for you?"

A stillness came into the camp. Then with a rush the accused man tried to break away, but the soldiers swarmed him, mobbed him to the ground, then brought him erect, his arms twisted cruelly behind him.

Spears struggled to his feet and grabbed Travis by the arm, thinking that now this man would be hanged. "In the name of God, you'd hang him for that? What is she anyway? Another year and she'd have been in some nester's shack!"

Rudely Travis pushed him away. "I'm not going to hang him, Mr. Spears. I'll let a jury do that for me." He pointed to the man Busik held. "Bring him along. You come too, Spears."

"What for? You got what you came for."

"We're going to backtrack a little," Travis said. "Back to the place where he found the girl." He locked eyes with Spears. "It occurs to me that if a man doesn't have the sensitivity to see the shame here, the crime committed, it follows that a jury of Dodge City buffalo hunters might not see it either. I just want to make sure, Mr. Spears, that this girl's family was killed *by the twister*."

251

9

Sergeant Ben Arness tended his duty well, not because he felt any particular dedication, but because he knew that Jefferson Travis would tack his hide to the stable door if he didn't. Grudgingly, Arness had to admit that the young lieutenant was as tough as any brigade commander he had ever seen. For a young upstart who didn't know much, he was positive as hell about what he did know.

The Indians who had been the terror of the plains just a few years before were now almost wholly dependent on the reservation for supplies. With the hunters slaughtering off the buffalo, the Indians were too lazy or too proud to plant crops, and seemed content to beg flour, salt, and anything else they thought they could get.

Then the nesters started straggling in, those who had been hit hard by the twister, and Arness saw that they were given enough staples to carry them along until they could get up a new soddy and round up the few head of stock they owned. With all his tasks Arness kept busy enough to forget for a time that Travis had pulled a sneaky trick on him, and how much he hated him for it.

Trooper Daniels and two men returned one day, bearing a dying man on a travois. It was late in the evening and Arness had him brought into the storeroom; there was no sense in having him bleed on the office floor.

"Found him crawling on his belly," Daniels said, biting off a chew of tobacco. "I sent two men to backtrack him. The twister got the rest of his family." He looked at Arness. "However, he's been shot."

For a moment Arness failed to recognize the man; he was dirty and hollow-cheeked, and pain drew his face into harsh, unrecognizable lines. "Ain't that Swain, from over near Buffalo Basin?" He turned and got a lamp and lit it; the light was growing poorer every minute. "Get some water and clean him up a little. We'll have a look at that wound."

Swain was forty-some, old for his age, for he had given youth to the land, hard land. First, that ten acres of rock and stump in Arkansas, then that forty acres of Illinois bottom land that had been worked out before he got it, and now, six years on the prairie, with nothing to show for it except a twister-leveled soddy, a bullet aflame in his stomach, and a mind full of overpowering regrets.

There wasn't much Arness could do for the wound except clean it; Swain was a doomed man, but he was making a fight of it, holding off until the last possible moment, and Arness wondered why, when it would have been easier to just let go and die.

"I'd better put this all down on the report," Arness said. "That goddamned lieutenant will want to know the details." He went back to the office and Daniels followed him. "The twister got the rest, you say?"

"Yeah, the old lady and his sons. The soddy just collapsed and buried 'em."

"Didn't he have a girl? What about her?"

Daniels shook his head. "No girl around, sarge. And we dug too."

"Well, if the wind took her, she ought to have been around someplace," Arness said.

"I tell you we looked, circling for over a mile around the soddy. That's how we come across Swain, crawling toward the reservation. Sarge, how come he's shot? You know, that ain't no .44 in him, not and make a hole like that. A buffalo rifle?"

Arness shook his head. "I wouldn't want to say." He sat down and began to write. "Kind of look after him. Make dying as easy as you can. If he wants a drink, just take what you need from Brewer's liquor cabinet."

"All right, sarge." He took a bottle and went out, and Arness never thought to tell him not to drink any of it himself. He finished writing up the details and then went to the storeroom. Swain lay like a frail ghost, alive only in his eyes.

Arness knelt beside him and said, "Can you hear me, Swain?"

The man nodded weakly.

"Do you know where you are, Swain? You're at the reservation. You got a bad one. No time to ride to Spanish Spring for the doc. Can you tell me who shot you?"

It required a supreme effort to speak, and then it came out as a whisper. "Hunter."

Arness knew the man didn't have the strength to say much, so he worked out a system whereby Swain could answer him without speaking. "Swain, I'll ask questions that you can answer by yes or no. You nod or shake your head. Do you understand?" he did, so Arness went on. "Did the hunter shoot you after the twister?"

Swain nodded.

"Were you in the soddy? No? Away then. Were you alone?" He watched the sideways movement of Swain's head. "Your boy with you? Your girl then. Yes, the girl was with you." He paused to think. "Well, you had to be under cover or the twister would have got you. In a buffalo wallow? Were you taking cover in a buffalo wallow?"

Swain nodded and Arness smiled, feeling that he was getting somewhere. "All right now, what about the girl? Is she dead? Alive!" A puzzled frown wrinkled his face. "Wait a minute now. The hunter was in the wallow when you got there? He was? More than one? How many? Three? Six? Ten? Ten hunters! Swain, did the hunters shoot you to take the girl?"

When Swain nodded, Arness stood up slowly. "All right, Swain, take it easy. We'll do what we can." He went out, looking for Trooper Daniels, and found him leaning against the far wall swigging from the bottle. Arness took it away from him and clouted him on the jaw, then ordered him to the storeroom.

He went back to the office and wrote some more in the report, detailing his questions and Swain's answers. It made sense, the hunters taking the girl. An unprotected woman was considered fair game to them; this was just a hard, brutal facet of living on the prairie, and Indian women, caught alone, would stuff themselves with dirt to cheat the hunters. Arness knew all these things, knew also that it didn't help to feel anger over it; there really wasn't anything he could do about it.

Just sit and write it all down on a piece of paper while a man lay dying in the storeroom.

The day was the hottest Travis had so far endured; they were moving toward the reservation now, the three buffalo hunters bound and tied to their horses, surrounded by troopers. They found the buffalo wallow where they had all hidden to protect themselves from the twister, but Busik found some additional sign, a spore of blood, and the tracks of army horses.

It was clear that all movement was toward the reservation.

Luke Spears had stopped pleading, stopped arguing the night before; he knew now that nothing he could say would deter Travis. In Spears' mind it was injustice for him to be brought along, for his responsibility ended when the guilty man had been singled out. He was sure that by the time Travis got through fooling around, he'd find his hides and wagons gone, stolen by his own men in his absence.

At last they came in sight of the reservation; a brassy noon sun was overhead, layering the land with an intense heat and glare. When they rode into the yard, Ben Arness came out, saw the girl, and let his jaw drop open.

"Good God! I've got her old man in the storeroom with a bullet in him."

Across Lieutenant Travis' unshaven cheeks came a new brittleness. He whipped his head around and looked at Luke Spears. Then he said, "Separate these three men and keep them under close guard!" He pointed to the one who had taken the girl. His name was Clayman, originally bound for California, but he couldn't find a wagon train that would tolerate him, and he didn't have the courage to go it alone. "I want him brought to the storeroom. Hold him outside until I'm ready."

He lifted the girl down, taking care to keep the blanket around her to shield her nakedness. Then he carried her inside, to Brewer's room, and put her on the bed. Ben Arness was hovering by the door when Travis came out.

"She hasn't said one word since we recovered her," Travis said. "Oh, why couldn't they have a doctor here!" He slapped his hands together impatiently. The tension of his duty was beginning to show on him; his face seemed even more thin and haggard, and his deep-set eyes more sunken. Small worries and larger ones kept pushing a wrinkled frown into his forehead, and the old optimism was gone from his voice, replaced now with a tired stubbornness, a determination to do the best he could with the inferior tools at hand.

"You look like you could stand some sleep, sir," Arness said.

"Later, later," Travis said irritably. "Is the girl's father still alive? Tell me about it." He listened to Arness relate the facts as he knew them while they walked toward the storeroom. Two haggard troopers guarded Clayman; the others, Spears, and the badly beaten man, were kept apart so they couldn't talk up a story between them.

"Bring him inside," Travis said, and opened the door. Swain rolled his eyes and stared at them as though he couldn't tell one from another, then he slowly raised his hand and pointed to the prisoner, his mouth working desperately.

"That's enough for me," Travis said harshly. "O'Donnell, this man remains bound and under strict guard; he is to speak to no one. Understand?"

"Yes, sir! I sure do." He gave the man a jolt with the rifle barrel. "Let's go, you son-of-a-bitch."

When the door closed, Travis took off his kepi and wiped his sweat-streaked face on the back of his sleeve. "If he dies, I've got a charge of murder to bring."

"In Dodge, sir?" Arness shook his head. "A jury of buffalo hunters would never convict him. It's the way the world is, sir. Buffalo hunters bring the money into Dodge, and even a merchant, if he was on the jury, would think of his cash drawer and not Swain shot in the belly." A trace of anger crept into his voice. "No one would want the buffalo hunters to get down on them. And they're going to hate you, sir."

"Do you think I give a goddamn about that?" Travis snapped. He knelt by Swain and touched him lightly, bringing the man's eyes half open. "She's safe now, Swain."

He tried to smile, and he thanked Travis with his eyes. Then the two men stood there while Swain's breathing turned harsh and ragged; he took in a huge breath and let it out in a long sigh. He never took another.

Without thinking, Ben Arness slowly took off his hat and said softly, "He was grateful, sir, for telling him he didn't have to hang on no longer." Then angrily he wiped

256

his knuckles across his nose and sniffed. "God damn it anyway, that's all they do, hang on, when there ain't nothin' to hang on for. And when one dies, another comes to hang on in his place." He jammed the hat back on his head. "I'll take care of the burial, sir."

"Yes, I'd appreciate that," Travis said, looking at Swain. "You know, sergeant, there'll come a time when all the Swains and the Pearls, who lived a lifetime being nothing, are going to be empire builders; that's what people will call them. Populating the prairie, as Wrigley said. Bringing schools and roads, hell! They brought blood and poured it on the ground, a man a mile, sergeant, a family an acre; that's what this land's going to cost, and there's no denying it."

He wheeled and strode out into the smashing sunlight, motioning for Luke Spears to be brought to the office.

"Sit down," Travis snapped. He took his place behind the desk and eyed Spears coldly; there was not one shard of sympathy in Jefferson Travis. "Mr. Spears, I'm not going to mince words with you. Swain died, and Sergeant Arness tells me you were there when he was shot. Now I've got a charge of murder to bring against Clayman, and I'm going to enjoy watching him hang for it." He picked up a stub of a pencil and some paper and spun them around so that Spears could write. "I want you to put down everything that happened, just as it happened, and then you're going to sign it, before witnesses."

Spears licked his lips. "God, I can't do that! Why, when word got out, I'd be shot in the back inside of a month!"

Travis tapped his finger on the desk top. "Mr. Spears, you're done for anyway. If you don't write me a correct and complete account and sign it, I'm going to turn you loose on the prairie without a horse or a gun, and I'm going to make sure every Indian on the reservation knows about it. How long do you think you're going to last out there?"

"Why, that's plain murder!"

"It's more of a chance than Swain had, or that poor girl. Make up your mind, Mr. Spears. I'll give you thirty seconds." He took out his watch and laid it on the desk.

Spears didn't need thirty seconds; he was writing by the time fifteen had passed. Travis watched him labor over

257

the paper, then he called in Arness and another soldier to witness the date and signature.

"Give Mr. Spears his horse and pistols and escort him a mile away from the reservation," Travis said.

This seemed to outrage Arness. "Are you turning him loose?" Then he shrugged and took Spears outside.

The beaten man was brought in; he was in considerable pain, for many of his teeth had been broken, and Travis suspected that his jaw was fractured too. He mumbled his story while Travis took it down, and it was signed with an X, and witnessed.

Then he was released and sent away from the reservation. Arness remained in Travis' office, and the young officer kept shuffling the two confessions. "You think I'm crazy, don't you, sergeant, letting two witnesses leave?" He smiled grimly. "A man can lie on the witness stand, sergeant, and he can be discredited by good cross-examination. But did you ever hear of a deposition being cross-examined or discredited?" He slapped the papers. "Here's my case, sergeant. Now have Brewer's ambulance hitched up. I want a detail of four men to escort me to Spanish Spring."

"What about the girl, sir?"

"I'm taking her along; she can't stay here. And even if she won't talk, sergeant, I want her on that witness stand to point her finger." The depth of his rage was apparent then, and Arness studied him carefully.

"Sir, every time I offer advice, you shut me up, but this time I wish you'd at least hear me out."

"All right. At least you're speaking to me again."

Arness grinned in spite of himself. "Well, what I've got to say is going to sound like I give a damn about you one way or another, and I don't. But I wish you'd think this over careful, sir."

"Meaning?"

"Well, the army around Fort Dodge is in sympathy with the buffalo hunters. Now if one of their patrols had run into this, most likely it'd have been written up in a report and let go at that. What I mean to say is, that if Clayman gets hung, a lot of people are liable to ask if this was the first time, or has it happened before. And the army at Dodge ain't going to like answering that, sir. Neither is Major Deacon." He scrubbed a hand across his weathered face. "Damn it, I don't like to sound as though I'm siding with Clayman—you know that ain't so—but I don't want to see a stink stirred up between the army and the buffalo hunters either."

"That happened when Clayman shot Swain," Travis said firmly. "I couldn't turn my back on this if I wanted to, sergeant. It's the way I am." He got up and turned toward Brewer's room. "Let's look in on the girl."

She was awake, lying still, staring at the ceiling, and when Travis stood by the bed, she moved only her eyes. She was pretty, in a big-boned, peasant way.

"How are you feeling?" Travis asked gently. "Can you understand me?"

She nodded, and he smiled to reassure her.

"We're going to take you to Spanish Spring, where you'll be safe. Wouldn't you like that?" When the girl did not answer, he looked at Arness. "Do you suppose there's something wrong with her? She doesn't say anything, just looks at you. I'm sure she understands."

Arness softly cleared his throat, then said, "Little girl, your father's dead."

"Why you clumsy—!"

Then Travis stopped, for the girl began to sob, with a grief made more terrible by its silence. He stared at her while her mouth worked frantically, trying to form words her voice box was incapable of producing. He could bear only a minute of this, then he wheeled and walked out of the room. Arness joined him a moment later and found Travis leaning against the wall, his face ashen.

"Mute," Travis said. "I understand now, sergeant; she was just a female animal to Clayman, just something to be thrown away." He waved his hand. "Go on, get Brewer's ambulance hitched up. I want to leave within the hour."

Major Deacon was seven hours out of Fort Winthrop on the Spanish Spring road. He rode in an army ambulance, with the driver, and four troopers bringing up the rear. The heat and the dust bothered Deacon and he sat glumly on the high seat, a cold cigar clamped between his teeth, trying to ignore the many miles he had yet to go.

A dispatch case rested between his feet; in it were his personal papers and dispatches from Lieutenant Jefferson

Travis. Major Deacon was suffering a twinge of conscience, for in assigning Travis to this detail he did so with the deliberate intent of using him and sacrificing him if necessary, for it was less tragic to lose an officer whose career had only commenced, than an officer whose career was already established.

Of course this was not the first hopeless assignment the army had suffered through; Ralph Deacon had lived through one or two when he had been younger, and expendable, himself. This was why his conscience troubled him, for in Jefferson Travis he now recognized value in spite of youth, and judgment, a sense of justice that was not misplaced by odds. The young man had honor and a capacity for greater things, if he could be spared.

Major Ralph Deacon was going to spare him, if he could.

It was bad to have to sacrifice a young, unproven officer whose worth had not yet been established. But it was criminal to sacrifice one whose worth was rapidly becoming apparent. In going to Spanish Spring, in supporting Travis, Major Deacon was placing his own future on the block, yet he disregarded the risks. Fort Dodge was commanded by a general, and generals always protected themselves. And Fort Winthrop was an outpost, with only a tired major in command; he had no illusions about who would win in a test of political strength.

Still he had to try, because a damned young, inexperienced officer was trying, and this, in a way, was shaming Deacon to try with him.

They made a meal stop at the stage relay station, and quite coincidentally, the stage came through, which gave them an opportunity to catch up on the Spanish Spring gossip. Deacon ate alone, but the room was small enough for him to hear every word that was said, and in this way he learned of Swain's murder and Clayman's arrest.

Changing horses, Deacon and his detail moved on, at a faster pace now; he was in a hurry to get to Spanish Spring, for this was a development of tremendous importance and he could only speculate on the final results. The dead nester would be stoutly defended by politicians interested in clearing the buffalo hunters out and opening the land for farmers, and likely some Eastern newspapers would get hold of this and play it up. This would set the defenders of the hide hunters into action; they'd make a fight of it to protect their interests, which ran into several million dollars a year.

By George, he didn't want anyone turning this into another Dred Scott affair, and it could; a good many momentous things started out innocently enough.

Travis sat in his office in Spanish Spring and looked out the open door at the brassy sunlight. The sky was rinsed to the palest blue, and the country around had a purple cast, as though it stretched so frighteningly far that God tinted it so you could not see the full enormity of it.

A bath, a shave, and a change of clothes refreshed him; then he went out and down the street to Doctor Summers' house. Hope was in the kitchen humming to herself when Travis stepped into Summers' office. The doctor was grinding some white pills into a powder, and he went on with this while Travis sat down. When he had finished, he glanced at Travis and read correctly the embarrassed expression on the young man's face.

"Would you rather read a report of my examination, or have me tell it to you?" Summers asked.

Color came into Travis' cheeks. "Really, doctor, I know what goes on, you know. When I was fourteen, my father took me to a farm to watch a mare bred."

"I hardly consider that ample qualification," Summers said wryly. "But no matter. There's nothing wrong with her, no real harm done. Of course we ought to wait a few months to be positive of that." He poured the powder into paper sacks and folded them, then turned around to face Travis. "She's a husky girl, Mr. Travis. Perhaps we can find work for her someplace, housekeeping or something. Too bad this had to happen though. People will always remember it and point."

"Why do they do that? Why don't they point at a man because he broke his leg?"

"You answer that," Summers said, "and you've gone a long way toward solving the world's trouble." He slapped his thighs and stood up, reaching for his bag. "Got to peddle my pills. Hope's in the kitchen."

Travis went to the rear of the house while Summers slammed out the front door. Hope Randall was plucking a chicken; she wiped her hands on a towel and poured a cup of coffee for him. Then she sat down.

"You look older, Jeff."

"I'm a hundred years old," he declared. "And I wish I were ten again and running barefoot in a clover field with my dog." He laughed. "His name was Fleas and he was of mixed parentage, but he was a good dog. A farmer killed him with a pitchfork one day for scaring his horse, and no one ever did anything about it."

She regarded him steadily. "I could have guessed that last part, Jeff. But you'll break your heart, defending people who won't defend themselves."

"What would you have me do, Hope?"

"Just what you are doing," she said softly. "And one of these days I hope you'll find time to marry me."

10

It was dusk when Lieutenant Travis reached the archway to the barracks compound and saw the ambulance parked in front of his office. He stopped and stood there for a moment, trying to imagine where it had come from. Certainly it had brought a visitor of field grade; few below that rank rated an ambulance and a mounted escort.

His first guess was Major Griswald from Fort Dodge, and Travis walked on to the office with misgivings; he did not like Griswald, his opinions, or his manner. Two troopers whom Travis had never seen before stood on the porch. They came to attention as he stepped inside and saw that it wasn't Griswald at all.

Major Ralph Deacon was studying some papers. He raised his head as Travis saluted.

"At ease, Mr. Travis." He got up from behind the desk and waved Travis into the chair. "I hope you're not assuming that I've taken over your detail by occupying your chair." He shuffled his papers together and stuffed them into his dispatch case.

With a touch of nervousness, Jefferson Travis sat down and looked at Major Deacon. The lamplight struck the older man's face harshly, blocking it in defined shadows, giving his expression severity. Deacon opened his cigar case and bent forward to offer one to Travis. A match passed between them, then Deacon said, "Mr. Travis, can you smell trouble in the wind?"

"I'm learning how, sir."

"Mmmm, well, I could smell it all the way to Fort Winthrop." He crossed his skinny legs and rested his hands on his knee. The cigar bobbed as he rolled it from one side of his mouth to the other. "You're very prompt with your reports, Mr. Travis. Very well written too. Very complete." He tapped his dispatch case. "I have a letter from Major Griswald requesting that you be relieved of your duties and returned to Fort Winthrop to be given a less exacting task. General Thomas C. Wrigley also wrote to me; he demands that you be withdrawn and a more experienced man replace you. Mr. Brewer, the Indian agent, wrote a letter to me complaining that you disrupted a beef issue and spread discontent among his charges. Mr. Travis, you seem to have a talent for antagonizing people."

"Yes, sir, if you want to look at it from their point of view."

Deacon's eyebrow raised. "Suppose you tell me your point of view then."

"May I speak freely, major?"

"It was an invitation," Deacon said. "Let's dispense with the protocol. We'll get more accomplished that way."

Jefferson Travis wiped a hand across his mouth and wondered where to begin. "Since I've assumed my duties, I've tried to pinpoint responsibility for the conditions that exist, and I've concluded that it's impossible, as such. My first impression of the homesteaders was that they were a thieving bunch. However, I now believe differently; they are more victims than perpetrators, major. General Wrigley, through some vague Indian Treaty stipulations and squatter's privilege, has taken charge of the decent land." He smiled. "I'm not suggesting that much of it is decent, but there *are* a few springs and water holes about that will support small-scale subsistence farming. Wrigley claims control of this land and leases it to these people. Frankly, I seriously doubt the validity of his right to lease. But, be that as it may, he extracts what little money these people make, money they desperately need to live and grow on. In my opinion, he holds them in virtual slavery, much in the same manner as the New York landowners during the Dutch rule." He puffed on his cigar a moment. "The first contact I had with the cattlemen did not leave me with a favorable impression of them. They were arrogant and strong-willed, and I thought they were overly eager to take issue with the homesteaders. But this did not prove to be the case. Most of their grazing land is now Indian reservation, the homesteaders have been rustling them blind, and I now realize that had they been less tolerant, less peaceful, men would have been hanged before now. I came to terms with them, major; I found them quite reasonable." He paused and frowned a little. "As you know, Mr. Brewer is dead, and I hesitate to speak of his shortcomings now, but he was a man in a hopeless position, and, I believe, quite ill-fitted for the job. But I couldn't say what man would be fitted for *that* work; he would have to be a master diplomat, an excellent politician, a sharp horse trader, and something of a petty embezzler to come out on top."

Major Deacon laughed softly. "Mr. Travis, that is an astute observation. I must remember that. But go on."

"The buffalo hunters are a scurvy lot, major. Yet I can't condemn a man because he has a dirty neck. They are a product of the country, born of necessity. Without the buffalo they would not exist at all, so they can hardly be at fault for doing what is required of them. Buffalo robes are in vogue, and 'beaver' hats, so the buffalo have to be killed, and hide buyers in Dodge pour money into the town, and the army is there to protect the money." He shook his head. "It isn't my intention to lay the blame at anyone's door, major. I only wish to keep the multitude of forces here in harmony with one another. Without that, none of them can survive long." He fingered the ash off his cigar and sat with his elbows planted on the desk top, his hands cupped together. "I'd very much like to be thirty, major, with the experience to tell me what is right and wrong. But I'm not. I can only function within the scope of my own conscience, and stay as neutral as possible." He then went into lengthy detail, relating to Deacon the aftereffects of the twister, and the steps he had taken to relieve the hardships of it. "Of course I'll put this all down in a written report," he said. "At the moment, Sergeant Arness is in charge of the agency. In a week or ten days I expect someone will be sent out to take over. Which brings me to a most unpleasant matter, major." Quickly, in an unadorned fashion, he gave Major Deacon all the facts leading to the arrest of the buffalo hunter. While he talked, Deacon listened to the subtle changes in Travis' voice and realized how deeply disturbed the young man was over this affair.

"Are you going to press for a speedy local trial and a quick hanging?" Deacon asked.

"No, I've decided to make a public matter of it. I realize, sir, that such a decision may be unfavorable with the major, and of course you may change it."

"Mr. Travis, you'll be forcing the entire command at Fort Dodge to stand behind the buffalo hunters in the matter. They've always supported the hunters and the money behind them; they can't reverse their position now. Do you fully understand that the commanding general may feel as you do, yet, by prerogative, must publicly take the other side? Mr. Travis, for that your career may be forfeit."

"Yes, I understand that," Travis said. "I could try the man speedily and get him hanged and have it blow over with just a local smell to it." He spread his hands in an appeal. "Major, I could let that man go too, but if I did that, I'd be endorsing the molestation of every homesteader in this area, especially if he had a woman about. So you see, a quick hanging smacks of 'lynch justice,' and turning him loose is an acknowledgement by the U. S. Army that we have no justice at all." He sighed and chewed the end of his cigar. "Major, this is undoubtedly my first and last tour of duty, and I wouldn't like to leave anything behind that I'd be ashamed of."

Deacon studied him carefully. "You're willing to air this in a federal court in Dodge, Mr. Travis? The defense will wheel out the big guns; they'll rip you to pieces."

"Yes," he said.

"Justice against money! That's what will be on trial,

Mr. Travis. The army policy." He snuffed out his cigar in a glass dish. "Dodge has needed a federal marshal for a year now, but no one wants to hire one. And the army has been nursemaid and protective father and whipping boy too long, but no one wants to change that either. If you win your case, Mr. Travis, some Washington politicians are going to have to overhaul their thinking and introduce some law out here. They'll have to give us more money, more men, and a sound policy. And I don't think they want to do that. They want the profit without the investment. The homesteaders are to shift for themselves, the hunters can do as they damn please, and the Indian has to stay where he's put as long as he's out of the way. But if you lose, Mr. Travis, it will signal in a new, prolonged period of lawlessness and bad politics, with every man shifting for himself toward his own ends. Do you think you have the right to gamble with the future of these people?"

"No, I don't," Travis said. "But I've got to take the right. Someone has to, major. I've got less to lose than perhaps the next man."

"You've got more to lose," Deacon said softly. "Well, I'd probably retire a major anyway, so that puts us in the same boat." He half rose from his chair and reached across the desk to offer his hand. "Now let's get together on our campaign strategy. I'm just the officer who can do a good job of prosecuting."

Lieutenant Travis had to return to the reservation; Sergeant Arness sent a trooper with word that the Indians were doing a lot of dancing and face-painting over the buffalo hunting. The kill was big this year and the Indians were scrounging around for powder and lead and talking war talk.

In going on to the reservation and leaving Major Deacon in town, Travis missed the transfer of the prisoner to Fort Dodge, six days' ride to the north. And he missed the communications the commanding officer of Dodge sent down to Major Deacon. The correspondence was essentially a threat with one end in mind, getting the charges against the hunter dropped.

The people of Spanish Spring were still busy repairing their roofs and fixing the twister damage, but the weekly paper managed to get published on time and the editor ran a well-written account of the hunter's arrest. He editorialized about the crime, voicing a strong opinion, and copies of the paper went East on the stage when it came through. Ralph Deacon considered this inevitable; some reporter was bound to read about it and pick it up, because people always took an interest in what happened to the downtrodden.

Arriving at the reservation, Jefferson Travis learned that over forty braves had taken their horses and weapons and left the reservation, striking north into the buffalo hunter's territory. With this immediate crisis facing him, he deliberately ignored Arness' report that the agency stores were being rapidly depleted and that with no money coming from Washington for another six months the Indians would starve if something wasn't done. Leaving orders with Busik and Arness to ready the detail and be ready to leave with him at dawn, he slept the clock around.

The rest made him feel better. He arose before dawn, shaved, had something to eat, and was outside preparing to mount his horse before the sky in the east rinsed to a pale gray. He had to chance that the agency help would be able to manage alone. Travis couldn't spare Arness or any of his men to do the job, not when there was Indian trouble afoot.

Through a hot, dusty day they traveled in a sweeping circle, trying to pick up some sign of the Indians, and they camped out the night in a dry wash before pushing on. In the early morning they came across a buffalo hunters' camp and found three skinners digging graves.

Turning the detail over to Sergeant Arness, Travis went forward and spoke to the owner. "Indians?"

"God damn Indians," the man said, spitting tobacco juice. There was blood on his pants leg; he had suffered a slight wound, but paid it no mind. "They hit us late yesterday. We wasn't ready for nothin' like that." He squinted accusingly at Travis. "Thought you sojers was supposed to keep the Indians quiet. Can't you do your job?"

"How many in the raiding party?" Travis asked, sidestepping an argument.

"Oh, thirty-five, maybe a few more. You didn't answer me, mister."

"What the hell do you want to do, argue or tell me about the Indians so I can round them up?" Travis snapped. "How many casualties did you sustain?"

"How's that?"

"How many got shot?"

"Three dead," the hunter said. "Four wounded, but not bad. I got hit on my——"

"And the Indians?"

"I guess we killed five or six. They took 'em along though." He pointed to the east. "That way, if you intend followin' 'em."

"I intend to," Travis said, and went back to his horse. He swung about and struck off in the new direction, still on a cold trail, but it was better than nothing. Three dead hunters to five or six Indians was hardly profitable for the Indians. He supposed it was that way every year, the Indians going on a few punitive raids and getting their ranks thinned out, gaining absolutely nothing by it, for the goverment wouldn't blame the hunters. They'd blame the Indians for having a warlike nature.

Arness took the point and Busik came back to ride with Travis. He kept chewing tobacco and squinting and swinging his head from side to side to peer at the inscrutable distance. Finally he said, "Sir, what we going to do if we find the Indians?"

"Put them back on reservation."

Busik seemed saddened by this. "Sure is a shame, sir."

Travis looked at him. "What is?"

"Ah, you can't blame 'em for having blood in their eye, with the hunters killing off the buffalo and leaving the carcasses to rot. And it's a damned shame we've got to fight 'em to make 'em go back. It don't seem fair, somehow, for the Indians to lose at both ends."

"Just chalk it down as another inequity," Travis said.

That evening they came across a homesteader and his family. They were repairing their soddy, and the two oldest boys worked with their rifles close at hand. Everyone seemed relieved to see the army, and the men came forward as Travis dismounted his detail by the spring.

"Name's Otis," the man said, extending his hand. He wore a faded pair of overalls, but they were clean, and he had shaved that morning; so had his sons. He pointed to the three women near the soddy. "My wife and daughters. These are my sons, Mike and Adam."

"Howdy," they said, and shook hands. "You look mighty good to us right now, lieutenant."

"How's that?" Travis said. "You have an Indian scare?"

"We sure did," Otis declared. "Around noon, a passel came through, made up for war, I tell you. Paint all over 'em, and their ponies. We ain't drew a decent breath since."

"Say," Adam Otis said, "ain't you the one who caught that hunter after he killed Swain?"

"News gets around," Travis said. "Yes, he's in Fort Dodge by now, awaiting trial."

Some of the pleasure vanished from their eyes. "Fort Dodge, huh? Well, I reckon *they'll* turn him loose. Too bad, too. We could stand a little law on our side." He looked at Travis as though he was presenting an argument. "We're not dirt, lieutenant. We came out here with two wagons, tools, enough supplies for a year, and six hundred dollars." He shrugged as though he realized this was getting him nowhere. "If you're after those Indians, I'd ride about seven miles east of here. Deer Creek has some water in it, and there's timber there. They were heading in that general direction."

"We may push on through and try to locate their camp," Travis said. "They already raided a buffalo hunters' camp and killed three men."

"Good for them!" Mike Otis said.

Travis shook his head. "We've all got to try to get along," he said. "It's hard, I know, but the only way."

"Sure," Otis said, "but it's hard to care about people that don't give a damn for you."

That was, Travis thought, the whole thing in a nutshell. He turned to his horse and stepped into the saddle and led them in the direction of Deer Creek.

Shadows began to lengthen and the prairie turned dark, although the heat of the day, imprisoned in the ground, radiated from it like a dying fire in a sheet-iron stove. There was a cold-ration stop of forty minutes, and cinches were loosened and the horses fed and watered lightly.

He kept thinking ahead, wondering if the Indians were camped at Deer Creek. It seemed logical that they would be, for they needed rest as well as the cavalry. But he wasn't sure of what he would do when he found them. Talking to them was out of the question. They had been lied to so many times that they refused to believe any white man. Fighting them seemed almost criminal. There were too many things in their lives to fight without adding the U. S. Army.

Yet he had to get them back, for their own sakes, and this was an ironic paradox, for no matter what he said, they would believe he wanted them on the reservation for the protection of the hunters.

He had a chance to talk to Arness when he walked over so where he sat alone. "Major Deacon is in Spanish Spring," he said. "When we get back you can take your complaints to him. I give you my permission."

Arness raised his head and looked at Travis, then said, "To hell with it."

"You quitting, sergeant?" Travis squatted beside him. "I'm glad to hear it, because you can't beat me. I'd always have the rank and you know it. It's too bad you choke on it; we might accomplish a lot together, if you'd accept it." He took out two cigars and offered one to Arness, and when the sergeant shook his head Travis jammed it between his lips, a little out of patience. "Here. Stop being such a stubborn jackass." He raked a match alight on the seat of his pants and held it cupped near Arness' face. Then Arness laughed softly and drew his cigar alight.

"The last time we smoked a cigar, lieutenant, was because I wanted to see you cough a little. Now I guess it's my turn to cough." He took the cigar from his mouth and made some hacking sounds, then laughed again.

"Arness, did you ever try being honest with yourself about the army?"

"What do you mean?"

"Did you ever try to accept the truth for what it was? That you'd given a lot of years and felt that you hadn't got fair return for it?" Arness looked at him and Travis knew that he had hit on a truth. "Ben, what is it you want most from life? Give me an answer."

"A home and wife and some kids," Arness said. "I can't remember what it's like to sit under my own roof, lieutenant. For twenty-seven years I've seen young officers

270

come in the army and get married and raise their families, but it's not for an enlisted man, sir."

"Some do it."

"A wife of mine wouldn't live on Suds Row." He drew deeply on his cigar. "Look at me now, near the end of it, and nothing to show for it but nine hundred dollars in the St. Louis bank." He shrugged and stared at the ground. "Grace Beaumont is the only woman I ever asked to marry me. I felt I could, not having much more time to go. Still, it's not that easy, always being army, knowing you're no good for anything on the outside, and knowing you'll have to be out someday."

"So it suited you to have me 'push' you out, is that it? That way, if it didn't work, you could always blame me and not yourself." Travis shook his head. "Don't do that to me, Arness. I don't want any part of it." He got up and looked down at Arness. "It takes a man to stand on his own two feet. Maybe you like the army because there's always an officer around to give you an order, and when it goes sour, you can say it was his fault and not yours. The army isn't something to lean on, Arness. You've got a little part of it to hold up. And I wish to hell you'd try and do that."

"Where'd you hear that, at the Academy?"

"As a matter of fact, I did. It's still true." He started away, then turned back. "When we get to Spanish Spring, ask Major Deacon to make out your retirement papers. Or else get a transfer out of my detail."

"What for? I thought we were beginning to understand each other."

"Just understanding something doesn't make it right," Travis said, and walked away. Busik was stretched out on the ground, a hand over his face; he stirred when Travis came up.

"Get the men mounted, sergeant. Let's get on with our Indian hunting."

A few minutes later they were again moving toward Deer Creek, and in an hour they came upon it, a trickle of water in an irregular slash across the flat face of the prairie. The night was dark, with only a splinter of moon to help them, and Travis led his men slowly and quietly along the creek for better than a mile and a half.

Then he stopped and let them bunch up. Ahead was a

271

grove of trees, and he thought he saw a camp there, the flicker of a small fire. Leaving Arness with the detail, he and Busik went forward afoot for a closer look.

It was the Indian camp. The horse herd was being guarded on the other side, two braves moving around them constantly. The fire was built low in the creek bed, and in that way shielded from the view of anyone approaching from the north or south. And even if a man traveled along the twisted course of the creek, he might stumble on the camp before he saw it.

There was no accurate way to count the remaining Indians, but Travis thought that thirty-five might be a fair estimate. He motioned for Busik to move back, and followed him, and when he rejoined his detail, he took off his kepi and wiped his forehead.

"You want a flanking maneuver, sir?" Arness asked. "We can catch them in a cross fire."

"I don't want anything of the sort," Travis said testily. He wondered whether or not he should berate Arness for presuming to advise him in front of the men, then decided not to. "We'll make a quiet camp here," Travis said. "Then, before dawn, we'll make a raid on the Indian ponies. It occurs to me that they can't make much war afoot." He looked intently at Arness. "And the first man who downs an Indian when we go in can figure that he's in more trouble than he ever knew existed. I want those Indians back on reservation all right, but unharmed. They've already had enough done to them."

11

In the creek bed, Travis' men waited silently, the horses held well back. Six hundred yards separated them from the Indian camp, and there was no sign of movement there either. Some of the troopers caught up on their sleep;

they were a calm lot, undisturbed over the prospect of trouble.

Travis stretched out on his back, his heels near the trickle of water, but he could not sleep. There were only two ways to disarm the Indians: take their guns away from them, or their horses. Fewer would be killed if he took their horses. Afoot, the Indians couldn't do much except return to the reservation. The scare would be over and the damned hide hunters could go on killing the buffalo until they were all gone. Then they could move on to something else, for it seemed to be their lot to destroy. Travis had read much about the mountain men, how they raped a country of her furs in a few years, and with their greed destroyed their own way of life. The buffalo hunters just might do the same thing, but the damage would be done by then. The Indian would have nothing to hunt, no way to live, and in time they too would vanish, killed off by "progress," or shoved out of sight on some reservation and forgotten.

About three o'clock he woke Busik and quietly the men mounted up and left the creek bed, easing in toward the Indian camp. Travis made certain he was on the same side as the pony herd; he didn't want to have to charge across that creek bed full tilt, and in the darkness to boot.

The Indians' ponies were bunched up, just clear of the stunted timber, and guarded by two mounted warriors who rode sleepily about. Travis moved close enough so that he could just make them out, then he waved his hand and the men moved into a line abreast to wait for his signal. He gave it with a jab of spurs and they thundered toward the pony herd, yelling and whooping, and the two guards wheeled to meet them. The Indian camp came alive with a rush, but it was too late. Travis and his men were into the herd, driving them out. Guns popped as the two guards fired at the soldiers, but there were no answering shots. Some of the Indians in the camp loosed a volley at the vanishing horses, then Travis and his men were in the clear, pushing the herd onto the flats, beyond hope of the Indians' recovering them.

Busik and the men gathered the ponies and held them, and Travis signaled for Arness to side him. When he drew up, Travis said, "There are still two mounted men in that camp, Ben. And two Indians on horseback constitute a danger. Let's go back."

"You're crazy, sir."

"I don't think they'll expect us," Travis said. "I want those two ponies, Ben. The Indians are going to walk back to the reservation so they won't forget this." He twisted in the saddle for a look around. "Two mounted men *could* try to take the horses back. Now let's go; I'm picking you to volunteer."

"All right, since you put it that way."

They made another approach to the Indian camp. It was in an uproar, braves milling about, shouting, blaming everyone else for the surprise attack. The fire was being built up, and the two mounted guards rode about, shouting at those on foot. They were so busy arguing that Arness and Travis made their approach unnoticed. They were almost into the camp before the Indians spotted them.

One of the mounted braves wheeled his horse and whooped, leveling his rifle to fire at Travis as he came at him. Bending low, Travis made a small target of himself and the bullet missed him somehow. Then they came together and Travis caught the brave around the throat and dragged him backward off the horse. Arness and the other Indian were clubbing at each other with carbines. A gun went off and Arness grunted, then fell, dragging the brave with him. There was the sound of a bone snapping when they hit the ground, but Travis was too busy to pay much attention. He dragged the brave he had unhorsed into the camp and dumped him across the fire. With a shriek the Indian bounded up and went thrashing off into the brush, trying to put out the blaze in his breeches.

Travis was in the middle of the Indians, surrounded completely, and a rush of fear filled his chest, but he beat it down and dismounted as casually as he could. The Indians started to crowd about him, their half-naked bodies vivid with paint, their bronze faces cold and angry. He rammed his way through them and knelt by Ben Arness, who lay on the ground, clutching his stomach. Blood stained his fingers, but he managed a weak smile.

One of the Indians grabbed Travis by the shoulder as though to pull him away, and he was stopped by a shout.

Travis looked around as a tall, well-proportioned brave stepped toward him. He wore broad white streaks across his nose and cheekbones, and he carried a Henry repeating rifle, the brass receiver dull and tarnished. A hoary ring of corrosion crowned the muzzle, for Indians never understood the necessity of cleaning their weapons.

"The soldier dies," the Indian said, speaking to the brave who had bothered Travis. "Leave this moment to him." He pointed to the Indian Arness had dragged from the horse. His neck was twisted at a grotesque angle, broken in the fall. "We have our own dead."

"Ben," Travis said, "how bad is it?"

"Hotter than—any whiskey I—ever drank," Arness said. He looked past Travis, at the Indians circling them. "Got yourself in—a tight one—this time, sir."

"Never mind that," Travis said. "We'll get you a doctor——"

"Too far," Arness said softly.

"You can hang on," Travis said. "Swain hung on. Are you still a damned quitter, Ben? Is that the way it's going to end? You not wanting to play it if you can't make the rules? Go ahead and die then. Who the hell's going to miss you anyway?"

He stood up and turned his back on Arness. "Who is the leader here?"

"I lead," an Indian said.

"Don't I know you? Yes, you're the one who talked so much at the reservation. Well, I thought then that you were a troublemaker. I guess I was right." He waved his hand to include them all. "Go on back to the reservation. The fighting is over."

There was no change in the Indian's expression. He still kept his rifle pointed at Travis' stomach. "The soldier leader has a strong heart. Death is all around you, yet you speak of your terms. We do not go back, soldier leader. Many battles are to be fought before we die." A sound came to him then, so subtle that Travis did not hear it, but all the Indians looked around them.

Then Travis saw what had alarmed them. Busik and ten men circled them, carbines ready. They had come in afoot, very quietly. And they waited for Travis to speak, to give the order for them to fire.

"*You* may die now," Travis said, "if you choose. There

will be no more war with the buffalo hunters. You'll go back to the reservation afoot, for we have your ponies."

He didn't realize what an insult this was, for to return afoot would disgrace them in the eyes of the others. An Indian scorned another who lost his horse.

The rifle still pointed at Travis' stomach, and to quell his nervousness, he reached out and plucked it quickly from the leader's hands. A wail went up among them. Their defeat was certain now, and their future inevitable. This was just another degradation, and Travis supposed that the day would come when they would surrender on sight of a white man.

"Busik, rig a travois for Arness, he's been gut shot." He pushed the Indians aside and bruskly gave orders. "Have the horses driven to the reservation and corralled there. They'll be returned to their owners when each one steps up and surrenders his rifle and ammunition. The rest of you form a column of twos and we'll follow the Indians back, at a respectable distance."

"Herding them, sir," Busik said, "is going to be hard on their pride."

"It will hurt less than a bullet," Travis said, and walked to his horse and stepped into the saddle. He observed the activity from this advantageous position, for he thought that it might have some effect on the Indians, the conqueror sitting above them, watching them. A travois was made and Arness transferred to it with some groaning. One of the troopers kicked out the fire and the Indians were marched off. They still carried their rifles, but Travis expected no more trouble from them. He had destroyed their confidence when he disarmed their leader, and the effect of this would take a while to wear off.

At dawn they were moving across the prairie, the Indians in a straggling knot a quarter of a mile ahead of the cavalry. Arness bobbed along on the travois, making a rough trip of it, but he endured his pain as silently as possible. When they came to a point that Travis reckoned as due north of Spanish Spring, he called Corporal Ardmore aside and instructed him to kill his horse riding for Doctor Summers. They would wait at the reservation.

That afternoon they passed near a homesteader, and he came out with his brood to watch the parade of Indians pass by, and when the cavalry passed, they all cheered and clapped their hands. Travis wished he could stop them, for it was bad enough to humiliate the Indians without rubbing salt into bleeding wounds.

He planned to march straight through to the reservation, with only a few rest stops, for dismounted men were very vulnerable on the prairie. They saw some skinners at work, and, to the north, they could hear the near-constant boom of heavy caliber rifles as hunters went on with the slaughter. Toward evening a good-sized herd thundered southward, passing them over a mile away. The dust hung in the air for an hour after they had gone by, and later, just before dark, a knot of horsemen rode down on them, hunters looking for stragglers and wounded from the herd.

When they saw the Indians afoot, they forgot their intent and changed course, making for them.

"Forward," Travis shouted, and brought his detail to the gallop. He planned to intercept the hunters' path, placing himself between them and the Indians, and his reckoning was correct, for he arrived just as the hunters drew up.

A huge bearded man was their leader. He pointed past Travis to the Indians and said, "How come you ain't killed 'em? Ain't that your job?"

"I know my job," Travis said. "Don't interfere with it."

The hunter looked at the eight armed men behind him, and at the dusty troopers, then laughed. "Well, sonny, you just ride on and we'll do it for you. Pete! Hank! Skirt that flank and put a couple of shots in 'em for the hell of it."

"The first man who lifts a weapon will be killed," Travis said. "At the ready!"

Spencers were flipped up and hammers came back. A surprised look came into the hunters' eyes, as though they had bitten into a nice piece of cake and found it full of walnut hulls. The leader, who wore a bone-handled pistol at his hip, put both hands on the pommel and looked at Travis.

"Sonny, you don't really mean that, do you?" His eyes hardened as he said, "Pete! Hank! You heard what I said?"

"You do it," one of them answered. "You're the boss, Swilling."

"Yeah, I am at that," Swilling said flatly. "Say, ain't you the bastard that shook up Luke Spears' outfit?" He

277

grinned. "Well now, this is more interestin' than the Indians, ain't it, men?" He took a hand off the pommel and put it on his thigh, near his holster. The flap was unfastened, hanging loose over the butt of his gun, and Travis considered his own weapon, secured against his hip. He was at a bad disadvantage. "We ran across Spears on his way to Dodge, sonny. Gave him and the other fella two horses. Spears lost his outfit, and he's offering three hundred dollars in cash to the man who kills you."

"Do you need three hundred dollars?" Travis asked, sparring for time. He watched Swilling's hand, and when it moved, he cast himself off the horse and hit the ground rolling, tugging at his pistol holster.

Swilling's first bullet spewed dirt over Travis' shirt sleeve, and the second plucked the kepi off his head and sailed it into the grass. Swilling never fired a third time, because Travis came to one knee, sighted his .44 Smith & Wesson, and shot Swilling dead center in the breastbone.

The man fell off his horse like a half-filled barley bag, and the horse shied when Swilling rolled against his legs. The rest of the hunters remained very still, staring at a row of .57 caliber Spencer carbines. As Travis got up and retrieved his kepi, he noticed that the bullet had rent the hard round top of it, and he tried not to think about the troopers and the way they had held their fire; perfect discipline. No soldier worth two bits would act without an officer's command.

With amazing calm—at least on the exterior—he broke open his .44 and inserted a fresh shell, then holstered the weapon.

"Does three hundred dollars seem inviting to anyone else? No? Then turn those horses around and get the hell out of here!"

"You won't be so lucky when you meet Spears," one man said, then they wheeled their horses and went back the way they had come.

Travis' hand trembled when he reached for the reins, and Busik saw it. Travis felt shame because it showed. Then Busik laughed and said, "Sir, that wasn't bad pistol marksmanship."

"Thank you, sergeant." Travis was amazed at the effect of Busik's brief words. His nervousness vanished and complete control returned. He looked at Swilling a moment, then said, "God forgive me, I don't feel like burying him. But break out the shovels anyway, sergeant."

"Yes, sir."

While they were burying the buffalo hunter, Travis rode over to where the Indians hunkered down in the grass. He did not dismount, and the leader looked at him, an expression of puzzlement in his eyes.

"Does the soldier leader kill his own people?"

"When it is necessary."

"The soldier is a friend to the buffalo killers. It is so. Is there now war between the soldier and the buffalo killers?" He asked this hopefully.

"No," Travis said, and returned to see how the burial detail was coming along. Busik wasn't putting the man down very deep. They were getting ready to shovel in the dirt when Travis turned to Ben Arness on the travois and stepped from the saddle.

Arness' face was gray, and pain etched deep lines in it. He looked at Travis and tried to smile. "Thanks for—sending for Doc, sir."

"I only wanted it on the record that I tried," Travis said, trying to sound casual.

"You going to—miss me when I'm—gone?"

"Wait until you go," Travis said. "Maybe you'll just bleed some of the contrariness out of you. That's what they used to do in the old days."

"Wish I had a—drink."

"With a hole in your stomach it'd leak right out," Travis said. "Come on, Ben, be tough. For once in your life, live up to your reputation."

Busik came up. "Finished, sir."

"Then let's get going."

In the very last of the daylight they moved on toward the reservation headquarters.

Arness was put in a room and made as comfortable as possible. In Brewer's medicine chest, Travis found a hypodermic needle and some morphine, and from a leather-bound instruction book he found the proper dosage and method of administering it. This gave Arness relief from the pain and he sank into a deep, undisturbed sleep.

With the pony herd safely guarded in the corral, Travis set about his task in the morning to trade the horses for weapons. Word was passed about the village, and the response was better than he had figured on. Nearly sixteen braves came forward and surrendered their guns and took their horses back. For Travis this provided an insight into the Indian way of thinking. Their war had gone badly and since they had suffered defeat, they believed their gods frowned on the enterprise and were willing to abandon it.

Still there were some hardheads who would not give in, and he knew they had to in order to completely squash any notion they might have of breaking out again. So, taking Busik with him, he went into the village. He thought it best to go without more men behind him, to carry further the idea in the Indians' minds that the soldiers were superior.

Travis pushed his way into the first lodge and turned it upside down looking for guns, and when the Indians offered resistance, he knocked one down and kicked another. He knew that this was a bold move, but they seemed to respect boldness, and often took no action just to see what was going to happen next. He found four rifles and some corroded ammunition, and then refused to part with any of the ponies when the braves wanted them back. All guns, he told them, that he had to get himself, were not worth a pony.

He gave them an hour to think this over, and by two o'clock his corral was empty and all the rifles and shells were locked in the storeroom.

This was, he hoped, the end of the Indian trouble for a while. He didn't think it would ever end permanently.

Quite late the next day, Major Deacon arrived in the ambulance, drawn by two lathered horses, with his four-man escort. Doctor Summers was with him and he rushed inside to have a look at Ben Arness, who was still stubbornly clinging to life.

Ralph Deacon sat down in the office and accepted one of Travis' cigars. Dust powdered the major's clothing and he had sweated through the back of his shirt. After he had blown a wreath of smoke to the ceiling beams, he said, "That damned General Wrigley is a pain in the butt, isn't he?"

"Yes, sir, a genuine pain."

Deacon shook his head. "Five years ago he was just a defeated Rebel. But the war's over and the Union generals are writing their memoirs and the Wrigleys now become proud, gallant foes, all remembered kindly. Naturally they take advantage of it and try to wheedle favors."

"What's the general been doing, sir?"

"Camping on my doorstep, that's what he's been doing. Good God, Mr. Travis, since you arrested that hunter, Wrigley thinks the army has entered into the partnership of marriage with him. He's been telling me how to conduct the prosecution until I'm sick of it. He's even volunteered to go to Dodge and testify. That's why I came along with Summers. The reservation will be a relief."

"Any word from Fort Dodge about the trial date?"

"In ten days," Deacon said, his thin face full of concern. "I think the commanding general wants to get this over with before newspapermen get out here from the East. There are some advantages to this geographical location. The Indian scare didn't turn out to be much, did it?"

"No, sir, they really weren't in a position to make war against the hunters."

"But they always try. How many dead Indians am I going to have to explain away to the Department of Interior, Mr. Travis?"

"Well, none, sir. We stole their horses and marched them back to the reservation. Then I traded the horses for the guns."

Slowly Deacon removed the cigar from his mouth and stared at Jefferson Travis. "Do you mean to tell me Arness was the only man who was shot?"

"No, sir. I killed a buffalo hunter. There was a group of them bent on shooting a few Indians. However, the argument was personal. Spears has offered three hundred dollars to the hunter who kills me. This fellow, Swilling, was eager to collect it. In the exchange of shots, he was killed."

"Is that how you got that crease in the top of your kepi?"

Travis laughed and took it off. "Yes, sir. I thought I'd wear it as a reminder of how close a man can come to getting killed and still be alive." His expression grew sober. "Major, I haven't gotten us into any more trouble, have I? I mean, they're not going to make anything out of this Swilling affair, are they?"

Major Deacon shrugged his shoulders. "I don't know.

Their version of it isn't going to agree with yours, I can tell you that." He got up and walked around the room, trailing cigar smoke. "This evening, I'd like to go over our case with you, Mr. Travis. You're familiar with court-martial procedure?"

"Yes, sir."

"Well, I imagine it'll be similar, only with a federal judge presiding. The army will want to keep as much control over this as possible. That's why it'll be held on the post, to keep newspapermen out. The prosecution will present its case first, then the defense will get a crack at us. Naturally we can recall witnesses for cross-examination." He came back and sat down. He seemed nervous, unable to be still. "Having practically memorized the two depositions you took, I've come to the conclusion that we're going to be outfoxed there."

"How's that, sir?"

"Well, if we introduce them, the defense will place Spears and the other man on the stand and dispute the depositions. Whether we like it or not, I think our safest course will be to accept Spears as a hostile witness and keep waving the deposition under his nose if his story happens to be different. But we'll talk about that later."

The connecting door opened and Doctor Summers entered the room. He tossed a .44 Henry rifle bullet on the table and then tamped tobacco into his pipe. "If that had been one of those new .44-40 '73 Winchesters, he'd be dead. It didn't do too much damage. I sewed up two minor holes in the large intestine, but the bullet didn't penetrate too deep."

"Is Ben going to make it?" Travis asked.

Summers shrugged. "Fifty-fifty. Depends on what complications he has, if any." He shook his head. "It's tough to say when you can't get the bullet out right away. A couple days should tell." He looked from one to the other. "Don't hold the wake yet."

"Hardly," Deacon said.

"Would you care for a drink?" Travis asked. "Brewer left some pretty good whiskey behind."

"Fine," Summers said, and sat down. He crossed his legs and sucked on his pipe, adding a strong flavor of shag tobacco to their cigars. "Hope sends you a kiss," he said, chuckling. "You want me to give it to you?" His amusement increased when Jefferson Travis' neck got red.

"There," the young lieutenant told him, "drink your whiskey."

Summers tossed it off, then wiped his eyes. "You say that's pretty good? It's a cross between formaldehyde and rubbing alcohol." Then he handed the glass back to Travis. "Fill it up again. And my blessing to Mr. Brewer, wherever he may be. There is, I believe, a very slight demarcation between some men's heaven and hell."

Ralph Deacon looked at him curiously. "Where's all the compassion for human suffering?"

"Buried in an ocean of tears," Summers said. He leaned back in his chair and smiled. "Gentlemen, before I die, I want to be called out in the middle of a stormy night, to drive eighteen miles through the mud, and when I get there I want to find a man who is healthy as hell, and just wanted to tell me so. What a refreshing change!" He looked at Jefferson Travis. "Say, you *are* going to marry my niece, aren't you? I'll bring your first four children into the world for nothing. You can't ask for a better bargain than that." He held up his empty glass again. "Just a little more, and don't worry about me. I turn morose when I've had too much to drink."

12

With a beef ration taking place on Thursday, Janeway and five of his men drove a herd of cattle onto the reservation early Wednesday morning, and that afternoon Otis appeared with three gaunt animals. Later, five more homesteaders showed up, one of them driving a solitary steer.

To the penny, Travis knew how much cash was in the agency safe, and he knew there wasn't enough to buy all the cattle; not and pay cash for them. Busik was in charge of the holding pens and the weighing in, and Travis and

Major Deacon observed the proceedings. In deference to Deacon's rank, Travis offered to turn the issue over to him, but Deacon declined, saying he would rather watch.

Before the weighing began, Travis gathered Janeway and the others around the scale and had it checked out against the test weights to assure them that the agency was dealing honestly. Travis allowed the homesteaders to weigh in their beef first, and Busik kept a record of it. The cattle were hardly in prime condition, and Travis understood that they were being sold to get a little "building" money to repair various bits of damage done by the twister.

Janeway's cattle weighed in at an average of fifty pounds more than any of the others, and Travis questioned Busik about this. He didn't think that Janeway's graze was that much better.

"Don't those bellies look a little round to you, sergeant?"

"Yes, sir." Janeway was standing right beside Busik, and the sergeant looked at him, then at Travis; he seemed reluctant to say any more.

"Well, sergeant, do you have an opinion?"

Otis and some of the others came over to lean on the pen rail; they could hear everything that was being said. Busik scratched the back of his neck. "Well, I wouldn't want to accuse anyone, sir, but I'd say it was possible they stopped at that seep about four miles from here and drank their fill of water."

"At six pounds to the gallon," Travis said, "that would add up." He turned to Janeway and found the man's face dark with resentment. "Well, Mr. Janeway?"

"Why, that's a hell of a thing to accuse a man of!"

"You couldn't prove it, sir," Busik said hastily.

"I suppose not," Travis said. "But I could confirm a suspicion, couldn't I? Sergeant, have Janeway's cattle weighed in, then held overnight. We'll weigh them again in the morning and see if they're any lighter." He tapped Busik's tally sheet. "Pay off Otis and the others on the weight."

"Yes, sir."

"Now, just a goddamned minute!" Janeway fumed. "You chivvied me into lowering the price of my steers, then you've got the gall to accuse me of watering in to

284

make more weight." He shook his fist under Travis' nose. "Someone ought to give you a good thrashing."

"Mr. Janeway, if I'm wrong, I'll be paying you full weight, won't I?"

"It's the principle of the thing, that's all! You going to pay me now or in the morning?"

"In the morning, after they're weighed again," Travis said.

Janeway turned to Major Deacon, who sat on the top rail, smoking his cigar and chasing flies away from his face. "Are you going to allow that, major?"

"What he proposes is fair," Deacon said dryly. "He tested the scales to show he was giving honest measure. It wouldn't hurt you to go along."

Janeway kicked dust and took off his hat and flogged it against his leg. "All right, I stopped at the seep and they drank a little. Hell, they were thirsty!" He looked at Deacon and his unreadable expression, then at Travis, who just seemed to be waiting. Finally Janeway snapped, "Take thirty pounds apiece off of 'em if you feel like it!"

"Mark that down, sergeant," Travis said. He spoke to the others. "Sergeant Busik will pay you off. Mr. Janeway, would you mind stepping into the office for a minute?"

Travis turned and walked across the yard, Janeway following him, and then Deacon said, "I think I'll go listen to this," and jumped down off the top rail.

Inside, Travis poured a drink for Janeway, then another for Major Deacon when he came in. He sat down behind his desk and folded his hands. "I'm going to pay you in cash for twenty-one steers, and in army script for the other nine," he said.

Janeway halted the whiskey glass halfway to his lips. "Why? The others got cash."

"I don't have enough cash," Travis said frankly. "Army script is the same as gold. Mr. Janeway, I don't really see how you can object."

"Well, of all the damned crust! Before you stuck your nose in I got Dodge City prices for my cattle——"

"Which was unfair."

"——All right, all right! But then when a man takes pity on some thirsty steers and lets them drink a little too much water——"

"He shouldn't complain when he gets caught," Travis finished for him.

Janeway tossed off the whiskey and banged the glass on the desk. "Now you want me to take script when the homesteaders get cash. Let's see you make that right."

"You must have *some* cash," Travis said. "These homesteaders have none. And they need it to improve their lot. Janeway, somewhere along the line, you've gotten the idea that the ills of your fellow men are of no expense to you. You've got to put yourself out a little to help them. If you put as much thought into reaching a hand down to help some other man off his knees as you did figuring out a way to get paid for a few extra pounds per steer that crossed my scale, you'd be quite an asset to this country."

With a rush Janeway came to his feet, his fists clenched, and Major Deacon used a tone heretofore reserved for dressing down impudent young officers. "Sit down!" Janeway whipped his head about and stared at Deacon, who speared him with his eyes. "Mr. Janeway, I rarely repeat myself."

Slowly, Janeway eased himself back into his chair. Deacon kept watching him. Then he said, "Mr. Janeway, in my book, Mr. Travis is the best thing that's happened since Sheridan's march to the sea. You are fortunate that I'm not sitting behind that desk, for if I had been, I would have had you thrown off the reservation!" He let his voice rise until it was a shout when he reached the end of the sentence. He went on in a calmer voice. "Once, when I was a young second lieutenant, I shared Mr. Travis' tolerant views, and I also strained my God-given understanding trying to put up with men like you. My patience is now frayed a little thin, and in ten years Mr. Travis will find himself the same way. I suppose that's why we need the very young, Mr. Janeway; they will tolerate such nonsense from men like you, who should know better."

Janeway kept rolling the brim of his hat in his hands, then he got up and went outside and walked across to the holding pens for his horse.

"I suppose I should have kept my mouth shut," Deacon said. "But that damned man needed telling off, Mr. Travis." He sighed and searched his pockets for a cigar, and found one. "In the future I'll keep my nose out of your business."

"I'm grateful for the major's support," Travis said sincerely.

Deacon extended his hand. "My name's Ralph. Formality seems a little misplaced, since we're both in the same army." He slapped his lean stomach. "Who does the cooking around here? And is it fit to eat?"

Dodge City lay three days to the north, and they left Friday evening in the ambulance, Sergeant Slattery, the major's personal orderly, in command of the four-man escort.

Busik was placed in charge of the reservation, and since Arness' fever had broken and only time was needed to put him on his feet, Summers returned to Spanish Spring on horseback.

During his journey to Fort Winthrop, Jefferson Travis had stayed over five days at Fort Dodge and met the town first-hand, but that was hardly long enough to make acquaintances at the garrison, let alone friends. And this time, when the officer of the day showed them their quarters, the atmosphere was decidedly chilly.

Major Deacon was billeted with the staff officers while Travis was given a small room in the bachelor officers' row. He dined at a table with four others, but he might as well have been eating alone, for they cleverly blocked him from their conversation.

At eight o'clock an orderly summoned him to Quarters A, and he found Major Deacon on the porch.

"We only have time for a word," Deacon said, "which is why I waited here. Now we find out what the rules are going to be."

They went inside and were taken by an orderly to the colonel's drawing room. He was a tall, robust man, fifty-some, with a distinguished career behind him. A lieutenant introduced them.

"Colonel Keene, Lieutenant-Colonel Farnsworth, and Major Griswald. Would you all be seated, gentlemen?"

Major Griswald nodded coldly to Travis, and smiled a little "I told you so" with his eyes. Colonel Keene was a bearded man, the commanding officer in the general's absence, while Lt. Col. Farnsworth acted as executive officer. He was older than Keene, rather thin and wan in complexion, and his military career had been not only difficult, but rather uneventful.

"Gentlemen," Keene said in a very soft voice, "I thought it would be best if we all sat down and had a talk before the proceedings begin tomorrow morning. First, since the case is going to be tried here, Colonel Farnsworth has agreed to handle the prosecution."

"I understood that I was to handle that, sir," Deacon said bluntly.

"Quite so, but the general—who regrets his absence—thought Colonel Farnsworth more suited." He frowned slightly.

"But sir," Deacon protested, "I'm fully familiar with the case. As you know, I was on the spot."

"Precisely, Major." Colonel Keene was patient. "We want no hint of partisanship in this case. In any case, I hardly think it's worth making an issue over."

"Very well," Deacon said resignedly. "I assume, sir, that the charges remain unchanged."

"Yes, generally speaking," Keene said. "Major Griswald, who is acting legal officer, gave the whole matter his studied attention, and felt that a conviction would be more certain if we disregarded the actual killing of Swain, and based our case on the girl's attack."

"Why?" Jefferson asked.

They looked at him in much the way parents do when they believe children should be seen and not heard. Colonel Keene said, "Lieutenant, what difference does it make what a man is hanged for?"

"Two charges, sir, enhance the possibility of his hanging," Travis said.

"Well, we don't wish to debate the matter, Mr. Travis," Griswald said coolly. "I believe our judgment in this case is sound."

"I trust, major, that it's more sound than your auditing of Regan's books."

Griswald surged erect, his face livid, and Keene held up his hands. "Now, we're not going to argue. Mr. Travis, that remark was highly out of order! I want to hear no more of it!" His glance touched Major Ralph Deacon. "I'll expect, sir, that some measure of reprimand be taken against Mr. Travis for his impertinence."

"Impertinence, sir?" Deacon was a picture of inno-

288

cence. "I was assuming that Mr. Travis made a conjecture based on fact. I have, sirs, his report, as yet unforwarded, concerning certain discrepancies in the auditing of Regan's books. And it was my understanding that the trading post was going to be reopened. Yet when I used the crossing the place was still padlocked."

"There has been a change in policy," Farnsworth said, in his reedy voice. "We've canceled Regan's trading permit and have no intention of reopening the post." He glanced at Colonel Keene. "Must we discuss the matter any further?"

"I think it will bear a great deal of discussion," Deacon said firmly, prodding the point. "Can it be, gentlemen, that there's been some sleight of hand between Regan and Major Griswald that has been settled in the privacy of the immediate family?"

"*You're* out of order!" Keene snapped. "Don't mince words with me, major! By God, I won't put up with it!" He turned his wrath on Jefferson Travis. "Haven't you stirred up enough?"

"Yes, sir, I suppose so. But the colonel must admit that I can't be blamed for the twister."

Deacon laughed aloud, for he had been jolted by this blunt honesty at their first meeting, and it was amusing to see the shocked surprise on Colonel Keene's face. Griswald came to his feet, shouting, and Keene pounded his fist on the table to restore order.

"Gentlemen, we are accomplishing nothing," he said. "Can't we agree on the charges?"

"Yes, sir," Travis said. "Murder and rape, sir."

Keene's frown was a thundercloud. "Mr. Travis, you are a witness, and that is all. We're setting the charges, whether you approve of them or not. You will hold yourself in readiness on the post until the time you are called." He looked at Major Deacon. "Now you go ahead and forward any report you want, and I'll kill it before it ever reaches the general's desk. Is that clear? Colonel Farnsworth and Major Griswald have prepared their case carefully, and they're going to present it. I think that will be all, gentlemen."

When they were outside, Deacon said, "I hope you noticed how rank was pulled, Jeff."

"Pulled? I thought we were being smothered by it." He

bit off the end of a cigar and put a match to it. "You hit pretty close to home concerning Griswald. He was probably taking a bit for his own pocket, and in turn letting Regan have a little more rope to swing."

"Well, it happens in the best of armies," Deacon said. "Can't blame them for wanting it hushed up. I've hushed up a few myself." He hesitated, as though considering a point. "I don't understand why they want to charge Clayman with rape and not murder. To me it weakens the whole case."

"How can they drop one? The charges are specific."

"By presenting all admissible evidence in one direction and not much in the other." He looked through his own pockets for a cigar, then took one offered by Travis. "I'd like to know for certain whether or not Keene really wants a conviction. He covered up for Griswald—" He let the rest trail off. "Well, we'll know more in the morning when the trial opens."

Travis spent the rest of the evening writing letters to his family, and it was a chore because he couldn't keep his mind on his writing. Yet he managed to fill several pages and put them in an envelope, then took it to the officer of the day, who would see that it got on the east-bound train.

He slept poorly, and in the morning dabbled listlessly at his breakfast, then went to his room to put on his parade uniform, supplied by the Fort Dodge quarter-master for the occasion.

The trial was being held in the headquarters building, and the parade ground was crowded with buffalo hunters. As Travis pushed his way through and gained the porch, Luke Spears turned from a group of men and stared at him. Spears was shaved and wore a tight-fitting suit. A derby was perched on one side of his head, and he came over to Travis, smiling without warmth.

"Well, if it ain't the little soldier boy. Say, I heard you had a little fun on the prairie not long ago. I sure hope you buried Swilling deep. He always had a fear of dying out there and being ate by varmints." He reached out and poked Travis on the chest. "You going to testify against poor Clayman? Well, you go right ahead, and when you're through, I'll be in Dodge waiting for you."

"Don't waste your time," Travis said coolly.

"I don't look at it that way," Spears said. "I just add up the cost of six wagons loaded with green hides, and the wages I paid out, which are all gone now, and shooting you becomes real pleasurable. If you don't come into town, I'll likely meet you somewhere on the way home. And I won't bother to bury *you*."

He wheeled then and went back to his friends, and Travis went on inside to sit in the hallway until he was called. At nine o'clock, the prosecutor, Colonel Farnsworth, made his charge to the court, but this took place behind closed doors and Travis heard none of it. Then a side door opened and a junior officer came in with the Swain girl. Travis was at first surprised to see her, then he reasoned it out quickly: Colonel Keene had sent an officer to Spanish Spring for her, and to make sure it was done quietly, he had taken the stage both ways. Very clever of the prosecution, Travis admitted to himself, and then wondered how deeply this cleverness extended.

He was not called until the middle of the afternoon. The Swain girl had already corroborated the charges to the satisfaction of the court.

This was a closed hearing, with only the court and the accused present. The room was small and drab, and the shades were drawn. He was sworn in and took the stand to the left of the judge.

Lt. Col. Farnsworth asked all the questions: they were simple enough, dealing with every phase of the girl's recovery, and and the subsequent arrest of Clayman. The two depositions had already been introduced as evidence. Travis had an opportunity to see Clayman's legal counsel, two distinguished civilians who more than likely had a formidable reputation for acquittals, and he wondered who was footing the bill for them. Clayman's buffalo-hunting friends, or someone with high military rank, who had an alliance with the big moneyed hide buyers? He supposed he never would know.

Farnsworth was very good with questions; all of them could be answered yes or no. And the defense counsels were very quick on their feet every time Travis tried to volunteer a statement. They lost no time in having it stricken from the records as voluntary. So he ended up sketching in what Farnsworth wanted sketched in, and he never got to tell them about Swain dying in the storeroom with a buffalo-rifle bullet clear through him.

That night, Major Deacon came around and they sat until quite late, talking it over, trying to decide how it was going to come out. The prosecution was resting its case on the statements of two people, Travis, and the Swain girl, who could only answer by nodding her head.

Neither Deacon nor Jefferson Travis liked this, but they couldn't do anything about it, not and continue to pursue a military career.

The next day, when he returned for cross-examination by the defense lawyers, it seemed that one did all the talking while the other did all the thinking, for after a few questions, Mr. Skyler, who talked, always went back to the defense table to listen to Mr. Lavery.

"Mr. Travis," Skyler said, approaching the witness. "You're an ambitious young man, aren't you?"

"Leading the witness," Farnsworth said, as though he didn't really care.

"Rephrase your question," the judge said.

"Are you an ambitious young man?" Skyler repeated.

Travis wondered how a man answered such a question. By saying no and having the army put it on record, or saying yes and opening himself for a low punch?

"I suppose I am," he said.

"Did you see the accused attack the Swain girl, Mr. Travis?"

"No, sir."

"I see." He went back for another conference and brought back the two depositions. "Do you recognize these? The prosecution has entered them as evidence."

"Yes, I recognize them."

"This deposition, signed by an X, how was it obtained?" He regarded Travis with some amusement. "Voluntarily, or by threat?"

"They are signed," Travis said. "And witnessed."

"I quite understand that," Mr. Skyler said. "And I understand a great deal more, Mr. Travis. Isn't it true that you rode into the buffalo camp and demanded to search it?"

"I told Spears I *wanted* to search it."

"Ah, yes, that was it. You considered it your right to invade their privacy?"

"We were searching for those left homeless or injured by the twister, and it was suggested to me that I examine Spears' camp. To answer your question, I considered it a duty to search it."

"And when Mr. Spears objected, you threw him to the ground; isn't that correct?"

"I was defending myself. He reached for his pistol."

Mr. Lavery hissed and Skyler went to the table for a whispered conference. Skyler came back. "Mr. Travis, we'll skip all that. Isn't it true, that in order to ascertain the identity of the defendant, who is accused of molesting teh Swain girl, you threatened to hang another man?"

"Yes," Travis said. "But why do you insist on calling it molesting when the charge is—"

"Just answer the questions," Skyler interrupted sharply. "And at the reservation, Mr. Travis, isn't it true that you threatened to turn Mr. Spears out on the prairie afoot and unarmed, unless he confessed?"

"Yes, but you don't bluff a man like Spears."

"Your Honor, can we have that last stricken?"

"Strike it out." He looked at Travis. "Just answer the questions."

Skyler said, "Mr. Travis, wasn't the other man beaten and threatened also?"

"Not beaten in relation to his deposition."

"Threatened then?"

"I used harsh words with him," Travis admitted. "You don't get anywhere with a man like that by——"

"Your Honor——?" Skyler said.

"Strike it out," the judge said. "Mr. Travis, please just answer the questions."

"He's twisting my words and meaning to suit his case!" Travis said indignantly.

"I'm through with the witness," Skyler said smoothly, returning to his chair.

"You may step down," the judge said.

"But that's not all there is to it," Travis protested. He looked at Farnsworth, who was paring his fingernails with a pocket knife. Anger made his cheeks stiff, and he stepped down and walked from the room, his heels trouncing the floor.

In the hallway, where he met Major Deacon, he found himself still too angry to speak, and he went outside to stand, trying to cool off.

13

Neither Major Ralph Deacon nor Jefferson Travis expected the trial to last more than two days, and when it went into the fifth, they expressed a common worry, for the defense was making a strong bid to discredit Travis and the depositions.

Unable to attend the trial as a spectator, Travis picked up information through Deacon, who had enough rank to find out what was going on. With the prosecution resting on the testimony of Travis and the Swain girl, and backed only by the two depositions, the defense attorneys had a free hand in kicking the supports out from under it all.

They drew their witnesses from the buffalo hunters, several of whom swore that they had been on familiar terms with the Swain girl from time to time, and even went so far as to maintain that they had her father's blessing, since they always paid, cash in hand. The buffalo hunters made a good impression on the court with their behavior and dress; they all wore dark suits and ties and spoke softly without swearing, and every lie became the truth.

Spears was put on the stand, and no amount of cross-examination by Lt. Col. Farnsworth could shake his testimony; he was a man set upon by an impetuous young officer and an irresponsible army. Clayman was innocent, for the girl went along of her own free will, and when Clayman took the stand to tell his story, it was of a life well intentioned, but misspent. He claimed to have been an orphan with little religious upbringing, and his only crime was to take the girl to his blankets without benefit of clergy. It was true that her father had been shot, but only in self-defense. They had argued over price and Swain had lost his temper.

It took half a day for the defense to sum up, and forty minutes for the prosecution. The court then adjourned until ten the next morning, when the judge would announce the verdict. That night Travis ate his supper in Major Deacon's quarters, and they talked.

Jefferson Travis had some outspoken opinions: "Colonel Farnsworth just threw away the charges, major. The man is either a fool or he's making sure Clayman is acquitted."

"It wouldn't be the first time the army whitewashed anyone," Deacon reminded him. "You must have been in grade school when Colonel Chivington perpetrated the Sand Creek Massacre. A lot of people wanted him drawn and quartered for that, but the army fooled around and slapped his wrists and turned him scot-free. A few years later, Colonel Carrington went through his brief and tragic fiasco at Fort Kearney. He was recalled, of course, but he was never court-martialed for his part in the gross mismanagement of the campaign." He sighed and opened his cigar case. "Jeff, the army wants this over and a right decision rendered. You were the principal witness and you weren't on the stand an hour. It's obvious that you were only supposed to give token testimony."

"Something ought to be done about it!"

"Nothing can be done about it," Deacon said flatly. "And you know it."

"Yes, but that doesn't make it any easier to take." He accepted one of Deacon's cigars, and a light. "That poor Swain girl, unable to answer the lies told about her."

"In the old days they used to have the sacrificial lamb," Deacon said. "But in the army we use anyone who's handy. Including second lieutenants." He leaned forward and added, "Jeff, be thankful they didn't ruin your career. But bear in mind, they would have if there hadn't been any other way."

"Major, Clayman will be acquitted, won't he?"

Deacon hesitated a moment before answering. "Yes. It's in the cards. I suppose I knew all along how it would be, how it had to be. But I don't want you to turn bitter over it, Jeff. I don't want you to think everything you did was for nothing."

"Well, wasn't it, sir? Can you honestly say that it wasn't?" He let his anger out; it put strength into his voice.

"Nothing we do, good or bad, is totally for nothing," Deacon said. "If I knew whether you were really army, I'd know you understood that. It's a slow, tedious game we play at, Jeff, and sometimes, measuring it by the span of a man's service life, it doesn't seem like we accomplish very much, but we really do. You put it all together and we do."

"If the next forty years are going to be like this, sir, I don't want to think about them."

Deacon studied him carefully. "Thinking of resigning, Jeff?"

The young man shrugged. "Right now, sir, I feel like poking some staff officer in the nose." He drew on his cigar until he was calm again. "I suppose that's not very 'army,' sir, to want to poke a colonel in the nose."

"We don't do it in the army," Deacon said softly. "There's no mark on your record, Jeff. Why don't you be glad of that; it gives you a chance to go on, to try again."

"Is it worth it, sir?" He shook his head. "Right now I don't think it is."

Someone knocked on the front door and the orderly, who was in the kitchen washing the supper dishes, went to answer it. He came into the parlor a moment later and said, "It's Major Griswald, sir. He offers his compliments and——"

"Invite the major in," Deacon said, and got up to have a drink ready.

Griswald came in, his heels clicking smartly on the bare floor. He sailed his hat onto a corner chair, and took the drink in his left hand so he could unfasten his collar.

"Well, the beastly affair is over," he said. "My, that's good whiskey." He glanced at Travis briefly. "Cheer up, Mr. Travis. There will be other days in court."

"Will there, sir?"

Griswald laughed. "You have to learn how to ride with the punches, Travis. Isn't that right, major?"

"It helps to minimize the bruises," Deacon admitted. "How is the verdict going to go, Griswald?"

"Guilty," he said, then sat down and crossed his legs. "A telegram arrived last night from the general; the whole complexion's changed." He looked at Travis. "You look surprised. Don't be. The buffalo are being killed off rapidly. In three more years there won't be any hunters on the prairie. There's no sense coddling a dead horse. Travis. Makes sense, doesn't it?"

"So you're going to hang Clayman because it's no longer profitable to let him go," Travis said. "I don't like the reason."

Griswald finished his drink. "Travis, we're hanging him because he's guilty. Justice has been served and you're Queen of the May." He got up and flourished his hand. "You've done a good job, Mr. Travis. Damn it, though, for a while there I thought you were going to put salt on my tail, but all you ended up with was some feathers."

"I may get a little meat the next time," Travis said frankly.

"Then I'll have to watch myself," Griswald said. "And I'll be watching your career closely, so see that you make no mistakes." He looked at Deacon, who was sitting there, glancing from one to the other, and staying clear of this. "Travis, my boy, if we didn't keep our eye on one another, we'd all be thieves. The easy way out is always there, and generally we'll take it because doing right is often one hell of a lot of trouble. For myself, I'm glad Clayman is going to be hung; the buffalo hunters have been out of hand for some time." He reached over and put his glass on the table. "Well, I must be going. Colonel Keene's giving a small, private party, to celebrate, I suppose. In the morning he'll send the general a wire, relaying the verdict, and then he can forsake his Arkansas mud baths and come back; the smoke will have cleared by then." He got up and buttoned his blouse and put on his hat. Then he walked over to Travis and offered his hand. The young man stared at it for a moment, then accepted it and Major Griswald laughed. "Happy hunting, Mr. Travis. I'm sure we'll both enjoy it immensely." Then he winked broadly. "And if Deacon proves too much of a bastard for you, transfer into my command. I can always use an able officer."

He went out then, as briskly as he had come in, and when the front door slammed shut, Jefferson Travis wiped a hand across his mouth and stared at Major Ralph Deacon.

"Well, Jeff, why didn't you poke him in the nose?"

"It's nothing but a damned game," Travis said softly. "I thought I'd made an enemy in Major Griswald, but it isn't so at all. He'd tear me limb from limb if he had to, or thought it would suit some purpose, but there wouldn't be anything personal in it. Would there?"

"No," Deacon said. "Why didn't you hit him?"

Jefferson Travis shook his head. "I don't know. Do you?"

"Yes," he said. "I know. Because you're 'army,' Jeff. Like it or not, you're a career soldier, in until sixty-five, retirement age. You'll cuss and fume and swear you'll get out, but you're army and there isn't anything you can do about it, because you're made to soldier. Griswald knew it, sensed it; most career soldiers can sooner or later. Myself? I wasn't sure. Not until you sat there and listened to him without flying off the handle." He got up and poured two drinks, handing one to Jefferson Travis. "Are you going to stick around and watch Clayman hang?"

"No, I guess not, sir."

"What are your plans?"

Travis thought for a moment, then shrugged. "Go back to Spanish Spring and start all over again, I suppose. And hope for better luck next time."

"Maybe you'll get it," Deacon said. "You've brought a few problems to your door though. Spears is going to be looking for you and the buffalo hunters are going to blame you for Clayman's hanging."

Travis drank some of the whiskey and enjoyed the fire in his stomach. "Spears doesn't really scare me much, sir. If he wants a fight, I'll accommodate him." He looked at Deacon. "The reservation's a mess; I'll have to straighten that out as soon as I get back or the Indians will leave." He sighed. "That will be a thankless job, I can tell you. And there isn't any real peace around Spanish Spring. I'll have to do something about that before I get much older." He raised his glass until he could see the bottom, then set it aside and leaned back. "Major, what the hell am I going to do with Ben Arness? He and I never hit it off on the right foot, and he even made up his mind that he wanted to leave the army. It's really my fault because I've ridden him too hard."

Ralph Deacon laughed. "Jeff, I've know Arness for

twenty years and he's threatened to leave the army periodically. But he can't leave. He's a soldier, and he's stuck, the same as we are. Sure, he hates young lieutenants; he hated me once, but young lieutenants sometimes get to be old captains. Give him another year or so, Jeff. He'll come around. He always has." Deacon chuckled. "He'll marry that Beaumont woman and she'll take some of the starch out of him."

"I expect I'll take a horse back," Travis said, rising. He seemed eager to leave, as though his duties were pressing and he just had to get at them. "I'm going to work on General Thomas C. Wrigley and see if I can't break his stranglehold on the homesteaders. Of course, it'll pay to keep an eye on those cattlemen too; they're a rough lot, bent on having their own way." He stopped talking and turned his head as someone knocked. The orderly answered the door.

He came to the parlor and said, "A Mr. Jamison to see Mr. Travis, sir."

"Show him in," Deacon said.

Eldredge Jamison was a man in his young thirties, very well dressed, and he carried a malacca cane with an ebony head. A celluloid collar forced him to keep his head high, and he swept off his beaver, holding it in the crook of his left arm.

"Have I the pleasure of addressing Lieutenant Jefferson Travis, commanding the Spanish Spring detachment?"

"I'm Travis." He neither smiled nor frowned. "How can I be of service?"

"By hearing me, sir, and I shall be brief," Jamison said crisply, his voice full of the brittleness of New England. "I wish to inform you, sir, that I have been appointed Indian agent to succeed the late Mr. Brewer. I've had experience before with the army, and I want it clearly understood that I'll brook no interference whatsoever. The Indians are under the jurisdiction of the Interior Department, while you represent the War Department; the name alone implies its purpose. If I need you, I'll summon you. In any other event, do not disturb the Indians, as I intend to instill in them Christian habits and various agricultural pursuits." He bowed to Major Deacon. "I've disturbed you. I'm sorry. Good night."

They stared at the door after it slammed shut, then

Travis laughed, a soft rumble in his throat. He did this twice, then a gale of laughter poured from him and he and Deacon slapped each other on the back and held each other up, laughing until tears ran down their cheeks.

Finally they checked their mirth and Deacon picked up the bottle of whiskey and empty glasses. "You want to kill this for the road, Jeff?"

"Pour," Travis said, and sat down, feeling strong and mature and completely at ease, completely satisfied with himself and his lot.

Will Cook is the author of numerous outstanding Western novels as well as historical frontier fiction. He was born in Richmond, Indiana, but was raised by an aunt and uncle in Cambridge, Illinois. He joined the U.S. Cavalry at the age of sixteen but was disillusioned because horses were being eliminated through mechanization. He transferred to the U.S. Army Air Force in which he served in the South Pacific during the Second World War. Cook turned to writing in 1951 and contributed a number of outstanding short stories to *Dime Western* and other pulp magazines as well as fiction for major smooth-paper magazines such as *The Saturday Evening Post*. It was in the *Post* that his best-known novel, *Comanche Captives,* was serialized. It was later filmed as *Two Rode Together* (Columbia, 1961), directed by John Ford and starring James Stewart and Richard Widmark. Sometimes in his short stories Cook would introduce characters who would later be featured in novels, such as Charlie Boomhauer who first appeared in ''Lawmen Die Sudden'' in *Big-Book Western* in 1953 and is later to be found in *Badman's Holiday* (1958) and *The Wind River Kid* (1958). Along with his steady productivity, Cook maintained an enviable quality. His novels range widely in time and place, from the Illinois frontier of 1811 to southwest Texas in 1905, but each is peopled with credible and interesting characters whose interactions form the backbone of the narrative. Most of his novels deal with more or less traditional Western themes—range wars, reformed outlaws, cattle rustling, Indian fighting—but there are also romantic novels such as *Sabrina Kane* (1956) and exercises in historical realism such as *Elizabeth, By Name* (1958). Indeed, his fiction is known for its strong heroines. Another common feature is Cook's compassion for his characters, who must be able to survive in a wild and violent land. His protagonists make mistakes, hurt people they care for, and sometimes succumb to ignoble impulses, but this all provides an added dimension to the artistry of his work.